Knife River

Knife River

A NOVEL

JUSTINE CHAMPINE

THE DIAL PRESS

NEW YORK

Published in the United States by The Dial Press, an imprint of Random House, a division of Penguin Random House LLC, New York.

THE DIAL PRESS is a registered trademark and the colophon is a trademark of Penguin Random House LLC.

Hardback ISBN 9780593447208
Ebook ISBN 9780593447215

Printed in the United States of America on acid-free paper

randomhousebooks.com

2 4 6 8 9 7 5 3 1

FIRST EDITION

Book design by Ralph Fowler

For Mary

Knife River

2010

Her bones were discovered by a group of children playing in the woods. It was October, a Sunday morning, and the ground was crisp with fallen leaves. Two boys and a girl. I don't remember who told me that. They stumbled upon the skull while digging around gathering rocks. They were going to build a little wall, a fortress in the trees. I think about this moment often; these three small bodies loose in the wild, their bright hats and coats just a speck, a flicker, beneath a grand canopy of oak. Their cold, delicate fingers gripping mossy stones, hauling them one by one to the site of the fortress. Laughs muffled by acres of dense wilderness. The children spread out, searching for the perfect pieces to build a foundation. And the girl, eyes narrowing as her tiny hand grazes bone. I imagine her lifting it carefully, silently, from a bed of dirt while her brothers gallop in the distance. Moss clings to the edges. A loamy, muddy smell hangs thick in the air. There are worms. One black beetle. The skull is nearly intact, missing only its lower jaw. Later on, a fracture surrounding a hole is noticed on the left temple. But in this moment, the girl holds her discovery in her hands, this piece of a body, untouched and unseen for fifteen years. The subject of so much anguish and longing, hundreds of hours of searching, now uncovered in a chance moment of play. She doesn't yet scream, or run to find the boys. She crouches there in the leaves and examines the smooth edge of the eye sockets, the remaining teeth, long and yellowed like an animal's. The gentle slope of bone, just barely thicker than an orange peel, hooked over her thumb.

What did the girl think of then, in those seconds before she dropped the skull back into the dirt and sped off toward home? Every good dinner this unearthed stranger had ever eaten, every happy day she'd ever had, every friendship, every argument, every habit and routine and hidden talent and movie watched and lover taken, her taste for black coffee, loose-fitting clothing, the color blue, winter over summer, eggs over easy, books on cassette, each time she'd felt infuriated or bewildered, each new idea sprung into her mind, each memory, each daydream—all these things, all the glimmers of life that made her into a woman, had once been kept safe inside this very piece of matter, this delicate shell of a thing. Soon, the children reappear with two adults in tow. Then more people, dogs, police tape wound around trunks. A news van stuck in the mud. Someone made a cross out of dried palm fronds and nailed it to a tree. There were cameras, a helicopter. But first, there were my mother's bones.

1

I was at home when I got the call.

It was my girlfriend's home, really, though I'd been living there with her for a year. Sarah was a dermatologist. A calendar keeper, a salad eater, a former horse girl. The only person I'd ever known whose under-the-sink area was spotless and organized. Every morning I got up hours after she left for work and walked around the house, trying not to nudge anything astray. In the beginning, I thought that feeling would pass, that soon enough I would relax into the house and all its surfaces would feel like mine to leave dust on. But still each night I found myself zipping all my toiletries back into my travel case so they wouldn't mingle with her vast array of expensive serums. She had a very involved skin-care routine. Eleven steps, at least. All day she swooped in and out of bright, sterile rooms squeezing and lancing people's skin, then came home and fussed with her own face. She fussed, too, over mine. Occasionally I opened my eyes on a weekend morning to find her already alert, staring at some spot on my shoulder or chest, with a detached laserlike focus. She was always forcing me to apply sunscreen.

We met online. Our first date was at an apple orchard. I drove out from Queens, where I was staying in a friend's spare room after breaking up with my last girlfriend, to New Jersey, where Sarah lived. I wound up spending the weekend. We picked too many apples. We made three pies and stayed up until dawn each day explaining all the intimate details of our most formative life events, punctuating the explanations with sex and pie eating and some light crying. We agreed that I would return the next weekend, and then the next, and then soon I was moving in.

My friend, the one I'd been staying with, eyed me wearily as I tossed all my clothes into a duffel bag.

"On to the next one," she said flatly. Her fifteen-year relationship had come to an abrupt end that summer, and though she insisted that it was fine and for the best and didn't cost her any sleep, I sometimes heard her crying in the night and throwing things at the wall.

"That's one way to look at it," I said.

"Well, Jess." My friend rapped gently at the doorframe, surveying the bedroom with a vacant expression. "It was good having you here."

"I'll come see you still. I'm not going to Siberia."

"Not exactly."

"Less than an hour away."

"That's a long hour."

I knew what she meant. I felt a little bad leaving her alone in the apartment—it was large and drafty, and full of furniture she'd shared with her ex. I felt some chagrin, too, for having come there with so much gusto after breaking up with one woman, only to leave for Sarah with similar gusto two months later. In the ten years since I'd left home, I'd never had my own place. When I could, I gave cash for rent to a girlfriend, or to a friend in the between times. All my things fit into a few bags, a fact that had recently begun to bother me, so much so that I'd actually told Sarah I had a storage unit somewhere out near Philadelphia, where I once lived. And I did have one there for a while, years ago, to stow a mattress and bed frame I'd been given, but I stopped paying the bill and the locks were soon changed.

Every New Year's Day, I'd privately resolve to learn how to stay happily in one place for a while. Before Sarah, I'd even made plans to go to Maine. I knew someone there, an older lady named Maria who'd since retired from the office I worked at and lived Down East full time near her family. She was actually my boss, but she'd always been soft with me, patient with my errors when I was new, interested in my day-to-day. We kept in touch, emailing a few times a year. She had a daughter who had a job with the parks service, tagging and monitoring the breeding population of peregrine falcons in Acadia. Every so often, Maria sent me pictures taken on hikes up towering, silvery rocks where the birds nested above the tree line. Below were lush valleys of pine and a vast ocean, capped with froth. The pictures, the whole idea of a life in this place, tranquil and pristine as it appeared on my computer screen, tugged at something in me. I didn't see why I couldn't go there myself. Not just to visit, but to live, work, make some kind of home. After all, I was always longing to be outdoors. But then the newness of the year grew stale, and in September I met Sarah and forgot all about the falcons and Maine.

When I pulled up to her house the day I moved in, Sarah was standing out on the front steps waiting for me. Within minutes she'd affixed a security sticker to my windshield, adding, "I put you on the gate registry so you can come and go freely." Her beige two-story was one of a dozen nearly identical beige or white or pale yellow houses on the block, which was one of a handful of cheerfully named, freshly paved streets in the development. Everything sat in a horseshoe facing a scenic reservoir with a walking path. There seemed to be a different gazebo around each corner, though I never saw a single person inside one.

"You don't have much stuff," she said, eyeing the mismatched duffel bags scattered around the back seat. "Is this everything?" I nodded. In the time we'd been dating, Sarah hadn't come to visit me where I was staying, or met any of the few friends I had. She didn't ask much about my transcription job, either. It didn't bother me. I actually preferred things that way. I liked driving out to her place on Friday afternoons. I loved emerging from the tunnel into the gentle, blue light of day and whizzing past all the ugliness of the gas stations and motels and on ahead toward the quiet leafiness of her neighborhood.

Our whole relationship was built on these weekends. Each one was so simple and calm. We would have breakfast on her deck and then go to the garden center to buy potted geraniums or deer spray or whatever she needed for her yard. There was something oddly perverted about it all for me: the way she wore cardigans tied around her shoulders, and that she was friends with all these straight moms in the clean, gated community where she owned a home. Sarah was eleven years older than me, and she'd been married once before to a woman named Francis. A real estate lawyer. They separated right before beginning IVF. I didn't understand how urgently Sarah still wanted children until we'd already been living together for a few months. She'd talked about it some before, and I believed her, but the idea of it all seemed so far away, so irrelevant and intangible to me, and was always quickly brushed aside by the glittering newness of our relationship, buried under all the surging lust and discoveries of one another's interests and fears.

Sarah kept a binder from an upscale sperm bank in her study. In it were the detailed profiles of about 150 men, all around my age, with good teeth and advanced degrees. I first saw it one night after dinner when we were talking about her marriage and all the ways it had gone wrong. Sarah exhaled slowly when she was finished, deflating back into her chair and swirling the wine in her glass.

She took a long look at my face and said, "You're very mature for your age." This elicited in me an unnerving combination of arousal and revulsion and panic. It was the same thing teachers often said to me growing up.

But here, in this moment, I was an adult. I was twenty-eight. I'd been on my own for just over a decade by then, but still every day I felt that my life was something lent out to me in error—tenuous, and always just about to slip from my grasp. Sarah then rose abruptly from the table and trotted to her study, returning moments later with the sperm binder held out before her. It included laminated pictures of the donors engaging in their various pursuits. There were a lot of action shots, mostly scuba diving or skiing. A couple of mountain climbers. Sarah had a system of categorization, I soon learned. She'd stick a red tag on the donors she was definitely interested in, a blue one on the hard passes, and yellow on whoever needed further consideration. I darted my eyes between the page and her face, trying to assess her reaction to whatever we were looking at, but I could hardly tell anything. Her decisions were a mystery. Why did all the blonds get a yellow tag? When she spent a solid three minutes examining the picture of a young man in a chef's hat, affixing sugar flowers to a tray of masterful-looking pastries, and then made an indecipherable sound under her breath before unpeeling a red tag from the sheet, what did it mean?

I couldn't help but note the differences between myself and these strangers. Numbers thirty-one and twenty-three both had tall, aquiline noses and got quickly tagged with red stickers. Mine was blunt and plain. A forgettable nose on a pale, oval face, unlike number fifty, who had a deep golden complexion and a prominent, square jaw. He was pictured standing triumphantly on the end of a dock, holding a large fish on a line. Sarah tagged his profile red without hesitation, as she did with three and twelve, who both had smatterings of freckles and thick, muscular necks.

Once she commented on donor number nine. "This one kind of looks like you. You know, if you were a man." I could see what she meant. We shared a similar lanky figure and dark, deep-set eyes. Even our mouths were set at the same kind of lopsided angle, giving the impression of a permanent smirk. On this page, she placed no sticker at all. I wasn't sure whether I felt dismay or relief.

We went through the binder often. It was one of her favorite after-dinner activities. One day, she just removed all the tags and we started back from the beginning. Some of her judgments were the same, but many had changed, and this gave me some sense of solace. Like maybe it wasn't all as meaningful as I'd imagined. Maybe there was more fantasy to it than hard desire. I brought this up one night before dinner. She seemed relaxed; it was the beginning of a holiday weekend and we'd just gotten a large mulch delivery.

Waving my hand over the binder, I said, "Do you think it's possible you're more interested in the *idea* of all this than in actually having a child?" Sarah stared at me, a sautéed cremini mushroom speared on the tongs of her fork. Sage oil dripped off the mushroom and back onto the plate.

I tried to explain myself. "Like, it's fun to look at these guys. I mean, it's so weird. Who are these people? Why do they all scuba dive?" I smiled, but it didn't catch. She put her fork down with the mushroom still on it and leaned forward, placing her hand beneath her chin. "I'm just saying, it seems like you're having a hard time actually picking one. The kid would probably never meet the guy anyway."

"Choosing a donor is a really critical part of the process."

"Sure, but I just thought you'd have decided by now. If you were seriously going to go through with this."

Within minutes, the conversation devolved into an argument, and then a real fight about the difference in our age, the pace of our relationship, the preciousness of her time and how it was waning, her uterus growing older and less hospitable to new life with each passing day. Images of little hands, feet, the outline of a head or shoulder pressing out against the taut skin of her belly swirled in my mind. I felt nauseated and a little hot. I pressed my glass to my forehead.

"I'm just not ready to be *needed* like that," I told her.

Sarah smiled blandly. "This isn't a joint decision. I'm going to pursue this"—she tapped her nails on the binder's cover—"motherhood, a child, the next important phase of my life, regardless of who I'm in a relationship with. *Waiting* for the other person to be ready is what got me here in the first place."

Sarah, surely wanting to make a point, left the sperm binder out on the kitchen table for another week. I couldn't bring myself to move it. After this argument, the house and everything in it all seemed to belong to her completely. Every blade of grass and salad plate, all her Italian-made shoes lined up in the closet—she'd given it all to herself. She was an ambitious person. Disciplined. A hard worker. She had plans: an eventual child, a practice of her own. Every so often I'd ask what made her want to be with me, live with me, let me raise a child alongside her.

The first time she scoffed and said, "You are the exact *opposite* of Francis." After a minute of silence, she added, "I think you're a kind person. You have a lot of growing to do, but you're actually much wiser than I was at your age. I look forward to seeing what you become." She gave me a congenial pat on the shoulder and went to go soak in the bath. A couple of days later she said, quite abruptly, "You must think I'm some sad old woman."

"I don't think that," I told her. I really didn't.

"Reeling from her divorce," she continued. "Trying to shack up with some young thing."

"Well, you have succeeded in getting me to shack up."

"Divorce is fucking horrible." Her voice began to crack. She dropped her face into her hands and held it there, cradling it slowly. "You think you're over it and then—" She gave a swift, hard kick to the table leg. Water sloshed around in my glass. "It just hits you." I got up and dimmed the lights, then unclipped her hair from its tight, high bun and began to rub the back of her neck. The muscles were hard and knotted beneath the skin. She said, "I'm really glad you're here."

I wanted to give Sarah money for letting me live in her house, especially after our donor argument. I wanted it to be a show of my impermanence. A clear sign that I could not have a family with her. She refused. I insisted. I could see that she was offended by my continuing to offer, but my guilt didn't subside. I felt fraudulent, somehow. Like I'd been given a lovely gift intended for someone else and kept it for myself, wearing it around for everyone to see, flaunting something that I didn't deserve.

I began doing things for her, like picking up the dry cleaning and groceries and making pitchers of sangria for her friends who came over every Thursday night. They were moms from the neighborhood, around Sarah's age. These women either had good, serious jobs, or didn't work at all. They took punishing group exercise classes and always smelled delicious. They were a little fascinated by me, I think. By my age and my relative manginess, and the work I did transcribing medical reports for a periodontal surgeon's office. I'd catch one or two just staring at me sometimes, their eyes moving from my heavy boots, up along my jeans, before finally resting on my hair. Sarah had once revealed to them that I cut it myself with kitchen shears every few weeks, twisting it together and hacking off whatever fell below the base of my neck in one rough chop—a fact that elicited shrill, bewildered laughter from the group. Overhearing this from the kitchen while dicing white peaches for the sangria, I considered popping my head around the doorframe and explaining that I'd first started the habit at thirteen because there just wasn't any haircut money, and how by then I'd already emerged as someone who couldn't quite comfortably walk into a salon *or* a barbershop, so doing it myself worked out fine in the end anyway. For maybe a whole minute I stood there, knife suspended in motion, imagining how I'd say it before deciding it wasn't worth the trouble.

I'm sure Sarah was the only lesbian they knew. It was the kind of group that previously, maybe just a decade earlier, would never have befriended her, though now seemed quite proud to be able to say they not only knew a gay person, but went over regularly for drinks. Drinks made by her *partner*. I cringed all the way down to my gut when they used that word. It made me think of cartoon Westerns, little mustachioed men in oversized chaps swinging their pistols around against a backdrop of desert cacti. I didn't mind these ladies, though. Honestly, I was a little fascinated by them, too. They liked to get tipsy and complain to me that their husbands didn't go down on them enough. And they fucking loved the sperm catalog. It made them crazy. After the first pitcher, they always began flipping through it, howling and cackling as they read each man's stats. They liked to take different things from each page—one man's height, the MBA and eye color of another, until they created what they all agreed was an ideal specimen. Then the most severe mom, a former equities analyst named Dana, would engage the group in a weird game where everyone guessed the price of one vial from a selection of attractive men. Dana, referring to the cost index in the back, gave approving nods to the closest guessers.

Somehow, I liked Sarah more in the context of these other women. She made sense among them. She laughed easily and could commiserate about the same kinds of things. It renewed my appreciation for her orderliness, the way she formed habits easily and stuck to them. What drew me to her to begin with was her reliability. Every day she did the same things, the same way, at the same time. Not once did I see her fall into bed without washing her face and applying under-eye cream. I took comfort in the sound of her setting the coffeemaker for the next morning, the gentle rattle of the grinding, the click of a small machine. Then her quiet steps, drawing closer in the hallway. Occasionally, while finishing off the rest of her friends' sangria glasses as I loaded up the dishwasher, I let thoughts about a new life creep in. I imagined what it would be like to stay there, right where I was. I could get a lawn mower. I could extract decaying leaves from the gutters. And maybe I could settle into loving Sarah the way old couples describe, a kind of contentedness that comes at you slowly. A new island turning lush over a lifetime. Maybe I would even come around to the idea of starting a family. But the next morning always came, and I'd know deep down in my heart that we had no business sharing a life together.

It was my sister, Liz, who called. I was in the garage digging through a storage bin for Sarah's snorkeling equipment. She had ideas about us going to Mexico over Thanksgiving—our first holiday together. At her suggestion, I'd gone part time with my transcription job, spending just a few mornings a week at the dining room table with a headset on, listening to tedious recordings and typing up long blocks of text to be printed and filed away along with bright, gory images of diseased and injured gums. The practice had gone through a lot of transcriptionists before me, and I think they would've cycled through me, too, if I wasn't so good at understanding the dense accents of the two Hungarian periodontists. I'd lied my way into the position in the first place, claiming I'd done similar work before, putting a then-girlfriend's phone number down as my most recent reference and cobbling together a phony college diploma online to include in the application.

I suspected the hiring manager could tell my résumé was a sham, but she let me do a practice recording anyway and then said I could start work immediately. The job came as a badly needed stabilizing force in my life, something I could reliably survive on. Sarah called it a stepping stone.

"You've been with them for too long," she said. "Why don't you move on to the next thing?"

"I kind of like this."

"Well, why don't you become a periodontal technician? Or even a periodontist?"

"I didn't take this job because I'm, like, interested in mouths." I waved my hand over the images on my laptop screen—close-ups of someone whose gums had receded so far down to the root the full lengths of their teeth were all exposed. "I just kind of found my way into it."

"I pursued dermatology because it was what my father did, but now I love skin." She nudged me on the shoulder. "I'm *interested* in it." A few hours later she was on her computer researching resorts on the Yucatán Peninsula. Before leaving for her first appointment in the morning, she asked me to see if I could find us two pairs of flippers from the storage bins.

My sister started speaking before I'd even gotten the phone up to my ear. *I need you to come home.* I knew instantly what she meant. It was the heaviness in her tone. The shadow of relief and excitement hovering above each word. There was a hint of pleading. Anxiety crackling in her pause. We rarely spoke, just on birthdays and at Christmas, and sometimes the anniversary of the day we last saw our mother alive.

"Bones were found," she said. "They think it's her. I need you back here. When can you come?"

I stood there for a moment, dumbfounded, a straw gardening hat dangling from my fingers. Liz repeated herself twice more. As she spoke, the room began to shift. Everything—the plastic bins, the flippers, a spider's web quivering on the window—seemed to shrink down to a doll's size. It all looked fake, like a movie set, like I could blow the walls down with a forceful breath. When I finally spoke, I felt like I was operating a puppet. A mouth that wasn't mine, my voice coming through it from somewhere very far away. I wanted to sit down but found that I could not command my legs. For fifteen years, I'd imagined this exact moment. I thought it would crash into me like a great wave, lifting the dam on a lifetime of anger and fear and wondering. It was the wondering that ate me from the inside—there was no refuge, no depth of dreaming that could stifle it. I'd always thought getting this news would feel like being ripped back through time. I thought it would knock me to the ground. Instead, I found stillness.

Hearing my sister say it again and again, *they think it's her,* all the subtle rhythm of the world ground to a halt. There was nothing but trapped air hovering in the garage. With each outward breath, I grew more faint. For years after our mother went missing, everyone wanted to talk to us about closure. They told us that the saddest, most tragic thing of all, the thing that broke their hearts the most, was the fact that we didn't have closure and might never get it. It was amazing to me how comfortable grown people were with sharing their own idea of heartbreak over what happened. I would ask myself, what do they want me to say? What am I supposed to do with this confession? I felt obliged to take care of them, somehow.

One of our mother's co-workers, a woman from the county clerk's office named Patricia, came over with a lasagna around the time the investigation was beginning to turn cold. We'd never met before. My sister showed the woman to the table, which was stacked nearly a foot high with unpaid bills and catalogs and crusted-over plates. Patricia handed the lasagna to Liz, who handed it to me without breaking eye contact with Patricia. I held it awkwardly against my chest for a long moment, looking back and forth between the two of them, before placing it down on the table atop all the clutter. Soon we were hearing more about closure. How sorry she was that no one could give us any, and what a glaring vacancy our mother's absence left in the records room. I smiled sympathetically at the woman, already beginning to drift away from myself, eyes glazed over. While I was smiling, Liz was starting to fume. The woman continued to tell us how sad she felt. Within seconds, my sister had her by the elbow and was escorting her to the door.

"Thanks for the lasagna," she spat, slamming the screen shut and flipping both locks over with a force that made the frame rattle.

I tried Sarah at work three times. The receptionist told me she was in the middle of handling a large cyst. I texted her, simply, *Call me. Urgent.* What more could I say? What kind of an explanation did I owe her? Sarah knew about what happened. It came up on our second weekend together. She'd been asking repeatedly about my family. She referred to her own family as *my people*. Her people were in Maryland. Horse people. Boat people. She kept framed pictures of them in the house.

I stepped carefully around the truth, instead offering little anecdotes about my sister and the town we came from—one of the northernmost places in New York, not far from the Canadian border. An asteroid the size of a small house fell there the year my sister was born. I hadn't been back in a long time. None of this seemed to satisfy Sarah's curiosity. I didn't really expect it to, she had an investigative nature. She liked to grab hold of little threads and pull, following them to their ends. She wanted to know about everything. I listed some more trivial things, then mentioned the real important thing at the end—my mother going missing fifteen years ago. Fast and quiet, like I was trying to sell a car with mechanical troubles. She snapped her head around and looked at me seriously. She had a few questions, the kinds of things everybody asked. *What happened?* That was the one every person started with. It always made me want to laugh.

I would sometimes say, "That's the sixty-four-thousand-dollar question." Some people chuckled somberly, understanding that was the easier reaction for me to digest. Others looked at me with pity. Without a doubt, that was worse. It always made me want to give them a punch in the gut.

"It was a long time ago," I told Sarah, feeling like I needed to reassure her.

"It's about half your life," she answered. "That isn't much." This took me aback. Normally, sharing this information sucked the air out of a conversation within minutes. But Sarah seemed fine sitting there with it, turning the facts over in her head. In a way, I was more attracted to her for it, but another part of me thought about just leaving in the night while she slept and stealing something expensive on my way out. Sensing my nervousness, she deftly changed the subject to where we might have brunch the next morning. I relaxed back into the warmth of her bed, and we didn't discuss it again.

It took me less than twenty minutes to load my things into the car. I flew in and out of the house, barefoot on the cold driveway, tossing grocery bags stuffed with clothes into the trunk. Dashing through the garage with my sack of toiletries, I knocked over a storage bin full of Christmas decorations. The lid popped off and dozens of precious, glinting ornaments went tumbling to the ground. The few that didn't break rolled out onto the driveway, colliding with the tires on my car and plopping sadly over a ledge of sod, finally landing in the neighbor's bed of winter cabbage. A dazzling blanket of shattered glass lay all around me. The tree topper, a large ceramic cherub, now headless, sat in three jagged pieces near my feet. I sliced open my big toe trying to navigate through the mess and let out a sharp howl, emerging out onto the driveway, swearing beneath my breath and gripping my still wet toothbrush in one hand. I tossed it through the open window down onto the passenger seat.

The woman who lived across the street was standing near my car, staring in horror as I limped toward her, blood trailing behind me. We'd met once before at a summer block party. I couldn't remember her name. I waved, panting. She arched one eyebrow in return.

"Everything is okay," I announced. I tried to smile, but could only muster a grimace. The woman took a step backward. "Would you please tell Sarah to call me?" I asked. "Tell her everything is fine, just tell her to call me back." The woman nodded. Not a minute later, I peeled out of the driveway, bits of Christmas ornaments cracking beneath my tires as I went.

2

Here's what I remember:

Her black hair swept up under a red kerchief, tied in a bow at the nape of her neck. For years afterward, I uncovered those hairs in odd places around the house. A strand caught inside the pages of an old book, snared on a garden trowel in the garage, among the broken remains of a ceramic mixing bowl pushed to the back of a kitchen drawer.

She wore dark jeans that morning. A white shirt. On her wrist, one thin silver bangle. The bangle knocked against the table as she and Liz argued. Gentle wind and sunlight poured freely through the open screen door. I upended a bottle of honey over my cereal bowl, letting enormous globs drip down into the milk. My sister leaned back in her chair. She was nineteen then, wickedly smart and unhappy. High school graduation was just around the corner. She wanted to study aerospace engineering in California, where all the best programs were. My mother hated the idea. Why go so far away? Where would the money come from? Liz had a folder of scholarship applications and late admission papers at the ready. She fanned the pages out and slapped them down. Our mother glanced at the folder and said dismissively, "I just wish you'd get a job in town while you think about it more, Liz. That way you can save some money and decide what you really want to do. Maybe you'll see you don't really want to be all the way out on the other side of the country." At that, my sister stood up and stalked over to the sink with no obvious purpose. Her body was ruled by anger. I remember my mother looking to me as if seeking another voice to anchor her pleas, but I was totally disinterested. California meant nothing to me. I didn't particularly want Liz to leave, but I also didn't care much if she stayed. I was thirteen; we were too far apart in age to have played together as girls or confided in each other as teens. She was a nervous, serious kind of person. Nothing like my mother and me, who could keep each other up late into the night, shrieking with laughter.

The fight cooled to a simmer and then, around eleven thirty, our mother left the house for the last time. Her final word to me was *mustard*. A reminder for Liz and me to stop by the store. It was the Friday of a long holiday weekend, Memorial Day, and we were going to grill hot dogs in the yard that night. A small sack of charcoal sat out on the back porch next to a couple of boxes of bottle rockets. That was another thing we loved together, my mother and me: fireworks. There was a big store in far western New Hampshire where we'd stock up during summer trips to Lake Winnipesaukee. She liked the loudest ones, the ones that really screeched as they spiraled up into the air. All this made Liz uneasy. She'd shout from her bedroom window, "One of you is going to get your hand blown into pieces. Then what will you do?" We waved her off. We loved watching the canisters burst apart in the sky, the lingering smell of gunpowder and burned paper. But most of all we loved igniting the fuse and then taking off in a mad, breathless dash to the edge of the woods.

I added mustard to the shopping list. Barbecue skewers, marshmallows, a canister of coffee.

"Okay," I told her. "I'll remember." And that was my final word. *Remember*.

Our mother went on walks all the time. It wasn't unusual. Especially when she was stressed. The town we lived in, Knife River, was tucked in the valley between two sprawling forests divided by the runoff of a towering waterfall. There were hundreds of trails snaking through the land, many of them originating just north over the Canadian border. Backpackers came through often. They camped out in the woods usually, or stayed in a motel near the central trailhead. I watched her lace up her boots on the porch. I watched her retie the bow on her kerchief. She slung a small backpack over one shoulder and headed out down the road. I watched, drinking the last of the sweetened milk from my cereal bowl, as her body disappeared around the bend.

I revisit this morning again and again. The images are copies upon copies of themselves running on a loop, forming deep grooves in the recesses of my brain. They are never quiet. I used to think I couldn't go on that way, the constant din, whirring and rattling, was so unbearable. A little echo that could not be snuffed out, no matter how desperate I became for a black and dreamless sleep. Now, I'm afraid I would die of loneliness without them. What would I have left to hold on to?

3

I pulled into Knife River just before midnight. Being there felt unreal, almost impossible. The storefronts and buildings were the same. The air smelled the way I remembered it. Pine and loam, chimney smoke. Knee-high grass swayed in vacant lots illuminated by streetlamps. A sign sat at the first stoplight, faded wood with red valentine hearts painted in each corner. It read, inexplicably, NIAGARA FALLS, 320 MILES SOUTH. It had been there all my life. There was a little white church, a little brick church, and an abandoned church all on the same stretch of road. A blue sleeper van with plaid curtains in the windows parked outside the Main Street grocery store. An enormous pothole next to the fire station. Two sugar maples side by side on a gently sloping hill. Turns and stop signs that I hadn't seen in years came vaulting back into my memory, or the memory of my body, as I drove to the house I'd grown up in without glancing at the map on my phone.

Liz and I stood out on the porch staring at each other after an awkward, stilted hug. The weight of our mother's bones hung between us. I eased my body against the railing, exhausted and numb below the waist from seven hours in the car, but also feeling faint from the rush of my heart, the gathering sense of dread burning a hole in my gut.

"I'm expecting a call from the precinct tomorrow," she finally said. "They should be able to tell us something."

"I think it's her."

"We can't know that yet."

"I just have a feeling."

"Feelings aren't facts." A prickle of anger rushed over me, then subsided. A ripple over quiet water. She'd been using this expression our whole life. I'd always hated it. I took a deep breath.

"You wouldn't have called me like that if you didn't feel it, too. The way you sounded on the phone—"

Liz put both hands out before her as if refusing a plate of food. She shut her eyes. "We just have to see."

My sister was only thirty-four, but the swaths of delicate baby hairs framing her face were bright silver. She frightened me a little, honestly, the way she stood so still under the yellow porch light, hardly blinking as we studied each other. The only part of her that felt truly familiar were her eyes; wide and dark with a black freckle on one iris. Everything else was like a strange costume. Her oversized smock dress and tightly coiled bun reminded me of the Mennonite women I'd sometimes see getting onto an unmarked bus near the Port Authority. Her feet were bare and I could see that her toenails were grotesquely overgrown, some sharply broken and yellowing. I could think of nothing to say that wouldn't plummet uselessly into the bottom of the abyss whose edge we both seemed to be standing on.

I squeezed the banister and a splinter caught under my skin. The wood felt damp, almost spongy. Nothing was kept in good repair. Paint peeled off the clapboard in long strips. The roof was missing shingles. Tall weeds grew up from the cracks in the driveway. I thought of turning around and driving back down to Sarah's. It was very close to being too late for that, but not quite. A sliver of time, growing narrower by the moment, still remained. I heard something rustling beneath the slats of the porch deck. Some animal.

As if sensing my nerves, my desire to run away, Liz went over to my car without a word and began hauling my bags in. "Let me bring you into the house now," she said, squeezing my shoulder a little too hard.

I walked carefully behind my sister as she led me around. She wanted to show me everything, as if for the past ten years I couldn't shut my eyes and see these rooms anytime I wanted, and sometimes, also, when I didn't.

"I can't believe how long it's been since you've come home." She said this in an affable kind of way, but with a pointed look. "Do you even remember all this?" she asked, tapping on an heirloom milk glass vase, then the upright piano we used to bang around on, and finally our parents' old vinyl turntable from when they were newly married teenagers.

"Of course," I told her.

"Huh," she replied. "I didn't think you would." We paused in the kitchen, surveying the table by the front window with its plastic placemats and novelty Easter egg salt and pepper shakers from decades gone by. I could see the porch light reflected in the corner of the glass, the shadowy outline of my parked car to the left of it. Liz turned to face me. She reached her hand out and prodded me gently on the cheek, then nudged one of my earlobes. Her touch felt vaguely affectionate, but also tentative, like she was checking to see whether I was truly there in the flesh.

"You look a little older," she said.

"Well, yeah."

"Your face has thinned out. And you didn't have this the last time I saw you," she said, pointing to a tattoo of a toad on my arm. My old roommate was apprenticing when we lived together and I let her practice on me. A toad was the first thing I thought of when she asked me what I wanted. There was no deeper meaning.

"Are you still smoking cigarettes?" Liz asked. I told her I was. "I can see it in your skin," she muttered, tapping her finger at the tail end of my right eyebrow. "Only a little, though. I don't think most people would notice." She nodded briskly and we moved along.

The floor still creaked in all the same spots. Without thinking of it, I ducked my head beneath the low doorframe leading into the living room. I knew to jiggle the one hallway light switch a little to the left before pushing it up so the light wouldn't blink on and off. A deep and consuming sense of familiarity filled me from the head down. Our school portraits still sat in plastic drugstore frames on the bookshelf. On the sofa, an old pink and orange granny-square throw. Before it, the same coffee table with the nicked-up cherry wood legs. An oversized book, *Songbirds of North America,* was flipped open to a photo of nesting warblers. The radiator growled and hissed beneath the front window.

Our mother had loved this house. She moved into it at seventeen, pregnant with Liz, newly married to our twenty-five-year-old father, who'd moved them both from Vermont to Knife River after taking a job at one of the last remaining factories where he'd work for three years before it, too, shut down. He used most of a modest inheritance to purchase the house, which by then had sat uninhabited for some time. There were raccoons living in the attic. Wet, rotting wood beams holding up the ceiling in the basement. A large, mysterious hole in the wall between the kitchen and living room. She managed some of the repairs well enough herself, papering over cracks in the plaster and stacking cinder blocks where the foundation slouched until they saved enough money for a carpenter. Even years later, she refused to rip up the pea green shag rug in the living room, telling us, *It'll come back in style eventually,* or change out the ancient, humming refrigerator. *It's still ticking,* she'd say.

Her voice flickered in my head, clear and bright. I spotted her old crocheting basket tucked on a shelf next to the fireplace. A thick layer of dust caked the handles. Cobwebs hung between the needles.

"You haven't changed things much," I commented, trying to keep my voice level.

"It's good like this. Why would I?" Liz looked at me expectantly. What had she wanted? An admission of regret? An apology for leaving her alone in this house all those years? We'd argued over these things in the past, after I moved away and didn't want to get on the phone to rehash the minutia of our mother's case, already long cold, trying to find some glimmer of a clue. I wanted to get away from it all. Liz dug her heels in deep. *No one is forcing you to stay there,* I would shout at her. *No one has a gun to your head.*

This was always met with a wounded laugh. *My choices disappeared the day Mom did,* she liked to say. I always thought it was too dramatic, almost practiced. It seemed to me like a crutch. An excuse to remain on the outside of her own life.

Maybe she just wanted me to recognize her sacrifice. Here I was, the sister she'd raised to the threshold of adulthood, who left at the first possible chance and stayed away while she remained tethered by fantasies of a miraculous return. *What if Mom comes back one day? And you're not here, and I'm not here, and some strange people are living in the house who have no idea who she is? Someone needs to be home. What if something comes in the mail someday, some new information, and we never get it?*

I never allowed myself these kinds of ideas. They didn't even appeal to me. It was more painful, I thought, to keep the door open a crack like that. Easier to just slam it shut, but I knew it wasn't so simple for my sister. I thought about her every day—just nineteen and saddled with the care of a young girl and a house, no sign of when she might be relieved of it all, and an investigation led by a small, ill-equipped police force that steadily lost its steam with each empty lead. Months faded into years and Liz never seemed to edge toward acceptance. The odds of our mother being out there somewhere in the world, life intact, were so negligible, so thin, I could never bring myself to lean on them for solace. But Liz was stubborn and wracked by her own contrition.

The idea that our nightmare might have been avoided were it not for their fight at the table that morning seemed to eat at her, infiltrating the very fiber of her being, until every scrap of marrow turned sour with guilt. *If I hadn't been so harsh then she wouldn't have gotten so upset, and then maybe she wouldn't have gone out for that walk.* What could I say? Perhaps that was true, but it just as easily might not have been. Who could say what particular sequence of small things—a restlessness in her legs, a particularly luscious ray of sunshine coming in through the screen door on a light breeze, a restful night's sleep the day prior—invisibly led us all to the moment she walked away from our home for the last time?

Liz led an isolated, odd kind of life, but at least she *had* one. She slept beneath this roof every night. She went every day to her job at the bank, sitting behind a window counting out money with her fast, precise hands. She never married, didn't date. People talked about her. In the beginning, it was all pity. She'd go into the bakery and walk out with a free loaf of bread. An old acquaintance took it upon himself to come by and remove the wasp nest from our side door and clean out the gutters. Everyone worried after her. Everyone seemed to want to lift away a little bit of her pain, piece by piece. But years passed, and the pity gradually turned to mockery as she grew from a girl struck by tragedy into an unkempt, unsmiling woman. A frigid woman. A dour woman. A crazy woman. The kind of woman with witchlike hair who gets shouted at by teenagers in speeding cars.

Liz led me up the stairs. There I noticed a stained, wrinkly sheet tacked up over the window at the end of the hall.

"So the light doesn't come in," she explained. "It gets in through the crack beneath my door and bothers me." Her voice was terse. I nodded, trying not to let my gaze rest too long on a panel of wallpaper peeling down in one long, yellowed curl. She opened the door to our mother's old bedroom. Silently, we both stood at the threshold and looked inside. I could tell she'd been cleaning it. There were vacuum tracks on the carpet. But the bedding hadn't been changed. I recognized the same lavender chenille duvet and oversized, outdated sham pillows from so many years ago. Atop the dresser, three perfume bottles with a scant half inch of deep amber liquid inside. A pair of jeans with the price tag still on sat folded by the hamper.

My sister, suddenly seeming mortified, slammed the door shut in both our faces. I felt my hair blow back off my forehead and settle down again. She clenched her fists into tight little knots. "I'll bring some towels to your room."

"Don't worry about it," I said.

"You'll need towels."

"I don't think I want to sleep in my old room up here."

"Where, then? Are you going to sleep in your car?" My sister scoffed and crossed her arms over her chest.

"I'm just going to set up down in the den, if it's okay with you."

"Fine." I watched her clip down the hall and then turn sharply at her bedroom door. "I wake up early," she said. "You'll probably hear me in the kitchen. If you need towels—"

"I know where to find towels."

"Good night, then."

I gave a limp wave as she disappeared into her room. From the outside, I could hear her turning the lock on the door. I wondered how long she'd kept a habit of that, locking her own bedroom at night. Was this some leftover fear from years gone by? We were, I remembered, always afraid of being watched. Afraid that whoever took our mother from us could be just outside, lurking among the trees, ready to come for us next. Maybe she started doing it after I moved away, uneasy at being a lone woman in such a creaky, drafty old house. Or maybe it was simply a reaction to my sudden presence at home again. Perhaps *I* was the thing that lurked. My stomach turned. I felt painfully out of place, oversized and awkward, like I'd shoved myself into a child's playhouse and was trying not to knock anything over. The air was stifling. I could smell the dust on every surface. On my way back down the stairs I grabbed the loose strip of wallpaper by its tail end and yanked, ripping the whole thing off the plaster in one fast movement.

. . .

Hours later, after Liz was asleep and I'd managed to choke down a little food, I sat on a stump on the other side of the road, staring at the house, smoking, and sipping alternately from a cup of instant coffee and an airplane bottle of vodka I dug out from beneath the passenger seat of my car. I felt too jittery, too skittish, to safely rest my head anywhere. Some bats fluttered out of a gutter pipe, dipping and swooping among the crab apple trees in the front yard. Fallen fruit had turned pungent in the grass and drew dense little clouds of winged insects, attracted to the sweet rot. I had five missed calls from Sarah. Just that same morning, I'd felt so desperate to explain everything to her, but all that had already begun to feel unimportant and far away. I'd gone somewhere Sarah couldn't follow. I didn't know how to explain what it was like here, but I finished my cigarette and called her back anyway. She answered on the first ring, her voice tense, bordering on panic, then quickly morphing into astonishment as I told her the news. For a minute, we were both quiet, listening to each other breathe into the phone.

Finally, she spoke. "You must be in shock."

"It's a lot to take in."

"I thought something horrible had happened. I mean I came home and saw the Christmas decorations broken all over the driveway and the door was just hanging open. All the lights were still on. I thought, what the fuck happened here? It looked like you'd been abducted."

"That woman across the street didn't come by? I told her to talk to you."

"Dierdre?"

"Dierdre, sure."

"She texted me. She thought you'd gone insane."

"Well."

"Are you okay?" I heard myself burst into laughter at the question. I couldn't stop. I could hardly catch a breath. It was such an absurd thing to ask, and I was so exhausted.

Sarah raised her voice. "What is funny to you right now?" she asked. "What in the world could possibly be funny to you at this moment?"

It was funny that just twelve hours earlier I'd been digging around for a pair of snorkels in the suburban garage of a woman I'd met on the internet. That before we lived together I wanted so badly to spend every moment with her, but within a week of moving in began to harbor a secret hope that she would break up with me, or kick me out during an argument, or that someone new would sweep me into a frenzy and I'd have a good reason to leave. And then that on this day, of all days, in the single snap of a moment, my mother emerged from the depths of my memories and became a possibility to me and my sister again. Her body, some touchable piece of her real self, existed somewhere. Someone had seen something. Some thread in the mystery of her absence had come loose, and now I was home again.

"You're in shock," Sarah declared, her tone superior and final as my laughter subsided. "That's all this is."

"I guess that must be it."

"I would've come with you, Jess, if you'd waited just a couple hours. You shouldn't be alone during this."

"I'm not alone," I said. "My sister is here."

"You never talk about her. When's the last time you even saw each other?"

"Well, we don't live close by."

Sarah was quiet. I could imagine her sitting in the kitchen with the lights dimmed, a glass of white wine on the spotless countertop before her. Of course, Liz and I could have seen each other more often than we did.

The last time was four years ago, shortly after her thirtieth birthday. I was living in Bay Ridge with a girlfriend, and Liz was in Manhattan for two nights at a conference her bank chain was holding. Because she never missed a day of work, and was the only teller with a spotless manual bill-counting record, and everyone knew what she'd been through and felt a little sorry for her, the manager put her name in the pool of outstanding regional employees to be recognized with a banquet dinner at the Times Square Marriott, after the CEO's Christmas address. Liz seemed a little annoyed by it all, like the weekend away was a real imposition. I met her for lunch at a diner near the train station a few hours before she needed to head back home. It was strange seeing her in such a busy, noisy place.

I remember looking at her in her skirt suit and clip-on earrings, drinking a chocolate milkshake in our cracked vinyl booth amid all the rush, and feeling like I'd made a lot of mistakes. Yes, I'd managed to move away and take care of myself. I was working for the periodontists by then and it was fine, it was enough. But my sister felt like a stranger, and I could barely even talk about what happened. There was no point in getting into it with anyone, I reasoned. It was too messy. Too scary. Too complicated and weird. A turnoff. I learned to push all of it far to the back of my mind during the day, but then at night I'd go to sleep and be faced with my dreams, which were staggeringly lifelike, always more or less the same thing: me, alone, running from something in the woods and eventually coming upon my childhood home in Knife River. Awash with relief, I would nearly collapse trying to make it to the front door in time, but something would always go wrong. The house moved farther away the closer I got, just keeping itself barely out of my reach. Or I would come to the porch and find the house abandoned, full of rats and bats and spiders. Or the house would fall over like a Styrofoam prop when I went to twist the doorknob open. Or the house would have a family of strangers living in it who would throw me out, disgusted and angry. I would try to get drunk enough before bed that no dreams could find their way through to me, but it didn't always work.

And there was Liz, just on the other side of the table, loudly sucking the last of her milkshake through a straw. I couldn't honestly say she was a happy woman, but she didn't seem afraid like me.

"You like living here?" she asked me as we walked out onto the street. Contortionists struck nauseating, spine-bending poses before a crowd on the sidewalk. Nearby, a man lay unconscious in a mess of his own vomit. Hundreds of people buzzed and jostled within our view. I steered us away from a German family, fighting with each other over a large foldout map.

"I don't live anywhere near here. I live in Brooklyn. That's a different borough."

"Oh. Do you like it there, then?"

"Mostly, yes."

"That's good," she said, her voice trailing off. "I'm glad you're happy."

Inside Penn Station she gave me a brief, passionless hug and got on the escalator. Watching her disappear into the maze of tunnels, I felt an icy loneliness start to creep up from the tips of my toes. I turned abruptly against the sea of commuters marching toward me and shoved my way back down the corridor, into the first bar I saw—an express TGI Fridays, where I sat at the visibly filthy bar and drank three tequila sunrises in quick succession.

4

We know that she was seen after leaving our house.

We know she waved to a man who was collecting his mail at the edge of the road as she passed by. He came to the police the day after our missing person's report went out. They said hello and she continued down the road, where she paused to speak with someone inside an idling pickup truck.

"I couldn't see the driver," he said. "But they seemed lost. I think she was giving directions." First he said the truck was blue, then said it might have been gray. He thought the plates were from out of state. Later, his wife, who caught a glimpse while coming back up the road, said she thought the truck was white. We know she stopped at the coffee shop on West Street. Her friend was working at the time. She used the bathroom, filled up her thermos at the dispenser behind the counter, and sat for a while on one of the tall stools facing the window.

"She seemed fine," her friend later said. "Maybe a little stressed. I think she had a disagreement with one of her daughters that morning." Her friend gave her a brownie and they chatted before a large group came in. "I got busy filling everyone's order. I don't even remember Natalie leaving the shop."

Her picture was stapled up on community boards and telephone poles as far south as Lake George. A couple of backpackers staying at the motel saw one and came down to the precinct, claiming they might've seen her sitting on a rock at a trail fork. "It looked like she may have been waiting for somebody."

"Did you speak to her?"

"No."

"Did you see her speak to anyone?"

"No."

The backpackers were shown the same photos of her again and soon backpedaled, telling the cops, "Maybe it isn't the same woman. It's hard to be sure." Calls came in from other people claiming to have spotted her out in the woods, or in a nearby town. Most of them were useless, a few were flat-out pranks.

"Situations like this attract a lot of sickos," the sheriff explained to us. "Don't let it get to you."

It got to my sister. She checked a huge topographical map out of the library and tacked it up on our wall, marking every place our mother had been seen with X's. Tangles of thin red ink lines wound through the mountains like veins spreading out from the same spot at the foot of the valley. Every night for weeks she stood before it, holding her pen and staring, unmoving, as if something would reveal itself to her if only she stayed still and quiet enough not to scare it away. Sometimes I drifted off atop a pile of blankets on the floor only to rouse awake hours later to the sound of her marker squeaking across the map, her breath strained and heaving. During this time, we moved nothing from its place. We never turned the lights off. We slept in brief shifts on the floor or on the sofa in the front room. Our mother's bathrobe remained slung over the back of a kitchen chair, exactly where it sat since her last morning at the table with us. A part of me honestly believed she might simply walk through the door and ruffle my hair. The idea of her being gone, really and truly gone, was still years out of my reach.

Our aunt, our mother's stepsister, flew in from her retirement community in Arizona to stay with us for a little while. We'd only met her once before that time and there was no genuine feeling of warmth between us, but she remained, dutifully, for two months feeding us and folding laundry and keeping in touch with the police. She joined us on sweeps of the forest. These sweeps were attended at first by large swaths of people from the community. They wielded lanterns and leashed hounds, spreading out over the land like a guerrilla force. A few of my teachers came. I recognized others from the pharmacy or grocery store, and some as the parents of a handful of my classmates. Many, still, were strangers to Liz and me. My aunt seemed wary of these people, the ones whom no one knew. She tried to keep a wide berth between us and them. Scouring the fields and trails like this gave me a terrible, hopeless feeling. Every little sound spooked me— wind rushing through the tall grass, a dog barking, thunder rolling in the distance. Each place seemed so utterly empty. Nothing but trees and dirt and heaps of rocks that could tell us nothing. I knew some- how that she wasn't there. I couldn't feel her.

One night, early on in the searching, I told my sister, "I can't feel her heart beating." Liz momentarily lowered her flashlight and looked at me, her face twisted in horror. I tried to explain. "I would know if she was somewhere out here."

"Just shut up," Liz snapped. And we kept walking, arms linked, into the blue dusk. A pair of women's underwear was uncovered in some brush, stirring a ripple of panic, but was quickly determined not to be a match. There was a sock, too, half hidden beneath a rock, but this also meant nothing in the end.

The party's numbers dwindled as days passed by. Within a month, just six of us remained. Then, around the time we stopped combing the woods, the sheriff called. A man had been pulled over in the early hours of the morning speeding down an unpaved road by the forest.

The sheriff told Liz, "Fucking flying. Mud blowing up all around the truck." The man was drunk. Agitated. He refused to produce his license and attempted to drive off. One cop held him against the hood while the other searched him, finding a cracked woman's compact mirror in an inner pocket of his jacket. The man became red-faced, nearly hysterical. Without being asked, he said he had no idea where the mirror had come from. Then, just moments later, he claimed it belonged to an old girlfriend. His fingernails were caked with dirt.

"It's Nick Haines," the sheriff said. "Do you know him?"

My sister's face was pale and shining with sweat. She looked up at the ceiling for a moment and then placed her hand on the small of her back, as if trying to steady her body against a powerful wind. I was standing across the room, holding our cordless phone to my ear and watching her.

She answered quietly. "I've heard her mention that name before." The officers bagged the compact and brought it to our home later that same night. Liz recognized it right away. "That's hers," she said, crossing her arms protectively over her chest.

"Are you sure?"

"Yes."

"Does this look familiar to you?" The man pushed the bag toward me.

I inspected the little mirror. It was green and white plastic poured into a swirled marble pattern. The name of a popular drugstore cosmetic brand was stenciled in gold on the top. I'd seen the same compact a hundred times. It was the kind of thing you got as a promotional item, bundled with lipstick or mascara. Certainly my mother owned one. I could picture it in her hands, dropping it into her bag as she walked out the door. Though I'd also seen the very same one at other people's houses, too, as part of the usual clutter on a nightstand or bathroom countertop. Liz and the policemen all looked at me expectantly. I felt a tightening in my chest.

"Yes," I finally replied. "I've seen it before."

"Where?"

"Lots of places. Everybody has one."

"But it's something you remember your mother using?"

I nodded.

Liz jumped in then, slapping one hand down on the table and waving the other toward me in quick dismissal. "She doesn't know. She's a kid. I told you, my mother had that exact mirror in her handbag all the time. I'm sure of it."

They asked us then how we'd heard Nick's name. Did our mother talk about him? Had he been to our house? One of the officers produced a small cassette recorder from his pocket and placed it on the table. There was a silver star-shaped sticker on the cover. I could hear the faint whir of the tape rolling around and around inside. I'd never heard the name before. I shook my head and drew my knees up to my chest. I wanted to go to bed. I wanted to shut all the lights off. I wanted everyone to be quiet.

"We don't know him," Liz said. The cops turned their attention to her. "I just remember her mentioning him."

"When?"

"Maybe six months ago."

"To you?"

"No. She was on the phone with someone. A friend, I guess. I think he'd asked her out a couple times, maybe she met him for a drink." There came more questions about her dating life, how often she went out and with whom. Rarely, my sister told them. And she never talked to us about it directly.

"Then how do you know she rarely dated?" The questioning cop held my sister's gaze. I could feel her growing aggravated.

"I know her," she said.

We allowed the officers to look around the house. Of course they'd been over before. First shortly after we initially reported her missing and they did a quick walk-through, seemingly unconcerned. And then again after two weeks had passed with no sign of her and they came back for a whole afternoon, rigorously examining each room. My sister hovered nearby the whole time, asking questions. Both searches were meant to uncover clues about secret plans she might've had or strange people she may have been speaking with. It was all fruitless. Her call records proved utterly banal. Both credit cards were still in her wallet left on the telephone table, meant for us to use for groceries the day she disappeared. No withdrawals from her bank account. No hidden love letters.

This time, though, there was something specific. The compact. Where would she have kept hers? The officers sifted through our bathroom cabinet. They shined little flashlights into the pockets of every coat and handbag in the downstairs closet. If it was uncovered somewhere in our house, then perhaps it was only a coincidence with Nick Haines, perhaps it belonged to another woman, perhaps he was just innocently drunk and filthy with dirt, speeding down the road like that, and this was another false alarm, as the underwear out in the field had been. Then we would be right back where we started, a boundless void of exhaustion and disbelief, no reason to cling to, no way to find our footing. I couldn't tell which outcome I hoped for less. I looked to my sister, but her face revealed nothing. The delicate skin beneath her eyes was smudged by deep, purple shadows and her hair had a sour smell to it. She was already a poor sleeper, and our mother's unexplained absence had driven her into a long period of insomnia. She'd lie down on the floor next to the sofa, where I'd set up a makeshift bed, for maybe an hour or two before getting up and going to sit by the front door, staring out the window in a trance.

Our aunt had long since returned to Arizona. "Well, girls," she said before leaving for the airport. "I don't know how to tell you how sorry I am." Then we were once again surrounded by mess.

It grew every day. Stacks of unopened mail, crusted-over bowls, dirty laundry spilling out of a basket. I tried to help where I could. Once I began to parse through a mail pile, but quickly found I couldn't make sense of the tables of numbers and dates, sums of money owed or paid off. Every other word was a mystery to me. Liz, already an adult in the eyes of the law, snatched the papers away from me.

"I'll deal with this," she insisted, her voice shaking. "This isn't for you to think about."

A young social worker was assigned to check in on us biweekly. We always let her in through the back porch and tried to keep her in our small sunroom, away from most of the mess, but sometimes she went wandering toward the front of the house, around the kitchen and living room and entryway, all cluttered and stale smelling, and there wasn't much we could do. She had a clipboard and a little business satchel, which she never took off her body. She asked us the same things every time: *Where would you rank your sadness on a scale of one to ten? Do you ever fantasize about harming yourself or another person? What have your last three meals been? When did you last leave the house and where did you go?*

On her fourth visit, Liz got so annoyed she interrupted the girl and said, "How old are you?"

"I'm sorry?" the social worker responded.

"I said"—Liz took a long, slow breath—"how old are you?"

She looked around nervously. I could see she was trying to decide whether she could get away with ignoring the question entirely. I wanted nothing more than for her to get out and never come back, but I also felt a little bad for her. Even at thirteen I could see how unseasoned and anxious she was. Her whole job was to enter the homes of depressed, unwashed, erratic people and pressure them to go for a stroll in the fresh air.

Finally, she replied, "I'm twenty-three." My sister burst into a sharp, ugly cackle that lasted about two whole minutes. The girl and I looked at the floor. At the end of that visit, she compelled me to return to school, citing the law. I did go back, eventually, but it was never the same. My teachers were not only unwilling to expect anything of me, but seemed fearful of speaking to me at all. My classmates, too, treated me like a fractured piece of glass.

We never did find that compact.

5

The bones were hers. I knew they would be.

Liz spoke to both the sheriff and the medical examiner on the phone while I sat nearby, listening on the other line. They explained that the dental records had been a positive match. There could be no question now.

My sister's voice was stoic. "What happens?" she asked. "What do you do next?"

"We are going to do an autopsy—"

Liz cut the examiner off. "On what? How can you do an autopsy on an incomplete skeleton?" I cringed.

"We can look for clues that might suggest a cause of death. We're going to look for any signs of trauma, in this case evidence of sharp or blunt force, or ballistic trauma. A forensic osteologist is going to come from the university to review our findings." His voice was soft and hesitant. He sounded elderly. "In all truthfulness, the condition of your mother's remains is not ideal. Without any other material evidence found at the site, it's hard to make any promises."

"What if you can't find anything?" she pressed. "What then?"

"Liz," the sheriff said. "We are using every resource we have here to try and find answers for you and your sister."

"Are you going to arrest anyone?" A loaded silence wavered on the other end. I shut my eyes. I knew she was asking about Nick Haines. She'd believed fiercely in his guilt since the day the police brought over that compact, and after their lead on him cooled, she became obsessed. She called their office regularly, offering the most mundane observations on his whereabouts and behavior—someone told her they'd seen him emerging from the woods again, early in the morning. *Hunting season,* the police reasoned. His license was active. Or she drove by his hardware store and saw him tossing a length of rope into the dumpster behind the parking lot. *Well, he does own the shop,* they said.

I thought of a time, maybe two years after our mother disappeared, when my sister returned home very late at night. It was unusual. She was almost always in bed by nine. I walked halfway down the stairs and watched as she slid her coat off, her cheeks and fingers red from the cold.

"Where were you?" I asked. She didn't want to tell me, so I followed her all the way to the bedroom, pressing the question.

Finally, she said, "I was parked outside of Nick Haines's house." My mouth hung open in disbelief. Liz went on to say that she drove up his street with her lights off and parked at an angle, a pair of binoculars pressed to her eyes as she sat low down in the driver's seat. "For the first fifteen minutes, nothing. Then I saw him in his living room." Certain she had witnessed something damning, I waited. I could hardly breathe. Soon, though, I realized she hadn't observed much of anything. He sat in a recliner for a long time, drinking a canned beer. Then he got up and did something to the TV before sitting back down, this time on the sofa, soon appearing to doze off with his outdoor jacket still on.

In a soft voice I told her, "I don't think you should do that again." She went back three more times.

"It's much too soon to tell, Liz." The sheriff took on a paternal if not slightly condescending tone. "There's a lot we need to work through before making any decisions about that."

41

"Is there?" My sister nearly spat the words onto the ground before her. I could see her shoulders hunching up, her ears turning red.

"You don't have to worry."

"How long, exactly, do I not need to worry?"

"We're not going to have any clear answers overnight here. It's been fifteen years. The evidence is in very delicate shape—"

"The evidence," she said. I heard the sheriff take a sharp breath inward.

Then the medical examiner's voice broke through the tension. "Would you like to come to the county morgue to view your mother's remains?" Without a second's hesitation Liz answered yes.

"And you, Jess?" My heart pounded. I had no idea either of the men even knew I was on the call.

"Yes," I whispered. "Okay."

Much of our mother was still missing. The pathologists had her remains arranged on a metal table with her name and birth date written out on a little card propped up in the top corner: NATALIE FAIRCHILD, 04/15/1965. There was the skull—the first piece to resurface from the earth. Almost all of her spine was intact. Her hands were in fragments alongside both femurs, which were warped and discolored almost beyond recognition. Liz and I were left alone in the room. It was ice cold, covered floor to ceiling in pastel tiles. Her table was just one in a row of many identical tables stretching all the way to the door. Behind us, a wall-length dead-bolted refrigerator hummed and rattled. I thought about how many other people must have been inside, just lying in the dark with their own little name tags. My sister was incredibly business-like about the whole visit. She placed her handbag down on one of the stools that had been set out for us and approached the table, expressionless. I watched her click around in her pointy boots, pausing every few moments to lean in and squint at some piece of bone. What was she looking for? The bones appeared to me like part of a museum exhibit, abstract and artificial.

When I first got the call from Liz, I'd been jolted into action. Oddly energized by the news, I drove like a maniac through the night, not stopping for coffee or anything to eat. The thought of missing even a moment of any developments felt unbearable. But actually being there, in the glum chill of the autopsy lab, I was frozen in place, close to vomiting. I wanted to run out into the parking lot. I wanted to gouge my own eyes out even though I understood that I had already seen her bones, looked straight at what was left of her, which meant it could come back to me anytime, even in the darkness, even with my eyes shut, even without eyes at all. This, too, was now the territory of my memory. There were two deep sinks set among many jars of cotton tufts and unlabeled bottles of yellow liquid. An eye-washing station sat in the corner. Someone had left a faded '96 Olympics coffee mug next to the basin. I had an urge to throw it to the ground and then stomp my feet on the broken pieces.

What got to me was her pelvic bone. All the life in that awful, cold room had sprung out of it. My sister and I—breathing, standing, flush with blood. Every artery, every finger and toe, the precious velvet of our tongues, had been cradled to the threshold of personhood just there, coaxed into the world between the smooth curve of its halves. As I looked at my mother like this, she hardly seemed real to me. Less real, somehow, than before I had any proof of her death. This was someone I hadn't known since the age of thirteen. I'd lived more of my life without her than with her. I wondered sometimes how many of my recollections could be relied on. Was she really as funny as I liked to think? In my mind, she had long eyelashes and small ears and a low voice. How could I ever be sure? I wondered what she would think of my life. I wondered if she would have stayed in Knife River or ever remarried. Perhaps she would have had another child. I'd imagined so many different fates for her over the years, but they all washed away in the finality of this moment. She was gone. She'd been gone all this time. And here was proof, the kind I could lay my eyes upon.

Liz kept glancing over at me. I was waiting for her to break. She was the one who'd raked herself over nails, refusing to leave not just our town but our very house, unwilling to part with any of our mother's possessions. She was obsessed with the disappearance. I knew she went out to the woods and walked those trails, wandered the same swaths of land we'd covered with the search party so many years ago. So why, when finally brought face-to-face with the basest matter of our loss, was she so calm?

"Take a closer look," she said to me.

"I'm okay over here." I pressed my back against the metal cabinet.

"Look, you can see where her arm was broken as a teenager. There's a little mark here, a hairline. Remember she told us she fell out of a tree?"

"I remember."

"Come stand with me, Jess."

"I can't."

"Please." I shook my head and looked toward the door. The walls pulsed around me. There was a smell in the air, something loamy and damp, vaguely rotten, mixed with the sharp antiseptic fumes.

Liz lunged toward me and grasped my arm. Her touch was tender and firm. I felt like a feral kitten discovered hiding out in a crawl space. She looked right into my eyes and squeezed my wrist, pulling me toward the table where our mother sat like a pile of rocks.

"Do this for me."

And with that I cracked open. Tears rushed down my neck in a hot, urgent stream. Something shifted in my sister, too. I could feel it. She softened. We stood there leaning on each other. In my mind, I combed through all the time that had passed between this moment and the first moment that led us here, the moment we realized something was wrong.

For months, I wondered when I would see her again. Then, as time passed, I wondered *if* I ever would. Every year the wondering got smaller and smaller, something I kept in a little box at the back of my thoughts and visited only when I could bear to. I had to sort of catch myself off guard with it—usually late at night, alone, with the lights off, drifting to sleep. If she were alive somewhere, what would she look like now? What would she say to me? Would I recognize her voice? I didn't ever imagine her bones. I could only picture her alive, standing at the end of a long tunnel, growing smaller and smaller as I moved steadily in the other direction. A pinprick of light behind me. I cried thinking of how long she sat like this in the woods, beneath the dirt. I cried thinking of the seasons changing all around her. My sister squeezed my hand so hard it hurt, but I didn't pull away.

6

Here's something I've never told: I saw her.

It was three years after she vanished, the night before my sixteenth birthday. I was taking a shortcut toward home along the shoulder of a deserted road that ran between my street and an old dairy barn where kids hung out. It was only about five miles. Liz tried to forbid me from walking there. She didn't like how desolate it was, surrounded by pine trees and not a single streetlight or mailbox. By then, though, she was working full time at the bank and went to sleep early each night, tired after frequent double shifts. She no longer had the energy to put me in line, or wasn't quite sure how. I was angry and restless and secretive, only three years off from moving away. We'd had explosive fights over her trying to parent me, as I saw it. She slapped me in the face once, crying and screaming that whether or not she liked it, it was her job to protect me and I had to let her. After hitting me, she seemed a little scared of herself and backed off a bit. I can remember feeling not afraid of her, but worried for her. She seemed perilously fragile. Hardly capable of protecting anything, least of all me.

The night I saw my mother, I'd been out at the old barn with some friends from school. We'd all been drinking and smoking bad, dry

46

weed when a wave of panic overtook me. There were people all around, music playing on a stereo. Nothing was wrong. But still, I had the sudden feeling that a pair of hands were wrapped around my neck, pressing all the air out of my body. The room spun. My heart pounded. I felt a damp chill rush down through my fingertips. Everyone's smile looked huge and freakish, I could hardly tell anyone apart. All the noise, the laughter and screaming and singing, was flattened out by the blood rushing fast through my ears. The walls seemed to grow closer and closer. Finally, I slipped out of one of the doors unnoticed and stood out in the field, exhaling with relief.

The moon was full and low. Deep blue light shone gently down on the field sloping out ahead, sending glimmers through the tall grass. I started walking, soothed by the cool air and wanting to distance myself from the noise of the party. Dew soaked through the hems of my jeans.

When I got to the edge of the pasture where the road connected, I kept going. My heartbeat calmed. I took long, slow breaths and walked straight down the middle of the lane. As I walked, I thought of Eva, the girl I was in love with, and how impossible it seemed that I would ever get to simply grab her by the back of the neck and kiss her in front of anyone the way I saw guys do with their girlfriends all the time. I wanted to hold her hand in the daytime, out in the world. The way men looked at her made me want to throw myself in front of a train.

I thought of my sister and how tired she seemed all the time. I knew she was back at the house, probably asleep on the couch in her work clothes with a half-finished plate of food on the coffee table before her. Since she'd slapped me, we'd hardly spoken. I thought of my mother and how she used to hate it when Liz and I didn't get along. *You girls have to stop this,* I remember her pleading one night at dinner after we'd quarreled over the TV remote. *One day I'll be gone, and you'll only have each other. You may have your differences, but no one will ever know you like your sister does.* When she said that, of course, none of us knew that she would be gone in less than a year.

Guilt lapped at me. I walked faster. Just beneath the guilt was a prickle of fear. I didn't know how I was ever going to get out of Knife River but I knew that I had to. The idea of staying was quickly becoming less bearable than the fear of striking out alone into an unknown place. I didn't know what had happened to my mother, or what would become of Liz if I moved away. What I knew was that there was no certainty in a life. Nothing guaranteed. The world was full of unknowable forces that could sweep in entirely without warning and strike you out. You could go for a walk and never come home. It could happen any day. There was no one to appeal to, no one with the power to put things back together. And the world would just go on, absorbing the shock like it was nothing. I'd learned how quickly people forgot about even the most tragic things, and that no matter how dark and miserable life became you would still just wake up again and again each morning needing food and water and having to use the bathroom because even if you felt so depressed you didn't want to breathe you were still only an animal and your body would keep going with or without your will.

Right then as I was nearing the end of the road, something caught my eye. A brief flicker in the trees. I froze, startled, narrowing my gaze. And I swear to you, for a passing moment, just a fraction of a second, I saw my mother. She was looking straight at me, her expression neither happy nor sad. She looked as real as any other person. I was stunned. Seized with disbelief and fascination. The moonlight cast her in a silver glow. Her red kerchief moved in the breeze. Her eyes blinked. She leaned against a tree and appeared to breathe. I could see her chest moving beneath her clothes.

Then a dog barked in the distance, and I turned my head. When I looked back, she was gone.

7

"How are you?"

"Fine."

"You don't seem fine," Liz said sharply. She was picking through a large bowl of lentils on the kitchen table, sorting through the dusty, gray beans for little pebbles—also gray and dusty, and roughly the same size. She sifted each handful carefully through her fingers, feeling around and discarding the rocks in a cup set off to the side. "You have to be careful not to bite down on one of these. They're little but they'll crack your tooth right down to the nerve."

"I'll help you." I pulled my chair closer to the table and began to sort. The task was dull and bland and repetitive. It was even a little depressing, but as the minutes ticked by I noticed my shoulders relaxing. My jaw unclenched. I dropped another rock into the cup.

A week had passed since seeing my mother's bones on the table. I couldn't shake it from my mind. The name tag. The sharp, chemical smell of the room. When I tried to fall asleep I could still hear the flat, terrible buzz of fluorescent lights. I felt like I was going a little crazy, which scared me. The way my sister was made sense now that I'd been home for a little while and observed the routine of her life, the way she lived inside the contained squalor of our house. It was hard to tell if my presence was a welcome disruption for her, or something she was just managing to tolerate. We hadn't really fought, but the iciness between us was impossible to ignore.

"You know, a person can bite through a finger with only as much force as it takes to bite through a baby carrot." My sister offered this plainly, without interrupting her lentil sorting. After a few minutes, she carried the bowl over to the stove, where she dumped it all into a pot of water and lit the burner. "Humans have a stronger bite than orangutans, even." I stared at her. She stirred the lentils around with a long wooden spoon, gazing down into them as if something might materialize in the pot. "I've heard stories of women biting their abductors so hard their teeth actually break. Some crimes have been solved that way."

"Jesus Christ, Liz."

"I'm just talking."

"I don't want to think about that."

She shrugged. My sister had a way of getting obsessed with gruesome documentaries and books about missing people—kidnappings, murders, freak disappearances of all kinds. She saved newspaper clippings and old tabloid magazines with crude headlines. Whenever the nation turned its collective obsession to a new missing girl, my sister learned all the details and followed it like it was her own personal loss.

I remembered a time when one such girl was found alive and returned home amid a flurry of welcome banners and news crews. Some local church group was putting together a quilt for her. They were collecting personalized squares from any person who wanted to make one. Liz made one. She sewed it by hand, using a needle and thread to sign her name, and embroidery floss to illustrate a gold finch—a symbol of perseverance and hope. She sent a picture of it to me in an email attachment, along with a series of links to different articles about this particular girl's story. This was maybe five years ago. We hadn't been speaking regularly since an argument about Christmas, whether we would spend it together and who would have to travel. I refused to come back to Knife River. She stopped answering my texts. Then, in July, I got this picture of an embroidered finch in my email. I didn't want to tell her so, but it turned out nicely. She was very good at those kinds of things—drawing, beading, making small finely hewn things out of soapstone or wood. But this tendency in her, the way she threw herself into tragedy, both our own and that which belonged to strangers, made me a little sick.

I watched as she chopped onions, then stirred those into the pot.

"Are you happy here?" I asked her. "Generally, I mean."

She answered immediately, not looking up from the stove. "That's a pointless question." I opened a beer, unfazed by her sharpness. I could feel her thoughts churning around in her head, colliding.

She stood there silently, hunched over the stove, until the lentils came to a boil. Then she dropped a lid over them and sat back down across from me at the table, taking the beer from my hand and drinking half of it down in two gulps. "Why would you ask me that?"

"Just checking in. It hasn't been an easy week."

"Things are turning around," she said. "We'll know something soon." Beneath the table, I tore at my cuticles until they bled. I worried about Liz stacking all her hopes on the autopsy. The medical examiner's voice echoed in my mind: *The condition of the remains is less than ideal.* I thought of the excavated site in the woods, barely a dent in the vast scope of the wild. A little hope left me every time I pictured it— and her body, the impermanence of something so soft—becoming more and more an irretrievable part of the wild with every season. Fifteen years. If I thought of it in terms of apartments I'd lived in, loves fallen in and out of, birthdays, it began to seem like an impossibly long time. And more hope left me still when I thought of the long, long list of other names whose fates were never solved. For every girl who got a quilt, a thousand lay lost in the dirt somewhere.

"And to answer your question," Liz added. "Yes. I am happy enough."

"Enough?"

"I have my routine here." She set the can down sharply. "I like my job. It's very cheap for me to stay in the house. The yard isn't difficult to manage. And finally, a good pizzeria opened in town." Liz looked me up and down, her lips set in a hard frown. "I know you don't think I could possibly have much of a life here."

"That's not what I was saying at all."

"You think I'm not happy."

"No, it's just—" I scraped around for the right words but couldn't find any. My eyes landed on a thick stack of old newspapers by the doorway. Each page seemed to have been pressed against the others for so long, enduring swings through humidity and dry winter air, that they'd formed sort of a solid, petrified block. "I've worried so much about you over the years. I only want you to be okay."

She searched my face with her eyes, brow furrowed, then seemed to soften a little. Her shoulders relaxed. "Who do you talk to at night? Your girlfriend?"

"What?"

"At night. You talk to someone."

"I didn't know you could hear me all the way from upstairs."

"I can hear you."

"I'll try to be more quiet then."

Every night when we spoke, Sarah wanted to be brought up to speed, asking about the investigation, the pathology. Each question came with three others attached to it. She discussed my circumstances easily, with the removed interest of someone following a soap opera. I didn't feel like talking about it much with her. What I really wanted was just to listen to her rehash the drama from her group of mom friends, or hear how her search for the perfect neutral area rug was going. It was all so soothing and uncomplicated. The life I'd briefly shared with Sarah had begun to feel almost dreamlike—pleasant and surreal, but impossibly far away and hurtling farther out into space every day I stayed away from it. My first night back, I'd lain awake before dawn thinking that I'd stay a week, at most. I could visualize that length of time as neat, finite squares on a calendar. But days kept passing and now it had been two weeks. Still, I told myself that by Thanksgiving, surely I'd be gone.

I said to Liz, "Anyway, yes, that's who I talk to at night. My girl-friend."

"Does she love you?" My sister blinked at me, her face nearly expressionless. She'd always been incredibly blunt, even before our mother disappeared. I remembered her getting snapped at by teachers for her habit of asking personal questions. How much were they paid? Why were they no longer wearing a wedding band? Her peers struggled with this part of her, too. Her questioning, yes, but mostly the way she stated aloud the things other people implicitly understood needed to go unsaid. It was as if the unspoken boundaries of the social world were simply invisible to her. She breezed through them, hardly ever seeming to notice other people's horror. Honestly, it was a quality I often found myself envying. I wanted some of whatever she had that made her so unflinching in the face of truth, even when the truth was frightening or hideous.

"I don't really think so," I said, surprising myself a bit. "I think she *thinks* she does." I could see my sister didn't quite get it. She didn't nod or say anything, just kept staring. I knew she would sit like that, waiting, until I explained. "So, okay." I opened another beer. "We met online. She's older than me. She's a doctor. I think she takes a lot of pleasure in the fact that my life isn't as . . . developed as hers. That makes her sound like kind of a jerk, but she's not. She's just a control freak. I think she's secretly sort of insecure. I don't know. Her divorce seems to have really messed her up."

"What type of doctor?"

"Dermatologist."

"Oh," Liz said. "No one goes to those." I laughed, knowing my sister hadn't meant to be funny, but what she said wasn't that far from the truth. She'd never gone to one, I knew. I hadn't, either, technically, unless you counted Sarah's impromptu excavations of my pores under the bright lights of her master bathroom. Few people in town had ever seen one, I was sure. There wasn't even a gynecologist within an hour of Knife River.

"But she also wants kids, like, really soon," I said. "And I don't."

"Why would she want to have kids with you?"

"Fair question."

"You're not married, even though you could be now that they've finally changed the law in some states." Liz plowed on. "So she'd probably have a hard time adopting with you. And then it's not like you can just get her pregnant, so one of you would have to get artificially inseminated and then carry the fetus—"

"Okay," I said, interrupting. "Thanks. Yeah. It would be her, for the record. Carrying the *fetus*."

"Good thing. I can't imagine you abstaining from alcohol for nine months." Liz picked up the Easter egg saltshaker, sprinkled a little into her palm, and then tossed it back into her open mouth like it was a handful of candy. Then she got up and spooned some of the cooked lentils into a bowl, leaning over the sink to eat them. I knew she was mulling over everything I'd told her, taking it in slowly. Confessing aloud that Sarah probably didn't love me came as a strange relief. It was something I'd thought about for a long time but couldn't stand to admit. Now I started to wonder if it even mattered. I'd been looking for a way out anyway. Soon, Thanksgiving would pass, and before long we'd be in the thick of winter. Icy air. The year burning down to the end of its wick. All my things were gone from her house. How long would she really wait? How long did I honestly want her to?

"Well, do you love her?" Liz's words came out garbled through a mouthful of food. She stared at the wall as she spoke to me.

"That's a big question."

"It's no bigger than any other question I've asked."

"Why do you want to know so much about this?"

"Why can't you just answer?"

"I don't *not* love her. I definitely care about her. There was always a lot of attraction between us. But there's a lot of ways to love someone, right?"

"You should know more about that than me," Liz said quietly.

"I mean, in the beginning I did love her, for sure. But things got complicated between us and I started having second thoughts, and now I'm here and I just don't know."

"You don't have to be so afraid of being alone, you know."

"I didn't say I was."

"I'm alone here," she said, still gazing at the wall. "And look at me. I'm fine enough."

I did look at her. I could tell she felt my eyes traveling along her back. Her shoulder blades poked through the back of her shirt, which had a small tear on the seam. She had a buzzardlike hunch. When I'd asked about it the week before, she told me simply that her stomach hurt if she stood up too straight. *Like there's a little shard of glass poking at the side.* This didn't seem to strike her as a problem. She just lived with it. Water dripped from the faucet in a steady stream, hitting the thin aluminum sink bottom and making a tinny, hollow sound that felt suddenly unbearably loud.

Liz set her bowl down onto the counter and announced gruffly, "I'm exhausted. I'm going to sleep."

"All right," I said. "Good night."

"Good night." At the doorway, she turned around for a second and gave a wan smile before continuing upstairs.

8

The clutter was getting to be too much.

I'd been back home in Knife River for two weeks and was rooting around in the fridge when I noticed a magnet stuck to the freezer panel. It was one of those free calendar pads you get in the mail around the holidays, this one from a mechanic shop. It was six years out of date, yellowed and curling up at the corners. I peeled it off and tossed it into the trash. My skin began to itch, and I felt hot and restless, so I flung open the window. Crisp air filled the room. I was surrounded by piles of old things. A stack of ancient take-out menus, years of phone books, folded-up paper bags from the grocery store. All of it seemed to pulsate around me, pressing down against my skin and growing larger somehow with each breath. I threw all those things into the trash with the magnet, then grabbed a step stool and peered into the cabinets. There were cracked plastic cups, used coffee filters, bags of hardened brown sugar. I dropped it all down into the garbage at my feet. Some of it missed and fell onto the floor, clattering as it rolled over the tile. Soon I'd gone through every drawer and thrown out maybe a hundred dried-up pens and yellowed receipts. A cold breeze rushed against my neck.

When Liz returned home from work, she set her bag down on the floor and looked around slowly, blank-faced, at all the tied-up garbage bags and at me, out of breath and glistening, shirt sleeves rolled up to the shoulders. I was holding two old jars of home-canned peaches, lids bloated with fermented gas. I remembered getting these from a neighbor when we were teenagers—sort of a sympathy gift. People used to give us food all the time in the beginning. Later on, I looked back and felt guilty thinking about these people, most of whom we barely knew, taking the time to cook for us and worry after our nutrition. Much of what we ate for the first year came out of other people's kitchens. I couldn't believe these peaches had just been sitting around in the dust all that time. Liz looked at the jars in my hands, slowly unbuttoning her coat. I couldn't tell what she was about to do. I thought we might really have it out. Maybe she would even make me leave. Would I go to a motel? Would I drive back down to Sarah's and try to force the relationship into contentedness? Would I finally pluck up the gumption to move to Maine, as I'd long imagined? My heart pounded wildly. Then, without comment, Liz went over to the pantry and started tossing more old food into the trash.

We sifted through the whole kitchen together, purging years of expired sundries: relish turned greenish brown in a glass bottle, powdered cake mix full of dead ants, unlabeled cans, and rusted aluminum pie tins. Among all this, I found a scrap of paper with my mother's cursive. It read, simply, *crushed ice.* The sight of her handwriting sent a chill through me. The swoop of the *s*, an open loop dotting the *i*. It was like looking at a picture of her in a way. Unmistakable. I tucked the scrap into my pocket.

Liz found an unopened fifth of shitty vodka above the sink and we started to pass it back and forth as we cleaned, sipping straight from the bottle. I could always tell when my sister started to get drunk by how talkative she became. Her jaw muscles relaxed. She chatted easily about all kinds of things—tonight, a co-worker she hated. A woman who regularly showed up late and made popcorn for lunch every day in the microwave.

"Who eats a bag of dry popcorn for lunch?" Liz shouted. "A fucking weirdo." She listed off all the other objectionable habits this woman had at work, and then, as if to punctuate it all, stood abruptly and took the old jarred peaches with her into the backyard. I watched from the window. Grinning, she threw both jars down onto a tree stump with some real force. The glass burst into a million little pieces with a satisfying pop. Globs of putrid fruit landed in the leaf piles. Liz threw her head back, cackling up at the sky. Her face was harshly illuminated by the porch floodlight. She shouted into the open air, "This feels great." I was delighted.

Next, we worked our way through the dining room, tossing out bundled stacks of newspapers and tabloid magazines that were lined up under the table. Inside the broom closet, heaps of mail addressed to our mother sat jumbled inside grocery bags—sale fliers, insurance statements, Christmas cards. I dug through it all, dizzy at the sight of her name appearing again and again, almost multiplying, in my hands. Liz watched me intently. I think she was trying to see how I would react. I wanted to scream. Instead, I hauled the bags out to the end of the driveway and dropped them down with all the rest of the trash. We flipped over each couch cushion and got rid of old tissues and *TV Guide*s. We threw out a trio of rag dolls that sat inexplicably on the windowsill. I had no idea how they came to be in the house. I was happy to see them go. Their shiny button eyes gave me an uneasy feeling. Into the trash went a used mousetrap, a broken lamp, melted birthday candles in an envelope marked 10, six empty wine bottles. Fifteen sacks in total. We hadn't touched upstairs, but the place felt lighter.

By the time we were done it was late. Liz walked up and down the line of bagged trash at the side of the driveway. She looked a little anxious. "We don't have any garbage bags left now."

"I can go get some."

"The gas station closes in fifteen minutes. Go to the big supermarket across the river, they stay open late."

"All right."

"Get some bread, too?"

"Yeah."

"And half-and-half." I nodded, reaching around inside my coat for the car keys.

Liz asked, "Can you drive?" We'd drunk all that vodka on empty stomachs. The ground looked wobbly.

"Yes," I said, a little too loudly. "I can definitely drive."

The superstore had opened sometime in the last year. It was enormous, the newest branch of a national chain. Liz told me some people protested its opening, worried that it would bring too much traffic and drive the other, older store out of business. The protests were led by a man named Bill, who managed the original grocery and lived outside of it in a blue van with window curtains. He wasn't from here; he'd driven in one day from Ohio maybe twenty years ago and just stayed after finding work in the store and selling paintings from the back of the van at odd hours. Local landscapes and portraits done on small squares of plywood. I could remember walking around town and seeing him sometimes sitting on the bumper, sketching with a charcoal stick, one side of his mouth swollen with chew, white hair secured in a long ponytail. People generally liked him, and some showed up for about a week with homemade signs condemning the new chain, but before long, Liz explained, those same people were shopping at the chain themselves.

It was a little eerie looking, this huge store sitting in an otherwise empty field all lit up with white and orange lights. The parking lot sprawled out in every direction, asphalt in a once-vacant meadow. Some dented shopping carts sat upended at the grassy border. While grabbing my wallet from the center console I caught sight of my face in the rearview. I looked like an old paper bag. Like something dragged from the bottom of a ditch somewhere. My eyes were sunken, ringed with purple shadows. There was a little cut on my cheek I didn't remember getting.

I hadn't gotten much rest since returning home. The couch I'd been sleeping on was old and I could feel the springs cracking beneath my back every time I turned. The house itself made me jumpy, too; it creaked and moaned with the wind and seemed to do most of its settling in the early morning hours. I did try one night to sleep in my old bed upstairs. I was so miserable and sore on the sofa that I tossed off my quilt and marched straight up the steps, irate with exhaustion. I didn't turn the lights on. I didn't want to see what had once been my room. I just wanted a few hours of real, dreamless sleep. It didn't come to me. Frigid air leaked in around the warped windowsill. I could hear Liz's snoring from across the hall. After maybe an hour of earnest trying, I got up. Before going back down to the couch, I quietly cracked open the door to my mother's bedroom. Looking in, I had the feeling of doing something improper. Like staring too long at someone getting lifted onto a stretcher on the sidewalk. Dim, silvery moonlight cast shadows against the walls. Her furniture seemed to stare back at me. I couldn't bring myself to cross the threshold.

The supermarket was immaculately clean with white, unscuffed floors. Soft music drifted down from somewhere up above. Walking in, I could see no people other than a young man in a blue vest sitting behind one of the many cash registers. He yawned, looking at something on his phone. There was a refrigerator case full of roses. A tank with a few live lobsters scuttling around. An M&M's dispenser the size of a small corn silo. Beyond it, at the far end of the wall, red meat wrapped in cellophane seemed to stretch on forever along a mirrored shelf. It was strange to see a place like this near town. The grocery store Bill ran, which had not yet been driven out of business, was maybe a fifth this size, with brown and orange linoleum tiles and a wet, yeasty kind of smell. It held a sparse liquor aisle that Bill kept locked up on Sundays and every weekday before noon. Here, thirty different types of craft beers were displayed in an open cold case, bright lights shining down against the bottles.

Remembering the half-and-half, I turned the corner into the dairy section and spotted her immediately. Standing before a freezer, holding a carton of eggs in one hand, pushing her bangs back from her face with the other, was Eva. The girl I'd loved as a teenager. The sight of her took the air out of me again. Her hair was still dark and wild down her back, shining like ice on a river at night. Her posture still defiant and tall. We hadn't spoken in ten years. Not one word between us since the day I moved away from Knife River. I stood completely still, hoping to remain unnoticed. Many times I'd imagined what it might be like to run into each other again. None of it looked like this. I felt almost sick. I couldn't believe this was happening an hour before midnight, when I'd just spent the entire evening sipping room-temperature vodka from a bottle with my sister, hauling bag after bag of garbage outside. I wanted to leave. Fuck the half-and-half and the trash bags, I thought. We couldn't see each other like this, here. The problem was mostly me—my shirt was dusty and damp on the cuffs from some unlabeled liquid that had seeped from a jar into my hands while cleaning out the kitchen. I could almost feel the bags under my eyes. But I couldn't bring myself to look away from her hands. They were exactly as I remembered—long and graceful with delicately tapered fingers that seemed to glide over everything with the reverberations of some quiet, womanly magic. Like she was imbuing the world, piece by piece, with a spell.

Those hands were the first thing I ever noticed about her. I was halfway through high school then, two years into life alone with my sister. I was in a chemistry period in the middle of the day. The teacher, an ancient man with white hair coming out of his ears, nodded off at his desk. I remember summer lingering on through September that year; all the windows remained propped open and warm, fragrant air drifted in from the outside. No one could sit still. Then suddenly I noticed Eva watching me from a desk across the aisle. She was tapping her divine fingers against the back of her chair. Her eyes were wide and green. She wore a man's blue work shirt tied up at the waist. There was something vaguely dangerous about her presence. She was demure and commanding all at once. I had hazy recollections of seeing her around in the past, maybe a couple of years earlier, down at the far end of the hall between periods, quietly slipping out of the gym if we were going to have to run laps or climb the rope, but we'd never spoken before. Now we propped our chemistry books before us and started passing notes back and forth. It turned out she'd gone to live with her grandmother in a nearby town for a while, then returned after having problems at the Baptist girls' school there. When I pressed, she wrote back only, *it just didn't work out,* before getting up and leaving the classroom, unnoticed by our teacher. She was taller now than I'd recalled her being. And phenomenally, undeniably beautiful.

That year the other beautiful girls, girls I'd sensed hadn't paid any attention to Eva in the past, were suddenly trying to befriend her. I would watch from a distance as they surrounded her out in the empty lot where they set us loose during lunch, buzzing with questions and scrutinizing her with just barely veiled disdain. Eva received these girls coolly, keeping the conversations brief, hardly seeming to care what they thought about her. She didn't bother with being friendly. She didn't seem to worry about whether anyone liked her or not. We had most of our classes together that fall, and I always caught myself staring at her, studying those hands. At the end of September, she approached me in the bathroom and took my hand, turning it over silently, gently, palm up, a wry smile on her face, before writing her phone number on the soft skin of my wrist.

The gesture electrified me. I realized then how long it had been since anybody touched me at all. My sister hadn't hugged me in maybe a year. We were well past the point of concerned neighbors placing a hand on my shoulder. I stayed over at Eva's that weekend. Her bedroom was the attic space over her family's detached garage—her father and two older brothers lived in the house. They ran a small gravel processing plant together and never seemed to be around. Eva hardly mentioned them, she was so immersed in the little world of her attic. The ceiling and walls were painted a deep, hypnotic shade of blue.

She'd wrapped white Christmas lights around all the beams and rafters and kept her CD collection stacked inside an antique oven that sat, cobwebbed, in one corner. Her bed was two big mattresses pushed together and held up off the ground by a grid of wooden pallets.

She kissed me first that night. It was late. We'd gone to sleep hours earlier after tiring ourselves out watching *X-Files* and trying to smoke hash out of an apple. Before that, she asked me how it was going living alone with just my sister. She knew about what happened, of course. Everybody did. The question was abrupt. I blinked at her for a long moment, apprehensive. She waited. And then I found myself explaining everything, every detail that haunted me, every question that loomed and ate at me, everything I pushed all the way down into the secret quiet. Eva took it all in without a word, waiting until I was thoroughly finished to say anything. If it creeped her out, she didn't show it. She acted like it was something that could happen to any person— a sad, ruinous thing that was just as much a part of the world as earthquakes or lung cancer. Most notably, though, she didn't act as if it left any kind of stain on me. I woke up later that night to her hand pressed against my chest, her face softly illuminated by the twinkling lights.

"Hi," I whispered, eyes half shut. And then she kissed me, and everything that had ever caused me pain seemed to fade away.

I decided it would be worse if she were to spot me lurking around in the dairy aisle, so I took a long breath and walked up to her.

"Eva," I said. She turned, and in the fraction of a moment before recognition, I got to see her face as a stranger would. "Sorry to surprise you." My heart fluttered.

"No, it's fine." She seemed flustered, fumbling to place her things in the cart. "I'm glad you said hi." We exchanged a brief, awkward hug in the middle of the aisle. Both of us seemed unsure where exactly to let our hands rest or how soon to pull away. As we stepped apart she added, "I should say, I know why you're back."

"Oh."

"I'm really sorry."

"Thanks."

"Are you okay?" At this, I let out a strange, sudden laugh and pushed my hair back out of my face. "I know you're not okay," Eva said. "It's just what you say, I guess."

"I am kind of okay, actually. Today was a little better than the days before."

"That's really good to hear."

"So, people are talking about it then."

"Well, yes." She averted her eyes to the ground. "It was pretty big news here. Not much else going on, as I'm sure you remember."

"Yeah."

"But really just among the people who were here then. Like, the people who could remember her." She wrung her fingers together. I could see she was uneasy. "I just don't want you to feel like *everyone* is sitting around talking about it. You have enough on your mind already."

I nodded. The loaf of bread I was holding began to feel heavy. My elbows ached. I put it down on the shelf behind me.

"How is Liz handling it?"

"You know," I said. "Like Liz."

"Right." We stood there for a few moments just looking at each other. The quiet between us had a pulse of its own.

The boy in the blue vest from the front of the store passed by the aisle, slowly pushing a mop in front of him. Without looking at us he shouted, "We're closing in ten minutes." Needing something to do with my hands, I picked up the loaf of bread again and held it in my arms like an infant, close to my chest. Eva's eyes darted toward it, then scanned my face slowly, carefully.

I cleared my throat and said, "I can't believe I'm standing here talking to you right now. I had no idea if you still lived in town. I wondered about you all the time."

"Still here," she said. Her tone was flat. I let the words echo in my head, trying to weed out any feeling from them. It was impossible to tell if *still here* meant, still here because I found my place and came to be content, or still here because I couldn't figure out where else to go or what to do, or still here as in fuck you for moving away without any warning and never calling. Remorse rose through my neck and cheeks in hot little blooms. She could sense it, I think. The way she stared at me with her wide, penetrating eyes. I felt like a rabbit in an open field.

"How long will you be around for?"

My gaze drifted to our reflection in the freezer case. "Maybe a month. There's still a lot left for me and Liz to deal with."

"Of course."

"I should go," I said. "It's been a long day."

"Well, let me know if you want to get together? I mean, it would be good to catch up somewhere not here." She gestured to a twelve-foot pyramid of boxed ice-cream cones. "I can give you my number? Call it so I have yours, too."

My heart flung itself to the back of my throat. I told her yes, and then repeated it twice more. A hint of a smile slipped onto her lips. I was so tired and nervous, I kept punching the digits in wrong. Finally, she took the phone from me gently and put her name in.

9

Liz and I wanted to have something like a memorial in the woods, at the spot where our mother was finally discovered, but the only passable route was through a family's property. Technically, she was found within the boundaries of their land. The family lived in a log house set far from the road and shared a back border with the state forest, an enormous stretch of wilderness that extended into both Vermont and Canada, traversing Lake Champlain in a series of uninhabited islands. It was one of their children who found her skull in the dirt and came running that day.

No one really lived out there when I was growing up. The area wasn't possessed by the state or used by the county, and the road was half grown over with ragweed. A wild tract of no-man's-land. Eventually, zoning laws were changed and people slowly started to pull in temporary trailers and build water cisterns. Soon, foundations were poured. The area had to be added to the postal route and school busing schedule, though nearly all the children out there were educated in their homes. These people valued their privacy. A lot were sustenance hunters and land separatists. Liz told me there were occasional stirrings about some of them stockpiling unregistered weapons.

The family was reluctant to let us walk over their land. They had no phone, so our newly assigned detective, Jack Calloway, went over in person to ask for permission for us. It took some convincing.

"They've dealt with a lot of interference already," he explained over the phone. Liz was at work and I'd answered his call. I found myself pacing a tight circle in the kitchen as we spoke, anxious over being the only one listening to this new information. I worried I wouldn't ask the right questions. I didn't have my sister's shrewdness, her persistence. The detective went on. "You know, with the police vans and that one news crew that tried to drive in—they ruined a winter vegetable patch with their tires. The sheriff and I have already gone back twice since then with the forensics guy from the pathology lab."

"Twice? Why?"

"He wanted to comb the dirt again for fibers." He paused. "You know, sometimes there are trace materials from clothing or other things that can be helpful."

"Did he find anything?" I felt my throat tighten into a hard knot.

"No. I'm sorry." I let out a strange grunt. I wasn't sure what to say, and neither was the detective. I could tell by his voice he was very young. "But the good news is the family agreed."

"Great," I said. "We'll be careful not to disturb anyone. Liz just really wants us to spend some time there at the site."

"I understand."

"Listen," I said, pressing my fingers between my eyes. A dull aching beat at the back of my head. "Can you tell me anything? Anything at all."

"In regard to what, exactly?"

"It's been almost a month. And I just—" Tears suddenly stung at my eyes. I could hear my voice was wet and limp with them, too. All day I'd been fine. I'd transcribed a single, seventy-five-page report on corrective surgery for an advanced case of gingivitis on an elderly woman. I submitted the file to the record keeper. I sent my invoice to the office manager. "Sorry," I choked out. I stopped my pacing and grabbed a pad of paper from the junk drawer, thinking I should take some notes for my sister, then sat down at the table and took a deep breath. "I just feel like I need to know what we're waiting for."

"I know this must be really difficult—"

"It's miserable."

"All I can say is that once the pathologists finish their work, you'll have some more clarity. I don't know what it will be, but that's the first step for us to get through. We don't want to jeopardize any potential leads by going after someone prematurely. I know your sister has her opinions there, but we have to observe a protocol."

I traced a circle over and over again on the blank paper before me. It seemed there was nothing worth jotting down. No dates to mark on the calendar, nothing new about Nick Haines. I knew she'd be disappointed. *They could at least ask him a few questions,* she growled the night before. *You don't have to arrest someone just to talk to them.* I wished I could tell her something, anything, that might soothe her worry. That seemed almost more important to me than knowing for my own sake.

But there was nothing to tell her, and the police remained reluctant, despite my sister calling the office constantly. Each time she got the sheriff on the phone he told her the same thing; they'd held Haines as long as they could the first time around, there was never enough to bring him up on anything. By the time our local officers had obtained a warrant and first arrived at his home all those years ago, his truck was freshly washed and vacuumed. Not a speck of dirt beneath the floor mats, they told us. Haines claimed it was his weekly ritual. The detectives noticed the burned-out remains of a fire in an aluminum drum toward the back of the property, behind a shed. A foul, plasticky odor lingered in the air.

At this, Haines offered, "I burn my trash. I don't want to pay to bring it to the dump." The warrant was good for ten days, but they spent only one inside his house.

The police were lax in their investigation due to the smallness of our town, yes. They were only really accustomed to dealing with drunk drivers and shoplifters. The bulk of violent offenses called in were domestic, often involving the same people they'd already gotten on DUIs. And because Knife River was so small, half the cops already knew Haines. One of them had coached his junior high baseball team. The day we first reported our mother's disappearance was the first time I realized that no one else was ever going to care about this as much as we did.

We'd gone to bed the night before, anxious and reluctant, but still clinging to the hope that there was some simple explanation for her absence, that she'd walk back in the door and everything would be fine. There had to be some reason she didn't come back from her walk, I told myself. There just had to be. I woke up early the next morning to Liz pounding on my door. My stomach felt like a block of ice. When I stepped out into the hallway, she was already fully dressed, dried tear tracks all down her cheeks.

"We need to go to the police," she whispered. She and I rushed over to the station and insisted on speaking with the sheriff. It was Memorial Day weekend and the only other person there besides him was the switchboard operator, his young niece, who was filing her nails at the front desk. We explained everything in tandem, breathless, slapping our hands on the counter.

The sheriff ushered us back into his little office. A mounted moose head stared down at us from the wall.

"Nine times out of ten, a person isn't really missing." We blinked at him, utterly confused.

"No," my sister said. "You don't understand. She went out for a walk and didn't come back. Her stuff is still at the house."

"I'm telling you girls, she'll be back. This kind of thing happens more often than you'd think."

"No way, this isn't like that. She would never just leave."

"Listen," the sheriff said. "We wouldn't even *file* a missing person's report on an adult in such a short window of time." He smiled weakly at us, his eyes crinkling up at the sides. "Do you know why that is?" We

69

didn't answer. Liz was nearly shaking with rage. Her ears turned red. I could barely make sense of what was happening. "Because grown-ups who go *missing* almost always come back on their own in a day or two. Trust me."

"She would never go anywhere without telling us. Overnight? Never."

"Didn't you say you'd had a squabble with her?"

"Yes, but—"

"Well, then, there you go. It's a holiday weekend, she went out to blow off some steam and got sidetracked."

"But it's been a whole day."

"Not a whole day yet," he countered, glancing up at the wall clock. "But even if it were, I've seen it a thousand times. A woman goes over to her boyfriend's house and gets to talking and drinking and what have you and before you know it they're asleep on the couch and their family's in a panic thinking something terrible happened."

"She doesn't have a boyfriend," Liz shouted, rising up in one fast motion from her chair. The metal legs made an ugly, screechy sound as they dragged across the laminate floor. Some papers fluttered on the desk.

I looked up at her, stunned, but relieved. I couldn't bring myself to scream. I knew I would never be the one to demand action like this, to dig my heels in and raise my voice. Her chest heaved with short, hard breaths.

"All right," the sheriff finally said, hoisting himself up and grunting softly. I could see he was a little spooked. There was a particular look men got when they were scared of a young woman. Their smugness giving way to a widening in the eye, their mouth drooping at the corners. It was something my sister elicited easily. "You girls check around with her friends today. Find out if any of them have seen her. If you still haven't heard from her in another twenty-four hours, you call the station and ask to speak with me."

Talking to Calloway now gave me the same feeling of bewildered helplessness I'd felt in the office that day long ago.

"How much more time do you think it'll be before the forensics work is finished?" I asked.

"It could be a few months. It depends. As much as we want answers right away, you don't want to rush this kind of thing. You just can't rush it."

"Right." I wanted to laugh, thinking about how absurd it was that this young detective worried I might believe I *could* rush anything along, as if I hadn't spent half my life waiting on this, knowing the whole time I might never find answers. He gave me the family's address, and then his personal cell number. He encouraged me to call anytime, if I ever had any questions or needed anything. He promised to be in touch.

Three days later, Liz parked the car on the road at the top of the family's driveway. Heat roared from the vents. My hands were so dry they cracked at the knuckles and bled a little, stinging with each movement. We were waiting for a friend of hers. At first I thought I'd misheard. I couldn't remember her talking about any friends in town. But Liz just sat there, looking out ahead at the road like someone was going to show up any moment. I wasn't sure what to expect. Part of me thought it was going to be a man, some secret boyfriend I'd never heard mention of. Maybe someone from outside Knife River. But that felt impossible. My sister seemed to exist entirely between our home and her window at the bank, shuttling herself back and forth in her little blue car on the same schedule every day. I'd have noticed any deviations. It had been a little over three weeks, but I'd barely gone anywhere since returning back home. I knew when to expect the sound of her engine in the driveway, the click of her keys turning at the front door.

"You could've told me someone else was coming to our memorial," I finally said. She shrugged. I laid my head back on the seat. My frustration quickly faded into a resigned, tepid envy. A tiny part of me wished that someone was on their way to stand with me, too. Sarah probably would have made the trip up for this, I thought, if I asked. She would have been dressed appropriately; somber, but practical, ready with a funerary wreath and tissues in her pocket. She could have rattled off some kind of eulogy. She was good on the spot like that. But I didn't think to invite her, even when we spoke on the phone last night, and instead my imagination kept flickering back to Eva. I wanted her to show up, even though we hadn't seen each other again since the grocery store, even though we couldn't honestly say we knew each other at all anymore. She probably wouldn't have had anything to fill the painful silences with, nothing for me to blow my nose on. I wasn't even sure she'd arrive on time. But still, a little corner of my heart tugged and tugged.

Soon a dented white town car appeared in the clearing up ahead. It sped toward us, plumes of dirt and gravel flying up in its wake, and pulled over just off the shoulder by a heap of bundled firewood. A tiny old woman climbed out. Her spindly legs were dwarfed by large brown hunting boots. She wore bright pink lipstick. Silver hair hung loose around her shoulders. Liz turned off the engine and we got out of the car.

"This is your friend?" I whispered, baffled. Liz nodded.

As she walked toward us I could see she had a slight limp. She had to be in her early nineties. When she got closer, I saw that the top of her head barely reached my chest. Without a word, she pulled three white long-stemmed roses from her coat. I was speechless. I watched as my sister leaned down to hug her. I couldn't recall ever seeing a look of such genuine, unrestrained affection on Liz's face.

She introduced the old woman to me as Brenda, who pressed one of the roses into my hand and said, "Thank you for allowing me to join you today." I nodded, glancing from her to Liz and back again, waiting for someone to say the right thing. They reminded me of two owls perched in some bramble with their long, dark coats and shoulders hunched up in the wind, staring at me as the cold whipped around our bare faces.

"I guess we should get on with it then," I said, pushing my hands into my pockets.

I paused at the family's window as we passed by their house on the way into the woods. Through an opening in the blinds I could make out a room with pine walls and a stout cast-iron stove in the corner. Toys were scattered on the ground. Among them, a child in a plain, homemade-looking sack dress. Was this the same girl who'd stumbled upon our mother's bones? I stood on my toes, trying to get a better view. The child was holding a doll between her knees, fitting it into a plain little dress just like her own, oblivious to my presence. I felt choked up with an odd kind of gratitude.

In some way, I wanted her to know what a miracle her accidental discovery had been. She lay her fingers on a lost woman's skull by pure chance and reached fifteen years back through time, setting in motion a series of reactions that I hoped, still, might flood this ugliest, most impenetrable part of my life with light. Of course, there remained a thousand questions. Without the forensics results, Liz and I still had no clues into the manner in which our mother's life ended, or was taken. No way to assign blame. I still wondered about things like the last word she ever spoke, or if she felt any pain, but the certain knowledge that she'd been released from her body long ago was a gift I'd feared I might never receive. And there, just on the other side of the window, was the person who'd given it to me. A child. An absolute stranger. In another way, I felt protective of her. I worried she would be changed by this, that it would make her fearful of death and the woods and her own backyard. I didn't want her to lose out on the sanctuary of the forest. I didn't want her to think she could never be safe, alone, in the wild.

Brenda tugged gently at my wrist. "Onward," she whispered.

The three of us followed a series of yellow police tags through the trees. About half a mile from the family's cabin we came upon a clearing. There were deep tire tracks in the mud, emergency tape wrapped around stakes encircling the excavated area. In the center, an indentation as deep and wide as a bathtub. Earthworms wriggled in and out of the black soil, soaked through with weeks of heavy rain. I could see our breath rising in little clouds. The air was thickly damp and cold. I'd coaxed myself into coming out to the site because I knew my sister needed us to see it. But I also imagined that being there would somehow stitch together loose ends for me, that I would find myself inching nearer to the closure everyone thought I so desperately needed, if I just made myself stand there in the dirt, breathing the same air that once surrounded her, finally seeing where she'd lain.

It wasn't like that. Looking down, I saw nothing but a hole in the ground. Empty, dark, wet earth crumbling back down into itself. It didn't mean anything to me. I couldn't see her in there. I couldn't feel any lingering wisps of her presence. All around us was miles and miles of forest, dying as winter approached. Naked branches, stark and cruel looking against the bright light of day. Under our feet, a blanket of rotting leaves. We were only about forty minutes from home. I couldn't believe this was where she sat for fifteen years, in this unremarkable stretch of wilderness, while my sister and I struggled and fought and wept in each other's beds, trying to survive, somewhere just a short ways over the horizon. It was so depressing I felt like I might collapse. Liz seemed to be on the brink of it, too. I could see her face caving in. Maybe, I thought, this whole idea was a mistake. What did it matter if we came out here? How would this help us? We were far from the road, gazing down into an empty hole on someone else's land, cold and miserable and no closer to knowing the truth. Liz made a strange sound, like an animal being born. I wanted to put my hand on her shoulder but couldn't bring myself to move. My legs were stiff. I had no idea how I'd ever find it in me to hike back out.

Then, Brenda dropped unceremoniously to her knees. She wriggled under the police tape and sidled over to the edge of the hole, her coat dragging in the mud, hands caked with dirt. My sister and I looked at each other. Then, the old woman began to sing "Ave Maria." Her voice rang out of her tiny body like a church bell at dawn, strong and clear and sweet. It rose up to the treetops. It echoed far into the distance, funneling through felled logs and over the gems of dew that shook on moss-covered rocks. It soared like a ribbon over the canopy and across the river valley. It drove out the bleakness. Liz and I crawled under the tape and sat beside her, overcome. Our knees sank into the earth. I shut my eyes and listened.

As Brenda sang, images of my mother gathered in my mind. There were so many things I remembered about her. Small, fleeting things. A warped picture of her moment on earth. Her hands arranging some plucked wild daisies in a rinsed pickle jar. Her crouching behind a camera on a tripod, then running quick to join me and Liz seated, smiling on the front steps of our house before the timer went off. A vague recollection of her footprints in the snow leading to the mailbox. A hand on my forehead, checking for fever. She always dressed up for Halloween, even after my sister and I grew out of it. I could picture her in a shiny black witch costume, opening the door with a bowl of candy, green face paint sponged all over her skin, a big fake wart on her nose. Had she really worn a costume like that? Did I invent it? I lingered on the memory, turning it over like a leaf, questioning it.

I missed her every Halloween, every holiday, every time I poured a beer and remembered the way she always sprinkled salt into hers, saying she liked the way it made more foam. I missed her blunt sense of humor and her toughness. The way she spoke plainly to us, even when we were very small.

I thought of the story she told of her wedding, forced into quick fruition by her parents, held in an Elks Lodge basement, the dress straining against her pregnant belly. Some relatives got into a fight. One person got pushed through a screen door. She always laughed as she told the story. I never knew if I was supposed to laugh, too.

The groom, our father, gave it a fair shot at first, we were told. But once the factory went under he took a trucking job and was gone for longer and longer stretches of time, returning briefly and intermittently, bearing gifts of slightly damaged cargo. They had me to try and fix things, I think. Maybe our mother thought the presence of a new baby would keep him around more. But when I was six months old, he was given an ultimatum by his girlfriend, a woman in Vermont who called our house and declared herself his soon-to-be fiancée. I say ultimatum because that's the way my mother explained it, rolling her eyes and sort of half chuckling. She says she gave him one, too, breastfeeding me as she delivered it, and he left the next day.

Seven years after that, he was sitting in a parked car outside a grocery store when a blood vessel in his brain burst, killing him instantly. The Vermont woman called our house for the second, and final, time to let us know. Our mother relayed the news of his death to us nonchalantly. We were not devastated. In fact, we went out for pancakes later that same day. I missed that kind of coolheaded practicality she had. I missed the smell of her hair spray and perfume, and the sort of advice she gave: immediate, unsweetened. As I grew up, I looked for somebody who could give that same sort of hard-bitten guidance, but no one came close. I tried to give it to myself sometimes, but it wasn't quite the same.

When Brenda's song was finished, we tossed our three roses down into the shallow hole. Dusk crept up around us. Through the trees, the sky was turning a hazy purple. We walked back through the woods together in silence, looking toward the distant lights of the family's cabin.

10

The next day, I drove to the gas station to buy a lighter. The woman behind the register started to chat as she rung me up. She wanted to know if I was from town, and I told her that I was but had moved away.

"Here visiting?" she asked. I nodded. The woman clicked her tongue disapprovingly. I raised an eyebrow, impatient to get going. "All the young people go off to live someplace else, now." Curtly, she slid the lighter across the counter. It was true that Knife River had an aging population. I'd heard about it from Liz, who mentioned that our former high school had hit a record low student population last year. The town was considering shutting the whole thing down and busing the students to a larger school, thirty minutes away, that served four of the six towns in our county. The cashier made her way over to the front window with a damp rag. I felt a pang of guilt walking past her, and then again seeing her blurry figure from the parking lot, wiping down the glass in slow, wide circles.

I drove off, taking a back way home, along a street where an abandoned pizza place, a feed and seed, and a Dairy Queen sat in a row, their commercial property lines overgrown with dandelions. No one else was on the road and I slowed to a near crawl, studying the crumbling ecosystem of it all and thinking about how many changes this place had gone through.

A long time ago, things were made in Knife River—colored glass, cigarettes, buttons, train whistles, windows. There was a milk-condensing plant, a factory that made needles and thread. Another that mass produced lightbulbs, the first in the country to have the equipment to do so. The earliest of these operations opened in 1900, followed quickly by three more. People came to work in them, and then more people came to open restaurants and stores to serve all the factory workers. The town grew steadily each decade. A train station, a hotel, and a small hospital were all built in the same year. In 1930, Knife River was designated the county seat and an ornate, Grecian-style courthouse was built, the one where our mother had worked in county records. It must have looked as out of place then, on the dusty Main Street with its low-slung buildings, as it did decades in the future, diagonal from a chain pharmacy lit with blue neon lights. After work, her clothes and hair always smelled a little like the vast basement where all the files were kept—miles of old paper and dust.

A few factories were still operational when I was growing up, but I often thought about the way things must have felt back then in the town's early days; the constant churning, the momentum of hundreds of thousands of needed things cast into existence by the collective effort of so many bodies and machines. Now, only one factory remained: Blossom Dairy, which made evaporated milk. The rest of the buildings sat in various stages of decay. A few had been demolished and developed into strip malls. Another was the site of the new supermarket. These newer businesses were all brought in by fracking, something that began to creep in shortly after I moved away. The first man who agreed to have his land surveyed had a wealth of gas beneath the surface. News of his monthly royalties spread fast, and soon everyone was having their property checked. A little less than half of all title owners were sitting on gas, and about half of those managed to secure payments from the drilling company. Still, it was enough to change things. Stores sprang up, the diner reopened after a three-year hiatus. Then the state banned fracking and everything deflated once more.

After that, anger and resentment spread like a fast cancer. I heard about it on the news all the time, even in the city. This whole region was a favorite during election cycles. Losses seemed to stack up one after another with each new blow to the already crippled economy, most recently two big appliance manufacturers that went back on their contracts and pulled out within months of each other, relocating production to Vietnam, leaving people stranded amid a landscape of wind-eaten industrial parks and lush rolling mountains. Presidential candidates passed through from time to time. They all promised a return to industry while defending the elimination of shale gas drills.

I could remember one in particular I'd seen on the television in the periodontist's waiting room when I was coming in one morning to transcribe some old, nondigitized tape. The candidate stood in the center of an enormous assembly room. An American flag hung behind his shiny, coiffed head. He flashed a wet grin and swore up and down that each job, every single last one, would come back. Not only that, he said, but there would be more jobs. New jobs. Ones having to do with energy technology we'd never even heard of. Then the screen flashed to footage of him earlier that same day being led around a quaint, but depressed-looking, Main Street. I recognized it immediately.

"That's my hometown," I exclaimed, pointing at the screen. "I grew up there."

The receptionist looked up from her computer. She half listened to the segment for a minute before replying in her flat Hungarian accent, "Very nice."

From my car I could see remaining advertisements pasted up on the pizzeria's cracked windows, corners curled, tears down the center of the pictures. Bright orange, gleaming circles of pepperoni. Golden, bubbling cheese. Some vegetation grew inside what had once been a dining area, and had begun to find its way through the broken glass; long, leafy fingers creeping over upended booths, crawling toward the light.

The last time I was in Knife River, the place was open. I remembered eating there once as a teenager, burning my tongue on a pool of scalding, garlicky oil and walking around like I was on my way to the bathroom, snatching unfinished pitchers of beer from dirty tables and quickly swallowing the dregs, facing away from anyone who might be looking.

There were three middle-aged women standing next to the feed and seed, peering down into a low wire pen with some hens in it. I could see the chickens bobbing their heads, the shine of their feathers, a plywood hutch off to the side with some loose hay spilling out. One of the women said loudly to the others, *good-looking birds*. They nodded solemnly in reply, arms crossed, as the hens foraged around in the grass. I craned my head out of the window to get a better look. They were good-looking birds, black and white dappled feathers with blazing red faces. I stared at the pen for a while before realizing that I was nodding, too, as if I were part of their conversation. I wondered then if I might be lonely. The group of women looked up at me and I averted my gaze quickly, staring ahead at the road and pushing on the gas a bit too hard, like I'd done something wrong. The plain strangeness of being back here struck hard for the first time. I think I'd been so sidetracked by what brought me home, wrapped up in the mire of doubt and sadness, worrying about my sister, then dazed by my encounter with Eva, that I'd hardly stopped to notice the texture of things. Everything was familiar. Awful and comforting all at the same time.

I stopped at a red light next to the Dairy Queen. It was an old-format store, made to look like a barn with a red, plasticky roof and a sun-bleached plastic soft-serve cone jerkily spinning on an angle above the entrance. There were a few picnic tables out front. Around the side stood two people in aprons and hats, smoking, leaning back against the wall.

I thought I recognized one of them, though I couldn't place his face right away. The light was still red, and I rolled down the window a few inches to get a clearer view. He was maybe forty, with the shadow of a beard inching down his neck. He turned slightly, and then I realized. Howard. Jeff Howard, if I was remembering right. He coached my middle school track team. I hadn't particularly wanted to be on the team, but I was fast and restless, and my mother insisted on signing me up. I did it for most of seventh grade, until she suddenly stopped giving me the small quarterly payment required for participation. Then, not long after, everything changed and I hadn't thought about running or Jeff Howard in what felt like a lifetime.

He looked thinner, grayer, and a little hunched around the neck. It took me aback, seeing this whole person I'd filed away appear before me in the flash of a moment. I wondered why he was working here now, instead of at the school. I stared at him a little longer. My hands grew clammy. Something about his posture made me anxious. He tapped ash off his cigarette, then turned his head and our eyes met. Neither of us gave any outward sign of recognition, just stared at each other for a few seconds, before he flicked the cigarette into a nearby puddle and went back inside.

The light turned green and I drove on, leaving the window down to get some air on my face. I could smell burning leaves from a nearby property. We used to run in the rain, I remembered. A group of maybe twenty girls in matching green T-shirts and mesh shorts. Coach Howard, as we called him, never canceled for bad weather. I used to think he pushed us further when it was miserable outside. Our school didn't have a paved track, so we'd run through muddy fields, trouncing over ankle-deep creeks and abandoned carriage paths in the woods, down Main Street, across other people's farmland. I couldn't remember any competitions. Only these early morning practices. The group of us, a blur of color and swinging hair, and the coach behind us on his mountain bike with a cheap megaphone. I could summon his voice even now, crackly and muffled: *Girls, girls, keep it moving now.*

Then, as I was about to turn off onto the exit for the bridge, I spotted a low-slung white brick building with a few trucks parked out front. A bell rang somewhere deep in my brain. All my thoughts about the track team faded quickly. I slowed my car down once more, squinting at the waves of light bouncing off the metal roof, before realizing with a quick drop in my gut that it was Nick Haines's hardware store.

I'd last seen it years ago when Liz and I drove past after he'd first become a suspect. She'd stopped in the middle of the road, staring at the shop entrance, before speeding off and telling me, "I don't want you going near there again." People had all kinds of theories about his involvement. I didn't want to know them, but wound up hearing them anyway. She turned him down for another date and he lost his temper. He accidentally hurt her somehow and then panicked, killing her impulsively. He owns a *hardware* store, people liked to say. Rope, tarps, lye. Blunt objects. Sharp objects. Everything he could have needed. Others didn't believe he had anything to do with it. He was temperamental, no one could deny that. An off-putting kind of guy. But did that make him capable of murder? More likely she'd taken a bad step over the ledge of a gorge, or walked in the path of a hunter's stray bullet, or killed herself on purpose for reasons we could never know. But where, then, was her body?

We had theories of our own. Liz and I spent hour after hour dissecting her memory of the phone call she remembered overhearing; his name mentioned briefly, dismissive laughter before the subject changed entirely. Who was the friend on the other line? We made a list of all the women we knew our mother associated with. A few co-workers, Anne from the coffee shop, an old friend from childhood who lived in Winnipeg and sent Christmas cookies every year, someone named Sue she occasionally met for drinks, a handful of others I wasn't familiar with but my sister knew of. She brought all this information to the police herself, a sheet with every name and phone number in a neat column. I remember seeing her sitting at the table writing it all out carefully with a red felt-tip pen, our mother's old Rolodex next to her, her eyes fixed in pained concentration. I had to look away, I felt so bad. Not long after, we called Sue and the friend from Winnipeg ourselves. Neither had been contacted by the police. Neither said they'd ever heard mention of Nick Haines, either.

Liz kept at it, speaking to everyone she possibly could, questioning them, asking them to recount every conversation with our mother they remembered having. Some people hung up on her, likely put off by her harsh tone and unrelenting, impossible demands. A couple suggested gently that we leave this kind of thing to the cops. Some asked after me, wondering if I was okay, and if Liz would please put me on the phone for a minute. She wouldn't.

We started going around in person. It turned out that Anne remembered talking to our mother about Nick Haines. She'd told this much to the sheriff as soon as she learned he was a suspect. The sheriff, she said, took note but didn't seem overly concerned. My sister took small steps toward this woman as they spoke, gradually backing her into a corner of the shop. Liz had a frantic, wild glint in her eyes. I stood back by the door, chewing at my cuticles, heart pounding.

Eventually, the woman ushered us to a small table and said, "I just know that they went on a date once, and your mother thought he was a real creep. She said he got too drunk and made an ass out of himself. I don't really know what all happened. She was weirded out at first but then laughed it off. I never heard about it again." A group of elderly men came in to buy doughnuts. Anne got up to help them, paused, and gave me a quick squeeze on the shoulder. She said quietly, "I keep my distance from the guy. You girls ought to do the same."

I crossed the bridge and then pulled off to the side behind some tall grass. As if under a spell, I got out of my car and walked halfway down the ramp toward the lot where Haines's shop was. I wasn't thinking. Something else moved me. Once I could make out the hours posted on the window, I stopped. What on earth was I planning to do? What if I did look him in the eye? Accuse him, confront him, attack him? Did I really think that I could look at his hands, breathe in the air around him, assess the quickness of his breath in my presence and know, somehow, whether this was the man who'd taken my mother's life fifteen years ago? I walked back over to the grassy area and squatted, feeling sick. The ground swirled below me. A sour feeling rose up in my throat and then settled. I tried to get ahold of myself. I didn't even know if he was in there, or if he would know who I was.

I'd never actually seen Nick Haines up close in person. He'd always lived on the opposite end of town from us and hung around outside the bar in a cloud of smoke with men who wore hunting gear, had loud, gravelly voices, and always seemed to be chewing on something in the pocket of their cheeks. I was not necessarily more intimidated or wary of them than I was of other men, though I didn't like to walk right past them, especially if I was alone. The feeling of their eyes on me as I moved made the hairs on my arms stand up straight. And then, of course, Liz forbade me from ever going near him. She caught me by the elbow as I was leaving the house one night when I was fifteen. After two years of no body, no admissible material evidence, people had cooled to the idea of Haines's guilt. General interest in our mother's disappearance waned. Time was passing. Everyone else's lives moved on while ours stayed centered in grief and squalor.

"Listen to me," Liz growled, shoving me against the doorframe. "I know you're getting older and going out to parties, or whatever it is you're doing. But don't you ever go anywhere near his house. You don't go near his shop. If you see him, you get the fuck on the other side of the street. Do you hear me?" I nodded, stunned by her sudden show of authority. "If I even suspect you went anywhere near him, I will you lock you inside your room and you won't come out until you're eighteen." The idea of this was so absurd I scoffed in her face. Liz then twisted my arm and slammed me harder against the door. "You think I'm kidding? I'm dead fucking serious. I don't care. The school won't care. That school wouldn't even notice if you never showed up again. I'll shove your food through a dog door. It doesn't matter to me."

"What the fuck is your problem?" I said, pushing her away.

"My problem? My problem is that he thinks he got off free on this."

Her eyes flashed wildly. "The cops don't care about this anymore. No one cares about this anymore. Haven't you noticed? No one is looking out for us. He's just out there, walking around like any other man, and no one cares."

"How are you so sure?"

"What? That it was him?"

"Yeah. You've always been so sure. But how do you know? I mean how can you really know?"

"Do you remember when we were searching that field and you said she wasn't there? You said you couldn't feel her anymore." I nodded. "This is like that." She took a deep breath. "I don't care if you believe it or not. I just need you to promise me you won't go near him."

"Okay," I said, thoroughly startled. "I promise." And I did avoid him, along with anyplace I thought he might be. I worried sometimes I'd turn a corner in a store aisle and find myself face-to-face with him, or that he'd walk past me suddenly on a sidewalk or in the park, but months went by and nothing like that ever happened.

Then the following spring, just a week shy of the third anniversary, my sister saw Nick Haines in an altercation with a woman. I was there, too, though I didn't see it happen. We were at the home of her then-manager from the bank, a quiet, older man who lived on the eastern-most side of Knife River on the same street as the bowling alley, Dream Lanes, which would be shuttered by the time I moved away. He knew our situation and had offered to give us his old washing machine after upgrading to a new one. My sister refused at first, even though our unit leaked badly and had been on its last leg for some time. I was tired of mopping up puddles of cloudy water from the basement floor, the smell of mildew lingering on my hair, and pestered her about it all week until she finally relented.

We went to the manager's house on a Friday night. He promised to help us load the washer into our hatchback and then follow us back to our place so he could help haul it inside. I was amazed by the cleanliness of his home. The kitchen counters had no crumbs or coffee rings or dirty plates on them. A bowl of gleaming red apples sat on the table and I must have stared at them too long because the wife asked me if I was hungry. Soon the manager went to the basement to retrieve the machine, and I was seated with a plate of hot leftovers. The wife gave me some of the apples in a paper sack, along with a bag of winter jackets and snow boots that had once belonged to their daughter, who by then lived in Albany with a young family of her own.

Liz went back outside to flip our car seats down, and that's when she saw it happen. Halfway down the block in the Dream Lanes parking lot, a man and a woman shouted at each other. She ignored it at first, she said, because the bowling alley had a bar and was known to get rowdy on weekend nights. But then she heard a name, his name. Her head snapped up. She caught a flash of movement streaking across the lot and into the road. It was the woman, still shouting, hands held out before her as she looked down either side of the street. No cars were out, no people on the sidewalk. Liz took a few steps down the driveway and watched as the man drew closer to her, stumbling, angrily pointing to a row of trucks back in the lot. Within moments, he was in the street. "I recognized him right away. He was reaching for her," Liz explained. "But he was blind drunk, so he kept missing and tripping over his own feet." The woman then picked up a rock and flung it at Nick. The rock grazed his face and he howled, doubling over for a moment, before lunging forward with both hands aimed for her neck. The woman broke into a sprint, getting away just before his fingers made contact with her skin, and then Nick stood there for a moment, staring blankly, before going back into the parking lot.

"She got maybe a quarter way up the block before I saw him come back in his truck, speeding up right behind her," Liz said. "He was hunched over the wheel. I could see his eyes were wide open and he was shouting something, but I couldn't tell what." When the woman realized Nick was coming after her, she'd screamed. The manager's wife and I heard it from inside the kitchen. We looked at each other, alarmed, and went out to the driveway to check on Liz, whom we found crouching next to our car, her hands pressed to either side of her head like she was trying to block out a loud sound.

"He just tried to run her over," Liz told us. She repeated this twice, rocking a little bit on her heels. A ways down the road, I saw two taillights swerving fast around a bend, growing smaller in the darkness. I didn't know what to think. We both stared, bewildered. My sister flung one arm toward the street. "The lady jumped into some bushes. He didn't get her. I don't know where she went."

The manager's wife brought us back into the house and listened as Liz continued to describe what she saw. Her voice was now stoic, almost monotone. I noticed that she stared at the ground, eyes unmoving from a single spot, as she spoke. I glanced over at my bag of apples and winter coats sitting by the door. I felt exhausted. Almost too tired to be as frightened as I really was. I could feel myself dividing, my mind drawing a hard line between my racing pulse, my clammy palms and dry mouth, and the part of me that just wanted to go to sleep and not think of this. I felt bad for my sister. I could see how shaken she was, but in a strange way I wanted her to leave without me so that I could stay here with the quiet man and his nice wife and let them care for me and keep me fed in their warm, clean home.

Liz said again, "He was going to run her down with his truck, that's what he was trying to do. That's what I saw."

"What were they saying?" I asked. "You said they were fighting about something in the parking lot. Could you hear it?"

"She told him to quit following her," Liz said. "I heard her say that a few times. She told him he needed to take no for an answer."

"Did you recognize her at all?"

"No." My sister shook her head. "I don't think I've ever seen her."

"Poor girl," the wife muttered. She was standing at the window, pushing the curtain back and looking up and down the street. "I wonder where she went off to." The block was dark, and quiet but for a dull thump of music coming from the direction of the bowling alley. I imagined that the lady had just stayed in the bushes after escaping into them. There were paths in the brush, I knew, forged by deer. You could walk a long ways in there without ever being seen from the road. I'd done it many times. Maybe, I thought, she was in the thicket, just beyond our view, taking herself home.

By then, Liz's manager was in the front hall with the washer all wrapped up on a little moving dolly. He'd heard none of the commotion from the basement, and stared at us three with a peaceable smile, ready to get on with the task. My sister allowed this man to follow us home and set the machine out on our porch, but refused to let him inside. He was confused, I could see, and concerned that we wouldn't be able to get the washer set up without some help. Liz wouldn't budge. The manager looked at me to take his side, but I knew better than to press my sister after what she'd witnessed. He was a harmless man. Nice, really. Liz spoke fondly of him most of the time. But something had shifted inside her and reason could not move it back in place. Once indoors, she went from window to window, checking each lock, before pushing the telephone table in front of the entrance. At her urging, we slept in the same bed that night, and when I stirred awake in the early hours I saw that she was propped up, head resting on the wall, eyes open, just watching the room. I squeezed her hand and she squeezed back, and we stayed like that until sunup.

In the morning, we went to the sheriff's office to report what Liz had seen. He drank coffee from a large thermos while my sister explained everything. I couldn't quite tell what he was thinking. He seemed unmoved by her account, but his face was often inscrutable to me—leathery and sagging, so much loose skin creeping down over his brow bone it was hard to get a clear view in his eyes. Once she finished speaking, he looked directly at me and asked, "Did you see any of this?"

"No," I replied.

"Did anyone else there at the house see it?"

"The rest of us were inside. We came out when we heard a scream. I saw him drive off."

"So, only Liz actually saw this occur." He looked at both of us, arms crossed over his middle. I nodded, Liz sat still. A quiet moment passed. I asked, "What does it matter if only she saw it?"

"No matter," he said. "Just trying to get all the facts."

"Well, now that you have them, what do you think?"

"Lover's quarrel, I'd guess."

Liz slapped her hand against the arm of her chair and nearly shouted, "He tried to mow this woman over with his truck. I'm telling you this wasn't some little tiff. I know what I saw."

"That's bad behavior, no question. But this lady, she hasn't given us a call. If it gave her that much of a scare, then she'd be the one in my office telling me about this right now."

"So this means nothing to you, then? This changes nothing about our case?"

"I'll certainly take note of it. I can promise you that much. But I can't go knocking on Nick's door now, three years down the road, because we got a third-party account of some argument outside the bowling alley. If the woman came forward, then maybe we could do something, depending on what she had to say, but you girls aren't giving me much to work with here."

"Well, what if she did come forward? Are you saying you could arrest him?

"Again, that would depend on a lot of different things."

"Like what?"

"Like what her story is." The sheriff rubbed his hands over his eyes and looked over at the clock. It was getting to be lunchtime. He drank the last of his coffee and locked eyes with my sister. "You say you don't know her, but if you saw this lady around town, could you recognize her?"

"Yes," Liz said. She nodded evenly, but I could tell she was uncertain. Her voice wavered around the edges, and I noticed her gaze shifting downward and to the side for a brief moment as she answered.

The sheriff seemed to notice, too. He paused before saying, "Well, if you ever spot her in any trouble again, you can give us a call yourself. We're here for you girls."

I left the office that day feeling that I had, in some way, done something wrong. I felt that I'd failed by not running back into the house and dialing 911 right away, by not reacting with the same quaking shock as Liz, by not being out there with her when it happened in the first place, by her side, seeing it with my own eyes, too, and then by not knowing the right things to say to the sheriff to make him care about it.

My stomach hurt. Liz gripped the steering wheel tightly as we drove home. I recall thinking that my whole idea of what happened the night before was formed not just through someone else's witness, but through her memory of that witness. Within a moment, just a second after, it could be reached only through her remembering, and that remembering could not arrive without first shaking through the filter of my sister's language, bound by the limits of the spoken word. If I wanted to look back at what happened out there on the street, I had to rely not just on her memories, but on my interpretation of those memories. I could replay the scene a hundred times, but it would never really be mine. All I had to myself was the distant sound of a scream, and then a glimpse of Nick Haines's taillights going around the bend. And even these recollections, then only a day old, had already been combed through to the point of warping.

These thoughts made me dizzy. I pulled a thread loose from my sweater and wrapped it around one of my fingers, pulling tighter and tighter until the blood was trapped above the knuckle and the skin turned purple and swollen and began to throb. I counted to thirty and then released the thread, relaxing back into my seat as the blood gradually resumed its normal course. I could feel my pulse slowing down. My breaths grew deeper. I still felt a little dizzy, but in a controlled way.

I asked Liz, "Do you really think you could recognize that woman if you saw her somewhere?" My sister looked ahead, silent. I studied the side of her face. Shallow wrinkles fanned out from the side of her eye. I couldn't remember them being there before, but I also couldn't remember the last time I looked at her profile so closely. They must have just appeared one morning, I thought. I wondered if she ever noticed them, and if she cared.

"Did you hear me?" I asked.

"Yeah," she said.

"Well?"

"I don't know, Jess. I'm not sure."

Since moving away from Knife River, I'd looked Nick Haines up on the internet many times. The conditions needed to be right. I had to be in a bold, impulsive kind of mood and I had to be almost blackout drunk. There weren't a lot of pictures of him. He was one of many blurry faces in a group shot of local business owners taken at the American Legion. Another from a defunct dating website. Two old mug shots from a DUI in Vermont. He was incredibly plain. Limp, grayish-blond hair clung to his scalp. He had small, dark eyes and chalky skin. It wasn't a face anyone would look twice at, but still sometimes I sat up for many hours just staring at him on my computer. I stared until my eyes hurt. I looked for so long he began to hardly seem like a real person at all, more like a character, a bad man from a children's story. I asked aloud if it was him, if he had done it, speaking as though my voice could somehow reach him. I hated to think of myself like that, slurring my words in a dark room, gazing into the glow of a screen, interrogating not a person but the idea of a person, a stranger. Once, I had even called his store. *Hello?* he'd said. *Hello?* I stayed silent on the other end, my hand clapped over my mouth as though he were actually in my apartment looking for me. After a moment, he hung up, and I went to the bathroom and vomited.

My hands shook as I drove back to the house. I badly wished I hadn't taken the back road home after buying the lighter. I would not, I silently vowed, mention to Liz that I'd gone by his store. I felt weak and a little stupid for promising myself that; I wasn't a minor under her care anymore. I could go wherever I wanted. Still, though, I felt like I'd endangered myself somehow. I called Sarah from the road. It wasn't so much that I missed her, or wished she were there with me during the drive, but her voice would be familiar. An anchor into another life.

"Are you busy?" I asked.

She said, "I'm having lunch now, actually." Her voice didn't bring me the wash of comfort I'd expected. I could picture her in the geometric glass atrium at the center of her building. The pavilion had five different medical practices all spinning out in a starburst from this glorious, sun-filled room with its floating orchids and tall, artfully potted palms. I'd been there once to drop off her wallet on a workday. She was drinking a green juice with another woman, a doctor with a short, effortless haircut and visibly expensive shoes. Sarah simply took the wallet and thanked me briskly for dropping it off, but didn't introduce me to the woman. I left quickly, before the silence between the three of us could bulge any further, but I did think about it for the rest of the day.

"I can talk for a minute, though," she said. "How are things going?"

"Fine," I said. "Everything's okay."

"You sound sort of rattled."

"No, no, just tired maybe."

"Any news?"

"Nothing yet."

"Well," she sighed. "I finally got that area rug."

I turned off onto a long side road as she spoke, cutting around the center of town. No other cars were in sight. I sped up, accelerating until the woods alongside my window passed by in a solid, reddish blur. I had Sarah on speakerphone in the cup holder. Her voice echoed through my little car. She described the rug in detail. It was hand knotted. Cream and beige. Minutes passed and she was still explaining the process of finding it, then picking the right spot in the house to put it in. I hit a bump in the road and the car flew for a moment, making my stomach flip. My mind raced between the rug and the roof of the hardware store glinting in the sunlight with Nick Haines somewhere beneath it—breathing, talking, probably laughing. Living like any other person. Images muddled: the hole in the ground, my sister hunched over like a buzzard, Brenda's boots dragging through the dirt.

Then, suddenly, a raccoon appeared in the middle of the road. I swerved to avoid it and skidded onto the dirt shoulder, coming to a grinding halt just inches from an enormous pine tree. A strange, breathless scream escaped me. I gasped for air, my forehead on the wheel.

"What's going on?" Sarah asked. "Are you all right?" Instinctively, I felt around my face and midsection, searching for anything that hurt.

"I'm fine," I said. "Just hit a pothole."

"Oh." I could hear her chewing on something. "Well, anyway, that's what happened with the rug." I heard myself replying, continuing the conversation somehow. Minutes passed. The check-engine light blinked on and off. I wanted to get out of the car and walk around a little, try to shake my nerves off, but my body felt too heavy. Sarah said, "I've got to run. I have a patient in ten minutes."

I drove the rest of the way slowly, shaken up and exhausted, looking only at the next section of road and telling myself that I just needed to make it to the stop sign, then the stoplight, then through the intersection. *Just do the next right thing.* An old ex, a recovered alcoholic, used to say that to me all the time. I'd pretended it made no impression on me, but I said it to myself all the time. I said it aloud, quietly, there in the car. I had the same kind of feeling I used to get all the time as a kid, that I wasn't *quite* able to keep myself safe and cared for but had to figure it out anyway, on the fly, and make it look decent from the outside. It worked, but things were always a little off. And like a bird in the wild with an injured wing, I went to absurd lengths to hide anything that was going wrong, a tendency I could never shake. I still had the feeling that I was cobbling things together, doing what I needed to make everything appear passable. I found regular work, but I'd lied my way into it to begin with and never really cared about what I was doing. I had some friends, but when I went to the emergency room with a massive ruptured ovarian cyst and stayed for three days, I didn't call anyone. It was the worst pain I'd felt in my life. So bad I fainted twice in the cab on the way there and then, after forcing myself to walk upright and nonchalantly to the intake desk, vomited on the stack of check-in forms before falling to the ground.

When I woke up after surgery, a nurse came into my room with a cup of ice chips. She asked me how I was doing. "Fine," I told her. "And how are you?"

11

The next day, three sharp knocks came at the front door as I was setting the table for dinner. I froze. Liz was out picking up our order from the pizzeria. I had no idea who would just stop by our house unannounced. Brenda maybe, but it sounded like someone bigger than her. Two more knocks. I took a steak knife from the cutlery basket and carried it with me to the door. I felt silly looking down at its cheap pearlescent handle and flimsy, water-spotted blade. It would snap in half, probably, with the first good stab into anything. But I was still jumpy. I'd tried to shake Nick Haines from my mind, but my body hadn't caught up. Every strange sound sent a tremor through my gut. Each shadow loomed tall. Hiding the knife behind my back, I swung open the door.

There stood a young, muscular man in a pair of pressed khakis. He had a gun in a hip holster and dark glasses hanging from the collar of his shirt. He, too, seemed to be holding something behind his back. I was sure I'd never seen him before.

He smiled. "Detective Calloway. We've spoken on the phone." He stuck his hand out. "I'm sorry to disturb you at home." I must have looked bewildered because he quickly added, "I was the one you spoke to about your mother's memorial."

"No, of course," I replied. "I remember."

"I just wanted to drop by to bring you these." From behind his back he produced a small bouquet of lilies. "A belated token of our sympathy. You and Liz have been in all our thoughts."

Quickly pushing the knife into my back pocket, I took the bouquet with both hands. A tiny black beetle crawled along one petal. I wondered why exactly he would choose to show up at our house without warning right around dinnertime, but then felt guilty for being skeptical of his kind gesture. It was a good thing, I told myself. I should be glad that someone from the sheriff's office cared about how we were doing. There was nothing to read into.

"Again," he said. "I'm sorry to disturb you at home."

I cleared my throat. "You're not disturbing. Thanks for these, really nice of you."

"Least we could do."

"Can I get you anything? Water?"

The detective looked back at his cruiser. The driver's side door was ajar. On the dashboard I could see another cellophane-wrapped bouquet. Pink roses. "A quick glass of water. Before I head out."

Calloway glanced around the kitchen as I rummaged for a glass. He looked oversized, almost cartoonish, standing in our old house with its tiny doorframes and sloping walls. Having a cop in here again made me feel a little sick. It reminded me of the earliest months of our case, the night they first brought the compact over, freshly confiscated from Nick Haines, the sound of them digging through our mother's things, rifling around in her nightstand. Once the lead went cold, they stopped coming. I wondered, with both hope and dread, if Calloway's visit was about more than just the flowers.

"So," I said, handing him the cup. "Do you have any news from the medical examiner?"

"I'm afraid not."

"You haven't spoken with him?" He shook his head no. He seemed genuinely disappointed to have nothing to tell me. I nodded, and watched as he gulped his water down.

Calloway was younger than me, probably five years, with a handsome but simple kind of face. He reminded me of a guy in a Macy's commercial. I could easily imagine him leaping around against a white background, the glare of studio lights reflected in his shiny President's Day sale wing tips. He reminded me, too, of the men in Sarah's sperm catalog. If she were here, she would have given him a long, hard look, mentally calculating the sum desirability of his genes. His fingernails were short and neat. His Adam's apple bobbed up and down as he drank, like a fishing lure. I guessed he would have been an elementary student when my mother went missing. Maybe in his last years of grade school, learning about fractions and the Constitution. Thinking of him like that, small and oblivious, stoked my anger. He was still oblivious, standing in the kitchen with nothing to tell me. I wanted him to get out, go back to his cruiser and drive off to give those roses to whatever girl they were for, but he was already at the sink filling up his glass again.

"Has anyone spoken to Nick Haines?" I said. "Obviously, I know you weren't on the team yet when they first brought him in, but—"

Calloway cut me off. "You know, I was telling your sister, the sheriff doesn't want to make any decisions about speaking with him before the autopsy comes back."

"But he was the original suspect, I think it would make sense if—"

"I know," he said, interrupting me again. "And I know it must be very frustrating for you."

"It is," I replied, feeling acutely aware that he did not know, could never actually know how frustrating it was. If he did, he'd understand that frustrating wasn't even the right word. Maddening, agonizing. Or, simply, painful. Frustrated was how I felt when I dropped my keys into the crevice between the car seat and console and couldn't quite reach them with my fingers.

"I'm aware that you're both anxious for things to move along here, of course you are." He paused. "But we have to leave room for the possibility of other perps. Too early to rule that out."

My grip tightened around the cellophane-wrapped bouquet. I felt unsteady on my feet. The house was silent but for the crunch of the plastic and the ticking wall clock over our table—a kitschy, bird-themed one that chimed on the hour with the song of one of twelve different songbirds of the Americas. Liz found it at a rummage sale when we were kids, and within a couple of weeks she could do an eerily perfect imitation of each song.

Calloway shifted awkwardly on his feet. "If you come to the station, maybe we can all have a conversation about it. I don't want to speak for the sheriff. But I can tell you we're being very careful here, for your sake. We don't want to blow any leads prematurely."

"We'll do that, then. We'll come to the station."

"You're welcome anytime."

"You can expect us soon," I said, feeling like I was almost making a threat.

"All right." He glanced around. "You on your own here tonight?"

"No. Liz should be back any minute."

"Well. You give her my regards, okay?" The detective took himself to the front door, stopping in the entryway to leave his empty glass on the telephone table. His boots left deep imprints in the rug.

"What a fucking drip," Liz said. She was miffed over Calloway's sudden visit, particularly upset that she hadn't been home for it. "I bet he came early in the evening hoping I wouldn't be here. They're all afraid of me. What does he think? He can give us some flowers and we'll forget about how badly they've mangled everything?" *Mangled.* She spat the word out like a mouthful of dish soap. Specks of pizza sauce flew from her lips. She shoved a paper napkin down into her collar. "How did he seem?"

"He seemed fine. I don't think he's, like, the brightest guy in the world. But he was polite enough."

"He wasn't nervous?"

"Why would he be nervous?"

"He's a child." Liz wiped her mouth with her wrist, leaving a smear of orange grease. "No experience whatsoever. It's bullshit that he has this job at all, no less is assigned to a case like this one." She blew air forcefully from her lips and rolled her eyes toward the ceiling. "But that's what happens here. He was one of the few kids that didn't move away. They were probably thrilled to hire him."

"I asked him about interviewing Haines. He told me they didn't want to act too soon, like they were worried about overlooking other culprits. Then he suggested we come to the station ourselves to talk with the sheriff about it directly."

"Oh sure," Liz said, rolling her eyes. "We can go talk to the sheriff. Why the hell not." She slapped her slice of pizza down onto the plate and sighed, her forehead crinkling in exasperation. "At least Brenda will get a kick out of this," she muttered.

"You have plans to see her?"

"We watch *Wheel of Fortune* together sometimes."

"I had no idea you liked *Wheel of Fortune*."

"I like Brenda."

"How did you become friends with her, anyway?"

"She comes into the bank at the same time every week to deposit her social security check. We've known each other for years now. I don't really notice her age that much." Liz slid another slice of pizza from the box and shook salt and pepper all over it, like she'd always done. "Brenda's lived around here forever. She was born just down the road from our house, the eighth child in a family of ten. Two of her brothers are still alive, one of them lives in town. During the Depression, there wasn't enough food for all the kids, so she would go out and shoot possums for herself to eat. Once she told me she shot a dead rabbit out of a hawk's claws as it was flying above her."

I nodded. It wasn't hard to imagine. There was something very tough and precise about Brenda. Capable. You could drop her into one of those military training exercises where they leave you in the woods with just a point of flint, I thought, and she'd probably come crawling right out, pissed off and sated with raccoon meat. Yesterday I'd nearly driven off the road after being surprised by a raccoon from within the bubble of my own car. I shut my eyes, cringing a little at the thought.

"You know," I said, my memory stirred. "I saw Jeff Howard yesterday. The track coach? I was driving and noticed him outside the Dairy Queen. It looked like he works there."

"Yeah," Liz said. "He doesn't do the sports stuff anymore. He got into trouble."

"What do you mean?"

"It was around the time you moved away. There was a rumor he'd been groping some of the girls, so one of their parents went to his house and a fight broke out. He and the father started throwing punches, and when the mother tried to pull them apart Jeff threw her into a wall. She had to get stitches. This is just what I heard at work, one of the other tellers knew the family." Liz shook her head, clearly disgusted. "He never tried anything with you, right?" She stared at me, unblinking.

I picked up my drink and swirled it around. While I'd never felt threatened by Jeff directly, the story wasn't shocking to me. I could still conjure the feeling of being that age, running with a pack of girls, and the way our newfound, unspoken vigilance pulsed between the group of us. Our faces were still soft and childish, but our clothes had just begun to fit differently. We all sensed the steady approach of yet another layer of danger in the world, one more vile and insidious than anything we'd been warned about before. Nothing like the deep end of a pool, or speeding cars coming around blind corners at dusk, or a hunter's stray bullet in autumn. This was different. For this, we understood, we would be held responsible, always, for keeping it at an arm's length. And that other people, even adults—maybe especially adults—may well refuse to acknowledge it until one of us had been personally broken by it. And even then, it didn't feel like a guarantee. When we ran over the hills and into the woods, it felt like running away from something we couldn't yet name, like we could never get far enough no matter how fast we went.

I knew my sister understood this feeling, too, but I just shook my head and said, "No. He never did."

"Anyway," Liz said. "I like talking to Brenda because she knew Mom."

"What?" I said, slamming my drink down on the table, thoroughly stunned. The wave of cold nausea I'd felt just a moment ago halted in place. "What are you talking about?"

"They used to work together at the high school."

"Are you serious?"

"Yeah. When Mom first came here she did clerical work for a little while in the offices there. Brenda was a teacher for, like, thirty-five years, and then she became an administrator. She knew everyone. Mom was still pregnant with me when they met."

"How could you not tell me this? I don't understand how we could have gone through that whole day out in the woods with the singing and the roses, staring into the fucking ground like that, and I didn't even know she knew her. What were you thinking?"

"You didn't ask."

"I didn't *ask*? Of course I didn't ask. Why would I ever think to ask that?"

"You seemed totally disinterested in that whole day, honestly. It was like I had to drag you out there."

"What are you talking about? I'm the one who spoke with Calloway to make sure we could even walk on that family's land."

"How helpful of you."

"It was helpful. And you're supposed to tell me something like this. I know you know that. You were purposefully keeping it from me, you were just waiting to casually drop it into conversation like this. I think you like that everyone knew but me."

"That's not true."

"You've always acted like anything having to do with Mom belongs only to you."

Liz glared at me. I pressed my hands against the back of my neck and took deep, slow breaths. Finally, she spoke. "Well, I thought we'd talk about it sooner or later. I'm sorry I didn't bring it up before that day." Her tone was acquiescent.

My shoulders softened. I was captivated by the idea that there was someone close by, someone in my sister's life and now in mine who'd known my mother in the past, when she was a young woman, before I even entered this world. I'd spent so much time wondering about her life before me: what she was like, how people saw her, what she wanted for the future.

"What does Brenda say about her?" I asked, my voice quiet and tentative.

"She says Mom was a sweetheart. Everyone liked her."

"What else?"

"She kept coming in right up until she went into labor."

"And?"

"Um," Liz fiddled with her shirt cuffs. "Back then everything was on paper, obviously, and they had these ceiling-high shelving systems for all the mail and the records, but even on the step stool she couldn't see into the top compartment, she was so petite."

"Really? I remember her being tall."

"What?"

"In my mind, she's a tall woman."

"Mom wasn't tall." Liz looked at me seriously. "She was only five three, like me." I got a churning feeling in my stomach, like I was teetering on a high ledge. What other myths about her had I been carrying around with me? Where had I found them in the first place?

My sister and I sat at the kitchen table for another hour, picking at the pizza and piecing together who our mother was as a young married woman, new to town, through snippets of Brenda's stories. Watery visions rippled out before me: my mother walking through the offices of the school I'd eventually attend, Liz kicking around inside, ready to emerge. Every day the same lunch: crunchy peanut butter with pickle slices on cinnamon raisin bread. On her break, sitting at an empty picnic table out by the baseball field, sun in her eyes, drinking a can of ginger ale, sketching fantastical pictures of animals and flowers on a piece of scrap paper. Her contractions starting as she stood by the Xerox machine, warm copies overflowing from the chute and fluttering to the ground as she crouched over, gasping for air.

Eleven years younger than I was now, she'd become a parent. I pressed my hands against my abdomen under the table. The family line ended here in this kitchen. Liz would never have children, either, I was sure. If our family had remained intact, maybe things would have gone differently for the two of us. It was an alternate reality I imagined from time to time. A version of the past where we hadn't been derailed by tragedy. I watched Liz line up the Easter egg salt and pepper shakers precisely in the center of the table. My sister would have gotten her way with college, somehow, and gone on to study aeronautics. She was entranced by planes, rockets, birds, missiles—anything that flew.

In my earliest memory of Liz, she is willing something into the air; a balsa wood glider carefully pieced together from a pattern of her own invention. I can conjure the image of her gluing the wings together, brow furrowed, dark eyes shining with expectation. I watched her stand up on the roof of our house and wait for the wind to pick up. The little plane flew. It caught the air and sailed in a graceful arc over our copper beech trees and across the street, eventually coming to a gentle stop in the neighbor's grass. Sunlight beamed off her grin as she climbed down the gutter pipe. My brilliant, stubborn, strange sister. She was like a god to me then. I was floored by her independence. Every summer, she'd take a pair of kitchen shears and cut her hair short. "It's too hot for all this," she would say, leaning over the growing pile of fluffy black curls in the bathroom sink. She wore men's work overalls and let her eyebrows grow wild. She asked question after question until she understood something, and if no one had the answer she would go on a dogged search through the library until she got all the information she wanted.

Even though I was only eight when Liz started high school, I could see how painful those four years were for her. It still pained me to think about it. Her curiosity was boundless, but there was simply nothing for her at that school—low funding, limited facilities. Half of the building was unusable after a shop-class soldering iron was left on and the whole corridor was scorched. It was still like that when I entered ninth grade years later, which is why half of my classes were held in a series of leaky, rusted trailers set up in a field across the street. Liz was fiercely intelligent, but never a faculty favorite. Our mother once returned home from an evening of parent-teacher meetings and asked why nearly all her teachers had complained about her "lack of respect." *No idea,* Liz replied, barely glancing up from her aeronautics book. Their disapproval made me defensive of my sister. I knew they'd never understand her, and even though we weren't very close, there was a part of me that wanted badly to shield her from their criticism. My history teacher, who'd had Liz in his class a couple of years before me, spotted me in the back row on my first day freshman year and mockingly asked if my sister had managed to *learn any manners yet.* It made me want to give him a sharp kick in the groin. Back then, I liked to privately entertain fantasies of a life where these same teachers might chance to catch Liz as a guest on a news segment, offering expertise in a sleek dark suit.

Looking at my sister across the table now, I could still see the girl who'd captured my admiration so easily on the roof of our house, her little plane soaring overhead. She'd changed a lot since then, much of her spark dimmed by years of fear, frustration, isolation. But even so, I could sense that same keen, stubborn intellect in the way she spoke and asked questions, in the stunning precision of her embroidery. I watched as she dusted some crumbs off the placemat and got up to toss the empty pizza box into the trash. She spent a few minutes rustling around the kitchen, returning to the table with an apple and some honey poured on a cutting board. This was something we ate often growing up. Silently, she and I passed a knife back and forth, slicing the apple into pieces and dragging it through the pool of honey. The floodlights on the house across the street blinked on, illuminating an empty porch.

My sister cleared her throat then and said, "Brenda knew Nick Haines, too, by the way."

My throat tightened. "How?" I asked.

"She had him as a student. He graduated a few years before our parents moved here."

"And?"

"She thinks the same thing I do."

"You're saying Brenda believes he's guilty?"

"Yes," Liz answered, her tone firm. "She's always thought so. Since the beginning."

"But what does she say about what he was like? When she had him as a student, I mean."

"She thought something was wrong with him."

An icy stillness passed over my body. Liz went on, speaking plainly, seeming not to notice how unnerved I was. "Like once, she walked into an empty classroom and he was in there pinning a girl against the wall. When they saw her, the girl ducked under his arm and ran out without even taking her book bag. She looked terrified and didn't come back to school for the rest of the week. Brenda went to the super-intendent about it but he didn't do anything."

"That's disturbing." My voice stumbled over the syllables. I noticed my tongue had gone a little dry.

"Yeah. And she's said he would show up drunk to school sometimes."

"But does this all mean—"

"That he did it?" Liz said. "That's what you're going to ask, right?"

"I guess, yeah."

"You tell me what he was planning on doing to that girl in the classroom. Or what about the night I saw him try to run that woman over, what do you think his intentions were? You think he was just kidding? Just a friendly prank?"

"Of course I don't think that."

"You tell me what he was doing speeding out of the woods at the crack of dawn that morning after Mom went missing. He wasn't coming back from a hike."

"I know."

"He wasn't out there collecting litter. Doing his part to prevent forest fires."

"I know that."

"That was *her* compact in his jacket. You know it was. Can you look me in the eye and tell me you honestly believe that was a coincidence?"

I couldn't. I could barely look her in the eye at all. She drummed her nails on the table and stared at me so intently I could almost feel the heat of her gaze boring through each layer of my skin. I knew we were on the precipice of a conversation we'd had a hundred times before, where her belief in his guilt surrounded her like an impenetrable wall and all my doubt fell flat before it.

There'd always been a part of me that wondered if she was right about Nick Haines. I'd never even heard his name before the police came to our house, asking about him and the compact. As a kid, I had a hard time grasping the idea that someone whose face I couldn't even imagine had destroyed our life like this. By the time I'd gotten along in my teen years, I was so tired of thinking about it all the time that I did everything I could not to. I discovered how easy it was to maintain a baseline of mild drunkenness, just a light buzz, throughout the days. It was the best distraction I'd found, like a little miracle cure, and other people hardly seemed to notice. Then in adulthood, the things that didn't make sense to me as a kid started to come into sharper focus. I wondered about him all the time, sometimes obsessively, sometimes even dreaming about him. It no longer felt so unthinkable that this man could have been the one all along. Instead, I often thought, why *not* him? In all departments of life, I'd found that the simplest explanation was usually right.

But my doubt always rolled back in, reliable as a tide. I'd ask myself, what if in all the time I'd spent fearing Nick Haines, wondering about him, building him up like a monster in my head, there were others? Other shadow men, hiding right out in the open? What if he was just one in a world full of dangerous people, a bad one to be sure, violent and repulsive, but not *the* one? Not the one who'd taken a life from me and Liz. Certainly there were others out there. Just yesterday I happened upon one driving on a quiet road in the middle of the afternoon, standing outside an ice cream shop. The world was full of people running their stores, minding their business, taking smoke breaks after lunch, going about their lives. How could I know who we were searching for? How could I be certain?

"I'm not saying it was a coincidence," I told Liz. "But I'm not sure that it wasn't."

She glared at me, lips thin and hard, then went upstairs to bed.

I sat there for a few minutes, drumming my fingers on the tabletop and staring out the window onto the side of our porch. A ripped page of a grocery flier fluttered in the breeze on the top step. I watched it tumble down to the yard, getting caught in some wet grass, finally blowing over to the driveway, where it lodged beneath the front tire of my car.

I was exhausted, but before going to bed I pulled my laptop out and scanned through job listings for the parks in Maine, just to clear my head a bit. I sorely needed a moment of distraction. There were new postings since I'd last looked. A few for the coming spring, seasonal trail maintenance ahead of the busiest summer months. I wondered if I should take something part time like that while I kept my transcription work. I read through a few more, yawning, dreamily imagining a time when I could leave Knife River again and wake up in a new place, one where I could spend my days walking outside in the sunshine, thinking of nothing but forging a clear path through the trees.

12

Eva texted me an address. I was a surprised when the message came in. We'd had no contact since our run-in at the store a couple of weeks ago, and in that time I'd wondered, cringing a little, if her parting suggestion that we catch up sometime was given out only of awkward politeness. But there was the address. She didn't couch it with niceties. Just the street name and lot number, with some instructions on how to find her front door.

I left within minutes. The sun was high and bright in the sky, beaming down on the treetops and casting a glare in my windshield. It took me about a half hour to reach the long gravel driveway that cut through an open meadow. Partway down, I passed a white farmhouse with some trucks outside. *Don't stop there*, she'd texted. *Keep going until you reach the first turn, then go right, right again, and stop at the clearing at the end of the small road. Make sure you park behind the shed.* Some hound dogs followed my car, barking and leaping, before running full speed in the opposite direction at the fork toward some smaller animal.

The property seemed like an old dairy farm with all its dilapidated fences squaring off the land. Some rusted watering troughs sat out in the tall grass. This place was on the opposite side of town from her old house, the one with the attic bedroom we'd spent so much time in years ago. There wasn't much nearby. Down the road, an unused rock quarry I'd swum in as a kid. Across the street, a small church with a for sale sign out front and an ill-maintained cemetery in the yard. Beyond that, miles and miles of forest.

I took the first turn onto the small road and entered a dense thicket of pine. Branches scraped against the sides of my car as I passed through and I could smell the bitter sap coming through the air vents. Something snapped beneath my tires as I drove, giving me a jump. I thought I must have made a mistake. I seemed to be driving into nothing and the little road was growing ever more narrow, but turning around seemed impossible. With the headlights on, I could just make out the shape of a little clearing far down ahead. As I drew closer, I saw a small house. A cottage with a green tin roof sat next to a wide, shallow stream. I could hear the water babbling as I pulled through the end of the pine gulch and stopped, cautiously stepping out of the car.

I was nervous. Here there would be nothing to distract from our conversation—no humming refrigerator cases or soft grocery store music floating down from the ceiling. Just the two of us, in this strange little cabin. I wasn't sure what we would have to talk about. White mushrooms grew in abundance along the path up to the door, moss sprouting in the crevices between each stone step. There were ferns everywhere—tall, ancient-looking ones with delicately frilled tips casting shadows over baby sprouts in the exposed riverbed, sheltered on the other side by rocks worn smooth against a gentle current. Bright yellow leaves dropped down from maple branches and landed on the water's surface, spinning slowly downstream. There was something enchanting about it all, and a little eerie. I approached the doorway, which looked to be at one time painted red, and knocked. Still thinking I must have somehow gotten the directions wrong, I took a wide step back, expecting a stranger to appear before me. I had a whole apology thought up. I was ready to speed back down the pine trail. But within a moment, there was Eva.

The cabin was warm inside, heated by a stout wood-burning stove that sat in the center of the room, its smoldering innards glowing orange through the iron slats. Pushed up against the far wall was a stack of firewood. The smell of rich, dusky smoke lingered over everything. There was a freestanding sink with an old water pump connected to the side. Above it, three cast-iron pans hung on the wall on bent nails. As I walked farther into the room I could smell the dark roast of coffee mingling with cedar. Above was a narrow opening in the ceiling, a ladder pitched on a tight angle nailed into place just beneath it. I turned around to look at Eva. She was still standing by the door, her hand resting on the lock. She seemed hesitant, like she might reconsider our meeting at any moment and send me back out. The quiet between us grew unbearably heavy.

Finally, I asked, "You live here now?"

"Yeah."

"What is this place? It looks like some kind of old farm."

"A long time ago, it was. This is my sister-in-law's property. She and my brother live in the main house and they let me stay in this place." She turned the top lock on the door and stepped a little nearer to me, half smiling. "Her great-grandfather built it. He used to trout fish in the stream just outside, and would sometimes spend the night here. When I moved in it was kind of a wreck but my brother helped fix it up." I nodded, easing myself down onto a worn bench by the woodpile.

"Can I get you anything?" she asked. "A drink?"

I needed one desperately, the way I needed my fingers or legs. I could almost feel the slick cold of a tumbler against my palm, hear the muted clink of an ice cube bobbing at the top, taste the smooth bitterness sliding down my throat and shooting me right through the middle, dropping a screen over all my fears and inhibitions.

This was a woman I'd thought about every day since the first moment we met. She consumed my thoughts as a teenager, existing as a star at the center of my world—the very light I lived off of. Years later, when I was in love with other people, I thought of her still, even when I was in the depths of that blinding, ecstatic newness with someone I hadn't yet found any fault with. I thought of her when I saw lithe, dark-haired women sitting at the other end of a bar. I thought of her when I was alone on the train late at night, lulled half to sleep by the car rocking its way through the shadowy tunnels. When I was doing my laundry or walking home from a movie, I wondered what she was doing at the same moment. Where was she, and with whom, and did she ever wonder the same things about me?

When I moved away, few people had cellphones. When I finally tried calling the line to her father's house a year later there was no answer—it just rang and rang. As time passed, I'd look around for her name on the internet but never found anything. Sometimes she began to seem unreal to me. Like a dream I'd once had that was slowly shifting further out of focus. Being near her again, seeing the light catch in her hair, knowing that everything I remembered was true, made my knees weak. More than I wanted to sink down into the hazy, familiar cover of a drink, I wanted not to fuck this up.

"No, thanks," I said, shaking my head. "That's all right."

"Nothing at all?"

"I'm okay."

Eva nodded and then went around the cabin pulling all the curtains closed. She checked the dead bolt on the door and tested the doorknob twice, then came over to sit next to me on the bench. I watched her inhale, lips parted, about to speak, then close her mouth. She glanced at the door and back at me again before leaning forward and kissing me on the neck. I was stunned. Of course I'd spent a lot of time in the past couple weeks imagining what this afternoon might be like, wondering what she wanted out of it. I bent toward caution. For all I knew, she really did just expect to catch up. I worried I was alone in reflecting on our former relationship with so much ardor. A lot of time had passed, and leaving town so abruptly the way I did—no notice, no goodbyes—must have left her few reasons to think back on me with any fondness. But here she was kissing me. Her lips moved up my neck and over my jawline.

Sarah's face flashed in my mind and I was hit with a sharp pang of guilt. I tried to reason with myself, flipping through all the things that might make my kissing Eva back feel less like a betrayal: that afternoon in Sarah's office building, her staunch reluctance to introduce me to the woman she sat with. The dearth of genuine concern in her reaction to my telling her the news, my whole explanation of the situation Liz and I faced. She was rational and cool, she had smart ideas about it, but she addressed it all like it was one of many things on her checklist for the day. There was the time she called me a troglodyte during an argument. Or the time she took my dick out of the nightstand and let three of her curious, wine-drunk mom friends from the HOA handle it like a show-and-tell curiosity.

But then, in fairness, she'd opened her home to me. She always held my hand as we fell asleep at night. She was bright and efficient and competent, someone who happily dispensed advice on things like establishing a tax-advantaged IRA and when to turn the mulch in your flower beds. Second to second I swung between feeling awful about what was happening—a deceitful ingrate with no impulse control, exactly the kind of person Sarah would pinch her face up at, and feeling somehow more emboldened by the very thought of that face. What did it matter? All the things that were important just weeks ago seemed inconsequential to me now. Thinking of them almost made me want to laugh—putting the raked leaves from the front lawn into the right kind of bags so the management company would pick them up without fining us, getting to the dry cleaner before they closed, planning a snorkeling trip in Mexico. It was just noise now.

All these thoughts vanished the next moment when Eva wrapped her legs around my waist. She ran her hands over the back of my head, pulling at my hair and biting gently along the top of my ear. I remembered how hard I'd fallen for her when we first met. Back then, I would have thought nothing of walking into a burning house for her. I still felt a ripple of infatuation. A sense of devotion bordering on psychotic. The kind of attraction that hijacks your brain so completely you are operated by something else. A parasitic, feverish love. How did any part of it manage to stay alive, dormant, inside me all these years? How did I live so long in so many different places where nothing reminded me of home, seeing other women, scraping together a living of my own, and come back only to find myself breathless at the sight of her?

I lifted Eva up by the backs of her thighs and carried her, still hooked around me, down to the rug in front of the wood stove. She looked up at me from the floor, flat on her back, hair spilling in every direction. Flashes of heat from the burning coals pulsed against my cheek and neck. I traced my finger down her chest, flicking the buttons on her sweater as I went.

"Off," I said, gesturing to her clothes. Who was I? I couldn't believe I was in this strange cottage in the wilderness, making such blunt commands. She knelt before me, pulled her sweater over her head and let it drop to the ground. I watched her dress fall from behind it, then her bra. I hooked two fingers under her chin and pulled her toward me in one motion, bringing her face to mine. I wanted everything about her body so deeply it almost hurt; the place where her thigh edged into the darkness between her legs, the dip at the base of her neck, two freckles on the pale shell of her ear. Kissing Eva gave me the same feeling I had in flying dreams—the sensation of being held aloft over twinkling city lights by some warm, unwavering gust of air. A sense of lightness so intense that I was no longer confined to a body, but simply part of the world's natural motion. She undid my belt and slid inside me, and I gasped, buckling against the curve of her palm.

It was as if no time had passed between us—like we'd been going about our lives while this moment just waited for us both to find our way back to it, to allow it to unfurl, and now that we had I could see there was no way to stop. I felt the pull of it. A tide sweeping me out over the ledge of the far horizon, deep down into something I had no name for. There was so much about her I no longer knew, and couldn't make sense of in the moment. Why had she been so careful to check the locks on the door? Why hadn't she ever moved away? We were both avoiding real conversation, the kinds of practical questions I knew we both wanted answers to. What lay behind that? These thoughts came to me as fallen leaves in a fast current. I felt them brushing up against me and then rushing past. I had no interest in looking back as they became small in the distance. I didn't care about anything but her lip brushing against my neck, the urgent pleading in her moans, her back lifting into a perfect arch as I moved inside her.

Afterward, we looked at one another in a sort of confounded awe. Hazy, golden light filtered in through the checkered curtains. The day was drawing to a close. I could feel all the things we wanted to ask rattling around inside us, unsaid. There would be time enough for it later, I hoped. I was intensely aware of the fact that she and I, in our present selves, were strangers. And neither of us wanted to be the first to pierce the exquisite quiet that cradled our bodies.

As the light grew dimmer, I felt that my continued presence would only erode the magic faster. She seemed to understand these same things, saying only, "Talk soon," as I got up and gathered myself to leave.

13

Liz dressed up for our meeting at the station. She'd really had to get after the sheriff to lock in an appointment. He wasn't busy, anyone could tell that. Just reluctant to engage with my sister. She wouldn't let it go. A full ten days after Calloway had come by, it came time for our meeting. I kept looking over at her as we walked in from the parking lot. She was wearing mascara and blush. Her hair was smooth, twisted back into a neat chignon. It was a Saturday but she wore her work clothes—a stiff black knee-length skirt with a starched white button-down. A green scarf was tied in a knot over the collar. I always thought that part of the dress code was a little ridiculous. People walked into the bank like they walked in anywhere else, in worn denim and work boots. And there was my sister with the other tellers, all women, all in this starched, flight attendant sort of apparel.

"What?" she finally snapped. "Why are you staring at me so much?"

"It's nothing." I shook my head. "I'm just not used to you wearing makeup or anything."

"I'm trying to look presentable."

"You do. You look very nice."

Liz rolled her eyes. "I know what people think of me," she sighed, staring straight ahead at the road. "I want them to take me seriously. This is important."

We waited in the lobby a long time. The black-and-white-checked linoleum floor was sticky with some kind of lemon-scented mopping fluid that hadn't been wiped clean. Some of the tiles lifted at the corners. There was a fake miniature Christmas tree and a tray of cookies on the reception desk. Gingerbread men. I watched a line of tiny ants march from a hole in the corner of the wall toward some loose crumbs. They broke the pieces down into even smaller bits, then carried it all back to the hole in perfect formation, the weight divided among them. I got up and crouched near the desk, squinting to get a better view. I wanted to know how they were able to all work such an efficient, complex system without speaking. They were so small. How were they able to communicate? How did they agree on anything? Liz would probably know the answer.

I turned around, about to ask, but she scowled and motioned for me to get back in my chair. The receptionist was flipping through a catalog, circling different gift baskets with a red marker. I sat down, then got up a minute later and poured myself a cup of Sanka from the little coffee station. The taste was so revolting I shuddered. I poured in four packets of sugar and tried it again. Still horrible, but I gulped it down anyway. I needed to go through the motions of pouring something, holding it, swallowing. I finished the first one, and then had a second with another four sugars. Liz watched me with a hawkish expression, shaking her head as I gathered up all the scraps of wrappers and mixing straws in my hand and walked them across the room to the trash.

I stood at the window and looked out onto the parking lot. A few squad cars sat in the spots closest to the building. It was snowing a little, just a sprinkling of flakes that disappeared as soon as they hit the ground. A skinny wild turkey pecked around the sparse grass underneath the station's sign that read Knife River Police in faded blue lettering. Two doors down, a small cargo truck pulled up outside the old grocery store. I could see Bill getting out of his van and greeting a man with a clipboard. He looked no different than how I remembered him, down to the same brown leather jacket. They both signed something, and then a young boy helped Bill carry in four crates of oranges while the cargo driver turned back down the road.

Directly on the other side of the street was a department store, Carson's, which had been in business for 112 years. The same family still ran it. Driving past it to get home the day I'd returned, I'd been surprised to see it still open, but quickly remembered why. There were no shopping centers nearby, and the closest mall was over an hour away. A lot of locals lived without an internet connection. And so people came to Carson's for their jeans and shoes and blenders and wedding bands. As I watched, two women emerged from the front entrance, laden with shopping bags. Their blond hair glowed beneath the streetlamps. Together, they loaded everything into the trunk of a station wagon.

I remembered going to Carson's when I was thirteen, just months after my mother disappeared, when I found myself in sudden need of a bra. I'd already tried on hers and my sister's, which were both comically large on my spindly frame. I knew Liz was in no position to take me shopping. She could barely get up to brush her teeth. So I walked in there one day after school and found the lingerie department. While the clerk was distracted with a fitting, I gathered up a whole armful of bras and went into the fitting room. I tried them all on until I found one that was wearable but still loose enough for me to grow into, with as few bows and frills as possible, and brought the rest back out to the rack. I left quickly with the bra still on my body, its tags cutting into my ribs as I hoisted my backpack over my shoulder.

That was the first time I stole, and I hated it. But before Liz got her job at the bank and after we'd eaten through absolutely everything in the house, I'd had to do it many more times. I went to the grocery store and shoved a pack of precooked breaded chicken breasts and a block of cheddar cheese into my sweatshirt. Before leaving, I hid behind a pyramid of canned pie filling and stuffed as many jars of peanut butter as I could fit into my backpack. Bill often gave us steep discounts on food if he happened to be working at the register when we rolled our cart up to the front, always without explanation or acknowledgment, as though the pitifully low number on the till was nothing out of the ordinary. But still, it wasn't always quite enough to tide us over in those months. Each time I slunk out the automatic front door with hamburger or pancake mix hidden in my school bag, I had to pass by a missing persons flier of my mother that was stapled to the bulletin board over the basket return. Eventually I tore it down and shoved it into my bag along with the stolen groceries.

It wasn't always food. We needed things like toilet paper and tampons, lightbulbs, toothpaste. Once when I was miserably sick with the flu, I dragged myself to the drugstore and slid a value-sized bottle of NyQuil under my coat. I don't know if I was good at it, or if everyone just gave me a pity pass, but I never hated doing it any less.

Eventually, the receptionist ushered us through a door and down a long hallway. Liz walked ahead of me. She smoothed her hair as we rounded the corner toward the sheriff's office. It looked the same; even the bulky gray desktop computer hadn't been updated. He sat behind his desk with Calloway in a chair to the right of him. The sheriff was the only person still left working in the local precinct who'd actually been on the job when our case was first opened. The force in our district was small, but there was a high turnover rate. One fledgling officer from Liz's graduating class had flipped his patrol car, drunk, and was discovered, unconscious and upside down, by another cop who heard the commotion on the radio. A heap of meth was discovered beneath his passenger seat. Some who managed to stay out of trouble, like Calloway, got to take a special training at the academy in Albany and be promoted to detective.

"I am here to ask you to reconsider speaking to Nick Haines again," my sister said, her voice calm and measured. She kept her hands clasped in her lap. Calloway looked at the sheriff. She added, "*Before* the autopsy comes back." The sheriff looked exhausted, and his chin drooped toward his chest. Liz saw it, too. I could almost feel the heat of her rising anger.

He hoisted himself up in his chair. "Do you have"—he paused to clear his throat. A deep, wet, toadlike gargle filled the room. Everyone waited in silence—"any interest in knowing *why* we're holding off on interviewing anyone in relation to your mother's case?"

A moment passed and he forged on without reply. "It's because we don't want to do anything to weaken it. You two are well grown now, so I have to be straight with you. We're scraping an empty barrel. There were no good leads then. You combine that with all the time that's passed, not a single tip coming in, and we find ourselves in a tough situation."

"But he knows by now that her remains were found. Surely he knows about it. Every day that goes by gives him more time to concoct some kind of story."

The sheriff shook his head. "Think of an old house," he said. Liz's face stiffened. "Let's say you want to build an addition on it, but the foundation is crumbling and the support beams in the basement are full of termites. If you just go in and build your addition without fixing all that, the whole thing will come crashing down on you. You have to start with the root problem before you do anything else. In this case, your mother's remains are the root. We need to see whether they can give us any information, any clues, before we know what direction to take. We don't want to put the cart before the horse here." He looked pleased with his explanation, and peered across the desk at the two of us with an easy, conciliatory kind of smile.

My sister seemed ready to tear his head off his body. I could see her tensing her hands into tight fists in her lap, her jaw flexing as she clenched her teeth.

"Let me just ask you this," I said, cutting into the tension. "Do you personally believe Nick Haines was involved? Setting procedure aside, what's your feeling?"

"My feeling," he repeated. "You remember what came of it when we spoke with him in the first place? Nothing. We found nothing. Nine times out of ten, if you're speaking with the perp you know it right away. Very few people leave no mess. And fewer kill a person out of nowhere like that, no motive, no incident, no ongoing relationship. That's very rare."

"He had something of hers, though."

"What? The compact? Don't make too much of that. It could have been anyone's. You see, what you've got with that is a confirmation bias." The sheriff turned to Calloway. "You can see that in the file, we found something on his person. A woman's mirror, looked strange at first but turned out 550,000 of the same one were manufactured in '97 alone, distributed at just about every drugstore in the region."

This was a fact I'd never heard before. For a moment, I questioned whether it was true, but then decided it was too specific a fact to be made up. Clearly they'd done some digging on it at one point. Yes, our mother had the same one. But so, too, did half a million other people. I wondered whether Liz already knew this, but she wouldn't meet my gaze. Calloway, still sitting off to the sheriff's side, glanced among the three of us like he was watching a game.

"Okay," I said. "But still, why was he speeding around early in the morning?" I glanced again at my sister. She was staring directly between the sheriff's eyes. "He was upset. He got emotional when the patrol officer asked for his license. That's unusual, right?"

"He was intoxicated, if I recall correctly."

"Yes. Same as when he took her on that date. And like he was the night Liz saw him fighting with that woman in the street."

"That's anecdotal. He may have been drunk on either of those occasions, we can't know for sure and it doesn't matter much either way. Bad dates happen every night."

The receptionist shuffled in, dropped a stack of papers onto the desk, picked up two large envelopes, and left. "Look," the sheriff said, rubbing at his temples. "I'll be frank. Is Nick Haines kind of an off-putting guy? Yes. I wouldn't be the first to say so. He's not going to win any popularity contests. But I've known him since he was a young man. I've watched him live in this town for the past fifteen years. He keeps his shop running. He's gotten into a couple bar fights in the past, but nothing too serious. He keeps mostly to himself these days."

I took a good look at the sheriff's face. Leathery, rough skin. A sagging lower lip. The whites of his eyes were yellowed, with little red veins snaking around the iris. I added up the years in my head, trying to guess how close he was to retiring and getting his pension. It couldn't have been far off.

"Don't think I didn't wonder about Nick back then," he said. "I did. Of course I did. We had him pinned as a suspect for six months. But we never found any just cause."

"What happened, then?" Liz said. "If he had nothing to do with it? Because I don't see any other explanation. I don't know what else makes sense. You can talk to me about motives and probability all day long, but sometimes things are just what they seem."

"There's a wide range of possibilities we can't discount yet."

"What?" I asked. "What possibilities?"

"Could have been a bad encounter with a through hiker, someone come down from Canada, perhaps. She might've crossed paths with someone camped out in the woods. We had a lot of drifters out there in those days." I remembered running past dense conifer thickets during track practice and occasionally seeing old tents, half dilapidated, with towels hung on nearby branches. Sometimes there'd be a pan or a plate on the ground nearby. Once I spotted a gentle curl of smoke emerging from a vent fashioned out of a foil-lined rolled oats canister. The sheriff's suggestion didn't seem totally impossible, but I also couldn't recall ever hearing about anybody getting harmed by one of these people.

"Well, how can you be sure it wasn't someone else in town?" I asked. "I know what Jeff Howard did to that one girl's mother. He was here then, living in Knife River, when she went missing."

"Your mother ever have a problem with him?" The sheriff looked back and forth between us, his eyes suddenly serious. I shook my head. Liz stared straight ahead for a minute, stone-faced, before telling him no.

"He never came to your house? Did anything funny?" We told him no to this, too, and his face relaxed. "Look," he said. "That was a terrible incident. He'll never go near the school again. And I'll tell you, as bad as the girl's mom was hurt, she got him worse before one of my guys went and broke it up. Nailed him in the eye so good the pervert's half blind now." He let out a dry little chuckle and looked over to Calloway, who gave an acquiescent smirk in reply. The sheriff composed himself and said to us, "But all this was years after you first came in here to report your mother missing. Just doesn't add up. Totally different situations." He looked again to Calloway, who nodded confidently, then back to us before saying, "If it wasn't a drifter, best chance is someone she was seeing that you two didn't know about. Could be a guy from here, but just as likely someone from another town. Someone we're still not aware of."

"No." Liz raised her voice. "No. No. She definitely was not seeing anyone."

The room was quiet. I looked at my sister and felt a rush of anger that took me by surprise. Her refusal to examine the truth suddenly seemed so unreasonable, so childish, it bordered on crazy. I'd never really entertained the notion that our mother had some secret boyfriend, but how could any of us know that? I thought of the secrets I'd kept in my own life. Every time I texted with Sarah in the past couple of days and didn't mention that I'd fucked someone else, and fully intended to do it again. When I forged a college diploma to get my job. The months I'd spent orchestrating my move away from Knife River when I was eighteen, securing a room in an apartment seven hours downstate, without mentioning it to anyone, not even my sister or Eva, before just driving off early one morning. Everyone in the room had secrets of their own. The receptionist down the hall had them, the people walking in and out of the department store across the street. Surely, Liz had hers, too.

I watched her tap her fingers on her thigh, blinking at the men around us, who didn't seem to know what to say to my sister's vehement denial of any unknown boyfriends. How could she still recall our mother with such a narrow lens? Long ago, when I was still in my teens, I sometimes thought of her like that, too. Those first few years, especially, she was frozen in place in my mind as a kind of saint. I had dreams where she appeared before me, haloed in a soft yellow light. She didn't age, or raise her voice, or cast a shadow. But as time went on, I began to think of her as just a person—at once precious and inessential to the world, as all people are. I knew she had within her kindness and ignorance and brilliance and deceit, all stacked against one another, all present from birth. The more my grief ebbed, the easier it was to see her this way, and the easier it was for me to accept her absence. What stopped Liz from getting to that place? She kept this version of our mother, this idealized ghost of a woman, under fierce guard. A fruitless labor. I couldn't understand what good it did her.

In the end, I think mostly to get us out of the office, the sheriff agreed to reconsider further investigation of Nick Haines in the near future. He offered us, too, regular meetings with Calloway, saying, "That way you can come in and get your questions answered. Maybe every few weeks or so. He'll keep you both informed, and we'll all be on the same page as we work to get through this together." The sheriff used a slow, gentle voice like he was speaking to children. Calloway smiled at us, gave a little encouraging nod, and I looked immediately to my sister, trying to gauge her receptiveness.

Her lips were set in a hard line. Finally, she said, "We'll be back soon, then."

Out in the parking lot, I wanted to say something terse but wasn't sure exactly how, or what, and spent most of the drive home replaying the evening's conversation in my mind. The more I thought of my sister's stubbornness, the angrier I became. The sheriff's voice echoed in my mind: *turned out 550,000 of the same one were manufactured in '97 alone.* The feeling I got looking at Haines's picture, or venturing near his store, echoed in me, too. Was it manufactured or did it come from something real—some unfeignable, animal way of knowing? I wasn't sure what to believe.

"You know," I suddenly said, my tone sharp. "Our mother was just a person." Liz's face scrunched up, perplexed.

"Yes," she answered. "Obviously, she was." I sighed. I knew my sister wouldn't understand. It was exactly the kind of broad, purposefully overt statement that went right over her head. She took jokes and sarcasm at face value, and rarely used hyperbole. Coming back home was a daily exercise in remembering how to use her language once again.

"What I mean is, none of us can really know for sure what was happening in her life when she disappeared." I paused a moment, waiting for Liz to shoot back with something, but she just stared ahead, quiet. I went on. "Nick Haines isn't the only person in the world capable of something like this."

"No, but he's the only one who makes sense."

"Is he? Because they seemed to have a lot of other ideas."

"So, you trust the cops on this now," she muttered. "You think they have a better sense than Brenda and me."

"No," I told her. "I'm not saying I trust them."

"Then what, Jess? What are you saying to me?"

"I'm just saying there might be other possibilities."

"I don't understand how you can look at Nick, knowing everything we know, and say these things. He's an absolute monster."

"Of course he is," I said. If I was honest, there wasn't anyone in the world who scared me more. "But it doesn't do us any good to pretend we really know the truth. Because we just don't."

When we got to the house, Liz stepped wordlessly from the car and walked inside. She went upstairs without taking off her coat and shut her bedroom door hard.

14

S arah called me late that night. We chatted for a few minutes about her job and how she was readying the flower beds for winter. I was lying on the sofa in the den, where I'd still been sleeping every night even though it made my back ache. On the coffee table before me was a plastic cup full of gin. Every ten minutes I leaned over, took a gulp into my mouth, and let it sit there on my tongue, burning a little, before swallowing. Then I checked my watch so I knew when the next ten-minute increment would be over. My hands would itch as the seconds dragged on.

"Thanksgiving is coming up," Sarah said. I could hear her placing a dish down onto a surface. It sounded like she was in her kitchen, sitting at the island. "Where will you be?" Her tone was just barely clipped.

I sat up straight. "I don't know," I told her. "The holidays aren't really on my mind these days."

"So you aren't coming back down here."

"I didn't say I never was."

"I didn't say *never,* either. I was just asking about Thanksgiving. Maybe Christmas. I'm trying to make plans."

"Don't let me stop you."

"Well, I was trying to make you a part of them." Now her tone was hard.

"There's just no chance I could get away right now. I can't leave my sister alone during all this."

"So it's Liz you don't want to be away from?"

I paused, taken aback by her question. She let the silence sit there, swelling between us.

Finally, I said, "I told you it was, yes. What are you asking me?"

"Nothing. I'm only saying you've been gone about a month now. In the beginning, we were in touch almost every day. Now I hardly hear from you, and when I do you sound like you're on another planet."

"Well, I'm a little distracted. None of this has been easy."

"I know."

"Do you? Because you're acting like Thanksgiving dinner is something I should have on my radar these days."

"My life didn't get upended all of the sudden. Yours did. I'm not just going to keep everything on hold forever."

"I'm not asking you to."

"You know what, though." Her voice took on a prying, syrupy tone. "You don't sound so *sad* tonight. Maybe a little remote, but not depressed the way you did in the beginning."

"Why don't you just say whatever it is you want to say to me?"

"Oh sure, I can do that. I think you're fucking someone."

At this, my stomach dropped. Chagrined, I glanced around the empty room as if someone else might be there, listening in on everything. I took another gulp of gin without checking my watch. Sarah was a brutally practical woman. Even if feelings were at stake, she had this way of steeling herself emotionally and examining her own circumstances as though they belonged to a stranger.

"Some townie, I guess," she went on. "Probably an ex?"

"Wow. Really?" I said, trying to come off indignant.

"Does she have an ankle tattoo?"

"No," I said. "She doesn't."

Sarah began to laugh openly. I could picture her there in the kitchen, her bobbed blond hair spilling over onto the countertop as she heaved her bony shoulders. I tried, briefly, to muster a sense of contrition, but nothing came. When I placed this conversation in the lineup alongside every other pressing thing, it seemed flimsy and small.

"So, is it an ex?" she asked. I inhaled, but before I could respond she said, "You know what, doesn't matter. I don't need to know. I'm too old for this kind of shit."

"What happens now?" I said. "What do you want to do here?"

"I mean, it's best that we just end things. I think you know that. There's no point in trying to work this out."

I felt a bloom of relief followed by panic, like I was balancing on a narrow board between two tall buildings and realized suddenly that no safety net lay below me, no parachute hung on my back.

She continued. "It's better this way, honestly. I missed you after you first left, but as the weeks passed, I started to feel like I was coming out of a haze. Like I'd put myself under some kind of spell, being with you. I really tried to brush it off, probably because that was less mortifying for me, but now this." I could hear her pouring something into a glass. I thought I should respond somehow, but my tongue felt like a slab of rubber. No words came into my mind. Sarah continued. "It was stupid of me to ever ask you to move in. You're too young. You don't even know what you want."

"I guess I don't."

"And honestly, Jess, you're being stupid, too. Once this is all over, whatever that looks like, you're going to see there's nothing in that town worth sticking around for, and now, nothing for you to come back to. You don't have any attachments, that's your problem."

"Thanks for the tip."

"I'm serious. You need to learn to make some actual decisions about your life. You're completely unmoored."

"I think that's a little dramatic."

"Is it? Because it took you less than one afternoon to near totally remove yourself from my home. Which had also been your home, since you'd been living there with me for a year. And then *poof,* gone. Like a fucking magic trick. Which is funny, because you can't stand being on your own, but once you find yourself with somebody, you start trying to find some way to get out of it. You get something good and then you sabotage it before skipping off to the next new thing."

"I didn't sabotage anything. Are you kidding me right now? I didn't ask to come back here. I didn't make this happen."

"No, you didn't. But no one forced you to start fucking some high school girlfriend, did they? And you can't honestly tell me that you weren't plotting a way out months before your sister called you. I tried to ignore it, but I knew you were getting restless. You practically started choking when I talked about getting pregnant."

A tense silence hovered between us. Again, I could think of no defense. My face grew hot.

"What are you going to do with yourself?" she asked. "Have you even thought about it?"

"Yes," I said. "Of course I have."

"And?"

"I may go to Maine."

"Maine," she repeated. "Why?"

"I've been thinking about it for a while."

"I never heard you say anything about Maine."

We talked for a little bit longer. Sarah informed me that she'd found a pair of my reading glasses wedged between her couch cushions, and one of my sports bras in the dryer.

"They're going in the trash," she said. "I'm not mailing you anything."

I did not think that was unreasonable. I wished her luck with her fertility treatments, saying that I hoped she found the right donor soon. There came a strange sound on the other end, somewhere between a scoff and a sigh. And with that, it was over. I doubted we'd keep in touch. If we ever ran into each other, it seemed entirely possible she'd give me a once-over from across the room and then turn away, expressionless, as if we'd never met. I went to sleep weighed down with a heavy, nagging sadness. Not over having lost something—certainly I'd lost it willingly—but over how easy it was to lose. Just weeks ago I was sharing a dresser with this woman, and now that life had slipped from my grasp readily, like sand, and I hadn't even tried to fight it.

In the morning I had a text from Eva. She wrote simply, *Come over again.*

15

This time Eva opened the door before I got to the front step. We didn't even say hello. Within moments, we were on the floor in the kitchen, moving over each other desperately, feverishly, as though at any moment our hands might turn to dust. It was totally different than with Sarah. My mind didn't wander. In fact, I didn't have thoughts at all. We descended into some kind of blackness together. It was like sinking, slowly, to the darkest depths of the ocean. Weightless. There was no sense of the encumbrance of a body, or the room itself, or the outside world at all. We fell into a rhythm that felt utterly natural, breathing as one, the line that defined the boundary between our separate selves blurred beyond recognition. If I had my mind about me, I might have been scared by how easy it was, how effortlessly we slipped back into the kind of intimacy that laid me bare. Normally I found this sort of thing terrifying. With anyone else it felt like pushing down on a bruise, but with Eva, I was hypnotized. She saw a version of me that was unknowable to any other woman. She knew me when I was just becoming, and through that knowing she understood how to touch me now. I didn't want to turn away from that. With one hand I felt for a mole I remembered on her upper back, and when I found it, I had to stop myself from erupting into tears.

Afterward, we climbed the ladder into the loft and lay down together. Above the bed was a wide skylight, set into the ceiling just a little crooked. It looked like it had been installed recently. Through it I could see the craggy, naked arms of tall trees swinging wildly against the bright light of day. Leaves spiraled down toward us and then away, caught up in the changing wind. I thought about Eva waking up each morning in this spot, her eyes fluttering against the gathering dawn. I wondered how long she'd slept here, what she'd dreamed of. There was so much I didn't know. Just minutes earlier, down in the kitchen, I'd felt almost fatally crushed by the closeness between us, but now she seemed to recede somewhere beyond my reach, like a tide rushing back out toward the horizon.

"So," I said. "Should we talk?"

"About what?"

"I've been over here twice now, and I still don't know anything about what your life is like these days."

"You know me," she said, turning on her shoulder. Her hair slipped down over her neck in one fluid motion, long and glossy, so dark it looked almost blue. "Somehow it just doesn't really feel like any time has passed between us," she said. "You know what I mean?" I did know what she meant. "Besides," she added, flipping onto her back. "It's not like you've told me anything about you."

"What do you want to know?"

"Where have you been for the past decade? What have you been doing?"

I laughed. I wasn't sure where to begin, or what was even worth mentioning. The topic of Sarah, or any other women, was obviously off the table. My job was dull and kind of disgusting, and the last thing I wanted to discuss was the investigation.

"Well, I moved downstate to Queens first, then moved around a bunch. I was staying in New Jersey right before I came here."

"What's it been like?"

"It was hard at first. Really hard. But I don't know what I would've done if I hadn't left."

"Did you ever think of me?" She asked this so plainly, staring up at the skylight, without any trace of resentment or flirtatiousness, that it made me want to cry. I blinked, unsure how to respond. How could I explain that had she not, by the simple fact of her being, shown me what I wanted, I might not have come to know myself or felt that there could be a place for me in the world?

"I thought about you all the time," I said.

"Honestly?"

"Honestly," I said. "And what about you? How long have you lived here?"

"A few years now."

"You don't have a lot of stuff."

"Well, I wasn't planning on staying long. But then my dad got diagnosed with Parkinson's and moved into a small apartment closer to the hospital, and I started going over a few times a week to help him with things. It's not a far drive from here."

"I'm sorry."

"It's all right. He's not too far gone yet, but it's sad to see him this way."

"Of course."

"So, yeah. I've been staying in this cabin awhile longer than I meant to."

"Are you working somewhere?"

"I was. My sister-in-law got me this job doing accounting at the hotel." She rolled her eyes a little and sighed. "I'm looking for something else now, though."

"Accounting? Not what I would have imagined."

"No?"

"I used to think you might become a vet or something. You were so good with animals."

She used to scoop up fell chicks in the springtime, feeding them with an eyedropper and keeping them wrapped in a laundry basket until they grew large enough to live in the wild. She tended to stray, injured cats and left spoiled chicken out at the edge of the woods for coyotes. If a raccoon made a nest in the garage below her attic bedroom, she'd wait until winter was over to shoo it outside. I used to worry about her getting bitten, but it never happened. *Animals only bite when they're scared,* she would say.

"Yeah. I used to think about vet school. Maybe one day," she whispered, her gaze on the ceiling. I could sense her reluctance to talk any more about herself, and I was afraid to push things too far. Our conversation seemed to teeter on a delicate balance and I didn't want to break the spell.

We must have drifted off for a little while. When I opened my eyes again the sky was dim and I could hear rain falling against the tin roof.

"I should get going," I said. She gave a drowsy nod.

As I climbed back down the ladder I heard her say, "Come back again soon?"

I got a ping from the periodontal office on the drive back, asking if I could finish a large file a bit sooner than expected. They were getting sued, apparently, and needed to present all the plaintiff's records to their lawyer. They were offering time and a half. By the time I pulled up to the house, I'd decided to brew a pot of coffee after dinner and stay up late, knocking out as much as I could during those quiet hours. I'd always liked working that way, even back in school, uninterrupted by ringing phones or cars rumbling down the block, in a stretch of time that felt like it belonged just to me. When I was halfway up the steps, trying to remember if we had enough coffee left in the pantry, I heard someone call out behind me. I turned and saw our next-door neighbor in his yard, a hand held up in greeting. I gave a limp smile, fishing around in my brain for a name.

"Hello," he said, taking a few steps forward, traversing the grass that divided our two driveways. A familiar wariness came over me: stiff limbs, blank face, one shoulder angled back like I might turn around and run any moment. It wasn't his fault. It was the same unnerving feeling that came over me when any man approached out of the blue, or when I walked past Nick Haines and his friends outside the bar. This neighbor, I started to remember, used to work in his garage summer evenings, the door pulled all the way up and the lights on, his figure illuminated behind a workbench, bending up and down, lifting little tools, like a wooden man in a cuckoo clock.

I said hello and walked down the steps toward him. When we were both near enough to hear one another without shouting he said, "I saw you coming in the other day. I couldn't believe it was you." He awkwardly shoved his hands down into his pockets. "You're so grown now." I nodded, unsure how to answer. "You remember?" he asked. "Paul."

"Of course," I said, suddenly embarrassed. "Yes."

"That's good." His voice trailed off before he repeated it once again. "That's good."

A strong breeze gusted around the trees and then blew between us. I zipped my coat up. Some dead leaves fluttered down and fell around our feet. I wanted to get inside and take a closer look at the file I'd been sent, but felt that I owed a few more minutes of polite conversation. Sarah used to always get after me about that, my habit of enduring things I didn't want without question. Someone could have their elbow jabbed into me at a movie theater and I would just sit there, numbing into the pain, until the credits rolled. Or I would badly scald my tongue on a bite of hot soup and then swallow and keep eating it, the broth blistering the inside of my mouth. *You need to become a better advocate for yourself,* Sarah would say. *You treat yourself like an old dishrag.*

"How are you?" I said.

"I should be asking you that question."

"Oh," I answered, flustered. "That's fine."

"Like I said, I couldn't believe it when I saw you going up the steps the other day. It's been such a long time. But I knew it was you because of course I heard about . . . well, about everything. I expected you'd come home."

"Right." My toes curled up inside my boots.

"So," he said. "You're doing all right?"

I shrugged. "Some days are easier than others." Paul nodded.

He was older than our mother would have been, maybe by fifteen years. We never knew him very well, though he and his wife had brought us food once or twice after she disappeared, leaving the dish on the porch with a brief note. He was a widower, I recalled. His wife—Sharon, was it? Shelley? Or Shirley?—had been in and out of the hospital for years with some aggressive form of cancer that spread to different parts of her body. I saw her once right before I moved away, sitting on their front porch with a knit cap on her head and a crutch propped against the railing. She looked frail and had enormous purple bruises in the crooks of her arms and on the tops of her hands. A few years later, Liz told me she went back to the hospital and never came home.

I shifted my weight. I tried to calculate how much more time I needed to stay there, chatting with him. A yellowed leaf blew off the roof and landed on my shoulder. I brushed it off. Paul cleared his throat and glanced back over to his yard. I remembered that I once spent the night in their house when I couldn't stand another moment sleeping on the floor with my sister and the mess of unwashed bedding all around us, her map on the wall covered up with red pushpins, scattered notes around the telephone. The room itself had seemed to pulse, drawing nearer from all sides as I lay there listening to her fitful breathing and the ticking clock. I got up and crept out the door with no plan in mind, just needing to get out. For a while I stood on the porch, shivering. I looked up at the stars until I got dizzy. I still couldn't bring myself to go back inside, so I walked next door, where I saw Paul through the side window of his garage.

His back was to me, and he was startled when I tapped on the glass and said simply, "Can I sleep here?" He came outside quickly, glancing between me and my house. I could see he wasn't sure what to do, what his responsibility as an adult was in this situation. "I'll leave when it gets light out," I said. I must have looked desperate. He led me in through the front door, without conversation, to a spare room where I fell asleep almost instantly on a little cot, surrounded by boxes and bins overflowing with X-rays and medical records. It was the most rest I'd gotten in weeks. When the sun came up, I snuck back into my own home, quietly sliding under the quilt next to my sister on the floor where she slept, the telephone receiver clutched in her hand.

We'd never discussed it, but as he looked back toward me I could almost feel the memory hanging uncomfortably between us. I felt a little defensive, like I wanted to place a shield between him and any recollection of me as a kid. I didn't want him to be able to imagine me small and cold like that, needing anything from him.

One of his pupils was a little cloudy, magnified under thick glasses. "If there's anything I can do, you just let me know."

"Thanks," I said.

"Anytime."

He turned and walked into his garage. There were a few rakes and old shovels piled up against the porch railing, and throughout the yard lay coiled hoses of different sizes, a pile of bricks, birdbaths, tires, a wheelbarrow full of dirt that had begun to sprout something that seemed to be near death in the cold air.

I stood there for a few seconds, looking it all over, then took my cigarettes and gloves out of the passenger seat and walked down to the sidewalk, turning left toward town. My transcription could wait. Liz wouldn't even be home for another hour or so, and even though it was getting cold I suddenly felt that I didn't want to be alone inside. Surely Paul would have already noticed my sister's car absent from the driveway. How could I know he hadn't gone back inside and then watched from a window, waiting to see what I did next? I had no good reason to think he'd care, but still I felt like there was an invisible force field keeping me from going alone up the porch steps to my own front door in plain sight of any man.

I walked past the edge of our neighborhood and over a small bridge.

Fallen branches rushed along the river. Tall trees swayed in the wind, their leaves turning and rustling. A dark, purplish dusk began to set. Lots of the houses appeared vacant, the yards overgrown with weeds and shutters hanging by their hinges. A spring-coiled rocking horse sat in an otherwise empty driveway. The paint was warped and sun faded, but it was placed at an assertive angle right behind the curb, like it was standing ready to prevent anyone from driving onto the property, refusing to abandon its post no matter how many seasons came and went.

On the corner, a middle-aged couple idling at the stoplight stared at me from inside their car, their two heads swiveling slowly as I passed. I looked ahead even though I was acutely aware of all four of their eyes on my hair, my profile, my gait, the breadth of my shoulders. It was a stare I knew well; they registered me first, just peripherally, as a grungy young man. Then when I came into clearer focus and the subtleties of my body revealed themselves, their eyes sharpened. These were stares laced with discomfort, even displeasure, that I not only existed but was walking in public so brazenly as myself. That word, *brazen,* was one I'd overhead people use about me a number of times. Like maybe I could get away with looking the way I did if only a layer of abashedness came before it, like an olive branch of shame might grant me their continued tolerance. In another moment, in another place, I might've met this couple's eyes and given a knowing, barbed smirk. Maybe even a quick wave. This usually dispelled all gawking. It made people shrivel up. Almost inevitably, they became preoccupied with their own hands or something in the bottom of a shopping bag. But here, on this night, in this town, on an otherwise empty street with no other witness but the discarded rocking horse, I pretended not to be aware of them and just kept walking ahead.

After the couple drove off, I saw no sign of any other people. I thought of the woman at the gas station who'd admonished me for moving away—the town really had grown desolate. What would become of these houses in twenty, fifty, one hundred years? I sat on a large, flat rock where the river bent toward Main Street and had my cigarette. The rock had probably been sitting there for eons. It probably tumbled off a glacier in some distant geologic period, landed right here, and just sat, gradually eroding, while everything happened around it. Creatures lived and went extinct, never to be seen by human eyes. Industry boomed and disappeared. People settled in droves, built homes, then vanished. Once the houses were gone, the rock would still be there.

A breeze came and sent a shower of tiny orange sparks flying off the tip of my cigarette. The streetlamps began to illuminate, snapping on one after another with their dull buzz. I felt so small inside my body. Woefully impermanent and, worst of all, soft. I was vulnerable to so many things. Another person could lurch from the shadows and plunge a knife into my spongy, yielding middle. Some freak thing could fall from the sky and crush me to a paste. There was little I could do about it. I couldn't even guard my feelings against whatever gravity Eva seemed to hold.

16

The next time I was with her, just a few days later, a knock came at the cabin door.

We were sitting opposite on her couch, undressed, having a giddy, careless conversation about a trans-Canadian road trip we could take over the summer. It was my third visit to her place and I'd already been there for most of the day, completely ignoring my phone, letting myself fall for the fantasy of this long drive through the alpine meadows and wild, ice-capped mountain ranges. She talked about foraging for berries, taking her clothes off and plunging into a glacial lake. I could see it so clearly in my mind—the length of her body disappearing beneath the frigid surface, sunlight dancing over blue water. We'd talk about it, fuck some more, then lapse back into our dizzied planning.

She shrank away from most of my questions about her life in town, but the idea of driving away together like this, stopping in unknown places, leaving without a return date in mind, seemed to embolden her. Charting a course through the oblivion of the plains, the thought of sleeping out in the open, cloaked by a vast sea of stars—it all brought a glimmer into her eyes. Longing thrummed beneath her breath, I could feel it.

"When could we leave?" she asked. "June?"

"Maybe, yeah."

"We could spend the whole summer."

"We could," I said. "We can do whatever we want." This answer seemed to satisfy her. She grinned and crossed her arms, tilting her head to the side as she questioned me about edible wild berries and distances between cities.

The knock came as she leaned forward to kiss me, right in the fraction of a moment before her lips touched mine. Her face went pale and she gasped, jumping up and pulling on her robe. She yanked me by the arm over to the loft ladder. Pointing up into the bedroom, she mouthed the word *go* over her shoulder and ran toward the door. I was bewildered. As I climbed, I caught a glimpse of her checking her face and hair in the little mirror over the row of key hooks.

Up in the sleeping nook, I crouched at the opening and listened intently to the conversation below. My heart was pounding. I tried to silence my breath. There was a man's voice. Her brother, I soon gathered. He sounded like he was standing just inside the doorway.

"Sorry to bother you." He paused. "Are you all right?"

"Yes, of course," I heard her say. "Why?"

"You seem kind of startled."

"No, I was just resting. I had a shit sleep last night."

"Well, I won't stay. I just wanted to see if you needed any kindling for the woodstove. I brought some over in the truck."

"I'm okay. Thanks, though."

"You sure? Your bin seems low."

"I'm fine."

"I'll leave it anyway. It's supposed to snow on Thanksgiving next week."

"Leave it on the porch?" she said. "The wood out back has to dry out; I forgot to cover them when it rained the other night."

There were two large aluminum boxes behind the toolshed where I parked my car. I knew they were clamped shut, I saw them on my way in just hours earlier. I shut my eyes. I could hear the light tap of her pacing in the kitchen, the sound of her brother grunting as he hoisted the sack of wood up the steps and dropped it onto the porch. They chatted for a few more moments. Her voice was strained. My muscles were growing numb, crouching stock-still by the ladder. After a little while, he said goodbye and returned to his truck.

When I heard him driving off, I climbed back down and got dressed before sitting on the edge of the couch. I watched her check the locks. I could tell she didn't want to talk. She lingered at the sink, fussing unnecessarily with some dishes before turning around to look at me again.

"Expecting somebody else?" I asked.

She sat down opposite me, opened her mouth as if to say something, but then closed it, looking sideways at the ground. My stomach was turning on itself. I thought of how careful she always was to make certain the curtains were down.

"I'm sorry," she finally said.

I shook my head, saying, "It's not like I had any expectations here." I meant it. I hadn't allowed myself any. I could play around with these grand, ridiculous thoughts about running off together into the wild north, letting the spell of it all course through me, but I knew it was just daydreaming.

"I have to be honest with you," she said. She looked close to tears, which worried me. I didn't want to hear whatever this was. Coming out into the woods to be with Eva was like slipping into an extra pocket of time, a secret part of the day only we could move in and out of. I didn't want to make it into something difficult. In a way, I didn't want it to become real, tarnished by all the matters of our actual, outside lives and ruined by consequence.

"I am sort of involved with someone else," Eva said. She studied my face for a reaction, but I kept still. "It's not . . . I mean, it's been on and off. It isn't what I really want, you have to understand that."

"How involved is sort of involved?"

"It's hard to explain."

"I'll try to keep up."

She rolled her eyes at me. "Don't feel weird about it," I said. "I was living with someone when I came here. I only ended things with her a few days ago, over the phone. Nothing to do with you, of course."

I smiled. Eva didn't.

"It's someone you kind of know," she said.

I scanned through everyone it might be. The list was short. There was a girl with a bunch of neck tattoos who was always standing around outside the drugstore, but she seemed too young. Then I remembered someone we'd gone to high school with, was her name Joan? She was tall and broad and unafraid to start fistfights with guys, though I was almost certain she moved to Buffalo after graduation.

As if reading my thoughts, Eva said, "It isn't a woman."

"Okay," I replied. My heart stung. "Then who is it?"

"It's Jack." I blinked, not understanding. "Jack," she repeated. "Jack Calloway. Detective Calloway." Her eyes darted quickly up and down my face, waiting for a reaction.

I thought she must be kidding. My lips cracked into a dry half smile. I cocked my head to one side, waiting for her to tell me who it really was, but she didn't say anything else. My mouth went dry.

"You're serious?" I said. "That's really who it is?"

"I knew you were in town before we ran into each other at the supermarket," she said. "This is his first missing persons case, so he talked about it a lot after getting assigned." All the blood seemed to rush out of my head and pool down in my ankles. "Don't say anything yet," she said. "Just let me try to explain it to you."

"Please, yes," I said, my voice thin. "I wish you would."

"One of my brothers got to know him a year ago, so he was always hanging out. And then I became friendly with him. He wasn't an asshole. I mean, he isn't an asshole."

"Oh my god," I said, getting up and walking over to the sink. I splashed some water on my face. I could feel Eva's eyes on my back as I twisted the faucet off.

"He kept other men from bothering me," she went on. "And then one thing kind of led to another. It was easier for me to have him around. It made my whole life simpler. No one questioned me anymore. Everyone left me alone. My family quit asking me when I was going to get a boyfriend or get married. Guys in town stopped asking me out. There were no more rumors."

I turned around. "Does this mean you didn't date other women after I moved away?"

"Of course it doesn't mean that," she said, narrowing her eyes. "Don't be arrogant."

I sat back down next to her on the sofa and she began to explain how she met women on a dating website and then drove to see them elsewhere, out of town, where they lived. One of them she saw for a while, almost nine months, before the woman declared she was no longer willing to date someone who wanted to keep her a secret.

Talking about all this made Eva sad, I could tell. She was peeling at the skin on her cuticles so hard they'd begun to bleed, though she barely seemed to notice.

"You don't get it because you haven't been living here," she told me. "Things haven't changed that much. When we were kids, no one was out. There wasn't such a thing as *out*, here. You remember. Now there's just this one older guy who works at the library and some music teacher I've never even met who nearly lost her tenure for bringing her girlfriend to the school play. And while we're on it, my last job, the one at the hotel? I didn't quit. The manager, the woman who knows my sister-in-law, fired me out of nowhere. She said it was because they could only keep one accountant, but it was right after another woman who worked there had started a rumor about me."

"What kind of rumor?"

"She saw some picture I was tagged in online, before I even knew it was up. Wasn't even a new picture, it was taken at my ex's birthday party over a year before." She described how quickly the rumor spread, and the picture itself: her sitting in the girlfriend's lap, the girlfriend's hands resting on her upper thigh, the picture taken the exact moment she kissed her on the neck. Shortly after this, Eva let Calloway take her out for a drink, to quiet people down.

As she spoke, I thought back to the first place I ever lived after leaving Knife River. I'd looked through the classifieds in the back of some lesbian magazine I found at a natural food store in a neighboring town, and spotted an ad placed by someone in Queens who was looking for a roommate to supplement the rent. She wanted someone by the end of the following month. I'd been secretly saving money for a while already, socking away canned food and toilet paper in the trunk of my car whenever I thought Liz wouldn't notice it missing. I only needed a place to go.

My first morning there I sat in bed, looking out the window onto the East River, watching white swells break against the concrete barrier. I couldn't believe that I'd woken up in a completely different life. No one knew me. The woman whose apartment it was didn't even know my last name. After I reached out, we'd agreed to meet at a nearby bar and she sized me up quickly, asking how old I was and where I came from. For some reason, I blurted out Toronto, which surely sounded like a lie, but she didn't care. I paid her first and last in cash, as was her preference, and then drove my car, where all my worldly possessions were still stashed, around the corner to her building. She had a lot of parties, which she always invited me to join. In those days, I never really felt in the mood for them, but I always went anyway because I couldn't get over the feeling of wonder and bliss brought on by being in a room full of women who wanted each other so openly. They danced and kissed and touched each other without any hint of fear or self-consciousness. For weeks, I cried every night before bed. Not out of sadness, but from the sheer relief that this kind of life was real, and it could be mine, that it *was* mine, and that it had always been happening out there somewhere, waiting for me to find it.

"Anyway," Eva said, picking at a loose thread on the couch cushion. "We obviously don't live together. He thinks I'm with this fundamentalist group. My sister-in-law is, like, deep in that world. Tongue speaking and apocalypse stuff. She's nuts. She got my brother roped into all that, too, so I let them both think I'm into rediscovering my Baptist roots."

"And Jack buys that?"

"Yeah. He suggested we get married, thinking that would be a way to get around it. But I told him I wasn't ready."

"When did that all happen?"

"Three months ago. He hasn't brought it up since."

"You know I see him, like, regularly," I said, a nervous heat rising up my face. "He's been by our house. Two weeks ago Liz and I went to have a meeting with him and the sheriff at the station."

"I know."

"Of course," I muttered. "You know, I'm going to have to be in touch with him a lot while I'm in town."

"Yeah," she said, her voice frayed with guilt. "I've thought about that."

"How could you not say anything?" My nervousness was turning to anger, and I heard myself asking again, now more loudly, "Seriously, why? Why didn't you say something?"

"I'm sorry," she said. It sounded like maybe she was near tears. "I feel horrible. I thought I'd see you once and that would be it, but then every week I would tell myself just one more time. I'm really sorry I didn't tell you."

I stared at her. "You know what?" I put my hands up in the air before me. "I don't care. I actually wish you never told me."

"What do you mean, you don't care?"

I began gathering up my things—my jacket and gloves and cigarettes—and making my way toward the door. "I mean, I'm going to leave right now like we didn't just have this conversation. It's your business. I can't tell you what to do."

I gave her a brusque kiss on the shoulder and left, walking quickly around the back of the cottage, behind the shed, where she always asked me to park. I knew she was watching me from the window, but I didn't look back.

Her brother was out in front of the main house, loading split logs into the woodshed as I drove past. He barely looked up at first, but then stopped in place, staring at me through the windshield as I approached. I tried to keep my face turned down, but we'd already caught each other's eye. I could see him in the rearview still staring, now frowning, squinting at my license plate as I turned onto the road.

17

"What's wrong with you?"

"Nothing."

"You seem weird." Liz studied me, arms folded. "I know something is wrong."

I looked up from my computer. It was Saturday, and I was making my final edits on the large file the periodontists had sent over to me a few days ago. The lawsuit was over a surgery on an elderly man who'd fallen in the bathroom and broken his top teeth against the side of the tub. They'd had to place twelve titanium screws in his gums. The patient and his lawyer were claiming two of them were inserted incorrectly, causing unrelenting pain and emotional distress. It was one of the more interesting files I'd ever transcribed, but I was so distracted I had to play the recording back every few seconds, forcing myself to follow along with the technician's voice.

"Where were you yesterday?" Liz asked.

"When?"

"I came home in the afternoon because I'd forgotten my lunch, and you weren't in the house. I called you but you didn't pick up."

"Oh. I was out buying shampoo."

"We have shampoo."

"Well, I wanted the kind I like."

"What kind did you get?"

"Can you please—" I said. "I'm trying to finish something here." She stood there like a mannequin, staring at me as I typed. Minutes passed and my sister didn't move.

Eventually she repeated the question, adding, "Where did you go to buy it?" She hated being lied to and knew, always, when I was trying to pull something over on her. That was what she used to say when she suddenly found herself having to play parent to me whenever I was going somewhere or doing something or seeing somebody I didn't want her to know the truth about: *I know you're trying to pull something over on me right now.* My sister seemed to have a line into my head that could not be severed. Years of distance hadn't weakened it.

"It made me anxious," she finally said.

"Anxious?"

"When I came home and you weren't here. I worried."

I closed my screen and looked her in the eye. I felt guilty for making her nervous, and then even worse thinking of all the hundreds of times she came home to an empty house and had to sit with her fearfulness, have dinner with it, carry it up the stairs to bed with her all while, miles away, I was sitting with my own fear, and never even let her know. I wanted to throw my head into Liz's lap and scream until all my breath was gone and my throat was raw and sore. I wanted to admit everything to her, how bad I felt about leaving her alone and what Eva had confessed to me the day before. I wanted to ask her what to do.

"Well, I'm sorry," I finally choked out. "I don't want to worry you."

"Good. I have all the worries I can handle."

"I know."

"I'm going to Brenda's now. You should come with me." I looked at her, trying to decide if she wanted me there to assuage her own anxiety, or because she could sense my heart hurting and felt pity for it. "Let's go," she said. "Come on."

Brenda lived in a little brick house out by the high school. Her living room was pink, floor to ceiling—flamingo shag carpeting, silky drapes with matching tassels, two vases on the mantel full of dusty artificial roses. By the door sat a big ceramic poodle, also pink, with a hole in its back that held umbrellas. Liz walked in and dropped her coat over the side of a chair. She seemed at ease in this place, as comfortable as she was coming into our own home. Maybe even more so. I hung back by the door, watching her hug Brenda.

Liz looked her up and down, touched her on the wrist, and asked, "How're you feeling?" Brenda waved her off, smiling as she padded over to the sofa.

She pulled a bottle of scotch from beneath the coffee table and beckoned me over. "I fell down last week. Hurt my rib." Once the scotch was poured and I was seated, she lifted the side of her sweater and revealed a big, swollen bloom of a bruise. Its edges faded into a sickly green, while the center was dark with old blood trapped beneath the skin. Out in the woods she'd seemed so tough, sinewy and hardened like scrap hide. She kept pace with Liz and me on the way out to the site and didn't wince dropping to her knees in the dirt. Now I could see her rib cage move with each breath, the bones rippling beneath her papery, shriveled skin. Up close like this, without the big winter coat and hat, her body was undeniably frail. "It looks worse than it is," she said.

Brenda observed my face carefully, watching me looking at the bruise, only pulling her sweater back down when I turned to reach for the drink she'd poured me. Back in the kitchen, I could see Liz poking around, neatening things up. She opened the fridge and started checking the expiration date on everything, shelf by shelf. She sniffed a carton of milk and then tossed it into the trash. She took out a pack of chicken thighs and gave them a long stare, bringing the plastic right up to her nose and inhaling. I thought of the squalor in our own kitchen, the ancient jars of jam and long-forgotten potatoes, shriveled and sprouting, that were there when I first came back home.

"Your sister takes care of me," Brenda said, following my gaze. "I don't have any children myself. I have nieces and nephews, but only two of them live nearby and they're both useless."

"Good thing you've got Liz around, then."

"You have no idea. A few years ago, I slipped on black ice and broke my ankle. When I was laid up from that, I got a cold that turned into pneumonia. I've never been so miserable in my life." She took a big gulp of her scotch, swirling it around in the glass. "Your sister noticed that I wasn't coming by the bank to deposit my regular check. She called, but I couldn't even drag myself to the phone. When she saw how bad off I was over here, she started cooking for me and taking care of the laundry. She did it all. Got my prescriptions, shoveled snow off the front step. And then, you know, she would just sit with me and talk."

Liz was still in the kitchen, now standing at the counter dividing pills into a weekly container, her brow knit in concentration. She checked each bottle carefully, pouring the contents into her palm and dispensing the medicine with care.

Brenda said, "Your sister is a good person."

I felt almost embarrassed by her pointing this out. Even though we'd gone so many years hardly speaking, I never once felt that there was anyone in the world more connected to me than Liz. I'd seen her in her purest, most true form: a young girl standing on the roof with her balsa wood plane, sun in her eyes. We emerged from the same womb, were made of exactly the same stuff. We'd felt the same terror, grown new skin over the same loss. But here was this whole other side to my sister that I'd missed. She was soft and attentive. Gentle. And clearly, she wanted to be needed by somebody. Brenda was just an old woman who came into Liz's work, and now here we were in her house, settling in with drinks while my sister lovingly counted out her various medicines and vitamins.

I'd always known Liz was clever and tough. Courageous, even. She did what needed to be done, and I never felt that she didn't love me. But the way she touched Brenda's wrist, asked how she was feeling—

that version of her was like being in the company of a total stranger. Maybe, I thought, she simply couldn't look at me and not be reminded of the darkest time in her life. Caring for Brenda was something she chose, whereas I was foisted upon her out of duty. A burden, even though I did everything I could to make myself as low maintenance as possible. I hardly asked for anything. I made myself scarce around the house. Maybe that was the problem.

"Yes," I finally replied. "She is." My mouth felt dry. I finished my scotch and Brenda refilled my glass. I could feel her eyes on me as I looked around the room and then back at her, unsure of what to say. Wild white hairs sprouted out of her face. Her wrinkles were spectacular—deep and long, narrowing into a spray of faint lines surrounding her lips. Her hands, too, were like weathered tree bark. Liz and I must have seemed so young next to her. Stupidly, wonderfully, perilously young. *Wheel of Fortune* came on and Brenda unmuted the TV. We watched the colors spin around and around. Glitter and confetti rained down as the contestants jogged out from backstage, screaming as if possessed. Vanna White, dripping in silver sequins, strode across the screen.

"I watch to see her gowns, mostly," Brenda said. "This one's all right. I would give it a B-minus. My favorite one was in June of 1990. It had incredible gold sleeves." She whirled her hands about her shoulders. "They were very fashionable at the time. I always loved nice dresses like that, even though I never had the life for them. In my next life, I'll wear gowns."

I saw Liz slip out the screened kitchen door with a handful of stale rolls and reappear in the yard, where she stood out in the grass, breaking up the bread into little pieces and scattering it around in a circle. Within moments, birds flocked to her. It was biting cold but she crouched down on the ground, her coat pulled tight around her, and watched the frenzy.

Suddenly I heard myself saying, "Do you remember the sound of my mother's voice?" I wasn't sure why I asked this. It surprised me the moment it slipped out of my mouth fully thought up, like it had been crouching just at the back of my tongue waiting for its chance to be heard. Brenda turned the volume down.

She almost seemed to expect such a question. "I remember Natalie well. We worked in the same office for three years."

"Sometimes I'm afraid I don't remember her voice. I can hear it in my head, but then I wonder if it's really her or if it's just a stand-in I invented for myself." Brenda reached over and squeezed my hand.

"Would you tell me about what she was like then?" I asked.

"I remember her laugh better than her voice, to tell you the truth. She had a good sense of humor. She smiled a lot. People were naturally drawn to that, there was something very light about her."

"There was, yeah."

"She was very pretty, too. A lovely face. Big, dark eyes. And she could play the piano, as I'm sure you know."

"Did you ever get to hear her?"

"Yes. We had a little Christmas party in the auditorium for the office staff while she was still at the job, and she played carols for us. It was very sweet. She was quite artistic, too. Did you know that? She made a nice painting of the river valley behind the school that hung in the superintendent's room for a while. No idea whatever happened to it."

An old memory broke free from the mire; a landscape painting hidden underneath our old piano bench. I discovered it by accident one day when I knocked the bench over sitting down to practice scales, still taking the occasional lesson at my mother's behest, and a Masonite board was revealed, repurposed to hold the upholstery down around a stapled base. It was a fantastical wilderness panorama; vivid, psychedelic fields of flowers flowing into a glacial lake with one monstrous-looking fish bobbing at the surface. There were tall, fruited trees and both a sun and stars with human faces hanging in the sky. The character of it was at once crude and enchanting, what I think now must've looked like the work of someone with a raw jewel of talent that never

saw the light. The kind of earnest folk art that almost never gets recognized for its weird, cockeyed beauty. I used to like to lie down on
the carpet in the living room, half my body wedged under the bench,
and gaze up at it, finding a new detail every time. In one corner my
mother's initials were half covered by the fabric cushion's raw edge. I
never asked her why she used something as pretty as this, something
she'd spent some real time creating, as scrap wood for furniture,
though I'd always wondered. Where it was, how I'd stumbled upon
it—it all felt so secret, like something I had no business prying into.

Liz was still outside communing with the birds. Brenda and I
watched as Vanna White glided across the screen again, her blue chif-
fon train fanning out behind her like a cloud. My eyes glazed over. It
was scary how easily I could picture the hidden painting, conjure how
special it felt to me, despite never having thought about it once in all
the years since. There were so many empty, black stretches in my memory. All I had was a strange hodgepodge of moments, sounds, images:
a skeleton of my life, picked clean by scavengers. Then, occasionally,
something would come back to me, perfectly preserved, sparked by a
comment like the one Brenda made. What bothered me most was how
little control I seemed to have over what I could recall and what I
couldn't. There were weeks, possibly months, of the past that I couldn't
account for at all. Someone told me once that it wasn't unusual to experience that kind of thing following a tragic event. Post-traumatic
amnesia, they recited to me, seeming pleased to know the proper ter-
minology. What was I supposed to do with that information? How
could I redeem it for my own memories?

Brenda dropped another ice cube into her glass and swirled it
around loudly, redirecting my attention back to the present moment.
"Later on, after she went to another job, I ran into her on the sidewalk," she said. "She had this sweet little girl with her, just barely old
enough to stand on her own. Your sister, of course. I never saw a child
with so much hair, scads of it all over. Your mother looked happy. Totally at ease. When she was new in town and still pregnant, I worried

sometimes if she would be okay. Especially once that husband of hers started working on the road. Your father, I suppose, technically. But anyway, it's really hard for young women. I wouldn't want to be that young again. You couldn't pay me. And then to have no family here on top of it all, the pregnancy and that rushed marriage, I did worry sometimes. But seeing her with Liz, she looked so self-assured. I didn't worry after that."

Liz had quietly come back in through the porch door and was sitting on the edge of the sofa, listening to Brenda. I looked at her. She looked at the carpet. She was still covered with whorls of black hair, all up and down her arms. Her eyebrows met in the middle. She had spectacular sideburns.

Brenda went on, "When I heard about what happened years later, the first thing I thought of was that day on the sidewalk with her little girl. And I felt . . ." She paused, gazing at the wall. Her eyes darted around and she shook her head slowly. "I don't know how to tell you how angry I was. There aren't any words for it."

Before getting into the car later that evening, Liz walked around the perimeter of the house making sure all Brenda's doors were locked.

"You're very good to her," I said once we were on our way back home.

Liz was quiet for most of the drive, eventually saying only, "She's been good to me, too." They seemed to be at utterly disparate phases in life; one slowly grinding to a halt, the other still young and vital, but my sister lived in such stasis that their days were really not so different. Liz's routine was unwavering. She kept her world small. It was a relief to see that she had someone so earnestly on her side, to see proof that she was less alone than I had imagined.

18

"I wasn't sure if you'd see me again after last time."

Eva sat across from me at her little kitchen table, examining my face for a reaction. Nearly three weeks had gone by, and I wondered if she regretted asking me to come over. I wondered, too, if I'd made a mistake by saying yes. I did let the text sit on my phone, unopened, for most of the day while I worked on my laptop. Eventually, I couldn't stand it anymore and got into the car.

We'd stood around in the doorway for a few minutes, hesitating around the question of each other's bodies. Were we going to kiss? Were we going to talk about what happened? Her text was vague. I couldn't get a sense of her mood from it, and still felt mystified as I stood before her inside the cabin. Finally, I took my jacket off and walked all the way in. I spotted a box of stuffing mix on the counter and remembered that the day after next was already Thanksgiving. Just a few weeks earlier, I was sure I'd be long gone by now. I bristled at the idea and then pushed it aside. In this moment, I wanted only to talk with Eva. I gave her a weak smile and she seemed relieved. Soon we were sharing a pitcher of coffee.

"I told you," I said to her, leaning my elbows on the kitchen table. "It isn't any of my business."

"You did say that."

"And I meant it."

She gave me a pained, incredulous look. She opened her mouth to speak and then paused first to take another sip before saying, "If you were angry at me, I would get it." I nodded but said nothing. "Are you angry?" she asked. Her entire body seemed to pulse with nerves. I got the sense that she was truly, genuinely afraid that I would be upset and leave, and not see her again.

"I'm not mad," I said, realizing it was true as the words came out of my mouth.

"Really?" She sounded perplexed, a little skeptical.

"I don't feel great about it. But it's not like you owe me anything here, so how could I feel betrayed?"

I got the impression she was disappointed I wasn't more visibly wrecked, and wasn't sure how to proceed. Being in her place again gave me an uneasy feeling. Each sound—leaves falling against the windows, a branch rolling off the tin roof, wind sweeping over the front steps—jolted my attention. I found myself calculating how quickly I could vault up the ladder if someone came to the door, then wondered what I would do if they actually came up into the loft. I thought about the feasibility of climbing out of the skylight and escaping by way of the roof.

"He doesn't ever just drop by, does he?" I asked.

"Jack?" she asked. I looked at her flatly.

She glanced to the side. "No. Not if we don't have, like, plans." As she said this, her body seemed to shrink. "You're nervous after last time, aren't you?"

"I mean, it was jarring."

"I know." She shook her head slowly, then spoke again. "Listen, I told him that you and I know each other from a long time ago."

My whole body tensed up. "Are you serious?" I asked. "When? Why would you do that?"

"After you left last time, my brother asked me who I was hanging out with back here. I guess he saw your car leaving."

156

"Yeah, I saw him watching me drive out. I don't know if he actually got a look at my face or not," I said. "It was quick. I just kept going."

Eva looked around the room, her eyes moving as if calculating something. "Well, the next time I saw Jack he mentioned your case."

"What did he say about it?"

"The investigation? Nothing, really. He just said it was still going." I looked at her urgently. "I'm not keeping anything from you. Honestly." Her face flushed. She added, "You know what I mean."

"I'm seeing him tomorrow. Liz and I have a meeting at the station." I crossed my legs. "Though perhaps you already know that."

"I did not."

"All right."

"Listen." She ran her hands through her hair and took a long breath. I could see she was trying to figure out the right things to say.

She got up and sat down in the chair next to me. "I only said anything to him because I thought it would be better to get out ahead of it. I didn't want any rumors to start. Also, it seemed like it would be the easier thing for you, just in case my brother said something to Jack. I didn't want him to be surprised." A dry laugh escaped me before I could stop myself. Eva squinted, her jaw set. "What?" she said. "What's so funny?"

"I don't know."

"You're laughing."

"Just the idea of wanting to spare him any surprises." I pressed my hands into my face, trying to alleviate some of the pressure building inside my skull. My skin felt like it was made of wax. Eva tapped her nails on the side of the coffee pitcher. The woodstove hissed.

Eventually, she said, "I really am sorry to put you in the middle of something like this."

"I think you're the one in the middle," I said. Her face darkened, then softened, then shifted, and I couldn't tell what she was thinking at all. I added, "But maybe it's fine. Why shouldn't he know we're friends?"

"Oh, are we friends?" she asked.

"Aren't we?" My voice came out softer than I'd meant it to.

We stared at each other. The air between us crackled with something angry and carnal. I couldn't tell if we were on the cusp of an argument or if we would soon be on the floor, clawing at each other's backs, wrist deep inside each other's bodies. "I can't call *this* dating," I said, motioning around the room. My tone was not quite stern, but had a steely edge that made her briefly glance down at the floor. "If we never go anywhere outside, and we're sitting here tiptoeing around why exactly that is."

"What do you want to call it?" There was a hint of a challenge in her tone, like she wanted to see what I'd admit to. What I wanted was to spend every night with her, somewhere far away from Knife River, instead of drifting off alone on an old sofa next to the drafty window in my childhood home as every ghost from my past, newly resurrected, swirled around me, howling in my ear. I wanted to be out in the world with her, holding her hand, knowing that there was no one else waiting to take her in their arms.

Instead, I said, "I don't know."

In the end, we didn't argue or wind up on the floor. The conversation dwindled to a close and I left without feeling that I understood the situation any better than I had when I first walked in.

"Don't worry about running into my brother," Eva said. "He's at work right now."

"What about his wife?"

"She's always lying down with a migraine or nursing a baby. She won't be outside."

I nodded and gathered up my things. The bathroom door was open and I could see her hairbrush next to the sink, a wet towel hanging over the shower bar, some earrings in a little dish. As I reached for the door she stopped me, placing her hand on my chest and looking straight into my eyes. She said, "You and I aren't friends."

19

Calloway came out to the lobby to get us for our meeting the next day. The receptionist was gone, an open magazine and half-drunk bottle of iced tea sitting before the phones. The switchboard, too, was unattended. Red lights blinked up and down the panels, with a long line of different-colored buttons and switches corresponding to a series of letters. I glanced at it as we walked past.

"Cutting-edge technology," he joked, noticing my interest. An empty little laugh escaped my mouth.

His office was at the very back of the building next to the exit. There was only one chair in front of his desk, so we waited while he went into someone else's office to find another. Minutes passed. I could hear the metal legs dragging along the linoleum as he approached. Liz looked up at the ceiling, her lips moving as if in silent prayer.

"Good to see you both again," he said once he was seated across from us. A tall stack of manila folders blocked part of his jaw from my view. My sister stared, unblinking, waiting for Calloway to continue.

"Thanks for meeting with us," I said into the silence.

"Yeah," Liz said. He asked us then how we were both doing. Liz looked baffled at the question. She glanced to me and then back toward the detective before saying slowly, "We're fine."

"I know this is a tough time for you two. You're on all our minds."

I gave a quick, placating smile. He went on. "I had a chance to speak with one of the pathologists this morning." Liz and I sat up straighter in our chairs. Instinctively, I reached out and grabbed her wrist. "The good news is that they've found an aberration on the skull." He paused, looking down at a stack of papers in front of him. I could feel the beat of my sister's pulse beneath my fingers. "A left temporal fracture, four inches in diameter. In the center of the fracture, they noted an aperture with a two-inch radius."

"A what?"

"A hole, basically. An opening. The fracture and the aperture were noted in the initial findings but they couldn't definitively say whether they were incurred in the last fifteen years as some damage to the bone caused by natural forces. That's one of the things they've been trying to figure out." He looked down at the papers again, shifting in his chair. Sweat shined on his forehead. "But now they've concluded that these injuries are both antemortem. They happened before death."

I was gripped by an odd sensation of watching the entire conversation from above, perched invisibly somewhere on the ceiling. While I watched his mouth move, forming all these ugly and important words, I saw the tops of all three of our heads, the papers scattered over his desktop, the way the light hit a layer of dust on the windowsill and seemed to make it glow. A cold feeling spread in my stomach. I heard myself say, "What does this all mean?"

"It could indicate trauma, which could indicate a cause of death."

"So this will finally tell us what happened."

"Well, maybe," he said. "This is just one piece of the puzzle. If the pathologists can definitively identify the cause of death, then we may have a clearer sense of what happened to her, but there's no guarantee. Still, dealing with a lack of other evidence, and the poor condition of the remains, we're lucky to have this to go on."

We stared at him, both unsure of how to react. The word *lucky*, the quiet way he said it, sounded over and over in my mind. People used to tell Liz and me we were lucky to have each other. I felt, more often than not, lucky to be alive. Even when I didn't feel particularly lucky to be among the living, I felt I would be lucky to eventually die a natural death and never draw the same straw our unlucky mother had.

Calloway tentatively pushed a box of tissues across the desk toward us. Everything about him, the way he moved and spoke, was tinged with uncertainty. He didn't seem to know if we would receive this news happily, or with outward grief. He seemed almost afraid of us. Liz grabbed the tissue box and placed it firmly in her lap. She wasn't crying. She didn't even seem close to it. The box was printed with an insipid floral pattern. Liz gripped its corners so tightly they began to crumple. Within moments, either side of the box was flattened between her hands. She pressed it down into her lap and then pulled out one tissue, which she began to carefully pleat. We both watched her.

"How long?" she asked. "How much time before they know more?"

"That's still unclear, they said they needed an extension. Could be a few weeks, a couple months. Busy time of year, a lot of people using vacation days with the holidays coming up. I don't want to take a guess, then be wrong and let you both down. But they're working on it, you can be sure of that."

"Well, what about Nick Haines? Can't you bring him back in now?"

"We still think it's best to wait on that. Especially since there's some real potential in this discovery. I mean, they're reexamining the entirety of the remains with the fracture in mind, starting again from step one. It's too early to say what they may be able to deduce, but we wouldn't want to jeopardize any leads."

"So you're just going to wait around until they're done?" she pressed. "You're not doing anything before then?"

"Our hands are really tied for the moment, to tell you the truth. We have to leave the lab work to the experts, and god knows they never rush. But if they do manage to uncover something big here, it could change our whole approach." He drummed his fingers on the desk. "So, you know, we're just going to have to be patient a bit longer."

I couldn't stand the way he kept saying *we*, like he wanted to make us feel that the whole group of us—Liz and myself and him and the pathologists—held the same stake here. My sister placed the pleated tissue on top of the box she'd flattened and pushed it back onto Calloway's desk. It skidded across the surface and landed inches from his chest.

He looked at the box for a moment and then cleared his throat. "I wish I had more to tell you. But this is good news, this is hopeful."

Liz repeated the word *hopeful* aloud, though I could tell she was speaking only to herself. I nudged her on the knee. Calloway's phone lit up and he looked at it, reading something. When he set it back down, I saw the background image on his home screen: a picture of Eva in a white shirt tied up at the waist. It was taken at night, bright lights blurred in the background.

"You and I have something in common," he said lightly. My eyes snapped up, and I realized he'd been looking at me looking at the picture. My blood seemed to halt in place. He picked his phone up again and turned it so we both could see, tilting his head toward Eva's face.

"I hear you two go way back." He set his phone down again and shuffled some papers. I watched as he placed everything back into a folder and then slid it into a cabinet drawer, which he locked with a little silver key. His face looked exactly as it had since we first arrived at the station.

I took a quiet breath and said, "Yeah. We do."

He smiled a plain, inoffensive smile. "She mentioned you two caught up over coffee after you got settled back in town." I nodded. I could think of nothing to say.

"Nothing like an old friend," he said. "I'm glad you girls had a chance to reunite." All the panic I'd felt was replaced instantly with a kind of revulsion, toward both him and myself. I could feel my sister's eyes on me. I stared at the ground.

. . .

Liz was silent the whole way home. She walked into the house without a word, slipped her pumps off inside the door, and sat down at the table. I stood with one foot in the kitchen and the other in the entry, unsure whether we were going to have a conversation. She beckoned me over with a curt wave. I sat in the seat farthest from her, facing into the room, perched as though I might get up any moment and leave.

"So," she said.

"So."

"We learned lots of new information today."

"That we did."

"And I guess I know who you've been out buying your shampoo from, then." I looked out the window. Two squirrels were chasing each other up and down a tree trunk. I badly wanted to blink and transmogrify into one of them. I often got that feeling looking at wild animals, this aching wish to have been born in their body instead. It was always accompanied by a resentment of my own physicality and all the garbage that came with it, neck aches and shoulder tension and pressing concerns over things as stupid as how my voice sounded on tape and how well I tolerated dairy. The squirrels leapt deftly from branch to branch. "Hello?" Liz said. "Are you listening to me?"

"Yes," I told her. "I'm listening."

"I know you're seeing that girl. I remember how things were with you two."

"You know her name."

"Her name doesn't matter right now. Do you not realize how idiotic you're being?"

"He obviously doesn't know. Couldn't you tell? It's not on his radar at all."

"For now," she said.

Liz got up and poured herself a glass of water. She brought it back to the table and took a long drink. "I heard they were engaged." Her voice had a low, rumbling edge to it.

"They're not. He only *suggested* they get married."

"What do you think engaged means?"

"It means both parties agree and there's a fucking wedding in the future. She said no, so there's no wedding. And no engagement. I don't think it was even, like, a real proposal. They don't even live together."

"And you know that because you go to her house."

"Yes," I sighed.

"How many times have you been over there?"

"A few." My sister looked absolutely unhinged. Her face was bluish pale, eyes flashing as they darted around the room. She shook her head slowly for a long time. I could feel her anger gathering momentum.

"How many is a few?" she asked. "How often?"

"Like, maybe every week. I don't know."

She shut her eyes, sighing before saying, "Surely you understand it's not the sneaking around that I care about here." She spoke quietly. My skin prickled. "Go sleep with ten engaged women, married women, whatever. Any woman at all. It's not my business." She took a drink of water and then set the glass down so carefully it made no sound at all. "Did you know?" Liz asked. "When you started fucking her, did you know who her boyfriend was?"

"Of course not. Jesus."

"But once you found out you didn't stop." I didn't respond. Had I stopped? I certainly didn't want to. I couldn't honestly tell myself I even intended to.

"What happens when Calloway finds out? What then?"

"He's not going to find out."

"Oh no?" Her voice took on a hostile tone. "And what makes you so certain of that?" Before I could answer she continued. "He's a detective," she spat. "His entire job is to find things out."

"Well, he's not very good at it," I muttered.

Liz narrowed her eyes at me. "What you're saying, then, is that having some affair with your high school girlfriend is worth ruining the investigation."

"I never said that. That's not true at all."

"But you're willing to risk it."

"I'm not risking anything."

"Maybe today you're not." Liz took another drink of water. The lump in her throat moved up and down. Faint blue veins trailed around it in a ghoulish web. Everything about her seemed exaggerated; she was sickly pale, worryingly thin, her teeth looked like oversized dentures in her mouth.

"I don't think you remember how small a place this is, Jess." She shook her head slowly at me. "And secrets like yours—"

I cut her off, my heart pounding. "Like I told you, he has no reason to think anything and that won't change." I doubted myself as I began to say it, but brushed the feeling aside and tried to keep my face as placid and steady as possible.

"Now you are purposefully missing the point."

"I'm just—"

She held her hand before her like she was warning something from coming any nearer. Her fingers shook a little. "Listen to me," she said. "I've been waiting a long time for this. I didn't know if we would ever get another chance. I was really starting to think it would never happen. Then I got that call and—" Her voice broke up and she took a sharp breath inward. Nearly an entire minute passed before she spoke again. "I know it was awful for you when we lost her. I know that. But you were just a kid."

"I know how old I was."

"Then you should know that I was practically grown by then. I had a lot more life with her."

"What are you getting at?"

"I'm saying I think that this might not mean the same thing to you that it does to me."

I wanted to slap her across the face, though I felt also on some level that she wasn't being entirely unfair. Our loss always seemed to be more her territory than mine. Thinking of that made me want to slap her even more. As if sensing my growing rage, she leaned farther back against the chair.

"What we found out today about the autopsy, I've been waiting on something like that for so many years. I've been living here in this house, waiting around in this town, hardly knowing anything more than I did the first day this all began." She glared at me. "What do you want with that girl anyway? I thought you were living with someone. That woman you used to talk on the phone with."

"Well, you don't hear us on the phone together anymore."

"You broke up?"

I nodded.

Liz looked at me carefully before saying, "You don't have anywhere to go back to, then."

I dropped both my hands onto the table and stood abruptly. "I'm done with this conversation." I clipped around the kitchen, gathering up my coat and keys, and then said, "I can't talk about this anymore."

Liz shrugged. She didn't look at me but I could see she was furious. Her ears were red. Her ears always turned red when she was upset. I wanted her to say something but she kept her lips pursed into a thin line. What I really wanted was for her to fight with me, to try and stop me from leaving, but she just sat there in silence. I felt a great pressure building up inside my chest.

"By the way," Liz shouted, the last second before I let the front door slam shut behind me. "Your little girlfriend isn't putting you in such a great position here. Do you ever think about that?"

I got into my car and drove aimlessly for a long time, first following the dark, winding roads and looping around the crest of the mountain that sheltered our town before switching off onto the highway. Both lanes were desolate except for some tractor trailers and an empty state trooper's patrol car parked in the median. I sped past the exits, continuing north until the landscape grew barren and snowy. I clenched my jaw until I felt a sharp pain in my teeth, and then I gripped the wheel so hard my fingertips pulsed. Hot air rushed through the vents and cooled before it could circulate through my car. Winter was just around the bend and the night was frigid. Long, jagged icicles sparkled on the overpass ledges. My sister's voice rang in my head. *You don't have anywhere to go back to.* It made me want to drive full speed into a wall. I let out a brief scream. It didn't bring the kind of release I'd hoped for.

I remembered what my sister had said when I first returned home: *You don't have to be so afraid of being alone.* Friends and exes had made similar comments in the past. Sarah accused me of it just a few weeks ago. I imagined what it would be like to leave Knife River once everything had settled and go somewhere entirely new, rent someplace by myself, own permanent things. I had enough money saved. I still harbored my dream of going to Maine and working in one of the parks. But then, in my mind, I saw myself walking into a dark room, alone, and trying to go to sleep, alone, only to remain awake into the early morning hours with no other body beside me. I struggled to picture an existence without the rhythm of another person in the foreground— their throat clearing and faucet running, the mundanities of their working hours, their set of friends communing at our table. The machine of a separate life, humming away beside me, tugging me along.

I passed a tavern connected to a gas station in a lot before the next ramp. My mind flew to the bar, the low orange lights and soothing din of clinking glasses insulated by four thick walls. Inside it would be warm, other people's conversations flattening into a hum. I could sit there and collect myself, cocooned by the presence of other strangers. And suddenly I was swerving into the right lane, crookedly braking into an empty parking spot by the back kitchen entrance. Each breath drove the points of a hundred tiny knives into my lungs. I practically jogged to the door, bare fingers throbbing. All the windshields were opaque with frost. Condensation sat frozen middrop on tailpipes. I slipped on some ice at the top of the steps leading inside and tumbled down onto the asphalt, scraping my palms as I went. Someone getting into their car on the other side of the lot stared at me, keys dangling in their gloved hand. Little globes of blood wobbled on my broken skin but the pain barely registered. I gave a quick, assuring wave to the stranger, leapt up, wiping the blood down the back of my jeans, and scudded inside.

Nearly all the tables were full of people eating and laughing. There were only three other people at the bar, a group of women in nurse scrubs with a pitcher before them. The one on the end turned to look at me as I hopped onto a leather stool. My hands were still bleeding as I placed my order. Scotch neat. I realized I was shaking and gripped the underside of the seat to steady myself. I turned away from the nurses and toward the wall where two televisions played the same Canadian hockey game with the sound on. One of the men was slamming another up against a clear partition with screaming, cheering spectators on just the other side. They fought crazily, grabbing at each other's helmets, until two referees broke it up and the picture cut to a long commercial for psoriasis medication. Plates of sizzling meat and french fries emerged from the kitchen door and were whisked by on big trays to the dining area. I could hear the nurses having an animated conversation about their children. They all seemed to know each other well. Everyone around me did. I found some comfort in it all, being there with all these people instead of by myself in the car, but my thoughts still rattled.

Silently, I made a list of the things I knew I didn't want. I didn't want to stay in Knife River. I didn't want to leave yet, either. I didn't want to stop seeing Eva. I didn't want to hurt the investigation. I didn't want to know anything about the investigation, either. Every phone call, every meeting with the police was a sharp twist to the gut, but I didn't want *not* to know. I wanted to be there as we followed the trail. I wanted to know what happened, even if it would never lead to a conviction. Justice sometimes seemed beside the point. The point was rest. If the person who did this rotted in prison for all time, would I feel better? If he was drowned in a river, shot between the eyes, skinned alive, would it bring me some relief? My sister would say yes. She believed in retribution. I didn't disagree completely, but my greatest fantasy was simply a reversal of time, to go back in an instant and have our lives to do over, together. No sentence, no matter how long or grueling or torturous, could grant me that. I didn't want to sit and wonder if every passing stranger was the taker of my mother's life, and I wanted to be rid of the chill that shot through me every time I saw a man in town, trying to figure out what came from my gut and what came from my soused and deceitful brain. And of course, I didn't want to sit in the house, knowing that Eva was sitting in hers just miles away, knowing that we were thinking of each other, and not go to her.

A dull pounding throbbed behind my eyes. The bartender returned with my drink. The glass seemed to move in slow motion. Within an instant of the first sip, all the frantic buzzing in my mind parted. A crystal lucidity, like a beam of white light, shined through. My breathing slowed. My muscles relaxed. Warmth spread all down through me, and suddenly I felt calm.

I found myself thinking of Gator Planet—a roadside attraction in Florida I'd been to once a long time ago. It was just alligators. Hundreds, possibly thousands if you counted the fake lagoon teeming with babies the size of an ear of corn. The main display was built around one enormous tank containing an albino alligator—it looked ancient with its deep, craggy scales and rigid tail swishing around behind it in the water, like something transported from the distant past. I was there with a woman. The first girlfriend I had after moving away from home. She was unnerved by the albino alligator's eyes.

"It looks like they aren't attached to a brain," she'd said. I knew what she meant; there was something off-putting about the whiteness of them, bulging and opaque like two eggs, both set above a gargantuan, open jaw full of razor teeth. You could tell the eye was moving but couldn't tell what it was looking at.

We walked to the center of the park where there was a small stadium set up with a banner advertising gator wrestling on the hour. I held her hand in the top row of the bleachers while a sinewy, tattooed man rolled around in the mud with one of the snapping creatures. Everything felt foreign to me: the humidity like a thick syrup slowing my breath. The dank, sultry smell of the air from the moment we stepped off the plane—green algae, suntan lotion, gasoline. The way she didn't hesitate to kiss me, or how she tucked my hair behind my ear in public or in front of her family. We'd gone down there to stay with them over Thanksgiving, and by the second hour of dinner I'd fallen into a deep rift between a nagging sense of resentfulness and alienation, and one of enthrallment. They welcomed me into their home with genuine warmth, a home that was clean in a way I'd never really seen before. Nothing was piled up in corners. All the lights worked. I had no idea what to do with myself, no clue how to navigate the whole weekend with all their familial affection. I felt like an intruder.

Since our first date I'd been skirting my girlfriend's questions about where, exactly, I came from and what my family was like, and as they piled turkey and cranberry sauce onto my plate, I sat there between an aunt and a sister referring to my mother as though she were still alive and well. As the meal went on and their questions kept coming, I slid further into the lie. I said that right then she was probably making a pumpkin pie with my sister, as was their annual tradition. Listening to myself say these things left me both disgusted and exhilarated. I didn't want to stop. The fantasy of it was overpowering, this idea that I so easily could have what they had if things had just gone a little differently. Visiting Gator Planet was the last thing this girl and I did before flying back north. By then I knew we were going to break up soon. There was nothing wrong with her at all. She was pretty and thoughtful, she liked good music and had nice friends and we rarely argued. But I stood there outside the glass door of the gift shop, smoking a cigarette and watching her wander around all the shelves full of back scratchers and ashtrays made from dead alligator parts, and knew that we couldn't be together.

By now there were three empty tumblers before me. The group of nurses was gone. My thoughts drifted to Eva. I always missed her. In a strange way, I missed her even when we were together. Sometimes we'd be sitting in her cabin and I'd look into her eyes and see nothing but traces of our past selves. No one took care of me like she did. In the hardest times, she was my refuge. Maybe you'd think that the worst pain followed immediately after the disappearance—the utter panic of the first couple of days, the fruitless searching through empty fields. But that time came with its own numbness, a feeling not so different from slowly wading into ice-cold water. Needles at first, almost unbearable, but then—nothing.

The first thing to really break that numbness came around the two-year mark when we got a phone call at the house and I answered to a high, strangled voice on the other end. *Jess?* the voice said. *It's me, it's your mother, I'm alive.* My jaw hung open in disbelief. I didn't know what to think. Somehow, my first impulse was to slam the phone down but I couldn't make my arm move. The voice continued, *Why did you stop looking for me? Why didn't you save me?* Peals of muffled laughter erupted in the background. The caller, too, began to laugh and abruptly hung up. The police soon traced it to some local boys. Sixteen-year-olds. The sheriff claimed he'd give them all a talking-to, but I never heard about it again. I couldn't eat for three days. Eva watched me as I paced around her room, shouting and crying. After I started to wear myself out, she pulled a sharp, unsheathed field dressing knife from her underwear drawer, dropped a few old couch cushions from the garage onto the floor, and instructed me to stab them until I couldn't anymore. Chunks of foam and downy white feathers swirled around me. I brought the knife down so hard it slid between the floorboards. When I was done, she brought me a glass of cold water and rubbed gentle circles into my open palm as I drank it down.

When there wasn't any food left in my house and I couldn't bring myself to ask our neighbors for help or steal, she'd swipe some cash from her brother and we'd go to the diner where we'd eat french fries and milkshakes until we were sick. When I woke up next to her in the night gasping from a bad dream, she'd speak to me in a low whisper, coaxing me back to sleep. In the mornings, I'd find her head resting on my chest, her arm crossed over me. I would lie there just feeling the weight of it on my skin, soothed by the low drum of her pulse.

But she refused to hold my hand in public. I couldn't pretend I didn't remember that. At the time, it hurt me, but I was so tightly gripped by the belief that there was no other option, no other way of being, that I never let her know it. I couldn't even conceive of a world where it would be possible for us to walk in daylight as a couple. I'd never seen a place like that. I wasn't sure if there was any in the world. The glimpses of far-off cities I'd seen on TV and in movies felt like pieces of mythology, totally unreachable, and when there was ever a vague mention of something that looked like what I had with Eva, it was meant to be a joke, or some guy was getting off on it, or both girls wound up dead in a ditch somewhere. I never even heard anyone say the word *gay* in earnest. It got flung around as an insult all the time: the superintendent was so gay, it was really gay of the student council to choose "under the sea" as junior prom theme, high-waisted jeans were laughably gay back then. But if someone truly wanted to make the implication about a person, they would simply put their hand out before them and flick their wrist side to side saying, *you know*. There were always euphemisms, too. You could say someone was *that way*. Or suggest they were *a bit fruity*. If you meant to be more threatening you could say they were a faggot. It didn't always matter who it was about. Men were fags, women who dressed too much like men were also fags.

I never heard a word for someone like Eva. She seemed to hide in plain sight, invisible to everyone but girls like me, making herself known with a certain kind of smile, a stare that lasted a few moments too long, a certain willingness to linger in our presence. In junior high, I went to the public library and searched the card catalog for the word *homosexual* and, after finding nothing, consulted the single, outdated dictionary where there was an entry in painfully small font on yellowed, onionskin paper between homonym and Honduras. A disorder, it said. Or, more delicately, a *predilection*. I felt that I was doing something wrong even just by reading it. I reread the entry again and again, seeking some kind of recognition, but couldn't find myself between the lines.

The thought of all this made me feel ill. The careful pretending, with its many awful layers of shame and anxiety. The fear of discovery. I'd struggled so hard to get away from all that, I didn't want to return to it. I didn't even want to get close. I thought of the way Calloway looked at me across his desk, his bland little smile as he held up that picture of her face. I tried to imagine how he might look at me if he knew. I tried to imagine what he might do. Then I recalled the afternoon he dropped by the house unexpectedly with flowers, when I glimpsed the roses in cellophane sitting on his dashboard and he drove off, and I felt so relieved that he was gone and I didn't have to figure out how to make conversation alone with him in the kitchen. He was going to her. The flowers were for Eva. He loved her, in his way. That was clear. He'd asked her to marry him, so he'd thought about it with as much depth as he could muster and decided that what he really wanted was for them to be together until one of them died. Still, though, I wanted her. I couldn't help it.

Now, four empty glasses. I looked around and saw that all the diners had left the restaurant. A plate appeared before me. The bartender stood there with her arms crossed.

"Eat that," she commanded. "Now."

It was a small cheese quesadilla with some brownish guacamole glopped around the center. It wasn't quite warm. I folded it like a slice of pizza and began shoving it into my mouth, chewing mechanically while the bartender kept an eye from the glass-washing station. Her arms were thick and she had the kind of permanently annoyed expression that made me want to follow orders. I was the only customer remaining. Someone in a black apron went around flipping all the chairs upside down onto the tabletops. I finished the quesadilla and pushed the plate back. Walking to the door, I was careful to keep my steps in a straight line. I could feel the bartender's eyes on my back, studying my gait, watching to see if she needed to stop me from getting to my car. No one followed and then I was alone in the dark parking lot, digging around for my keys. I was sure it was still bitterly cold out, probably colder than when I arrived, but I couldn't feel it.

The house was dark when I got back. I felt my way to the couch and cocooned myself in a stack of quilts, not even bothering to take my clothes off. There was a pain in my stomach so awful I couldn't get to sleep, so I lay there until the sun came up and I heard the floorboards above me creaking as Liz got ready for her day.

20

Brenda took the news of the autopsy developments calmly. A week had passed and we were back in her cluttered pink living room, sitting around the coffee table. This time the TV was off. An arrangement of dried flowers blocked my view of Liz's face as she explained what the pathologist had found. I couldn't get a sense of her mood. She'd been cool with me since that day in Calloway's office, barely speaking to me until she asked if I'd like to come with her to give her friend the update. Her friend, she said, as if I wouldn't know whom. My sister recited what Calloway told us, word for word. I was relieved that she'd committed it all to memory. When I tried to conjure that part of the conversation, I got only watery images of a skull on a metal table, indistinguishable from any other skull in the world. It scared me to know that if someone were to present me with a lineup of five different skulls on a table, one being our mother's and the others being those of strangers who died a hundred years ago, I wouldn't be able to correctly point out the one that mattered to me.

"This is big news," Brenda said seriously. "Long overdue." She shook her head. It did feel that something precious had finally, suddenly, fallen into our laps and we were all trying to handle it carefully without really knowing how. "They'll be arresting Nick Haines then soon, I imagine." She pursed her lips in a prunish knot after saying his name, as if she'd just bitten into a lemon.

"I don't know," Liz said. "This means the forensics people are basically doing the analysis over again, so it'll take longer. Maybe well into January, at this rate. I guess the lab is backed up with people taking time off for the holidays. I've been wondering if I should even bother trying to schedule another meeting for this month." She rubbed her forehead, wincing a little and closing her eyes. "Before we left the station I asked if there was any way they could speed up the arrest, but according to them it's still too early."

"Too early." Brenda scoffed. "It's fifteen years too late."

"The detective's barely been alive much longer than that."

"So I hear."

"He stumbled over the word *aperture*. He's completely out of his depth."

"The pathologists know what they're doing. Soon they'll be through with their work, and there won't be anything left to wait on. No more excuses. They'll have to charge him."

"I hope that's true."

"He'll get his, don't you worry."

When Liz went to the bathroom I turned to Brenda and said in a hushed, urgent voice, "I have to ask you something. How do you know Nick Haines did it? Liz says you've always been sure." She gave me an odd little half smile but didn't say anything. I looked toward the powder room door and then back again.

Brenda shrugged. "I'll say to you what I've told your sister."

"Which is what?"

"I just know."

"But how do you know, though?" I edged closer to her side of the couch. "She's told me about what he was like when you had him in school. But is there something else? I want to know what makes you so sure."

"You don't feel sure of it yourself?" She gave a penetrating stare. It was too uncomfortable for me to hold so I glanced down at my clasped hands. When I looked back up Brenda hadn't averted her gaze an inch.

I told her sometimes I felt sure of it, but then other times not. A twinge of guilt shot through me, like I was betraying my sister and even Brenda in some way by questioning his guilt. Aloud, I recited the list of things that made me feel more sure: the state he was in the morning of the compact being discovered, their date gone wrong, the warning from her friend at the coffee place, the fact that no one could think of another person who fit into the logic of her disappearance. Naming them all aloud felt monotonous and assuring, like dragging the same needle through a deep, familiar groove. I'd repeated these things to myself and others a thousand times.

"But still," I said. "I don't know."

"You have a theory of your own?"

"Not exactly," I said. "I'm starting to feel suspicious of almost everybody these days."

I thought about all the times that cold, lurching sensation grabbed me in the last couple of weeks. I'd seen an older couple on the sidewalk the other day and could've sworn they whispered to each other about me as they hurried away. Farther up the street, I passed by Bill's van outside the grocery and saw him digging around in the back, a mess of painting supplies and dirty laundry next to a thin mattress. Our eyes met and then darted away abruptly, almost awkwardly, and I spent the remainder of the day wondering why he might find it uncomfortable to look at me straight on.

A couple of days before that, I was startled by the mailman out on the porch when I stepped out, not realizing he was there, and immediately threw myself back behind the door, slamming it shut, in a reaction that felt almost involuntary. Through a little gap in the curtains, I could see a baffled expression on his face as he dropped the rest of the mail into our wall box and returned to his truck, glancing over his shoulder at the porch once before moving to the next street.

Even buying cigarettes at the gas station just earlier this same morning, handing cash to the guy behind the counter and thinking he was staring at my face for a second too long, I wondered did he recognize me? Did he know something? Or catching a glimpse of our neighbor Paul hobbling around the yard, I noticed the way my shoulders and hands tensed up at the sight of him. It had gotten so bad that I'd run a couple of red lights just to break a quick second of eye contact with someone in the next car. My paranoia seemed to have grown a clammy little hand of its own and that hand, stealthy as a mountain lion, had a way of seizing me by the neck before I could even see it coming.

Wanting to tell Brenda something that at least seemed to border on reason, I brought up the disgraced track coach, wondering if she'd react the same way the sheriff had. "I mean, what if he had something to do with it? Do you know him?" I said.

"Jeff?" Brenda scoffed, her mouth falling into a deep frown. "He's a worm. Doesn't have it in him. Don't get me wrong, I'd like to see him rot in a dark cell. He may yet, for all we know. But yes, I knew him as a young man, and I don't believe it was him." I let out a strained breath and rubbed the back of my neck, trying to relieve some of the tension that had begun to build. She patted me firmly on the hand and said, "It's hard to be certain of things at your age. I remember that feeling. What are you, twenty-six?"

"Twenty-eight. You don't get that feeling anymore?"

"Never," she said. "I know what I know. I'm telling you, I graduated from that school, took two years to get my teaching license with a special program they had for young women back then, and came back to the English department. Worked there for decades. Later on, I went to the administrative side before retiring, but my whole working life I've been around teenagers. I know how to read them."

She went on to describe how the pulp, that was the word she used, of their character was just hanging out all over the place like a gutted trout. I understood what she meant, the way that you can plainly see who a young person is becoming, who they already are deep down, before the finer lines of their personalities come into sharp focus. My mother used to say that no one ever changes, not really, not their essence—another thing I wasn't sure whether I believed.

Brenda's hands moved gracefully before her as she spoke. Her nails were nicely manicured, painted pink and filed into an elegant almond shape. She wore a thin gold band with a single pearl setting on the right ring finger, nothing on the left.

"The first week of class every September," she said, "I'd make little bets with myself about the kids, and I never really got it wrong." She looked at me pointedly.

"So you bet yourself that Nick would go on to kill a person?"

"Well, my thoughts on him weren't quite that specific, though when I heard he was a suspect I wasn't the least bit surprised. He was just off. How else can I put it? I could see what a bad egg he already was at fifteen, sixteen years old. Nothing good in his future. I tried speaking with his parents several times, but they never cared. There was something empty about him. Vacant in the eyes."

"What kind of a student was he?"

"He never did any work, but that wasn't out of dim-wittedness. He was fairly bright, once you forced an answer out of him. But he had so many absences, rarely turned in assignments. We wanted to hold him back, actually, or at least threaten it, but the principal wanted him out of the school system. He'd been stealing from the shop room. Not small things, mind you. Big pieces of equipment the school couldn't afford to replace. And he was getting into bloody, wild fights with underclassmen every week."

"Were you scared of him?"

"A bit, yes." She nodded slowly. "I avoided being alone in a room with him. He never threatened me, it was just a feeling I had."

"I don't understand why my mother would've gone on a date with him."

"Oh, you know." Brenda gave a little shrug. "A single, young woman in a small town. There's not a lot of men to choose from. She probably just wanted a meal and a couple of drinks out of it, something to do on a Friday night."

Liz came out of the bathroom. She'd been in there for a while, I realized, and the way she stared at the ground, arms crossed over her stomach, as she walked toward us made me wonder if she'd been listening to our conversation with an ear to the door. She fluffed a few pillows and then swept some crumbs off the coffee table, trying to keep her hands occupied.

"I never married, by the way," Brenda announced.

"What?"

"You were looking at my fingers earlier. I think you must have been wondering."

"I was, actually." The moment unfolded without awkwardness. I hardly knew her, but still there was no sense that I should withhold anything out of a need to be polite. "Why didn't you?" I asked.

"My high school boyfriend, John, and I were engaged. But he didn't return from the war. I never fell in love with anyone else," she said simply. "Isn't that odd? In all that time, it never happened. Even when I came to feel that I had moved on from my grief. Days went by without a thought of him. But I never met anyone else who gave me the feeling John did. I'm not ashamed to say I slept around quite a bit, but it wasn't the same." She raised her hands and then let them drop, punctuating the gesture with a sigh. "You've been in love?"

"Yes."

"Are you in love with anybody these days?"

I'd met a handful of other old people who spoke this way, direct and totally unembarrassed, wanting to get in all the good, important, honest questions before their time was up. And they didn't seem to care much what your answer was. If you told them something that made it clear you were running your life into the ground or completely ignoring the true desires of your heart, they never chastised you or got hysterical trying to set you straight. It made me think that they knew there was time enough for mistakes to be corrected, for new paths to be forged out of thin air, at the moments when everything seemed ruined beyond repair.

I hesitated, thinking of all the times I'd gone over to see Eva. Just a couple of days earlier I'd been there, losing time tangled up under her sheets. Driving away, I always felt a strong pull to go straight back, a heavy kind of longing settling deep down somewhere in my chest. It didn't feel unlike love.

Finally, I said, "If I told you no, I think I'd be lying." My sister shot me a horrified look. Brenda glanced between the two of us for a moment. "It's not so simple, though," I added.

Brenda let out a tiny yawn. "It never is," she said.

Later that night as I tried to fall asleep, I remembered a woman, a self-described psychic, who called us at the house years ago. It was just weeks after our mother had disappeared, and we were still sleeping with the phone then, the receiver resting between both our heads on the floor in our mess of quilts. Liz answered on the first ring. It was after one in the morning. My sister put the call on speakerphone just as the woman began to say that our mother's body was in water. She couldn't say exactly where, but described a lake with a faded red boat house and two Adirondack chairs at the end of a dock. Liz grabbed her notepad and began to furiously jot it all down, tearing the pages off as she filled them and letting each one fall to the side. I remember the chill that came over me then, lying there in the dark still dressed in my day clothes, eyes crusted over with sleep, listening to the sound of this strange woman's voice fill our living room. There was a rowboat on shore, she said, half full of rainwater. This place had been neglected, forgotten about. You wouldn't find anyone nearby, she was sure of it. The vision came to her in a dream. Her voice had been utterly resolute, each word firm and clear. She wasn't trying to get any money, and she didn't seem interested in stringing us along in any way—she seemed only to want to tell us this because she was sure of it herself.

When we pressed her for more—who she was, where she lived, would she speak to the police, and, most desperately, did she actually know our mother, the line went dead. My sister tried to call back, but it had been blocked. She sat there for a second, totally still. I could make out the outline of her face. I thought about touching her on the shoulder, to comfort not so much her as myself. The call had frightened me. I wanted to feel the reassuring warmth of another person's skin. But before I could reach out, she stood up and flung the phone across the room. It crashed against the door and tumbled to the floor, its plastic face cracked open while the dial tone rang out into our drafty old house.

At first I was terrified that it was somehow true. Of course we told the police, who knew of no such place in Knife River but sent out a note to every precinct in the surrounding area with a description. Nothing ever came of it. Every night for weeks I had strange dreams about drowning in thick, greenish water, held under by an arm unattached to a body. But time passed, and eventually I was no longer afraid but angry. The echo of the woman's voice in my mind sent my blood curdling. Everything she told us had been garbage. I didn't care if she intended only to help. I felt conned somehow, manipulated into fear by a faceless, nameless person who could not even wait until sunup to tell us such a gruesome story.

Thinking back on it again, I felt a heave of dread. I was older and taller now, in some ways wiser, more sure of who I was, but lying awake in the same place where I'd heard the psychic's voice gave me a terrible sensation of time sliding backward. My face grew hot. I shoved the quilt off me and then, feeling exposed, pulled it back again. The woman on the phone had been sure. Wrong, but sure. Liz was sure. Brenda was sure. They were resolute. They knew their guts. Their certainty scared me. I badly wanted to be able to hang on to something like they did, a buoy to hold me aloft in rough seas, but each time I tried to grab on, it dissolved in my hands and I slipped back beneath the water's surface.

21

That week I saw Nick Haines in town. Whenever I'd imagined this moment, he was at a distance. And always where I would expect him to be: his shop, his house. My thoughts would not allow the possibility of surprise, though my dreams turned him into a monster, almost an extension of the darkness itself. I would be running down a desolate road, pursued by the dying light. Nightfall was not just the world taking its turn away from the sun in these dreams, it was something with eyes and a presence that breathed on the back of my neck. I'd look over my shoulder and see a liquid black consuming all in its path. Out of this blackness, a man that I understood to be Nick Haines. He disappeared and reappeared in different places. He reached for me.

Actually seeing him, the real him, the singular human who represented to me all this horror mystery, was unceremonious.

I was inside the post office when it happened, buying stamps for bills. Liz would not pay the utilities over the internet. Four people were ahead of me in line. There was just the single register, operated by someone who seemed to get up and disappear into the dim, cavernous back room for great lengths of time between transactions. As I waited, I looked out the front window onto the street. The day was clear and bright. Ice melted from the gutters and dripped steadily, pooling at the curb. There was a large, sheltered bulletin board just outside the post office, facing the street, where people stapled fliers and job listings or notices for lost pets or things they were selling or looking to buy. My mother's picture, too, for a while. It seemed odd to me now, this plea for the return of a woman put up among used trucks for sale. Surely, Liz and I must have posted her photo here and in Bill's grocery, though I couldn't remember being there or doing it myself, only ripping it down from the grocery store wall months later. I could remember the fliers themselves, the word *MISSING*, huge and imposing at the top of the sheet. Her face, her name, our phone number. We'd kept an enormous stack of them on the kitchen table. They were not laminated. When the rain made the colors bleed, and the information became illegible, Liz would go staple a new one atop the old.

Looking at this bulletin board, even the back of it, made me anxious. I moved up a spot. More people came in and lined up behind me. One woman was holding an armful of Christmas cake tins, all labeled on the sides with pieces of masking tape, a different name written on each one. A roll of bubble wrap peeked out the top of her tote bag. The lady behind her flipped through a stack of shiny red envelopes, checking the address on each one, her mouth moving silently. A couple of the people waiting were about my age and it seemed impossible that I hadn't gone to school with them, or otherwise encountered them, at some point in the past. But their faces sparked no recognition in me. There wasn't anything familiar about their posture, or the way they squinted into the daylight.

I shifted a little to the side to watch a young couple, out across the street, load a furnace into the trunk of their car. It was loose, uncovered. Some tubes hung out the back and slapped around as the two of them tried to hoist it over the ledge. Finally, they got it where it needed to be, but the trunk wouldn't close. I watched with interest. The woman went away for a few minutes. While she was gone, the man sat on the curb and looked back at the furnace often. She returned with a rope, which they used to tie the trunk shut. It stayed put as they pulled out of the parking space, and held tight as they made their way to the stoplight, but came undone once the car gained a bit of speed. I could see them brake to a full halt, surely discussing what to do next. Eventually, the couple drove on, very slowly, with the open trunk door bobbing up and down over the furnace.

One moment Nick Haines wasn't there and the next he was. He was outside the service door of the American Legion, diagonal from the post office. An American flag, a state flag, and a flag for missing prisoners of war waved in the breeze by the main entrance. Around the side, near a large dumpster and some parked trucks and delivery pallets, was the door Nick Haines appeared from. It was flat metal, without a knob. He bent down to prop it open with a brick. Perhaps he was delivering something, lumber or paint maybe, from his shop. He may also have been hired to repair something, or might have been drinking at the bar in there. The American Legion in Knife River was, like most chapters around the country, sustained by its bar. They were tax exempt and offered cheap drinks to anyone, regardless of membership. I'd never been, but it was popular with older men in town. When he stood up again, I saw that he looked the way he did in the picture I'd studied online—pallid and unremarkable, with a gaunt face. In an instant, any doubt I'd harbored over his guilt flew from my body and disappeared like a vapor. It wasn't that I no longer saw the reason of it, it was just that in this moment, seeing him in the flesh, reason didn't matter at all.

Instinctively, I took a wide step away from the window and tried to angle myself in a way that took me out of his line of sight, though I knew he couldn't easily see me from where he stood, and even if he did, he wasn't likely to recognize me. The line moved up one space but I remained in place. I could barely even blink. I didn't want to miss one second of watching him. He wasn't doing anything strange or interesting. He was staring down at his phone, reading something, holding a cigarette with his other hand. He looked like a man who might've killed a woman only insofar as any man did to me, which is to say that there was nothing obviously alarming on the surface, but I got a bad feeling anyway. It wouldn't be true to say that I hated men. I didn't. They just scared me.

Nick dropped his cigarette onto the ground. When he brought his boot down on the pavement to stamp it out, I jumped. Everyone in the post office turned to look at me. I got back in line and faced in the direction of the register, away from the window, my eyes on the floor. Muddy shoe prints covered the tiles. It looked like nobody'd ever cleaned them. That bothered me. If someone handed me a mop, I would've done it myself. My mouth was painfully dry. I couldn't get ahold of my pulse. My body throbbed with the sensation that I'd just narrowly survived something—shaking hands, racing mind, a cold clamminess along all my skin. When I turned around to look a few minutes later, Nick was gone. I paid for my stamps and left.

Driving home I felt nothing. Just blankness with a vague static hum behind it. I did some work on my laptop and felt nothing then, either. I paced around the kitchen, aimless, before finding a half-empty bottle of white wine in the back of the fridge. I drank from it directly, even though it had turned and tasted of vinegar—bitter and cold. When the kitchen clock chimed five, the tinny call of a warbler breaking the silence, I was so startled I dropped the bottle on the ground. It broke instantly. Jagged shards of glass scattered toward every corner of the room. My heart raced. There was a time in my life when I would have ignored the mess and simply walked around all the pieces, inevitably getting some of them lodged in my feet.

Now I got on my knees with a dustpan and carefully swept up every fragment I could find. I wiped around with a wet rag. One overlooked piece wedged into my ankle and I began to bleed. Dust got caught in the cut. It stung and dripped, the blood clumping up around the dust and turning dark as it met the air. Cautiously, I ran my hands over the floor, like I was searching for something small in an unlit room. My fingers came upon a remaining puddle of wine, and without hesitation I brought them up to my mouth and sucked off the remnants before

186

dipping back into the spill, licking more sour wine from my skin, carefully feeling around with my tongue for specks of glass. I was disgusted with myself, and still I brought my hand from the floor back up to my mouth until the puddle was gone and my lips were covered in a film of dust and grit.

Even then, my heart continued to pound. It infuriated me that I could be this frightened by the sound of a clock chiming in my own house. It made me furious at Nick Haines, and furious at the empty hole I carried around that could have been filled, could have been paved over with knowing, or with the closure that everyone lamented us not having, but instead grew larger all the time. I wanted Nick to be the one struck by fear in unassuming places, on plain and ordinary days. I wanted him to expect a little burst of terror around every corner.

Over the years, I liked to think about the various ways my mother might haunt her killer. I imagined her appearing on his doorstep, naked and covered in dirt, ringing the doorbell again and again. I thought about her inside his refrigerator, contorted into a pretzel on the bottom shelf, blinking at him as the light snapped on. I wanted him to have to see her out in his yard, leaning against a tree. In his basement, crouching behind the hot water heater, grinning in the dark. I wanted her face to flash in the mirror's reflection when he went to take a piss at a bar. I wanted him to open his closet and find her standing behind the clothes, staring straight at him when the hangers parted. This kind of thinking scared me more, in a way, but it made me feel vengeful, which was soothing. I felt entitled to take comfort where I could find it.

When Liz came home I told her everything. She listened, unspeaking, sitting next to me on the kitchen floor. She hadn't even taken off her coat. I went on about it for a long time. I described exactly where he was, what the weather was like, how I felt. I was being unusually open. The more I said, the greater my urge to disgorge. As I spoke, it occurred to me that she'd probably had experiences very similar to mine lots of times before during the course of life in town. Her face remained steady. She asked a couple of questions and I noticed that her voice was gentler than normal. Closer to the way she was with Brenda.

I talked about how angry and frightened I was until my throat grew sore. I kept going for a little longer after that, but at some point the words stopped forming and I let out a strange little sound, almost like an animal, shrill and jagged. I realized it was the sound of crying, or the sound that precedes crying. I didn't know what to do. I wanted to stop it but nothing seemed within my control. The sound came again. My sister then took her coat off and shoved her bag to the side. She swooped over me, arms open, like a great wild bird, and took me against her chest.

22

On Christmas, Liz and I brought trays of gingerbread cookies to a nursing home. I woke up early that morning to the sound of thudding in the kitchen, the ticking of the oven timer. My sister was holding a sack of flour when I walked in. She wore a black sweater with a single jingle bell secured to the neckline with a safety pin. I'd known Christmas was coming; every store I went in was playing carols and each day more and more cars passed by the window with fir trees roped onto their roofs. But it always seemed a ways off, something in the distance that I'd never reach. Liz brushed past me and grabbed a jar of molasses.

"Merry Christmas," she said. "I am making five dozen cookies. You can help me." She pressed a star-shaped cutter, sharp side down, into my hand. I looked at her, bewildered. "Every year I bring something to the old people's home," she explained, sliding a new batch into the oven.

"I would've thought you'd spend the day with Brenda," I said.

"One of her nephews always picks her up and takes her to a big gathering with their relatives in Ontario."

"Oh."

"The people in the nursing facility are very lonely. They don't get a

189

lot of visitors." A timer went off and she rotated the pan. "You can come with me to deliver them if you want. That would be nice."

We sat on either side of the table, cutting the cold dough and gently coaxing the pieces onto paper-lined trays. I felt queasy. I had a cup of black coffee, which only made my stomach worse, and then drank two more. There was a restlessness in my gut I could not fight off. My first night here, I'd come in the front door and seen this kitchen again for the first time in ten years, thinking I wouldn't be back for very long. I'd settled into the couch, my bag open before me with my clothes and things in a heap, then lain awake listening to the mundane noises of a home—the settling of beams, the dripping of faucets, a branch scraping a shingle—that I had grown unaccustomed to. Now I had a favorite mug. I could set the coffeemaker without looking at the dials. The house's noises faded into background static, hardly detectable each night, though my clothes were still stuffed into the bag I'd come with. Despite my resistance, I was getting used to it all.

I cut out another star and placed it on the tray. "You didn't remember it was Christmas, I think," Liz commented without looking up.

"You're right."

"How did you spend the day before? I mean, what did you do every year?"

I looked at her. It wasn't meant as a jab, just an honest question, though I still felt heat rising in my cheeks. The truth was that I always spent the holiday with whatever woman I was dating, usually with her family somewhere. This habit had taken me to California, Kansas, Florida, Mexico City. Even if I wasn't really in love with the woman, or her family argued at the table, I still got the same voyeuristic satisfaction from being there among them in their togetherness. These gatherings were always so charged, fraught somehow even when things ran smoothly. I played a small, erasable role in the web of everyone's relations. I could fade easily into the background and allow myself moments of imagining that these people were my people. At some point in the day, I always started to feel intensely guilty imagining my sister on her own in Knife River, the sun going down midafternoon and cold air finding its way through the cracks in the house.

"I'd usually spend it with my girlfriend's family," I replied.

"Which girlfriend? The dermatologist?"

"Whoever it was at the time."

"So you went to the houses of the different girlfriends' families?" I told her yes and she asked if the grandparents and grandchildren and various spouses were present.

"Usually, yeah," I said.

"And then there you were, this person no one had ever met, just sitting at the table with them?"

"Yes, of course," I told her. "I didn't sit out in the yard." We worked in silence for a while. Outside the window unblemished snow stretched as far as I could see. No one was on the roads. Our kitchen smelled of warm ginger and cloves. "I feel bad that I wasn't here with you," I said. "Now I wish I had come home instead."

Liz was quiet for a long time. I began to wonder if she'd heard me. Finally, she said, "I don't blame you for it."

By the time all the batches of cookies were cooled and wrapped, it was starting to get dark out. We walked cautiously, arms locked together, bags full of Tupperware containers swinging from our elbows, over the thickly iced driveway. Our breath appeared in clouds before us and hung in the air as we brushed snow off the car with our bare hands. "The Little Drummer Boy" was playing on the radio when Liz turned the engine on. Every time I pushed the volume lower, Liz cranked it back up, humming along cheerfully. As we inched down the road, I wondered if it would be too late to go get a small tree for the living room, before remembering that my sister had thrown away all our ornaments. She'd kept everything else, of course. It took fifteen years for her to part with all the old junk mail and expired pantry items. But the ornaments went right away on the first Christmas we spent alone. I could remember vividly the way her eyes looked as she carried the box from the basement, rattling with frail glass, out to the end of the driveway. I stood on the porch and listened to everything breaking as she dumped it unceremoniously into the garbage. We didn't talk about it then, or after. I remember we shared only a microwaved chicken breast that night, silently, off paper plates.

The residents of the nursing home were gathered in their shared living room when we arrived. Liz seemed familiar with some of the attendants. They greeted her warmly and took the cookies to the table in the center of all the couches, like they'd been expecting her. I hung back in the doorway. A uniformed aide rolled a plastic hospitality cart toward me. I hated eggnog, but I took some anyway. Quietly, he asked if I wanted something extra in it. I nodded, and he pulled a slim bottle of whiskey from a box on the bottom tier of the cart and poured some into mine and more into his. One of his hands had a tattoo of a skull with a bow tie under the chin, the other another skull with long eyelashes and a heart-shaped beauty mark above where the lips would be. I drank it all down quickly, and then we both had more. Warmth spread down my limbs. I sat in a chair by the window while Liz spoke to one of the residents. I studied the ice patterns on the glass and thought seriously about what I would do come spring. Things would have changed by then, I was sure. We would know more, at least. Maybe even have answers. Maybe an arrest. I couldn't stay here forever, sleeping on my sister's sofa. Soon, I told myself, I would contact my old boss, Maria, in Maine, and I would go there, finally. Once the ice started to melt, I'd do it.

Before we left, Liz and I joined the group around the Christmas tree. The lights cast our faces in an eerie, greenish glow. A man in a neck brace held a wind-up angel in his lap. It was maybe a foot long with articulated limbs and scraggly blond doll hair. He stroked the angel gently on the cheek. Liz squeezed my hand. For a moment, it looked like she might cry. Then the man turned the doll's key twice. The angel creaked into motion, spinning slowly in a circle with her arms rising up over her head and then coming back down, haltingly, to her sides as a snippet of "Silent Night" played from a music box hidden up inside her blue sateen tunic. Everyone watched. When the angel slowed down, we all looked to the man in the neck brace, and he dutifully wound her up once more.

Later on, while we were walking back into the house, I slipped on some crusted-over slush and landed hard, my knuckles hitting the corner of the wrought iron handrail. Liz watched me silently from the doorway. I hardly felt it, warm as I was from the whiskey and numb from the cold.

In the light of the kitchen, my sister grabbed me by the wrist and said, "You're bleeding." I looked down. She was right. Blood trickled down my fingers and settled into the crevices around each nail bed. Translucent flaps of skin peeled back over the scrape revealing raw, pinkish layers of flesh speckled with dirt. It reminded me of an uncooked pork cutlet picked up off a kitchen floor. "Don't you feel that?" Liz asked.

"Not really," I told her, rinsing my hand off in the sink.

"You get that from Mom," she muttered.

"What?"

"Nothing."

"You said something about Mom, what was it?"

"It's a holiday, let's not have any friction."

"Not exactly a party around here anyway."

"Drinking the way you do." She sighed. "Scraping yourself up and stumbling around bleeding without the slightest awareness." She reached deep into the pantry and pulled out a movie-theater-sized chocolate bar. We sat down at the table together. I held a paper towel around my knuckles.

"I never saw her do that," I said.

"I never *let* you see her do that." Liz looked at me sharply. We held each other's eyes for a moment. My sister tapped her fingers on the placemat.

Finally, I asked, "What is that supposed to mean?"

"It just means that I was your big sister and I didn't think it was right for you to have to hide her car keys or help her out of her boots if she was in a blackout."

"When did she black out?" I asked, surprised.

"Not every night, but not never, either. From time to time. Occasionally I'd hear her pull in the driveway when I was downstairs doing homework and you were already in bed, and I could tell by the sound of the tires if she could make it in okay on her own or not. If it sounded like she couldn't, I'd go out there and help her inside, sit her down with a glass of water, then go back out and park her car right." I looked at my sister, flummoxed. She peeled open the gold foil wrapping and snapped off a segment of chocolate.

I couldn't immediately place what Liz was talking about. My thoughts were scattered, disorganized. I flipped back through the ages of five, eight, ten, trying to see this version of my mother through the fog. I found her there on the porch of our little rental cabin by the lake, one room with a woodstove, the September before I started fifth grade. She was watching me dive over and over from the dock down into the brisk green water, a slim bottle of amber liquid in her grip. Then we were in the kitchenette, my mother stirring Hamburger Helper in a glass dish, a bottle of beer in one hand, beads of condensation forming on the neck. When she went to the bathroom I took a big gulp, and when she returned she looked at the bottle and then at me, eyebrows furrowed, but didn't say anything. The next day, she and Liz stood by the car together. My sister took the keys from my mother. Their bodies were tense. Then there we were, the three of us, driving the long trip home to Knife River. My sister in the driver's seat, staring out ahead, silent. My mother in the back seat next to me, nodding off, stroking my hair from time to time. It wasn't something I'd thought of in years. It never seemed important before now.

"You honestly don't remember seeing her drink?" Liz asked. My sister's voice was quiet now, a little hesitant.

"I mean, yeah, sure. Of course I do. But in a normal way."

"A normal way."

"It didn't seem very different to me than any other adult around, is what I'm saying." Liz stared at me. I felt an itch growing under my sleeve, and then another one crawling up my ankle. I went on. "Yeah, I guess I saw her drink a fair amount. But we were okay, we never went hungry or anything."

"That is true."

"And she never blew off work or got fired. She had that same shitty job for so many years."

"Also true." Liz looked me up and down before saying, "Remind you of anyone?"

"What's that supposed to mean?"

"I just meant what I said in the first place. You get it from her." I looked at the floor, annoyed and a little chagrined.

"It wasn't always so bad," Liz said. "I mean, when you were a baby she wasn't really that way at all. But things sort of escalated with time. Every year I noticed it more."

"This just isn't how I usually think of her."

"I'm not saying she was some kind of degenerate. I'm only telling you that I think she struggled a bit more than you realize. Maybe more than she cared to realize herself, honestly."

"What are you getting at?" I snapped, suddenly angry. "That this has anything to do with what happened to her?"

"Of course I'm not. I would never say that." Liz shot me a stony look.

"You didn't bring this up when we went to the police back then."

"It wouldn't have helped." She waved her hand around like she was shooing away a bee. "It wasn't the kind of information they needed to know. They were already trying to use intoxication as an excuse. I wasn't about to give them any confirmation." She scoffed. "Like they needed a good reason to be even more negligent."

I could still hear the sheriff's voice in my head the day we reported her missing, the way his lips formed around the words *she probably had a few too many and isn't done sleeping it off somewhere.* The suggestion had enraged my sister. If I had any clear thoughts about it at the time, it was only that they didn't know our mother, that they were casting broad assumptions based on other people, other women they'd seen stumble back home after a three-day bender. Not this woman, who in my memory was always sitting at the kitchen table when I went upstairs to bed and whose empty coffee mug was always by the sink, still warm from her first cup, when I came back down in the morning. I took some of the chocolate from Liz and let it melt on my tongue.

Now I wondered if he'd said it because he'd once spotted her plowing through a red light or swerving into the next lane. Maybe he'd pulled her over and heard her slur her words one of those nights when Liz had to go out and park the car. How would I know? I really only saw her within the little world of our home, through a child's eyes. My mother tried hard to insulate me from unpleasantness when I was small. She wasn't overprotective, I couldn't recall her ever hovering or looking through my things. It was more like she wanted badly to divert my attention away from anything ugly or disappointing, like a magic trick. I remembered getting a tetanus shot at a very young age, and the moment before the needle pierced my skin, she crouched beside me and opened her palm to reveal a caterpillar, orange with black and white spots, chewing on a jewel-green leaf the size of a quarter. Sometimes in the winter little drifts of snow would find a way through old, warped seals and pile onto our windowsills. There were nights when sleeping in our bedrooms was unbearably cold. When it got to that point, she would build a fortress of quilts and pillows in the center of our living room, near the fireplace. Makeshift tents, held together by a flat sheet knotted to the ceiling fan, that to me felt almost mythical. Rare and festive, a palatial igloo that appeared only in the darkest time of year, when knobbly icicles long as my arm hung from every branch and the outside of our house looked like a frosted cake. I could remember Liz standing on the outside of our tent with her parka zipped over her pajamas, looking in at us, frowning. She'd go from window to window, trying to seal up the gaps with duct tape or bits of loose cotton. Eventually she'd come inside and sleep next to us, but not until late.

It used to irk me, Liz's reluctance to join in our sanctuary. I faulted her for not seeing the fun of it, like I did, for glaring in at us from an opening in the sheets instead of huddling alongside in the warmth, playing around with our Ouija board or making shadow puppets by the glow of a camping lantern. Looking back now, I ached for Liz. She was young, too, and cold. Someone should have taken care of her, I thought. Not just then, with the blanket fortress, but all the time. It would be untrue to say I'd been blind to the cracks forming in their relationship. I saw them bicker and snipe at each other over all kinds of things. As I approached thirteen, I noticed it more. I thought maybe it was just because we didn't have a father, or very much money, and the absence of these things caused a strain at home. But a lot of people around, maybe most people, had neither of these, so I didn't feel particularly worried about it. And by that time my attention was getting drawn more and more to other places. Like girls, or the understanding that for the sake of my own safety this burgeoning attention needed to be subtle, imperceptible, maybe even look like scorn or mockery. Or the fact that no one would notice if I left school to smoke pilfered cigarettes under the bridge, or that suddenly I was a foot taller than I had recently been and there was much to learn about navigating a world full of places to crack your head or ram your knees. So whatever dawning awareness I might've had about my mother's shortcomings was always getting blotted out by something more pressing to my teenage brain.

I knew she was a kind person. Thoughtful and sweet. Anyone would've said so. But in hindsight, I couldn't deny there were loose ends she clearly struggled to keep tied up. If she managed to get one squared away, three more unraveled. One year our well water became contaminated and needed to get fit with a new underground filter after a disinfecting treatment. The prospect of handling this seemed to overwhelm her. Liz was the one who stood outside with the inspector, taking notes on a spiral pad. Our mother didn't see why we couldn't just boil water for drinking.

"Just until I can deal with the repair," she insisted. "Like the pioneers did."

Liz taped the paper with all the information to the fridge and replied, "We're not pioneers. You can deal with it today."

Liz wiped some chocolate shards into a small pile on the table. This was the same table where she'd once argued with my mother about going to California for school. Suddenly, I realized my mother's opposition to my sister's college plan was probably less about getting enough scholarship money and more that she'd come to rely on her for keeping our life held together. Somehow it hadn't dawned on me until now, but once it did the plain truth of their argument bore into me hard. She'd regarded Liz more like a spouse than a daughter when it came to the handling of important things. We hadn't had the same parent, really. Or we had two utterly different experiences of the same adult. Mine was undeniably the better one. I started to feel queasy about that for the first time in my life, right then in the kitchen with Liz across from me, rattling her jingle bell pin around while she stared out the window, glassy-eyed, thinking her own thoughts. My first impulse was to give it to my sister, the version of our mother that I had. I would have, I thought, if it were only possible.

By now I was starting to feel really sour with guilt. I wanted to let my sister know that I was sorry she needed to drive us home from vacation at fifteen, or stop doing her homework to park the car, or whatever other things she took care of that stayed hidden from me, and maybe always would.

Instead, I heard myself saying only, "If she drank a lot, that didn't make her a bad person."

"I'm not implying that she was," Liz replied. I nodded, pissed at myself for willfully missing the point so completely. I realized then that I hadn't even gotten her a Christmas present. What was wrong with me? Why hadn't I gone to the bookstore and gotten her something about birds or planes? It wasn't like I didn't have the time. I took the paper towel off my scraped hand and let the air sting my open skin. I had a dramatic urge to dash some table salt over it, but didn't want to alarm Liz. Before long, she said, "I'm not saying you are, either, Jess."

Before bed, we stood at the piano together and sang "Midnight Clear." If someone had asked me to play it this same time a year earlier, at a Christmas party or something, I would've shrugged and said no. It was a piece of music I hadn't even thought of in a long time. But here, in my old living room, my fingers moved over the keys easily, like the memory had been alive and well in me just barely under the surface, waiting for this particular moment.

23

The second day of the new year was unusually mild. Melting snow dripped steadily down from the roof and over the windows. I sat at the kitchen table early in the morning watching daylight glistening over the thaw. The first week of January was a sour time of year for me—a fresh slate of twelve months on the horizon and all their hopefulness curdling rapidly while the minutes came and went, expiring at their usual clip, as the veneer of attainability over my resolutions crumbled and February drew nearer and nearer. Usually I could convince myself there was no rush to make changes. Quitting smoking would be just as much of a pain in the ass some other time, drinking less would be easier once my life was in neater order, and transitioning into a new job would go much more smoothly once I'd dried out a bit. But this time around, the future didn't look like such a far horizon. It felt instead that I was already in it. Soon enough, the investigation would be over, and I'd be launched into the next phase of life whether I was ready for it or not. I opened my laptop and pulled up a bookmarked listing of jobs Down East. More trail maintenance positions, and something about tagging new seal pups when they sidled up to sun themselves on the jetty. There were a few decent-looking one-bedrooms on the rental site I'd saved, too. Just knowing it was all there, waiting, reassured me a bit.

Liz came down at exactly seven. She stood at the counter in her uniform, eyes glazed, stirring a heavy stream of white sugar into her coffee.

"Back to work," she said. I nodded. "You must have some new recordings to take care of after the holiday."

"Yeah," I answered. "A couple, probably."

"Good."

I watched as she took a tablespoon from the drawer, filled it to a heap with sugar, then ate it straight before placing her utensil gently down at the bottom of the sink and waving goodbye. I sat there at the table for a little while longer after she left refreshing my email again and again, hoping there really would be some new work waiting so I could tell myself I was busy, and there were other people relying on me for something, and have that be enough for the day. Nothing came. I was still waiting to be paid for a long transcription on a soft palate abscess I'd done before Christmas. I deleted three spam messages about urgent auto insurance renewal. I'd never once insured a car. Soon the screen went black from inactivity and I caught a glimpse of myself in the dull reflection: short pieces of hair stuck up from my forehead, a crease on my cheek from the throw pillow I'd slept on all night. I wished I could peel my own face off and toss it into the trash along with the coffee grounds.

I noticed Liz had left a basket of dirty laundry at the foot of the stairs. Eager for distraction, I took the hamper down to the basement and sat in front of the washer, staring at the clothes whirling around behind the window plate. Suds bubbled up as the machine rumbled its way through the cycle. One of her green polyester neckerchiefs from work was in there, a streak of color spinning with all the black. I imagined her sitting behind the till all day, sliding cash in and out of the drawers, feeding checks into the machine, sucking on those unbranded, foil-wrapped hard candies as the hours ticked by. Her skin sometimes had this filthy sweet, almost metallic, scent lingering over it when she came home. From coins, she explained. Once a week she fed barrel loads of coins through an automatic roller to be trucked off to the re-serve in exchange for paper money. They weren't supposed to do it for customers anymore, but I knew she routinely gathered up all the loose change from Brenda's house, under couch cushions or out of forgotten pockets or wherever, and returned the next visit with cash to slip into her wallet. There must have been a hundred ways my sister worried over this friend of hers. She took care of so many things, thoroughly and lovingly, without ever being asked. For years she'd been doing that. The washer let out a long, wet gurgle.

Once the clothes were dried and folded, I took them upstairs and placed them in Liz's dresser. While I was in her room, I noticed some smudges on the vanity mirror, so I went and got some spray to wipe it off. Soon I was cleaning dust off her little collection of perfume bottles. I shook out her quilt and laid it neatly back over the bed, folding it down over the pillows and tucking the sides like we were in a hotel. It occurred to me that she might hate me being in her room like this, lifting things and setting them down in slightly different spots, getting my hands all over the surfaces. But I wanted to take care of her and I wasn't sure how else to do it. All I really had was time alone in the house, waiting. I stood there for a little while just looking over all her stuff. She had a few tin cast models of commercial airliners in a row on a shelf by the window, arranged in color order. Midmorning light passed through the sheers and illuminated the planes from within, fill-ing the shrunken cockpits with a yellowy glow and casting long shad-ows of their wings over the floor. I wished I could put us both inside one and fly us all the way to Australia. Instead, I went back downstairs and vacuumed all the carpets.

Late in the afternoon, I stepped outside to have a cigarette and wound up at the top of an old ladder I'd found out back and leaned against the house. The day had remained mild and all the rooftop slush was loosening as the snowpack softened under the sun. Back when I was living with Sarah, she'd hired someone to come install a series of low-profile heated cables along her shingles. *It's important to prevent ice dams,* she'd explained sternly, looking at me with a tight mouth, as if I alone might attract enough problem ice to collapse the whole house while we slept. I told her I'd grown up not far from Canada, and I couldn't remember ever worrying about ice dams. It turned out you were supposed to worry about them. As I stood there on the ladder with a gas station windshield brush from the trunk of my car, I thought of Liz living under the gathering weight of ice every winter and wondered whether she knew that it needed to be cleared and was just too tired to deal with it, or too broke to hire someone, or too preoccupied with other worries to care. The thought of her trying to ignore beams groaning and creaking above her head each year made me brush faster. Half-rotten masses of dead leaves slid out from the buildup and moved toward the gutter. I scooped them up with my hands and tossed them down into the yard. A sharp, earthy smell bloomed all around me. My fingers were nearly numb.

When I was about halfway through, just as the daylight had begun to fade, my sister's car pulled into the driveway. She got out and stepped gingerly through the slush, watching me with her hand on one hip. We looked at each other, me on top of the ladder and her twelve feet below in the muddy grass.

Confidently, I said, "Trying to prevent roof damage." Liz squinted at me, silent. I went on. "When everything freezes over again tonight, this'll expand and put more pressure on the rafters." I knocked on the gutter with a closed fist. "Enough ice builds up, the whole thing could even cave in." I took a big whack at the half-frozen slab in front of me. A chunk the size of a personal pizza broke off and went tumbling over the edge, where it fell about a foot away from Liz.

She kicked one of the shards with the toe of her boot and walked around to the other side of me, giving my setup a long once-over. I was sure she was wondering when the last time was this ladder might've been used, her eyes resting for a moment on the rung locks that were noticeably rusted and creaked loudly, but felt secure enough.

"Don't kill yourself doing that," she finally said. I told her I wouldn't.

She watched for a bit longer with a wry half smile on her face before going back into the house without further comment. I made my way around the roof until darkness began to settle and the temperature dropped. By the end, more than half of the ice was cleared. I stood on the ladder for a little while longer, surveying the house from above in the moonlight. It looked small and manageable from this angle. Not quite real, like I was viewing it from the edge of a dream—the shutters and shingles and bricked chimney all tiny pieces of an imaginary house, a version of the house I grew up in. There was the window into my old bedroom, a glare of moonlight obscuring the view inside. There was the porch with its yellow lantern hung above the doorway. A mailbox with our name in fading letters. When I left, when I was finally gone again from this town and settled in Maine, and then wherever I found myself thereafter, I felt like I would always remember my home from this vantage point—me, balancing on the edge of it in the shadowy half-light, trying to take care, knowing that coming back here didn't mean I had really returned.

Blood rushed into my face and fingertips the moment I stepped indoors. Liz was sitting in the living room with an embroidery basket spilled out next to her on the couch cushion. All the many bunches of thread were tangled in a mass, and she was carefully separating them by color. Once she got a whole one loose, she wound it around a piece of cardboard and set it to the side. There were three finished: black, white, magenta. She had her fingers looped around a big knot and was teasing it apart carefully, parsing the blues from the orange. I sat in the doorway between her and the hallway. Watching this process gave me the drowsy feeling of syrup dripping slowly from one part of my brain to another. My muscles relaxed. Inside my boots, the sensation returned to my toes. I yawned. Liz wrapped a length of blue thread around some cardstock and set it to the side.

Finally, she said, "You know what I'd really like? A pineapple upside-down cake." She folded her hands in her lap and looked up at me serenely. "I've been thinking about one for months but I never got around to it."

"Since when do you like pineapple upside-down cake?"

"I haven't actually tried it before. I just saw a picture in a magazine awhile ago and thought it looked great," she said.

"With, like, the cocktail cherries on it?"

"The cherries seem essential."

"Yeah, I would have to agree."

"No raisins," she said. "People try to sneak raisins into anything."

"I'll make you one," I told her. "I'll go to the store tomorrow."

"That would be nice," she said.

24

I walked to the store the next day. There was barely any gas left in my car, and the daytime temperature hadn't yet dipped back below freezing. When I used to take this route as a kid, the house at the end of the road had a tall pine tree in the front yard with some kind of strange deformity. Bulging, spherical growths protruded down the length of the trunk and the top was bent at an abrupt angle, like the tree was trying to get away from itself. I used to be fascinated by it, wondering what exactly the name was for this disease, and how trees even caught diseases, and what year this one first became sick. On the porch, most times, sat an elderly couple on two rockers. When it was cold, they had quilts. In the middle of the summer, a large, frosty pitcher on a little table between them. They seemed to sit there and rock all day, looking out at the street. As I walked by now, it didn't look like anyone had lived on the property for a long time. The tree was still there, though. Somehow alive, and much taller than I remembered.

I paused on the bridge over the river and looked down into the rushing water. Chunks of broken ice tumbled over the rocks and passed by in a blur, crashing into each other as they went around the bend and spraying a cold mist into the air above. Someone had left a single red mitten on the end of the railing. I stayed on the footpath until the end of the next block, then turned onto the Main Street.

Right away I could see Bill's van parked outside the grocery. The curtains around the back windows were drawn and the cab empty but for a stack of folded shirts sitting on the passenger seat. As far as I could tell, he was still living in there full-time. I'd always been so used to him as a fixture in this one same spot, occupying this little corner of town in this way, that before now, I never really wondered why. He'd been in Knife River for years, steadily employed, and it wasn't as if there was a shortage of housing around here.

The thought gave me a tense, nagging feeling. Like maybe he wanted always to be able to get up and go with only a moment's notice. Just turn a key and be in another state, another country even, with all his possessions in tow before anyone could try and stop him. But then I realized that I hadn't wanted something so different myself. I don't know if I'd ever again experience the same kind of soaring, wild relief I had at eighteen the day I'd left and crossed onto the freeway for the first time. All the signs flying past, the landscape shifting, tall buildings emerging on the distant horizon. Even today, if I decided to, I could be fully packed and gone within a matter of minutes. It wasn't such a crazy thing to want. Probably a lot of people thought about it. Here, and in every other town in the world. All I really knew about Bill was that he painted and used to give us a break on groceries.

I caught another glimpse of the van in the sliding door's reflection as I entered the grocery store's vestibule. There was a blue-haired troll doll planted in the center of the dashboard and a big, rusty dent on one side panel, right above the front tire.

My phone buzzed while I was standing in front of the brown sugar, trying to decide whether it mattered if I used light or dark. I grabbed it quickly, hoping it was Eva, but it was my sister sending me a picture of the cake she'd seen. The photo looked to have been taken in an open desk drawer at work: a magazine clipping sitting atop a stack of time stamp cards and receipts. I took the dark sugar off the shelf and moved along. Texts between Eva and me had started to dwindle some after each of our visits. I thought about her a lot, but most times I got it in my mind to reach out, I stopped myself. There were the pangs of guilt over doing anything that might hinder the investigation, and Liz's voice echoing in my ear, questioning why I needed to be doing this— seeing this person, of all people, at this time, of all times. I'd go back and forth, first telling myself it was fine, mostly harmless, worth it, then put my phone down before I could hit send. I didn't know where, exactly, Eva and I stood with each other. I got the sense she wasn't quite sure about it herself.

There was one single jar of maraschino cherries in the store. A thick layer of dust covered the lid but it hadn't yet expired. I gave it a couple of shakes, watching the red syrup shifting around the fruit, so bright it almost glowed. Only one of the three checkout lanes was open. An old woman was in front of me, digging in her purse for exact change while the cashier spun a ring around her finger absently. The worn plastic dividers lined up alongside the narrow belt advertised a brand of frozen vegetable. I looked at the magazines on the wire rack. They were all about food and celebrities. Mostly new year, new-you diet plans with promises of zero-fat desserts that tasted exactly like the real thing or full-body shots of famous people I only vaguely recognized promising to tell all about their workout regimes. I read the text on the back of the can of pineapple rings I was holding. I wondered if we had measuring cups in the house. And then I spotted Bill over in the corner, tinkering with a produce scale. His back was to me but I could see his face reflected in the angled mirror behind the mountain of carrots on display. Beads of sweat glistened on his forehead. Little silver piercings shined in his ears. There was an open box cutter sticking out of his back pocket, and every few moments he reached his hand around and touched it, checking it was still in place.

I was surprised by how familiar even just the back of him was. If I saw him standing in front of me at a crosswalk somewhere else in the world, or looking at a painting in a museum, I thought I would recognize him right away. There was nothing remarkable about his posture. He wasn't short or tall or tattooed. He was just in the fabric of my memory of this place—one of many threads making up the tapestry of a life's beginning, the things you don't dwell much on but couldn't forget if you tried: a loose floorboard, identical at first glance to all the rest, under which treasures could be hidden. What branches on a certain tree in your old yard lent themselves to climbing. The face of a woman who doled out lunch in the school cafeteria, the way hanging folds of purplish, crepey skin nearly covered her eyes. Bill was somewhere in that tapestry for me, a figure in the background, digging around in the trunk of his blue van.

As I was leaving the grocery store, I saw him tapping his fingers on the box cutter again, wiping his brow with the other hand.

T he cake tasted much better than I thought it would. My sister and I ate the entire thing over breakfast the next few mornings. Liz had it contained in a pink, floral plastic dome specifically made for protecting desserts. I'd never seen it before. It looked old, like something our mother might've gotten at her wedding. I didn't ask. Each day I watched her pull the whole thing out of the fridge and uncover it solemnly, slicing two pieces with slow precision and handing me a plate.

The morning we finished, she leaned back in her chair and said, "This ranks third in my top-five cakes."

"What are the top two?"

"Coconut and yellow."

"I like carrot," I said. There were a couple of cardinals outside the window fighting with each other on a branch. One got shoved off and then reappeared a moment later from above, its wings spread upward in a dramatic arc and its beak wide open. I tried to guess what the issue between them might be.

Liz took my plate and placed it in the sink. "Thanks for doing this for me," she said. I told her I was happy to. I really was. She nodded briskly and then walked out to her car, scaring the cardinals off the tree as she backed out into the street. I washed the dishes and the cake dome, drying everything off carefully and putting it all back where it belonged.

A t the end of the week, a message from Eva finally appeared on my phone. An enormous wash of relief came over me when I saw her name. It was Friday, late. Liz was already sleeping upstairs. I could hear her snores rumbling, the creak of her bed as she turned. I was in the middle of cleaning a trail of coffee rings off the countertop. Reading Eva's text, I had thoughts about waiting until morning to respond. It would be better, I reasoned. No need to come off like I'd been waiting by the phone. But while I told myself these things, I was already on my way out of the house, driving over to her cabin, not stopping for gas even though I still hadn't filled the tank. The weather had snapped back to a bitter cold the day before and the road was slick and glittering with ice. When I got to the door, she handed me an envelope.

"A belated Christmas present," she said.

Inside, I found a stack of old pictures. The flimsy, glossy kind you used to get developed from disposable cameras. In the first one, I was sitting on a fence post on the edge of a wide field, smiling a little from the corner of my mouth. I must have been around fifteen. In the next, Eva walking through the same field of wheatgrass and flowering weeds, her hair held aloft by the wind. I was dumbfounded.

"After I didn't hear from you for a while back then, I went to your house to see what was going on," Eva said. "Your sister told me you weren't there anymore. She said you moved away but that she didn't know much else. I went up to your room and sat on the bed for a long time. So many of your things were still inside. I couldn't believe you were really gone. Before I left, I took these from your desk drawer." I closed the envelope and tucked it in my coat pocket. I wanted these pictures. I felt protective of them, even. If someone tried to take them from me I would've put up a vicious fight, though looking at the images was painful and made me reel with nerves. It felt like something I could manage only in small doses, alone. It wasn't clear to me why Eva wanted to give me these pictures now. Before I could ask, she said, "Why didn't you say goodbye to me?"

I'd stumbled over this same question a thousand times. I wished I could give her a good answer. Why did I just disappear on her like that? Not even a hint that I was thinking about leaving town. Sometimes I thought I didn't want to make it realer than it already was— I was so afraid then, so unsure that my plans would work out. I was scared that I was making a mistake, but not more scared than I was to stay. What I wanted was a clean break, to bring myself to a place where nothing felt familiar and no one would know about what happened. Everything about home was agonizing. Every strange man I passed in the street made me wonder, with agony, if the eyes that looked back had seen some horrible truth that I'd never know myself. Every place I went made me wonder about her final moments, a thought that filled me with such dread I could hardly stand up on my own two feet. There came a time when I didn't want to wonder anymore, and I didn't want to be reminded. And there came, too, a time when I felt that I could no longer tolerate the heartache of lying next to Eva through the night and then having to be careful not to lay my hand on the gentle slope of her lower back during the day when we might be seen. I was in love with her then. It was a deep, searing, consuming kind of love, and it saved me, but it lived in the dark and I couldn't bear it anymore.

"Everything just hurt too much," I told her, hoping that would be enough.

"I would have gone with you," she said. I wasn't sure whether I thought that was true.

"Would you have?"

"Yes," she said, her voice firm. "You don't believe me?" I looked at her for a while, unsure of what to say. She led me away from the entry and into the kitchen. I stopped at the woodstove, warming my hands, while she went over to the sink and drank down a glass of water, then cupped her hands under the faucet and splashed her face again and again before turning around and saying, "I cried every night for weeks. I'm not telling you that to try to guilt you or anything. I know you were just taking care of yourself, and all this was a long time ago. But think about what it was like for me here without you."

I had thought about it. There were times I thought about it so much I would've set my head on fire just to forget. She went to the woodstove and stoked the coals. Heat rippled through the kitchen.

"I'm surprised you hung on to these for so long," I finally said, patting the envelope in my pocket.

"There were a lot of times when I was cleaning stuff out and thought I should just get rid of them. Then sometimes I was really angry at you and wanted to tear them up, but I could never bring myself to do it."

"Liz would have kept them."

"Yeah," she said. "Your sister went a little nuts right after you left, though, so who knows." I knew what she meant but asked her about it anyway, wondering if they ever saw each other after that day in the house, and if they ever spoke. She told me that she'd once seen Liz standing out in the middle of the road late at night, barefoot, walking in circles and getting in the way of passing cars.

"Did you stop?" I asked.

Eva looked down at the floor. "No," she said. "I was driving with some friends. I didn't know what to do."

"Oh."

"I wish I made them pull over to help her." I muttered that it was fine, but it wasn't. The image of Liz in the road like that, walking in circles, alone, gave me a terrible feeling. Eva then added that they'd run into each other a couple of years later at the pharmacy and she seemed better then and had said hello when they passed each other in the aisle. "Anyway," she sighed. "I just wanted to give you those."

I thanked her. I was heartened by the way she held on to them for so long, believing that we might see each other one day in the future, hoping she could give them to me, but I also felt weak. Blood seemed to drop from my head and chest and pool around my feet. A little voice, my own voice, whispered at me from somewhere deep inside. It wanted to know what I thought I was doing. It was almost one in the morning. There were other people in the world who would love me if they knew me. But the simple presence of Eva's body, the sound of her voice, soothed me in a deep, primal way. Like someone gently scratching the center of my brain with a very soft glove.

"Sit down," she said. I went to the table willingly and she made us cups of chamomile tea. The tea made me tired and loose around the joints.

"I should go soon," I told her.

"You can sleep here."

"I shouldn't."

"Why not?"

"I don't have any of my things." We both knew this was a lie. My things didn't matter to me at all. She poured more tea into both our cups and once it was gone, got out of her chair and came over to mine. She hooked both her legs around my waist and sat on top of me. Her hair smelled like the smoke that rose from the stove embers. There was a fleck of ash caught in one of her eyebrows. I brushed it off very carefully, like I was handling an old painting that didn't belong to me. Her face radiated warmth. I wanted her so badly I felt like I might die. She picked up my hand and slowly kissed each fingertip.

I went to my car sometime later, exhausted. I wanted to sleep for an entire week. My body felt shaky and hollow. As I pulled out of my parking spot behind the woodshed, I berated myself for all the ways I'd been neglecting my health. I wasn't eating enough, I knew that, but I just didn't feel hungry. After four or five bites of food my stomach began to feel sore and bloated. I sometimes woke up with a mouthful of bitter, vile acid in my mouth, burning a trail down the back of my throat. I knew I was drinking too much. My eyelids began to droop. I gave myself a quick slap on the cheek to wake up.

Halfway down the pine trail, another pair of headlights rounded the bend toward me.

I hit the brakes and sat for a minute, frozen in place at the wheel. The other car had its brights turned up. Funnels of white light beamed out into the night, reflecting off the snow-covered branches and creeping out into the dense wood. It was eerie to see the forest lit up this way, so starkly and unnaturally, in the early morning hours. An owl perched in the brush, blinking its silvery eyes at me. Curtains of dark, leafless vines swayed in the wind. I went to switch my lights off and then stopped myself. Whoever was in the other car wasn't visible to me. I didn't want to be the one to show my face first. There was no way to pass the other driver from where I sat. Snowdrifts encroached on the narrow road and up ahead, beyond the car, was a wide swath of black ice that I'd skidded over on my way in. The drum of my pulse quickened.

Then the driver's seat door swung open. It was Calloway. I could see him stepping out, hands on belt. His walk was trepidatious, the veins in his neck and hands illuminated harshly by the beams. A heaviness gathered in my stomach. He kept a wide berth from my car and I realized, as he drew nearer, that his gait was swinging and unsteady. He came upon a patch of ice and slipped, breaking the fall with his elbows with a grimace before steadying himself upright against a low-hanging branch. There seemed to be nothing to do but roll the window down and say something. Instead, I pulled my hood up and watched him from the corner of my eye. A little square of yellow light from Eva's cabin shone in my rearview mirror.

Calloway took a wide step over another frozen puddle, close enough now to lean down to the driver's-side window. I could make out the rough shape of his face through the frost, two shadowy pits for eyes and a wide open hole where his mouth was. He appeared to be saying something, though I couldn't make it out over the roar of my heater vents. I turned the fan off and after a long, excruciating moment, rolled the window down halfway. Wet, frigid air rushed in. We stared at each other blankly. Then he recognized me.

At first he seemed genuinely bewildered. I could smell that he'd been drinking. He wasn't quite drunk, but his movements were loose and his voice had taken on a sloppy, dragging tone.

"Hi," he said simply. "What are you doing here?" Stupidly, I told him that I was just leaving, which of course he could already see and didn't satisfy his question at all. He asked me the same thing again, this time with a touch of urgency. Once more I told him that I was just on my way out. He looked at his watch, then at me, then back at his wrist again. He stated the time. Two in the morning. I nodded in agreement and we gazed at each other with mounting anxiety. It was clear that I would need to pull my car into reverse and accelerate backward down the pine trail into her little yard, allowing him space to drive into the parking spot in the front before I could leave. We negotiated this quickly and Calloway lumbered back to his car.

As I drew closer to the cabin I could see Eva standing in the doorway. Moments later, her face sharpened into view. She looked confused at first, then horrified as Calloway's car emerged after mine from the thicket of pine. Her hands flew up to her face and then dropped down as she looked behind her shoulder and back again, clearly frantic. There came a sudden roar from the engine of his car as he sped up to circle around me, screeching to a halt right in front of the cabin. I had an overwhelming urge to run him over, but instead I just sat there, dumbly looking between the porch and the wooded drive.

As he got out of the driver's seat to approach Eva, he slipped again on the ice and then began to shout before even lifting himself up. I noticed that she did not go to help him. She did not look at my car, either. It was as if I'd already left. They began to argue. I left my heat off, straining to hear. Eva demanded to know why he was there so late without any invitation. Calloway pulled something out of his jacket and tossed it to the ground. It looked like a foil blister pack of pills. She picked it up and examined it before handing the pills firmly back to him. He said something about her claiming to be sick. She insisted that she was. Their voices grew louder and more fraught as they debated whether she was well or not. Calloway began to angrily wonder aloud why I was there at all. I had the distinct sensation of watching this unfold anonymously, as though I were hidden at some distant vantage point in the woods. Then the two of them turned in unison and looked straight at me. I stared back, and for a moment the three of us just observed each other through the yellow light of her porch lanterns. Calloway then took a step toward my car. Eva lunged for his hand, but he was already off the stoop and moving swiftly, ragefully, across the frozen grass. Within a second I was peeling off, tires sliding on the ice.

Once I was well away from the property and off the main road, I pulled over onto a dirt shoulder and took the key out of the ignition. I didn't want to hear any noise—not the sound of human voices or the thrum of my car's engine or even my own breathing. I sat very still. Flakes of snow drifted down from the sky. I watched them land on my hood and then melt in an instant. More followed. I watched, mesmerized, as more snow emerged from the liquid black.

25

Eva and I spoke on the phone the next day, just briefly. She explained that Calloway had come over unexpectedly after his shift ended with some over-the-counter migraine medication. They had plans to see each other that night, I learned, but she decided she didn't want to see him and canceled with an excuse about a bad headache.

Before hanging up she told me, "I hadn't meant to give you those pictures then, either, by the way. I just happened to find them while I was digging around for something else and the next thing I knew I was texting you."

My sister and I didn't have our next meeting with Calloway until the end of the week. I dreaded it intensely. Every time I thought of it my gut lurched like I was on the edge of something steep.

I didn't mention anything to Liz. She was distracted that week anyway. The regional management of her bank was seriously considering consolidating some of the branches in the northeast over the coming months and she was worried about having to move, accept a very long commute, or lose her job altogether. The possibility of change disturbed her on a visceral level. She started coming home from work with a grim expression on her face. She would eat mechanically over the kitchen counter, usually not bothering to reheat whatever food she found in the fridge, and then busy herself with small craft projects until bed.

The combined uncertainty of our mother's case and her work, a position she'd relied on for the better part of two decades, left her in a state I'd never before seen. I noticed she was picking and rubbing at one spot on the back of her head. Her hair was beginning to wear thin in a little circle there, a gleaming patch of scalp peeking through. I could see it gaining in diameter by the day, which alarmed me because it didn't seem like the kind of thing that should be clear to a constant eye. I thought its progression should only be apparent to me after some time apart, the way we are surprised by a child's new-grown height after only six months or a year of not seeing them. But I'd catch sight of the spot when she turned to walk up the stairs to bed. It was shiny and red, about the size of a quarter. Then in the morning, I'd see it again and it would look crusted over, a bit larger, with more new skin exposed at the edges. I thought about saying something to try to stop her, but then decided it was better not to get into debates over how we each soothed ourselves.

The envelope burned a hole in my pocket all this time. I'd occasionally take the pictures out and look at the first one in the stack, but the sight of my own face made me hurt all over. I looked so soft and wounded. Young in a way that felt impossible. I seemed unreal to myself, and had an overwhelming, unfulfillable urge to enter the world of the photo and save this little, distant version of me. Finally, one night I took the envelope into the bathroom and locked the door. Why I felt like this needed to be done in secret, I can't say, except that it felt intensely personal. I sat on the side of the tub and flipped through each photo.

They all seemed to be from different rolls of film, with orange date codes spanning the years from when I was eleven to sixteen. I couldn't remember any of them being taken. There was one of Eva and me kissing. While I seemed totally unaware of the picture being taken, a blurry stretch of her arm could be seen holding the camera out before us. This surprised me. It was a small thing, but I could see that it was brave. The photos would have been developed at the drugstore in town. You dropped the disposable camera into a box by the cash register with your name and telephone number on it, then came back a few days later to pick up the film. Someone who worked there saw everything that went through the processor, who may well have been the same person to operate the front of the store. Back then I was always keenly vigilant of these kinds of things, all my movements veiled with a searing awareness for what others might notice and how they might react to me, what they might decide to do or say to me as a result of their own disgust or, more dangerously, their desire. I knew I'd always remember how to live that way. It didn't feel like something I could just shake off.

In the last photo, I saw my mother. It wasn't meant to be a picture of her. One of my sister's model airplanes was in the center of the frame, one of the more intricate ones she'd ever built. Her hands hovered above it, as she was in the middle of pointing out some of its features when I took the photo. A little control box sat beside the plane. I could vaguely recall sitting on the back step as she flew it around the yard with a remote control, shimmying up a tree to get it back whenever the wings got caught in some branches. She was well into her teens by then, and I think this plane was the last one she ever built herself. I almost didn't notice my mother in the background at first. I was about to slide the photos back into their packet and get on with my evening, but her face caught me. It was a little blurry. She was in motion, and seemed to be on her way out the door. Her hair was pulled back by a bright red kerchief, the same one I remembered her wearing often back then: little white flowers printed on the fabric, rolled edges sewn with delicate stitches. I held the picture close to my face. I placed it emphatically down on the counter and then, after minutes of stillness, picked it up again and put it on my knees. She looked so young. That was the thing that really startled me. She was just this young, smiling woman. I did have a few other pictures of her, but they weren't of brief, forgotten moments like this. They were posed and intentional, usually of the three of us smiling in our good clothes on some holiday. I didn't look at them very often.

Studying my mother's face here filled me with a nervous happiness. It was like running into her again by chance, catching her face flashing by on a passing train. Joy rippled through me the way a breeze moves a curtain before an open window on a warm day—quietly, unceremoniously. I studied the photo for a while longer, noticing different things in the frame. It seemed there were endless mundane details. The wall calendar in the background told me it was April. A bowl of oranges sat off to the side. Car keys dangled from her belt loop. Sooner or later I began to think of her bones laid out on the metal table. I knew they were still there in that same cold laboratory, waiting in an even colder closet for further examination. Once this entered my mind I could not make it leave. The joy fell right out of me, a stone plummeting down a well. I felt like vomiting. I did, actually, kneel before the toilet, hovering my open mouth over the bowl and making a weak, croaking sound. My stomach seized and turned on itself, but in the end, nothing came up.

Later, after I'd left the bathroom and stuffed the pictures into the bottom of my bag of clothes, I heard Liz calling to me from the kitchen. She was hunched over a cross-stitch hoop. Her needle vanished and reappeared on either side of the cloth. A bluebird was taking shape, pair after pair of finely threaded loops forming its chest. She wanted to tell me that her bird-call clock had stopped.

"The battery must have died. You're tall, would you reach up there and replace it?" People were always asking me to reach things for them. In the bookshop, at the liquor store. Old ladies in the supermarket who would discreetly follow me to the next aisle, ready to have me get the rest of the things on their lists. Dust fell down in dense, gray clumps as I pried the clock from its hook. I sneezed. More dust fell. The house was never clean no matter what efforts were made, it seemed.

Dirt seemed to multiply overnight. There was always a different crevice for it to hide in, gathering mass.

No batteries were left in the junk drawer or anywhere else I searched. I did find a little carton that once held batteries, but it was full of rusty paper clips. My sister was irritated and suggested I get out to the store to buy more before they closed. "I'm used to hearing their songs on the hour," she said. "I don't need any disruptions to my routine right now." In the past, I probably would've ignored her and gone the next day. I wasn't the kind of person who took care of errands with much urgency. But now I was so wracked with guilt over my run-in with Calloway, and anxious at the prospect of seeing him again soon with Liz right there, and generally keenly aware of how much I owed her, that I did what she asked.

Our neighbor Paul was in his garage when I walked out onto the driveway. He was sitting behind a worktable, bathed in a warm or-ange light. Folded next to him was a length of white fabric from which he carefully cut out little shapes with a pair of scissors. I took a few steps closer and watched. He maneuvered the blade delicately around the pattern, holding it all just inches from his face. I couldn't tell what he was making. A stack of thin, foot-long planks sat at the edge of the table. I looked at my car, doubting whether the fumes left in the tank would take me all the way to the store. Hesitantly, I approached Paul's side window and tapped at the glass. He jumped a little, dropping the scissors to the ground. His eyes grew wide. I could see it took a mo-ment for him to recognize me behind the glass. I leaned forward, one hand resting on the top of the shutter. The wood was soft and warped. Dirt caked in the edges. I could feel the shape of a house key taped under the highest slat.

"It's Jess," I said. "Could I borrow a couple batteries?" He looked relieved, and came around to the front rolling door, lifting it a little and beckoning me inside.

There were two space heaters angled toward his workstation. I crouched before one and warmed my hands, leaning my face down toward the floor and letting the hot air blast my cheeks. He observed me for a moment, then nudged one of the heaters closer to me with the toe of his boot. A lot of other detritus was on the ground, besides the fallen screwdriver—bolts, nails, little bits of discarded material. I could make out the remnants of a heavily faded hopscotch court in red paint on the poured concrete. No children ever lived there with him, to my memory.

Paul asked me what kind of batteries I needed and then went over to a wall unit of little shelves. He opened them one after another, rifling around through all the piles of junk.

"I was just getting started on a ship in a bottle," he said, his back to me. So far it looked like nothing, just a pile of sticks and strings sitting near an empty old jug. I felt a bit awkward just standing there among all the debris, waiting. As he searched, I stared at the back of his head. There was an old scar visible through a thin hatching of silvery hair. The skin on his neck looked sun weathered and loose. I realized I wasn't even sure of his last name. I must've known it at some point. I scraped around in my brain, silently, still staring at the scar, and couldn't even come up with the first letter. Suddenly I felt acutely aware of all the other many things I didn't know about him. The man was hardly more than a stranger to me. My pulse quickened and I started to wonder if I shouldn't go get in my car and take care of it, the errand and the gas—my own problems, myself.

As if sensing my trepidation, he turned around, batteries in hand, and said, "If you ever need anything else, just come by."

"Nice of you," I said, my voice dry.

"I mean it," he said earnestly. "I have all sorts of things on hand here." He turned slowly with his arms outstretched, like a figure in a jewelry box. "Actually, let me just—" He held up a finger, asking me to wait, then dashed into the house through the side door to get something from a closet in the front hall.

Back in the garage not half a minute later, he solemnly presented me with a finished ship in a bottle. I was impressed with it. When I first realized what he was bringing out, I worried that I wouldn't be, and I'd have to feign some polite awe, but his handiwork was finely detailed and exact. I turned the bottle over in my hands. He explained how the ship got inside. It was collapsible, and he built the whole little vessel on the worktable before sliding it carefully in through the mouth of the jug. Finally, he used an attached string to pull it back into its upright form. Tweezers were involved. Thinking about this tedious process made my fingers feel jittery.

"So, you make things like this in your spare time," I said.

"Make things, fix things. I'm retired now." He explained that he'd worked as a specialty mechanic for nearly fifty years. "Maybe one day I'll build an actual boat," he said. "I've thought about it for a while. It's a big project."

"Where would you sail it?"

"A lake, somewhere nearby. This would be a canoe." He set the finished ship down on the worktable.

"My sister used to make model planes," I said.

"Yes." He smiled. "I recall." Paul cleared his throat and shuffled his feet a little. Seeming to want to redirect the conversation, he said, "These little projects keep me sane. If I don't stay busy, this all turns to soup." He gave himself a little knock on the skull. I nodded. A strong wind rattled the glass of his garage window. "Blustery out there," he said. I didn't answer. It was obvious we'd about run out of things to say to each other.

As I made my way toward the door, he cleared his throat and said, "Hanging in there still?"

"I guess so."

It looked like he was considering placing his hand on my shoulder in a gesture of goodwill, but stopped himself. In the end, he left me with a simple *good luck*.

26

As the end of the week approached, I grew more and more worried about my encounter with Calloway and what it could mean for the case. Some new transcriptions had come in after the holiday lull, and I'd sit in front of my computer between sessions, knuckles clenched, weighing the likelihood that he'd tell anyone in the department about it. On one side I thought no, he wouldn't want to tarnish anyone's impression of his manhood. But then it seemed just as likely that his anger, all the indignity and confusion oozing from his wounded ego, would override any of that and he'd tell other officers if only to use their scorn to inflate his own rage even further. Give him a good excuse to retaliate by making our case an afterthought. Either scenario was punctuated with doubts about whether he even understood what he'd come across that night. In the pit of my gut there was nothing but a quiet yes. Though still, he wasn't the most perceptive guy I'd ever met. He seemed like the type whose belief in lesbians was tethered either in porn—two girls awkwardly hammering away at each other in a fake locker room while their fake boyfriends were engaged in a football game somewhere—or in a peripheral awareness of late middle-aged women, sexless in his view, with identical gray haircuts, clad in flannel and Velcro sandals. It wasn't hard to imagine Jack Calloway not understanding that someone like his girlfriend could actually want women in every way.

On Wednesday, I decided to go to the courthouse where my mother used to work. I'd grown so restless and nervous I'd been on the same page of transcription at the kitchen table for almost an hour. I felt like I was on a carnival ride, spinning around and around under a whirl of lights and music, sick to my stomach but unquestioning, like I'd always lived there, like I'd been born in that spot and only just noticed that the waist strap on my seat had been unbuckled the whole time. For fifteen years, I'd relied almost entirely on my sister and the police for theories, for the information that supported or eroded all my questions and doubts. What if Calloway really was bitter enough to sideline the investigation? How would I even know if he had? He could easily keep having us in to chat every other week, pretending that he was making an effort, when really the files with our mother's name were already tossed to the bottom of a pile somewhere, gathering dust in the dark.

I felt a panicky urge to do something, to take some sort of action that wasn't filtered through the police or Liz, and decided to try to speak with someone who'd known her back then. I didn't know the old landline number for her friend in Ontario, and it would surely be disconnected by now if I somehow managed to dig it up. The owner of the coffee shop, Anne, the last person known to have seen her, had since moved away to be closer to her grandchildren. Liz had mentioned this to me maybe a year or two ago on the phone, annoyed that the prices had gone up under new ownership and that they were no longer selling loaves of bread. But Brenda remembered my mother. She still lived here. There had to be other co-workers, people she was friendly with in the records room where she'd worked for years.

I stood up and walked briskly toward the front door. Patricia, the woman who'd come to our home so many years ago bearing a foil-wrapped sympathy lasagna. Maybe she'd talk to me. Maybe she was there in the clerk's office right now. It was midafternoon, well after lunch. I got into my car.

The courthouse sat alone off the town square at the top end of Main Street. It stuck out, tall and imposing with four white columns out front and three tiers of wide, low steps to the doors. In front there was a round patch of grass encircled by a decorative iron fence. During summer, roses bloomed there. Now there were scraggly tangles of branch and a few rotten-looking brown flower heads that clung. In the center of the circle was a green copper statue of Wynken, Blynken, and Nod the size of a modest garden shed. Water bubbled around the base, glinting and swirling and spouting up into the air every few minutes. Three children in a wooden shoe held rods with little copper stars dangling from the ends like fish. It had been commissioned as a first birthday gift for the mayor's daughter in 1930, the year that Knife River was designated as the county seat and there was a fever of industry, new factories sprouting up all the time. A plaque on the base read For Violet, with the poem etched in a smooth cursive underneath: *Wynken, Blynken, and Nod one night sailed off in a wooden shoe, sailed on a river of crystal light into a sea of dew* . . . I remembered some kid at school telling me that Violet died only a few years later from consumption. I had no idea whether it was true. I wasn't sure what consumption even was, exactly.

Inside, there was a reception area with a small flag of the state of New York on a golden plastic dowel. A college-age man sat on a swivel chair next to a fax machine. He had some kind of textbook in his lap, and a mess of papers spread out before him. He looked up at me when I walked in, then down again. I followed signs to an elevator and rode down to the basement level, where the records department was.

The doors parted onto a vast, dim room with a row of desks lined up before many more rows of tall shelving units. The only person immediately visible to me, sitting at desk and typing on a big, outdated keyboard, was Patricia. It wasn't until I saw her sitting there that I realized how little I was prepared for the possibility of actually finding her at all, let alone this easily.

As I stood there, thinking about what to do next, she looked up, and then within a second had sprung up from her desk and rushed over. My body tensed up. A stack of bracelets jangled on her left wrist and her earrings, silver beads, chimed gently as she moved. She shook her head in disbelief, her yellowy-blond perm shifting side to side, and before I could open my mouth to speak she'd wrapped her arms around me and squeezed me into a tight hug. It was not a quick one. I could feel our hearts beating on either side of our chests. She held me so hard I felt a light pop in my vertebrae, which was a little startling but not totally unwelcome. Seconds continued to pass and I started to fret about the position of my arms. I hadn't immediately raised them to hug her back, so they hung in a weird, loose dangle in front of me. I worried that if I moved now to place my hands on her upper back, it would seem like I wanted to extend the hug. So I just stood there, sort of leaning into Patricia's body, my eyes wide open, limbs limp and yielding as a yarn doll. When she released me, there were damp spots on the shoulder of my sweater where her face had pressed. She was crying very softly. I suddenly felt bad about the way Liz kicked her out of our house after we took the lasagna back then. I can't imagine we ever returned the dish, either.

"I'm sorry to just show up like this out of nowhere," I said. "I wasn't sure if you'd recognize me."

"Of course I do," she said. "You and your sister have been on my mind lately, with everything that's come up."

She wore light coral lipstick, which had begun to feather out into the fine lines around her mouth. Her teeth were bright white, almost bluish. A faint vanilla scent drifted from her spiral curls. We were studying each other openly.

I tucked my hands into my pockets and said, "You look the same." I immediately wished I could swallow the comment right back down. What kind of a thing was that to tell her? It wasn't a compliment so much as an observation. We'd only met the once. What point was I even trying to make?

Patricia led me through a heavy wooden door on the far side of the room into an empty break area, where we sat down on two orange plastic chairs. There was a basket full of bagged mini pretzels and Oreos in the center of the table. She smiled at me warmly and offered me a cup of coffee. I didn't want anything. I wasn't even sure I wanted to be there. I'd had an impulsive, guilt-ridden thought and now here I was, holding this woman's full attention under harsh fluorescent light. It was strange to be in this place where my mother had spent so much of her time. I imagined her rummaging around in one of the cabinets, peeling a coffee filter off the stack, leaning against the counter and looking at the clock. Past the doorway I could see someone in a green sweater standing on a step stool, pushing a file into the row of stacks. My mother must have done that same thing a thousand times, perhaps with the same step stool. Patricia's eyes were still a little red around the edges.

She asked, "So what brings you here?"

"Honestly," I said. "I don't know. I just wanted to talk to someone who was around back then." I suddenly wished I'd said yes to her offer of coffee, just to have something to do with my hands. I added, "Besides my sister."

"How is Liz? I haven't seen her around in a little while."

"She's all right. This has been really hard on her, of course."

"And on you, too, I imagine."

"It hasn't been easy, no."

"Natalie talked about you two all the time," she said. "We were all heartbroken here when she went missing. Devastated."

"How many people are still around from that time? Is it just you?"

"No," she said. "There's a few of us. Debra and Faye, they've been converting all the records onto the computer system."

"Is that what you do here?"

"No, I do certificates. Birth, marriage, divorce, death."

"That's all of them," I replied, wishing a second later that I hadn't said it. What did I know about what went on in a county clerk's office?

"Well, there's business filings and land deeds," she said, correcting me. "Name changes, adoptions, court case stuff. We even have to keep certified records of asbestos contamination in public settings; there was a major lawsuit in the eighties." Her voice trailed off. "There's only about twenty thousand people in the whole county, so we keep it all together in there." She gestured toward the back of the main room with all the shelving units. There were low-humming dehumidifiers scattered around, but the air still felt damp and weighty. "Anyway," she sighed. "Have there been any new developments in the case? It was in the paper in October but nothing since then."

"Nothing major yet. The forensic stuff is slow going. They're waiting for those results before doing anything. My sister's been trying to get them to speak with Nick Haines again."

"Right." Patricia nodded. "I remember."

"Did she ever mention him to you?"

"Natalie? No, no. I don't remember his name ever coming up."

I told her then that what I really wanted to ask her was whether there was anyone she was suspicious of back then, anyone she remembered my mother talking about or wanting to avoid, anyone she still wondered about to this day.

She paused, eyes unfocused as if in deep thought before shaking her head and saying, "There isn't anyone who comes to mind."

"Liz is convinced about Nick. But I don't know."

"No?"

"I mean, I feel like I don't know anything these days. Half the time it's like I'm feeling my way through a dark room, stepping around missing floorboards." Patricia gave me a concerned, sympathetic look and I twinged, embarrassed by my honesty. "But no," I said. "I don't feel totally certain. And I don't want to be so focused on one lead that I miss something important."

She told me she understood, of course, how painful a position to be in, how awful for the wound to be reopened after so many years. I wanted to say that it was less like a wound and more like a gaping hole that just sat there, as raw on this day as it had been on every other since she'd gone missing. *Things get lost in there,* I imagined saying.

We chatted for a few more minutes. Mostly about where I'd been and what sort of work I'd been doing. She told me she'd visited New York City four years ago and wanted to go back to see more shows on Broadway. She named all of the ones she'd gone to and I nodded like I'd either seen them or wanted to see them, though I hated musicals. We talked about Knife River, businesses that had opened or closed since my moving away, a fire in the elementary school, people around my age who'd gotten married. I only remembered the names of a few, and struggled to conjure an image of their faces.

Finally, she gave my knee a tight squeeze and said, "I pray for your mom, Jess. And for peace to you and Liz."

"Thank you," I said, shifting in my seat.

There was a woman standing around the corner just outside the break room door as Patricia led me back to the main room. Faye, it turned out, who'd been in the department for nearly thirty years. Patricia introduced us quickly and then went to her desk to answer a phone call. Faye gave me a thin smile and a brisk nod before excusing herself and disappearing into the stacks. I waved goodbye as I stepped into the elevator, though no one was looking at me, and rode up to the lobby. I felt deflated. I really thought I was doing something showing up like this, finally taking charge in the situation. *My* situation, really. I'd been so passive for years. I had a way of acting like what had happened belonged to other people more than me. Liz, mainly. But how could I pretend that was still true when I was the one lying up at night, staring at the ceiling, remembering the way her bones looked arranged on the coroner's aluminum table and then turning my gaze to the piano bench and feeling like if I just squinted the right way I could see her sitting there, running her fingers along the keys?

I was out on the steps of the courthouse, digging around for my lighter, when Faye appeared at my side, breathless and a little frazzled.

"Jess," she said, and brushed some hair out of her eyes. "I'm glad I caught you." She looked around quickly, back toward the doors of the courthouse and then around the front, scanning the benches and the sidewalk. "Did you ever meet Patricia's son, Robert?"

27

"I don't want to make a fuss or get anyone upset, but I overheard your conversation in the break room," Faye said.

Robert Miller was thirty-eight, she told me, just a few years older than Liz, living in a converted fishing cabin on the northern edge of Knife River. He was tall, square jawed, freckled, broad shouldered. Faye showed me a picture of him on her phone. It was a mug shot she'd pulled up on her work computer back in the records department and quickly snapped a picture of before closing the browser and finding me outside. We were sitting in my car, parked alongside the building. She was worried about being overheard by a co-worker or someone walking by. I stared at the picture for a long time. I'd never seen him before.

She explained that in the winter of 1997, when Robert was in his early twenties, she and my mother were leaving work together and caught him breaking into cars parked on a quiet street around the corner. They'd stayed late that night, picking up extra hours retyping a section of documents that had been damaged in a small flood after a pipe burst in the basement.

"It was dark," she said. "And we heard strange noises, then saw a figure darting around in the parallel spots. By the time we'd gotten close, he was already inside Natalie's car. I wanted to turn back and call for help, but she ran right up to him. She was pissed."

"Did you recognize him?"

"After a moment, I did. And I told her, that's Patricia's kid. She said she didn't give a damn and grabbed him by the collar of his jacket. She yanked him backward out of the car and slapped the tool he was using right out his hand. It was some kind of smoothed-down key he was using to try and get in the glove box." Faye described what happened next: This young man, Robert, shoved my mother hard and she fell down on the sidewalk and slid on a slick of black ice down over the curb. She got up, bleeding from the palms, looking like she was going to backhand him across the face, but then he reached into his pocket. "It seemed like maybe he had a knife or a gun or something." Her voice lowered as she told me this. "Maybe he didn't, I can't be sure. It was dark out, and we were both upset. But a floodlight came on across the street and he got startled and ran off."

"What did you do next?" I asked, my pulse hammering. We were so close to where this had all taken place, just a two- or three-minute walk. I could picture it clearly: the car she drove, a silver '94 Honda, a foot-sized sticker of a cartoon leopard on the bumper that I'd gotten from a quarter machine at a gas station and adhered when no one was looking. She hated it, but the thing wouldn't come off.

"It'll sound funny to you, but we both just went home. We stood there for a couple minutes, catching our breath, before we checked out her car. He'd only managed to grab thirty dollars in loose cash. Some of it in change. Her lock and handle were still working fine. So we just said good night and drove away."

"You didn't think of calling 911 or anything?"

"We didn't want to call the police on our friend's kid, honestly. We knew he was troubled. Patricia's nerves were already so frayed. She talked about him all the time."

"So you didn't tell her, either?"

"Actually, we did. The next day at work. She was very upset. She swore up and down nothing like that would ever happen again, thanked us for not calling the police. She told us she was on the edge of a nervous breakdown, dealing with him. Then time passed, and it just turned into an ugly memory." Faye was rubbing her hands together and buttoning her sweater to the neck. She'd left the courthouse in just her office clothes.

I pushed all the heat vents her way, turning the air up. "I don't think Liz ever knew about this. I know I never heard of it before," I said.

"Probably she didn't want to upset you girls. Your mother was a pretty tough cookie. She was more angry than scared the whole time, I remember that."

"So what's the mug shot from?" I asked, nodding toward the phone on her lap.

"Right," she said. "So then about six years later, he went to prison."

It was a home invasion gone wrong, she explained. Robert and another man intended to rob a house they'd scoped out in a nicer, neighboring town, thinking the owners weren't home, but the wife's pregnant sister was there, watering some plants, and they all three surprised each other, and the woman was shot. I asked if she died, and Faye told me no, not in the end, though she lost the baby, and never regained full movement of her legs. Robert had been arrested before, but never for anything like this. All drug charges and petty theft.

"He got a prescription for a sports injury while still in high school, and then you know how that goes. It's not a cheap habit." Faye looked at me seriously, adding, "Patricia is a nice woman, but she's had a lot of denial about Robert. He'd steal from her and she'd brush it off, sometimes even pretending like she'd lost the necklace or whatever it was herself, but you could tell she never really thought that. And then of course each time she bailed him out was always the last time."

"Where is he now?" I asked.

"He's still here," she said, not meeting my eyes. She described a fishing cabin that had belonged to Patricia's late father and how, once Robert got out of jail, she'd had plumbing and new windows added, setting him up there with a job and a car. The cabin was on the far side of the rock quarry, where I learned to swim as a child. My mind immediately snapped back to the psychic's phone call, her vision of a watery, seldom-visited place.

"He's supposed to be sober," she told me. "I don't know. He must have some probation man testing his urine all the time. I hardly ever see him. Last time was over the summer when he came to drop something off for Patricia. He looked all right."

The car suddenly felt too hot. I pressed my cheek against the window's cool glass, closing my eyes and taking my gloves off, dropping them into the console. It wasn't only too hot, it was too small. Somehow the undersides of my eyelids were burning. Silently, I combed through everything Faye had just explained. My mother disappeared three *years* before Robert went to prison. I had the impulse to get out of the car and just run off, leaving her there with my keys and everything, even though I'd come here hoping to find this exact sort of information.

Seeming to sense my anxiety, Faye gently told me, "I'm not saying I believe Robert killed your mother. I never saw them in the same place after the car incident, and she never mentioned him to me again. I have no idea what really happened to Natalie. But I do think he was about ready to pull a weapon on her that night, and like I said, when I heard what you were saying in there to Patricia, I thought of it. And I knew if I didn't come and tell you I'd never sleep through the night."

"You must think it's a possibility," I said. "You wouldn't have said anything otherwise." I asked her then why she never came forward with this in the past. If she thought Robert was a threat, why not go to the police when the investigation was new?

She shrunk a little at this, clasping her hands tightly in her lap. "Well, at the time, most of us thought the cops were right to name Nick Haines. I didn't feel like they were being misled or anything."

"It didn't occur to you to go speak to them anyway, though? Just in case?"

"Well, when I learned your mother was missing there was a moment when I did think of Robert. But only briefly. Patricia had this picture of him on her desk, a school photo from when he was maybe ten. It's still there. I'd see it every day and he looked so harmless and sweet. I knew a lot had changed since he was that young, but still it seemed a bit extreme to go to the precinct and basically accuse the boy of murder. Especially when there was already such a solid suspect."

We sat quietly for a few minutes, both adjusting to the weight of everything she'd said. Some grade school kids walked past the car, laughing and swinging their backpacks. The sun was shining clear and bright. I thought my chest might explode.

Faye added, "Then of course, after he shot that pregnant girl, I felt a little differently."

"But you still didn't go to the police," I said, trying and failing to keep the accusation from my tone.

"Well, I'm telling you now." She sounded a little defensive. We sat in silence for another moment before she squeezed my shoulder and got out of the car, shutting the door gently behind her.

28

Back at home, Liz looked at me incredulously from the other side of the couch. She had a big mug of tea in her hands and inhaled deeply, wrapping her other hand around the front trying to trap the steam under her nose.

"My sinuses," she said.

"I'm trying to tell you something."

"I know, I'm listening."

"What did I just say?"

"You went to Mom's old work." It sounded like she hadn't really taken the words in and was just parroting me, totally disinterested.

"Yes," I told her. "Earlier today."

"What gave you an idea like that?" Then her face shifted from bewilderment to anger. She lowered her mug. "What are you trying to do?"

"I'm not trying to *do* anything," I told her. "I just wanted to talk to someone who was there then. Like, in Mom's life. Someone who saw her every day."

"We saw her every day."

"You know what I mean."

"No, I don't." Liz crossed her arms.

"An adult, a peer of hers. A co-worker. Like, another woman who spent time with her away from home, away from her kids and everything."

"You think a co-worker knew her better than I did."

"I think a co-worker knew her differently than you, probably."

"Well," she said, a flicker of curiosity flashing in her eyes. "What happened?"

"First, I saw Patricia."

"Patricia."

"She brought us a lasagna that one time."

"I remember. She wouldn't stop talking." Liz scrunched her nose. "She was so emotional. More upset than we were, even. Her face was all pink and swollen. It reminded me of a deli ham."

"It doesn't matter, just listen," I said, waving my hand impatiently. I explained to her about Faye, how she'd caught me out on the steps and everything she'd told me in the car. It was exhausting to recount. My mouth kept getting dry, so I'd pause every few breaths to take a gulp of water. Liz kept saying, *and what then,* as if I was going to just leave her hanging. By the time I got to the end, she'd set her cup of tea to the side and become very still, her eyes laser focused on me.

"She never told you about the car break-in?" I asked.

"No. I wasn't aware of that." She seemed uncomfortable, partly because of the fact that something so dramatic had been unknown to her until now. But also, I thought, because I was the one to unearth it, reveal it to her; that it was within my power to keep secret if I'd wanted to.

"Do you think it's weird she brushed it off like that?" I asked.

"What do you mean?"

"Like, she was probably pretty upset about it, but is it strange that she would basically just ignore it? Act like it hadn't happened?"

"I don't think it's that weird." Liz stared down at the space between the cushions, her eyes glazed like she was lost in a thought. After a minute she said, "Brenda once told me that Mom had a *high pain tolerance.*"

I asked her what, exactly, was meant by that, and she explained a conversation they'd had once on the anniversary of the disappearance about her life, the kind of person she was, what she'd done before leaving the world. One thing Brenda recalled was being struck by how calm she remained during her contractions, how when she'd gone into a hard, fast labor with Liz at the school office she was the least panicked of everyone who swooped in trying to help.

"She didn't mean just a physical pain tolerance," Liz said, adding that Brenda had pointed out how our mother had raised two small children in a place where she had no one to fall back on after our father left. It was true that when we got the news of his death she'd seemed unaffected by it. At least as far as I could tell.

I wanted badly to change the topic. "So, do you know Robert? Or know of him?" I asked.

"No."

"He's only four years older than you. He would have been a senior in high school when you were a freshman."

"You know I didn't make friends in high school. I definitely didn't know older boys."

Liz picked up her mug again and took a long sip. I stood and walked over to the bookshelf, fishing around for the right yearbook. They were caked in dust. It seemed like Liz had never touched them. I remember her saying they were a waste of money and that perusing a book full of portraits of people she either didn't know or like would be the last thing she'd ever do for fun, but our mother had insisted on ordering a copy every May. *They're cute,* she said, *I'm sure one day you'll like looking back through them.* My mouth went dry thinking of her saying that now.

I found the right yearbook and sat back down, flipping through until I found Robert's senior picture. His extracurriculars were listed beneath. Sports, like Faye had mentioned. Student council. Under future plans it said, simply, *professional athletics.* There were some other black-and-white images of him scattered throughout the pages. One in a team shot, uniformed and straight-faced. Another one, candid, leaning against the side of a dark-colored pickup truck, keys hanging off his belt loop, handing a flower to someone out of frame and smiling. I held up the page with his portrait.

My sister shrugged, saying, "I don't recognize him."

"Maybe you see him around town sometimes?"

"I don't know that face."

I let out a hard breath and leaned back against the sofa, closing the yearbook with a snap and holding it against my chest like a shield. Liz stared out the window, absently rubbing the spot on her scalp.

Finally, I said, "Well, what do you think?"

"It's a horrible story," she said, watching a robin flit around just outside the window. "I hate it. I hate that this happened."

"Me, too."

She turned her head and met my eyes. "But it doesn't convince me that this Robert person is the one we should've been looking for all along."

"How can you be so sure?" I asked, my desperation shifting into anger.

"Because this one, isolated interaction doesn't come close to making him a stronger suspect than Nick Haines. We know they had a date and something went wrong. We know he had her compact." Her voice was steady, adamant. Nothing in it made me think her conviction had been shaken.

"*A* compact," I said.

"And I saw him with my own eyes trying to plow down a woman with his truck."

"Faye saw this other guy shove Mom to the ground while he was robbing her car," I retorted. I didn't really know whether I thought Robert was a more likely perpetrator than Haines. But my sister's refusal to consider any other possibility made me feel even more doubtful that it was him. What I really wanted was for us to parse through all the possibilities together, examining everything scrupulously and honestly, and then arrive at the same theory. I wanted to have some kind of belief we could share in, both lean on. I wanted to feel like I knew anything at all.

Liz took the yearbook from me, got up, and slid it back onto the shelf. She walked over to the window and fiddled with the curtain tassel, biting her lip.

"What do you think happened, then?" she asked.

"It could have been anyone," I said, the words spilling out in a rush. In the past fifteen years, Liz had never once asked me this question. "Some psycho stalking people out in the woods. A hiker on one of the trails, maybe they got into some kind of altercation. Somebody from her work. Somebody she met at a bar. Any one of our neighbors. Like Paul, from next door? When I went over for batteries the other night, he said he knew you used to be into flying model planes. Who would remember something like that and then bring it up? Why was he paying such close attention?"

"He does live next door," Liz said. "I don't find that strange." She looked at me pityingly, which only irritated me more. I went on.

"Or the track coach. How do we know he only assaulted teens? Or Bill, from the grocery store. Mom was into painting, too, you know. What if they were acquainted through that?" I stopped myself right before suggesting that maybe the sheriff had done it and that's why the trail had run so cold. I took a long, deep breath and tried to get back on track. "Maybe Robert was angry that she'd attacked him and came back another time when she was alone," I said. "Maybe she tried to fight him off and wound up dead. Faye seemed pretty sure he had a weapon the first time." I shook my head, trying to expel the image from my brain. "He shot a woman in a burglary. That doesn't that make you wonder?"

"I didn't say that." Her tone was curt.

"I'm going to tell the police about it at our meeting on Friday." There was an edge of panic in my voice. Once I noticed it, the panic spread, coursing through my body like a poison.

"Good," she said. "I wouldn't try to stop you."

"How are you not freaked out by this?" I asked. I stood abruptly, my heart thudding so heavily I was almost dizzy. "This could actually be something. Doesn't this scare you?"

"Of course it does," she said. "I've been scared for fifteen years. I hope you know that." She cast me a near-glare, not quite angry but bordering on it.

I knew she stayed awake, pacing, questioning, tracing lines on a map until her vision blurred. I was there. And once I'd left, on some level I could sense her, miles away, still pacing in the night.

"I know," I said.

We stood in an awkward silence for a minute, neither of us wanting to leave the other alone to stew. Eventually, she passed me a butterscotch candy from somewhere within her sweater. She took them by the handful from the bank. I didn't want it, but I opened it anyway and let it dissolve on my tongue.

She took a deep breath and said, "I do find this stuff about Robert extremely disturbing, don't get me wrong. And I don't think we should ignore it. We're going to tell the police. But, Jess, Nick Haines cleaned out his truck overnight when he knew the cops were coming for him. In those hours before they could get the warrant, he made that truck spotless." She shook her head, mouth drawn in a heavy frown. "Doesn't *that* make you wonder?"

29

The next evening, I was working at the kitchen table transcribing a long file about a young woman's soft palate surgery when Liz came up to me and yanked one side of my headphones down, asking if I had any new information from the police.

"No," I said. "Why would I know anything you don't know?"

"Maybe you heard something from that girl."

"We don't talk about this." I pulled my headphones back on.

I'd gotten a late start on the transcription because I'd spent hours that morning cleaning the floor. With ungloved hands, I dipped a rag into a bucket of scalding water and rung it back out. After one section of tile was done, I'd take a gulp of room temperature vodka from the bottle, then do the next section. My hands grew raw and red. My knees ached. I'd pause here and there to read everything I could find online about Robert's conviction. A lot was made of his high school sports career, and of the injury he'd sustained during a football game, a compound fracture of his left shin. The first operation had been botched and needed to be redone, leading to intense chronic pain and a prescription that ultimately brought him to the state of desperation he was in when the burglary went awry. The local papers took a sympathetic slant in their reporting. People seemed to view him as a sad case of lost potential, a golden child ruined by medical malpractice, someone who was worthy of a chance at redemption.

Liz opened the fridge and stared in, shutting it for a moment and then swinging the door open again. I could feel the cool air on my forearm from where I sat. It felt great. I found myself wishing I could just crawl inside the crisper drawer and stay there. I realized then that I might be hungover from the morning.

"We are out of groceries," Liz declared.

I took off my headphones, got up, and looked over her shoulder. There was a jar of mustard and some onions with long, green fingers growing from the tops. A bag of chocolate chips sat open on the first shelf. I could see little drops of condensation on the plastic, and more drops on the chocolate itself. They seemed to have formed together into one large, inseparable lump. The onion gave off a sharp smell.

"I'll take you to dinner," I said.

Before we left, I spotted her in the bathroom trying to arrange her hair over the raw patch.

We went to Larison's, a restaurant that had been in business for almost ninety years. It was also an operating turkey farm—a wide pasture backed up to the property, clusters of chicken wire enclosures dotting the muddy grass around a worn, plywood run that all the birds funneled down through into the barn at dusk each night. Perched on the hill's crest was a grand farmhouse with a wraparound porch. It was the first thing you saw if you drove into town from the west, a tall white sign on the lawn: Larison's Turkey Farm and Restaurant, with a list of offerings beneath: Turkey Dinners, Fresh and Frozen Turkeys, Livers and Giblets, Eggs, Cocktail Lounge. In the seventies, the family built a smaller home on the far corner of the land and converted the big farmhouse into an eatery with a shop operating out of the back. It was immensely popular, drawing long lines on Sunday afternoons.

A warm, familiar glow hit me the moment we walked in. The wood-paneled walls, rows of oil lamps on every cloth-covered table, a bar that curved around the whole waiting area, even the same ancient, rickety man I remembered from years ago still making cocktails. Our mother had taken us here every so often. Even back then I was mesmerized by the way he poured drinks, holding the spouted bottle high above the glass, the stream seeming to halt in suspended motion. Behind him were rows and rows of bottles—amber bottles, green bottles, cut crystal bottles full of sparkling red and purple liquids. Behind that was a long mirror that made it appear as though the bottles went on and on forever, extending the room into an unreachable, endless world.

Liz waved to the old man as we walked in. "That's Brenda's brother," she whispered. He waved back and my sister made her way next to one of the stools, leaning forward to greet him in a loud voice. "That's my sister, Jess," Liz told him, pointing back at me. I took a few steps forward and waved, smiling a little. His jacket had a name plate that said Hiram.

He leaned his elbows down on a folded rag and said, "I remember your face." His hearing aid made a shrill sound. He clapped at the side of his head until it stopped.

"Oh," I said. "I remember yours, too."

"You were about this small." He reached his hand somewhere below the bar where I couldn't see. "Otherwise, you don't look any different." Liz laughed, throwing her head back and showing all her long, crooked teeth. I felt a pang of affection for her in that moment. I loved her crooked teeth. I loved her wild, woolly hair and cackle of a laugh. I loved that she had people in this community who knew her and cared for her, and that she cared for them back with such earnest generosity. Some more people sidled over to the bar and looked toward Hiram.

"You two go have some dinner now," he told us.

As we walked through to the dining room I saw that people were still smoking indoors. Each little banquette table had an ashtray next to a dish of salted peanuts. Glowing tips bobbed all around us, sending smoke trails up the ceiling where a wispy fog gathered and clung to the peeling paint. The smell was deeply comforting; cigarettes mingling with grease and cedar wood. I was comforted, too, to find that the menu hadn't changed. It offered only one thing, twelve dollars for a bottomless plate. Dark or light meat, mashed potatoes, steamed corn, green beans, buttered rolls, giblet gravy. A waitress would come around with a big platter, refilling your dish until you flipped a color-coded coaster to the red side.

We sat down at a table next to a window that overlooked a pasture and I realized that I was truly hungry for the first time in many days. My stomach growled.

"I can't believe Brenda's brother is still working," I said.

"I know. He's had three heart attacks. When he turned ninety in September they had a big party for him, thinking he would finally retire. Now he says working here is the only thing that keeps him from dying."

"Do you think he enjoys it?"

Liz stared down at the table, her brow deeply knit, as though she was really considering the question. Finally, she said, "I think so. I think it keeps his mind sharp."

"They say that's important. If you don't do anything, your brain gets soft and you die sooner."

"I guess I'll work at the bank forever, then."

"You won't."

"I will if they'll keep me."

The waitress came by and piled food onto our plates. We ate in silence.

Once Liz had finished most of hers, I said, "I have a question for you." She nodded pleasantly. "Have you dated anybody? You never mention it."

I thought she might get offended or dodge the question, but she replied without hesitation: "When I was thirty, I dated a man for three months." This information boggled me. It turned out the man was a physics professor at the university in a larger, neighboring town. He was fifty. Never married. "We met on the internet. A dating website," she said, sensing my befuddlement.

"What did you put on your profile?" I asked.

"What does anyone put? Just, you know, regular things. My interests."

"Which ones?"

"Birds, first of all. He was a birder, too. So, we had that in common."

"What happened after three months?"

"He wanted a more physical relationship." She appeared to glare at me for an instant but then it seemed she was only making a face at something behind me that I could not see, maybe something that was not physically in the room with us at all.

"So, you weren't sleeping with him?"

"No, actually that's the reason we stopped seeing each other."

I asked why it never happened and she shrugged, shaking her head. "I just couldn't do it," she said. "I really did want to, and I could get close, but every time it was about to actually happen I would totally freeze up and end it."

"Why, though?" I was worried she would ruffle at my prying, but she seemed unbothered.

She chewed a bite of food for a long time, thinking, before saying, "It's really strange, right? Because I liked this man a lot. He was wonderful."

I listened as she talked about her favorite date they'd been on. He'd picked her up on a Friday and driven her to Montreal, where he'd reserved a room at a nice bed-and-breakfast on the river. They drank ice wine and walked through the botanical gardens, then went to the open-air market and the art museum and watched acrobats spinning atop metal hoops outside the basilica at sunset. He took her to an expensive dinner where she wore what she described as a revealing dress, which I could hardly believe.

"And that was probably the happiest I've ever been in my life," she said.

My mouth hung open. I had no idea about any of this, and was taken aback to hear her talk so openly about her happiness at all. "Well, that all sounds great," I said. "What was the problem?"

"It's crazy."

"I already know you're crazy."

She smiled for a flash of a moment before her face darkened again. "No, really," she said.

"Just tell me."

"Okay. I always worried he was going to kill me." I looked at her seriously. She threw her hands up in the air. "See? I told you. I know it's crazy."

"Well," I said, exhaling slowly. "It is and it isn't."

"Anyway, it doesn't matter now. I looked him up a while ago. He moved away to work for another university and he's engaged to some woman named Dana."

"Oh."

"And I felt like such an idiot because of course he hasn't murdered her. He wouldn't have murdered me, either. I could have had a life with him by now. And it's especially stupid, because it wouldn't have changed anything about what you and I went through. I mean, I could've waited around this whole time driving myself crazy, like I have been, or I could have had children by now with this guy and probably done all sorts of fun things, and any which way she's still gone and not letting myself be with him didn't bring answers any sooner."

"Don't be so mean to yourself. You've had a life. And you still have so much time left for a whole new one, whatever you want. You aren't even middle aged."

"I suppose that's true." She scraped her fork around the plate. "Dana, his fiancée, is a food scientist." She looked up at me expectantly. I told her I wasn't sure what that meant. "She consults with companies on how to make baby food puree more appealing to the babies."

"Ew, how do you know that?"

"I stalked her internet profiles."

"Right."

"She's from Quebec. Her bio says she enjoys scuba diving and wild-life photography. She went to McGill. She's five years younger than me. Oh, and she has a pilot's license."

"Well, fuck her," I said. Liz snorted. I gave her a gentle, affectionate kick under the table.

She cleared her throat and sat up straighter against the back of the chair. "I can't ask you about your relationship because I don't approve of what you are doing right now." She said this matter-of-factly, like she was telling me that the microwave was broken so we would have to use the stovetop. Her hands remained folded neatly beneath her chin.

"Uh, okay." I sprinkled pepper over my food. "I'm not in a relation-ship, just to be clear."

"You act as though you are."

My face burned a little. I couldn't bring myself to look at her straight on so I stared out the window. Cold rain splattered down on the glass. Turkeys were being rushed back into the night barn by a pair of young boys, their shadows stretching out over the icy grass as the last glim-mers of daylight dipped down below the horizon. I wanted to be out there running after the turkeys, exhausting myself.

When I was saving up my secret money as a teenager, readying my-self to move away, I picked strawberries for a small farm. I arrived early every morning and went up and down the rows with a metal wagon that held two bushels. When it was full, I'd take it to be weighed and sorted. The owner would give me cash, and then usually I'd go back down the row and fill the wagon again. By the time I left, my fingers were saturated with acid from the berries, and they began to burn hor-ribly as the midday sun came down. Everything I touched made my fingertips sting. I came to hate strawberries. The smell still made me gag, and certainly I would've said that I hated the work itself, but thinking of it again I felt a longing for the kind of physical tiredness that frees you from your thoughts.

"Are you in there?" Liz asked, tapping softly at her temple. I nodded. Guilt weighed down on me. I thought of our meeting with Calloway the next day. My nervousness had a life of its own, like a little animal was trapped inside me, crawling from end to end searching for a way out.

"Well," I said. "It shouldn't seem that I'm in a relationship because I'm not."

"What are you saying? You stopped seeing her? Did you end it?"

I lied. "There's nothing to end."

"Bullshit."

"Can we please talk about something else?"

The waitress dropped off a basket of rolls. There was a little dish on the table full of butter squares wrapped in gold foil. The butter was cold. Steam rose from the bread. I placed one hand atop the butter and the other around the rolls.

"It's been interesting to watch you since you came back home," Liz said. "In some ways, you've changed so much, you're like a different person, but then you'll say something and I'll look at you and it's like you never aged a minute. Your mouth moves exactly the same way it always did. It's been kind of nice having you around."

I was surprised. She studied me from across table like I was a pinned bug. "What's so interesting about it?" I asked.

"Just, you know, observing you."

"And what are your observations?"

"Well, it's kind of strange that you're still sleeping on the couch. But I get it, I guess." The waitress came back around and dropped some more ears of corn onto Liz's plate. She ate them systematically, chewing each row with precision and leaving the cobs totally clean. Between mouthfuls, she said, "And I think you drink too much."

"Really?"

"I guess it's more the way that you drink."

I stared uncomfortably at the dregs of the scotch in the tumbler before me. "Don't worry," she said. "I don't care if you drink or not."

"I wasn't worrying."

"You just seem like you need it really badly." I took my hand off the bread and pushed my glass to the side of the table, out of our direct view. "There's more," she said, bringing a turkey wing to her mouth and delicately gnawing. A few moments later, she placed a meatless white bone back onto her plate and continued speaking. "At first, when you told me you were moving away, I was really worried. There were so many terrible things that could have happened to you. I imagined all of them. Part of me thought you would come back in a month or two, but then of course time went by and you didn't. You never even asked me for help."

"You already had enough problems. I wasn't going to cause you any more."

"That's not the point." She picked up her fork and pushed around some corn kernels on the plate. "I'm trying to tell you that I think you're brave."

This left me speechless. While Liz finished off the rest of her turkey, I sat there, holding back tears, wondering what it really meant to be brave and why, before this moment, I never thought that I might be. I'd only ever considered Liz to be brave; brave for staying in the face of what we'd lost, for never running away and never forgetting, even when it would have been easier to. It gutted me to think that my sister believed I had any courage. I felt fraudulent, somehow. Like I would be found out sooner or later, the real depths of my fearfulness exposed.

"I didn't know what you would do when I called you back in October," she said. "I felt so alone up here. I was in a real state. I kept wondering if you'd show up."

"Of course I was going to come. I told you I was getting in the car right then."

"I know," she said. "But people can surprise you."

"Not about this."

People began to clear out of the dining room. A large birthday group left, then a couple of families. Soon it was just us and three people in the corner, looking over a map they'd laid out atop the table.

"When Brenda asked if you loved anyone, you were talking about Eva, right?" Liz asked after a while. I nodded. She clucked her tongue disapprovingly.

"What?"

"That's a terrible choice."

"Why?"

"You've already been together. It's never a good idea to return to an ex."

"How would you know that?"

"I've read it in magazines many times. And anyway, don't you feel a little ridiculous getting back together with a high school girlfriend?"

I looked down at the table. I did and I didn't feel that way—there was a part of me that saw my entanglement with Eva as a return to an old knot I had to undo, something neglected, long deserving of being made right. If I was honest with myself, I had no idea whether we had any real chance as a couple. We still seemed to be sifting through the relics of what we'd meant to each other as young women, newly emerging into ourselves, hidden together in plain sight. Whether or not we could grow beyond that, I didn't know, but it still felt worth it to me.

To Liz, I said, "It's complicated."

"Love doesn't need to be complicated."

"Did you get that from a magazine, too?"

"No."

"Didn't you love the physics professor?"

"No. Of course I didn't." She looked appalled at the suggestion. "Perhaps I would have, if we'd had more time together. I liked him very much. I was extremely attracted to him. But that's just chemicals. Love should be more than that. It should be dependable."

Dessert arrived and we ate our pie in a companionable silence. If I leaned back in my chair, I could see Hiram from the corner of my eye, slowly making his way around the bar, wiping it down carefully and stopping every so often to collect fallen lime slices and cherries off the ground. He hummed softly as he worked, and I thought of the day Brenda ventured out into the woods with us. The gentle way she led Liz and me through the brush and bramble to such a grim place, somewhere that felt almost unfaceable to me, and met our grief with song. She held the afternoon, and us, together with her steadiness and her soaring, unflinching voice. Sometimes it seemed like that was all that could be done: either find the person who could hold you afloat in turmoil, or be that person yourself to somebody else. Taking turns, getting through it, until your final day. I watched my sister scrape the last bit of chocolate sauce off her plate, and made a silent wish that she would always find that kind of help when she needed it.

30

Calloway kept our time brief, claiming to have another meeting to get to right after. As we went through the usual greetings, I swung between feeling absolutely certain that there was something pointed and jealous in his tone with me, and that it was all in my own imagination. He did seem tired, though I believed everyone was tired. I never knew a single person who would have said they were well rested. But he appeared distracted, too. He looked at his phone a lot, which I could see bothered Liz. At one point, he left the room without explanation and returned ten minutes later, with a cup of coffee in his hand.

Every time we met before he'd given the impression of being a little afraid. Maybe not of us directly, but certainly intimidated by where he found himself within our private circumstances. I could understand it. He was tasked with straddling the divide between the personal pain and worries my sister and I shared, and the professional, almost clinical, duty he had to the investigation as it existed within the law. It was not a job I would want.

Today, I couldn't say he was being rude. Was he cold? Terse, maybe.

"I wanted to start by telling you something troubling I learned about this week," I said, watching him carefully for any change in demeanor.

Nothing. He stayed leaned back, aloof, blinking at me. I told him all about Robert, how I'd heard from an acquaintance, a witness, about the car break-in and then his conviction years later. I repeated the name.

"You know this guy?" I asked.

"Robert Miller, sure."

"He's been in here, I guess." I motioned toward the downward corridor, where I knew the holding cells were located.

"Not since I've been on the job," Calloway said. "In high school, Coach talked about him from time to time. Sort of a legend on the field. More of a cautionary tale, I guess." His face lit up just a bit. "He was going to go pro, you know. A scout came up from Pittsburgh to watch him play once."

"Well, instead he became a crook," I said, wanting to stamp out the faint glimmer of admiration in his eyes.

"You say your mother never mentioned the name to either of you?" He looked quickly between me and Liz. I shook my head no. Calloway gave a vague nod and looked down at some papers on his desk.

I waited a moment and then asked, "Don't you find this interesting?" I felt for a second that I wasn't asking so much about Robert as I was about our entire reason for meeting, his job here at the precinct, his assignment to our case, the trajectory of his life. I wanted to grab him by the shoulder and give him a good shake. Instead, I said, "I mean, don't you think this could be a lead?"

"Well, anything is possible." He shot me a barbed look, brief, but unmistakable, before adding, "Though, I don't think it's likely."

"Why the hell not?" My voice went up sharply at the end. Liz shut her eyes.

"Someone strung out like that, who was just trying to get a few dollars? No way they'd do such a clean job."

"You could still speak to him. Take a look around his place."

"Search the man's property?" Calloway furrowed his brow. "We can't just show up like that, no cause, nothing outstanding. You know that. Besides, seems to me he's already made even with the law."

"For the burglary incident, sure, but what about when he broke into our mother's car?"

"That was never even reported."

"No, but he was about a second away from pulling out a weapon."

"We don't know that."

"This is a firsthand account I'm relaying to you."

"A lady panics in the dark, thinks she sees something she maybe didn't," Calloway said in a nonchalant tone. "She's had about fifteen years to blow it up bigger in her head, gets even more hysterical when she hears you digging for suspects. God knows what he had in his pocket. Could be he was just bluffing, trying to scare them away. Sounds like your mother was going to try and kick his ass."

"So, what? You don't think this is even worth checking out?" I stared at him, mouth agape.

"Didn't say that." He picked up a pen and twirled it around his fingers. "I'll bring it up with the sheriff. See what he thinks." Calloway wrote something down on a piece of scrap paper and slid it into a folder. He then told us that there was still no news from the pathologist, but when we pressed for some sense of timeline, it turned out they hadn't spoken at all.

"I don't understand," Liz said. "You didn't call him? He never called you?"

"I suppose we kept missing each other," he replied. Now my sister turned to me with an angry, open mouth, a picture of the same outrage I shared. When we'd met in November, he'd used the word *hope* with us, more than once. He suggested that we have some. He described the new findings as *promising*. Now, nothing. Before I could get a word out, Calloway said, "It's not actually standard for a detective to adhere to a strict call schedule with a pathologist. When they have something for us, they have it."

"I don't understand," Liz said, twice in a row. I could see that she really didn't understand.

"Like I said, I've never had to keep a regular call schedule with them before." He was speaking as though he was doing us a special favor by being involved with our case.

"And how many times before have you dealt with something like this?" I asked.

"Sorry?"

"I'm wondering how many cases like this you've worked on. Like, what are you comparing it to? Ten others like this? Three? None?"

"I'm not comparing it to anything. Each missing persons case is entirely unique."

"Is this your first missing persons case?" I asked, already knowing from Eva that it was.

"I don't see why that's relevant."

I briefly entertained a fantasy of grabbing the back of his head and smashing it down into the desk. In this imagining, his face cracked up and fell apart like brittle papier-mâché when it made contact with the surface. I thought of what it would feel like to sweep the shards of his face into my hand like breadcrumbs and blow them into the trash can.

"It's relevant because it indicates whether or not you would know if it's standard to keep scheduled communication with the medical examiner's office in a situation like this," I said.

"Are you asking me if I know how to do my job?" Calloway's cool, detached composure was starting to slip. His cheeks were red. I, too, felt a wild, uncontrollable anger rising through my body. Once I'd seen the top of a grain silo come loose in hurricane winds and bounce crazily around a farm, up in the air. It popped into the sky twenty, thirty feet and then soared along, dipping sharply downward and spiraling into the storm's grasp. It was impossible to tell where it would land, or when. Eventually it crashed into a large billboard and both the billboard and the silo went tumbling together, hopelessly mangled, into a field.

"I'm not the only one assigned to your mother's case," Calloway said. "As you know, the sheriff has been involved in this from the start."

"We haven't seen the sheriff in months."

"Have you asked to? He's here now." Calloway raised his voice just barely. "And he's here most days." Liz didn't speak. I could see she was confused by the tension in the room, and I wasn't able to tell whether she suspected why it was there. I still wasn't quite convinced of it myself. One moment I felt sure that he'd caught on to me and Eva, that there was no way he couldn't have after running into me that night, and then the next I thought it just as likely he was only being a peevish, immature man.

"He's never called us," I said.

"When have you called him?"

Just then, a spider about as big as a peach pit dropped down from the ceiling and hung there for a moment, swaying slightly on its translucent line, before falling onto Calloway's desk and scuttling rapidly toward him over a stack of papers. The look of its legs gave me a queasy, panicked feeling. Fine, glossy hairs were shooting off the sides, all eight of them moving in such fast synchronicity it almost appeared to glide on air. Without thinking, I stood up and grabbed a thick folder from the desk organizer. I slapped it down on the spider with such force Calloway's hair blew back from his forehead. I was leaning over far enough to see the pores on his nose. The corner of his right eye was bloodshot, delicate pink veins fanning out toward the iris. We stared at each other for a long second, both breathing heavily. I released my hand from the folder and sat back down. Silently, he picked it up and held it over the wastepaper basket, scraping the flattened insect into the bin with a tissue, a faint curl of disgust on his lips. Liz glanced between us, one eyebrow raised.

"Anyway," Calloway sighed. "Before you can ask if we've spoken with Nick Haines, no. We haven't. But I thought I'd mention to you that his name came up on my radar recently." At this, my sister squeezed the edges of her seat so hard I saw her knuckles blanch. "You know the Rocking Horse?"

"The bar on West Street," I said.

"Yes."

"What about it?" My heart raced.

"I've been made aware that he was involved in a fight there two nights ago, with three other men. It didn't result in any arrests, but it was bad enough that the owners called for us."

"What was the fight?" Liz asked. "What was it about?"

"A woman, I believe."

"You don't know?" I said.

"I didn't respond to the call. This information came to me from another officer."

Liz wanted to know what all this about the fight could mean. "He's violent," she said. "We know that. How many more ways does he have to show you before you actually do something?"

"We are doing something. I promise you."

"You're going to use this to arrest him, then?"

"No, I told you I wasn't a responding officer on this incident. I can't just go cuff him, days after the fact." I could see he was growing exasperated.

"The sheriff once said it was common to use misdemeanors as a way to bring people in for more serious suspicions," Liz said. I looked at her, impressed by her quickness.

Calloway stared down at the desk and shut his eyes before speaking. "Look, I just brought it up because I thought you'd be interested to know. It certainly perked my ears up. But clearly, our guys didn't see fit to charge him with a misdemeanor for this. Though if there's anything in the pathology report that even looks like it might have a shadow of Nick Haines on it, the sheriff and I won't hesitate to take action."

"Action," Liz repeated.

"Yes."

"And that would have to be after you actually manage to speak with the pathologist, then," I said.

"Yes." He crossed his arms and looked at me straight on. "It would be after that."

Out in the hallway, once we were out of earshot, Liz muttered, "I hate him so much." The walls were lined with photos of the sheriff and each officer, only four in total, and several group shots commemorating what seemed like Christmas toy drives from years gone by. My sister scowled at the photos, briefly pausing at a poster outlining the rules for deer season licenses. "What is this place even good for?" She spoke in a harsh whisper. "No one does anything. None of these people care about us at all."

Once we were already out in the parking lot, I reached into my jacket pockets and realized I'd forgotten one of my gloves. I felt around desperately for it but already knew that it was sitting on the chair in Calloway's office. I could see it there, in my mind's eye. I was sure it had fallen out when I sat down at first, and then I'd gotten too fired up to remember to grab it when we'd left.

"I forgot my glove," I said, stopping in my tracks. Liz made an irate, huffing sound. She had her coat zipped all the way up to the chin. The zipper pull had broken off at some point and she had a bent paper clip shoved through the loop instead. It wobbled as she dug for her keys. The sky hung low over town with a thick, hazy cloud cover. Everything was gray. The snow on the sides of streets was gray, the police station was painted gray, Liz's coat was gray. There was a stillness in the air that suggested more snow might come at any moment.

"I'm not going back to get it for you," she said.

"I wasn't going to ask."

"Do you really need it?"

"It's, like, ten degrees. Yes."

"Don't you have another pair?"

"This is the good pair."

"I know you don't want to go back in there."

Down the road, a couple of streetlamps blinked on. Liz pulled her hair out of its elastic and tucked it all down into the neck of her parka like a scarf, covering up her ears and cheeks.

"Just be quick about it," she said. "Dash in and out. I'll pull the car around."

When I came back in, the switchboard operator was on her knees, crouching by the row of plastic chairs, patting around for something that seemed to have rolled beneath them. She didn't glance up as I jogged past. When I got to Calloway's office, I saw immediately that my glove was sitting on the desk in front of him. He must have gotten up, retrieved it from where I'd been seated, and placed it in the middle of all his folders and paperweights and loose pens. I knocked once on the doorframe and walked in without waiting for an invitation.

Without a word, he picked up my glove with one hand and held it out before him, the way you might hold up a glass to be refilled with water. Our fingertips met for a brief moment as I took it from him. The warmth of his skin repulsed me. The softness of it. It made me think of his veins, all the inner workings of his body that ticked away in the dark beneath the cover of his outer person. Part of the revulsion was knowing that we shared this softness. He and I were barely different. If I were to touch the hand of my mother's killer, I would feel warmth there, too. People would sometimes try to console me and Liz by referring to this unknown person as a monster. *The monster who took her from you*, or, *only a monster could do such a thing*. Outwardly, I'm sure I expressed some gratitude, they were only trying to be kind, but privately I always thought that person wasn't a monster. They were just another human. And that was much more frightening.

I shoved the glove back into my pocket and gave Calloway a firm nod. He went back to shuffling his papers around. From somewhere down the hallway I heard the echo of a croaking, wet cough.

As I was about to cross over the threshold of his office, he spoke in a voice so low I almost missed it.

"Be careful at night."

"What?" I stopped in the doorway and looked back over my shoulder.

"There's a lot of black ice out there." He motioned out the window. "Harder to see it coming at night." A wan smile came over his face and then disappeared.

31

I went to Eva's unannounced the next day. I knew it was a risky, stupid idea. I tried to talk myself out of it many times. I didn't even know if she was home, or whom she might be with, but I couldn't sit still. Every time I tried to rest or work or put my mind onto something else, Calloway's words looped in my thoughts. On the drive over, I practiced a whole speech. I had a mind to really tell her how I felt. Not just about her, but about myself and the way I felt so eroded and caught between, but the moment she opened the door I blurted out, "You have to make a choice. I can't do this anymore." She blinked, then took me by the hand and pulled me inside.

A vase of pink roses sat out on the counter, droplets of water glistening on the petals. A pile of fresh laundry sat half folded on the table, filling the room with a warm, sweet smell. I repeated myself, though this time my voice wavered, sounding almost like a question that I was asking of myself.

"Why are you doing this right now?" she asked. "What happened?" She came over and unzipped my jacket and then slid her hand up under my shirt, resting her palm on the bare skin over my sternum. I felt that she was trying to calm me down, anticipating my outburst and wanting to extinguish things before they had a chance to erupt. I told her that nothing happened, that this had been on my mind for weeks. She insisted there must have been a reason. "This is unlike you," she said.

"What is?"

"Showing up so abruptly, even the way you're talking. You seem weird."

I told her then about our meeting with Calloway. I wondered if she already knew about it, but the way she cringed, taking her hand off my chest and shoving it into her back pocket, made me think they hadn't spoken. "I knew something was off," I said. "His whole demeanor was different."

"You might be reading into things too much."

"Jesus Christ." My voice broke as the words came out. I wanted to throw my fists against the wall. "How can you say that to me? He obviously knows about us. What really happened after I left that night?"

"I told you, he was tired and drunk, and we had an argument. It wasn't about you." I asked what it was about, if not me. A sharp, exasperated sigh escaped her mouth. She conceded that it was, at the start, somewhat about me. She emphasized *somewhat,* pausing afterward as though it would sink in better if I had to listen to the silence after the word. "He was pissed that I had someone over after I told him I wasn't feeling well enough to see him."

"And how did you explain it?"

"I told him you were coming to get something I'd borrowed."

"At two in the morning."

She insisted that he didn't suspect why I was really there. I told her it seemed to me he understood perfectly. Her denial both alarmed and impressed me. I could understand how she got to be so good at it, living two lives at once for such a long time, but it gave me a bad feeling all the same.

"He hasn't brought it up with me since," she said. "Not once."

"That doesn't mean anything," I snapped.

"You knew he was in my life." Her tone was suddenly serious.

Heavy. I felt like I needed to hold on to something to remain upright but I didn't want to seem frail.

"I only ever knew because your brother knocked when I happened to be here with you, and you panicked." I scoffed. "It's not like you were going to tell me."

"That's not true."

"Oh, okay." My voice took on a sarcastic, bitter tone. I hated the way it sounded, but I hated, too, what she was saying to me.

"I really was going to tell you. I just didn't know how. I was trying to find an easy way to do it." I tried to imagine what way would have been easy. If she had divulged everything the first time we spoke, in the supermarket, would that have been easy? I imagined the scene like I was standing over a roofless doll's house. There were the pyramids of canned food, the reflective tile floor, and Eva and me, two moving points on a map, our paths moments from intersecting. If she had told me then, would I have walked away? I wanted to say yes, but I knew that wasn't true. The truth was, I would have done nothing differently.

She went on. "Whatever happened to *it's not my business, you don't owe me anything*? Not too long ago you were standing right there in that same spot going on about how you didn't even care and you wished I never even told you. Now, this." She shook her head angrily. "What are you asking me for, Jess? You barge in here and tell me I have to choose, but is that because you want to be with me or because you don't want me to be with him?" She began pacing around the room, shouting breathlessly. "You aren't asking me to pick between you and him. You're asking me to pick between you and my feeling of security in this town. You don't even care that it could create real problems for me to break up with him and start openly seeing you. I could get kicked out of this place, for starters." Eva gestured around the cabin, eyes flashing. "My sister-in-law lets me live here for free, you know we don't really get along. She could boot me any day. She's threatened to before. My brother's totally under her spell, he wouldn't stop it. And I still haven't found another place to work after that shit went down at the hotel. It's not like there's a lot of jobs here."

I asked her what she wanted me to say. I didn't even mean it rhetorically. I really wished a hand would drop from the sky, down through the roof, and move me through the rest of the conversation like a puppet.

Eva's voice became eerily calm. "Let's just say I did choose. Let's say I sacrificed all that for you, took this huge risk. What's stopping you from up and leaving any day? Nothing's keeping you here."

"What do you mean there's nothing keeping me? My mother's case is the whole reason I'm even back."

"Wasn't enough to keep you last time." She shot me a bitter look and clipped over to the laundry pile. Her hands were fast and angry, folding the clothes and tossing them haphazardly to the side. I leaned against a beam by the doorway, watching in silence before saying, "What's keeping you here, then?"

"What?" She set down a folded shirt.

"At least I had a reason to come back. You act like you're trapped in this town. You haven't gotten a new job, you're afraid to date who you want, there's fuck all to do here. What's making you happy enough to stay?"

"I never said I was happy in Knife River. It's just where I live."

"It doesn't have to be."

"Well, I told you already, I check in on my father a couple times a week. His tremors have been getting worse."

"Your brothers and their families don't help?"

"They help, too," she said. "You know, this really isn't your concern."

"I know it isn't."

"So let's leave my decision to stay here in town out of it."

"Fine."

"I don't understand why we have to change anything," she said. "Why can't we just go back to the way we were doing things before?"

"What, you mean why can't you have me when you want me, and then do whatever the hell you want with your cop boyfriend while I pretend I don't care about it when I have to see him? That sounds good to you? I bet it does, actually. Why wouldn't it? You're the only one who doesn't get totally fucking fleeced."

"You're the one who suggested it in the first place."

"Well, that was stupid of me."

"You know I don't, like, *enjoy* being with him." She glared at me. "Not in that way. I thought you understood that." I did. I also knew what she meant about feeling afraid to break off on her own without a job, without the help of a family. Particularly if she started rejecting men in favor of women, particularly if the woman was me. "I'm not happy about any of this," she said. "But this is my life. I'm not going to make it any harder just so you can feel like you won something." I told her I certainly didn't feel as though I'd won anything.

It was starting to get dark out. The floodlight on her front step switched on with a loud, droning buzz. She asked me if I had anything else to say and I walked out silently to the picnic table by the woodpile and smoked a cigarette in response. I was miserably cold. Pain radiated from my fingertips. I wanted her to know what it was like to be un-afraid to kiss another woman in the middle of the day, in the middle of the sidewalk, and then walk home together without looking back over her shoulder. I wanted her to know that feeling, even if it wasn't with me. I thought about her life there in town, how she had to find a way around the rumors and suspicion, everything that she tolerated trying to make things easier on herself. Who was I to say that it was better to be brave or honest than to want to feel safe? Any person would want security for themselves, or at least the illusion of it. I didn't want to feel like Eva and I were on opposite sides of something. I smoked two more cigarettes, finishing the pack, then gathered all the butts and tucked them beneath a rock so I didn't have to look at them.

When I came back inside, Eva was in the bathtub. I sat down on the floor, leaning my elbows on the ledge, and watched the bubbles rippling around her knees. Her hair was coiled up into a loose bun and she was taking loud, purposeful breaths. The little room was hot and clammy and smelled strongly of rose oil.

"Get in," she said.

Without hesitation, I stood up and pulled my clothes off. The water was scalding. I lowered myself down gradually, allowing each section of my body to wince before relaxing into the heat. We leaned back on either end, our legs tangled together in the middle. Eva's breasts rose and then submerged, coming in and out of my view as the water's surface leveled out.

She asked, "Do you want to stop seeing me?" I shook my head no. "Are you going to anyway?" I looked away. This question I could not answer so readily.

I saw plainly that she was not perfect—she didn't seem entirely sure of what she wanted, or at least felt unable to break out and grab it, and she'd been dishonest with me. But what really hit me hard was the realization that her presence did not magically transform me in the way I'd long fantasized it would. Being together again did not make me suddenly good at, or even comfortable with, emotional intimacy. It didn't make me less distant and inward, or more reachable. I was still just my same self, ready to pack up and leave any day. And we were just two people wanting each other badly, persistently, against all better judgment. I exhaled slowly. Condensation dripped steadily down from the tin ceiling. It was made up of twelve squares, each perforated with a pattern of concentric circles. There was a space between the wall and the last square by the window, a tuft of insulation poked through the opening.

"I know you don't *like* being with Jack," I said. "I get it. But how do you actually feel about him?"

She raised one eyebrow at me and then stared down into the water, cupping it between her hands and letting it pour back down onto her knees. "There are times when I feel like I hate him, but I don't think it's actually him that I hate." I waited for her to go on. Wind howled outside the window. "In a way, he's my friend, I guess. That probably doesn't make sense to you."

"It might," I said.

"He cares about me, he just doesn't know me like he thinks he does." She shrugged and went on to explain how he'd installed the skylight over her bed in the loft because he worried she wasn't getting enough sunlight up there, and before they'd even kissed for the first time, he'd rushed her all the way to the hospital, an hour outside of town, at two in the morning with his police lights flashing because she thought she had appendicitis. He waited several hours in an uncomfortable plastic chair while they ran all kinds of tests, only to discover that there was nothing the matter. He wasn't even annoyed about it, she said.

"Do you ever feel guilty?" I asked. "Being with him like this, knowing he cares about you but you don't feel the same way?"

She used her foot to turn the faucet on and let more water in before deftly switching it back off with her toes. "What? You're worried about Jack now?"

"No. I'm just trying to figure out where your head is at."

"And I'm trying to tell you."

A silence fell between us. I sank into the tub far enough that the water covered my mouth. I took slow, careful breaths through my nose and imagined Calloway coming through the door, his boots making the floor creak, the cold outside air rising off his skin. A searing anger spread within my body as I thought about it. I hated him with a kind of intensity that I wasn't sure I'd felt for anyone else before, at least not in this same way. It seemed like something we shared, actually. A mutual pool of disdain.

"Anyway, maybe you'll just go back to your ex," Eva muttered.

"What?" The word bubbled out of me, my mouth still half submerged. I raised myself up. Soap lingered on my lips. "Who are you talking about?"

"The one you broke up with a little while ago."

"No," I said. "There's no chance of that. I promise you."

"Still, it's not like you'll stay around here forever." She crossed her arms under the water. There was a luring edge to her voice; this was a question posing as a comment. "I think about it a lot, you know," she said. "What it'll be like when you leave again."

The image of her sitting in my bedroom alone, years ago when I'd left, came to me. I wished I didn't know about that. I wished I could erase everything from my mind and go on with my life, oblivious to the tracks I'd already left in the world.

"I'm planning on moving to Maine," I said, surprising myself. I hadn't meant to discuss it with her. I hadn't even mentioned it to my sister.

"What's in Maine?"

"I know someone there. This nice retired periodontist who could maybe point me in the right direction. I want to work outdoors. I don't know, I just want to go someplace new. I've been thinking about it for a while and it feels like the time is coming up."

"I've never been there."

"Me, neither."

When the bath went cold we crawled up to her loft and had sex on and off until the middle of the night. I kept an ear out on the driveway, though I wasn't sure what I could possibly do if Calloway were to arrive. I wondered if he would hit me. Most men liked to say that they would never hit a woman, though that hardly seemed like it could be true since so many women I knew had been hit, at least once, by a man. I imagined him injuring me in a fit of jealous rage. Eva looked at me, a sliver of moonglow beaming down on her face through the skylight.

She appeared to be reading my thoughts. The air between us changed. She brought her hand up from below the sheet and slid three fingers into my mouth, gently at first, almost distracted, the way someone shifts positions as they're falling asleep. Then she started shoving them down, almost choking me, holding me in place while fucking me roughly with the other hand.

Driving over, my intention had been to demand a decision. Now, I just wanted her to snuff me out like a candle. In my mind, I drifted as far away from myself as possible. She pulled at my hair and sunk her teeth into my neck and I gasped, groaning, and envisioned a vast stretch of ocean; my body floating on the surface, disintegrating, lapping waves carrying me off in pieces. In the middle of it all she stopped and touched the sides of my face tentatively, as if wanting to reassure herself that I was still really there. We looked at each other, unblinking in the dark. I could make out the vague shapes of the nightstand and the trunk where she kept her clothes. I held my hands over hers. Things began to feel less depthlessly sexual and more about something else, something related to our fears and our smallness in the world. I knew that I was still in love with her, that all my old feelings for her had survived inside me all the time we were apart, lying quietly, waiting for this moment to emerge. There was something about it that mortified me a little, like my falling back into her so hard, so instantly, was a sign that though I'd moved away, I hadn't truly left. Some woman at a party in Brooklyn had once made a comment to me, after learning where I'd grown up, that we can never really leave where we're from. At the time, I thought she was just trying to be rude for reasons probably related to money or her own anxieties, but here I began to feel there may have been a grain of truth in it, whether the woman meant there to be or not.

Eva pushed me down onto my back and began to kiss the dip in the base of my neck. I was intensely aware of my breathing, the fragile lump of my throat beneath her lips, which was beneath her teeth. She rested there for a moment, exhaling into my skin. Before I could stop myself, I said, "When I leave town, I don't want to go without you." I could feel the reverberation of my own voice rumbling against her face. There was a stretch of silence. I began to wonder if she'd drifted off, although I could not make out the sound of her breath. Her silence was purposeful. It aimed to conceal her thoughts. I waited. Some animal crawled along the tin roof, I could hear its scaly little feet moving above our heads. I imagined the cabin falling apart, piece by piece. The roof flying off in a strong wind, disappearing over the horizon, all four walls falling down and getting overgrown with moss and ragweed. The front door drifting downstream on the creek, washing ashore in some distant place, cracked and bloated with water. In time, her voice emerged from the dark.

"I don't want you to go without me, either," she said.

It was the kind of exchange that would normally have left me feeling vulnerable and nauseated by my own tenderness, but in that moment, my tenderness was easy to accept. Neither of us seemed sure of what to say next. She climbed downstairs and returned with a glass of cold water. We both drank from it desperately, passing the cup back and forth and then pressing the cool, wet sides onto each other's necks. As I drank, the water spilled down my chin and pooled in the crease of my hip. Eva dabbed at it absently, wiping her fingers against her own thigh before drinking the glass dry.

I left right before sunup but couldn't bear to return to my house and face the day, so I drove in slow circles around the little park in the center of town, watching the Christmas lights twinkle in the blue dawn.

32

Paint was discovered beneath one of my mother's fingernails. A microscopic smear of particles, discoverable only with a powerful magnifying lens. Motor vehicle paint. Black, satin finish, from the chassis of a truck. I didn't even know they had her fingernails. Not all of them, it turned out. Just three. We didn't get this update from Calloway. We hadn't heard from him at all in two weeks. January faded into February, and not a word from the precinct had come our way. Calloway's name hadn't arisen again between me and Eva, either, though I knew she was still seeing him from time to time. Twice when I'd texted her, wanting to see whether I could drive over to her place, I'd gotten only a brief *not tonight* in return. It made me feel sick, but also a little grateful for the warning to stay away.

Finally, around the second week of February, Liz returned home from work an hour early. I was sitting at the table with my headphones on, finishing a recording, and hadn't even noticed her car pulling into the driveway. She appeared before me, a serious expression on her face, and motioned for me to shut my laptop. I pushed all my work stuff aside and stared up at her, a little anxious. I knew it was rare for her to leave the bank before her shift ended.

"I've decided it's time for us to call the medical examiner's office ourselves," she said. "We can't just keep waiting on Calloway." I shifted my eyes to the ground. Before I could say anything, she said, "I found the number already online. I know they normally communicate directly with the police, but there's an exception for next of kin. I read that they have to provide us with information if we ask for it." Her voice was stoic.

While she sat down with the landline and began to dial, I went to retrieve the cordless set from the other room so I could listen in. It took a few minutes to get connected to the right extension. We were routed first to the wrong department, then back to the operator, who asked for our last name and case number again. Liz spoke slowly and firmly, a pen already poised in her hand for notes. When we were on hold for the second time, she covered the receiver briefly and said quietly to me, "Let me do the talking." I didn't argue. The hold music was cheerful and heavily synthesized. It played on a short loop, enraging me every time it began again.

"Why don't they use something else?" I whispered to Liz. "This is, like, kind of inappropriate." She nodded in agreement.

A minute later, the medical examiner was on the line. He sounded somewhat surprised to hear from my sister. "I'd have thought you would have spoken with the detective by now," he said. "We faxed over microscopy results a couple days ago."

I could see the color drain from Liz's face as she listened. "No," she choked out. "He hasn't contacted us."

"Odd," he muttered. "Well, hold on, let me just pull this out for you." I heard some papers rustling in the background, and then what sounded like a metal drawer sliding open. The medical examiner breathed long, wet breaths into the receiver as he searched, clicking his tongue every few seconds as he sifted through documents. "Here we are," he said. "I've got it in front of me now."

Liz began to furiously jot notes, her brow knit in concentration as he spoke. The paint, he said, was heavy-duty, weather-resistant primer.

When he started to explain the paint's origins, my sister interjected. "How can you know it's from the chassis of a truck?"

"We were able to link this particular primer in the forensic database to an American manufacturer," he said. "Looking further, we learned that manufacturer serviced only noncommercial trucks until the year 2002." This was partly why the pathologist's work had taken so long; it was difficult to trace the material all the way to its original source. And then there was nail polish, too, he told us. Traces of it on the same fingernail. They'd had to work to isolate the different remnants, then analyze each separately.

My heart started to race. Our mother had been good with mechanics. She liked to fix our car troubles herself. But we'd never owned a truck. Who did? Most people around here. Most men, certainly. Nick Haines. Robert Miller was pictured in the yearbook with one, likely his own. But Eva's father and brothers had trucks, and our neighbor Paul, and half the houses on our street. So, too, did Jeff. I could remember him pulling up to our track meets in an old blue one with a tarp over the back, sour-smelling exhaust billowing from the tailpipe. I thought of Bill then with his passenger van and felt momentary relief, but it ebbed as quickly as it came. How could I know he hadn't also owned a truck at that time?

"If the chassis paint found its way onto her, then isn't it possible the nail polish would've found its way onto the truck?" Liz asked. The medical examiner agreed, going so far to say he thought it likely, but stopped short of making any claims toward a manner of death. They hadn't been able to draw a connection between the aperture on her temple and the presence of the paint. They might be able to, or not. They were still trying to learn more about the paint itself—what make and model it might have come from and when it could have gotten on her person. That could take another week or more, and the sample might not be substantial enough to draw any conclusions. All this information made me feel dizzy. I tilted my head down toward the table and rubbed the back of my neck. I heard the examiner say the words *soft tissue*. It made me want to step out of my own body, leaving my skin like an empty suit. The absence of soft tissue made things difficult. The absence of soft tissue made her unreal, unreachable, unrecognizable to me. If her hands were intact, if they'd been able to find her sooner, we might have known if her fingers dragged along an undercarriage or if she was holding on to something.

Liz asked more questions about timing and potential outcomes, but I was barely listening. I thought of every stranger my mother might have passed by on the through roads that day. How many of them would've been driving something that matched this description? What if she'd simply stopped to help some harmless person with engine trouble, and the paint meant nothing at all? What if it was from the day before, or she'd picked up some broken piece of junk on the side of the road while she was out walking and examined it, getting its dust on her fingers, before casting it aside? But what if she hadn't, and it really was from Nick Haines's truck? What if Liz's theory had been right this whole time? That morning he was first questioned, the police had done only a cursory search—glove box, back seat, long bed—but by the time they returned to his home with a warrant the truck had been thoroughly cleaned inside and out. The matter of her being had long since been scattered to places unknown, carried away by the wind or washed away by rain or destroyed by another person's own doing. Skin, hair, blood. Cars, door handles, sink faucets, floors, bedsheets. How could I ever know where she went in her last hours? What she laid her hands on, or what she might have run from?

Liz thanked the medical examiner and said goodbye. They hung up and I listened to the dial tone for a few seconds, a little dazed, before setting my cordless receiver down on the table. We shared a quiet moment. I tried to stretch my hand across the table to squeeze hers, but couldn't quite reach.

Finally, I said, "We should've asked what color it was."

"What?"

"Her nail polish."

"Oh," Liz said. She glanced over her notes and shook her head slowly. I wasn't sure I'd ever seen a person look so sad. Her face was the color of old dishwater. "I wish I had." I felt guilty for mentioning it and said that it wasn't important. Liz said it wasn't *un*important, and I had to agree. "I don't like that he said it was odd that Calloway hadn't contacted us already," she said.

"I don't think it's a big deal," I said, a film of sweat beginning to materialize on my palms. Liz folded her hands curtly before her atop the placemat and stared at me. I went on. "I'm just saying we probably shouldn't read into it. Maybe he was waiting on more details." By now I'd grown a little queasy.

"That's honestly what you think?" Liz sounded more defeated than accusatory.

"I don't know."

At that moment, a large piece of ice fell off the roof and came crashing down onto the porch steps with a loud, jarring sound. Water in a glass on the table rippled a bit and I could hear the plates rattle, just for a moment, in the cabinet above the sink, next to the window. The ice had fractured into three large sections and as the biggest piece fell away I saw that one of the bricks had broken. We looked at it.

My sister sighed. "Does he know?" she asked.

"Of course he doesn't." The lie felt cumbrous and sour as it came from my mouth. Even as I was saying it, I started to wish that I hadn't.

"How are you so sure?"

"It's fine," I told her. "You don't need to worry."

"I'm glad you came home, Jess." Liz said. "But sometimes I wish I were doing all this alone."

33

I woke up early that Sunday morning and slipped out the door while Liz was still asleep upstairs. An hour away in the town of Wolf, there was a Quaker meeting house. I hadn't planned on going. It wasn't a place I'd even thought about in years. But when I'd opened my eyes that morning, the image of it came to me; this little white house in the middle of a field. A mossy, sagging roof. Windows with green painted shutters. A small, old cemetery around the back with headstones popping up crookedly from the earth.

I'd been there once before, years ago, when I was about eight and our grandfather died in a hospice facility in another state. Our mother rarely mentioned him. I'd never even met him. Liz had once, but seemed unfazed by the news of his passing. Still, I remember my mother staying awake for two entire days after the phone call, scrubbing the house from crevice to crevice. Pretty, long-stemmed glasses I couldn't remember seeing before were brought out and washed to a sparkle. My bedroom carpet was shampooed with a vile-smelling blue liquid. She paused for brief, fitful rests on the couch before getting up to clean some more.

By the second day, Liz, made uncomfortable by all this, walked to the library. I watched her go, desperate to join, but instead I stayed home, tethered by a feeling of duty. I stood around in the doorways, watching my mother cautiously, the way you'd watch a funny-acting raccoon wandering around in the daylight. I was worried, and a little spooked. I couldn't tell what she was thinking. The next morning, a Sunday, my mother, who was not very clean herself after all this, brought me out to the car. Liz would not come out of her room. The two of us drove this same drive to the same little church where we sat on rickety wooden chairs in a wide circle with people I'd never seen before. No other children were present. Pale light floated down onto us from the vaulted window. We sat in near silence for an hour. Most everyone kept their eyes shut and their head bowed slightly forward as though they were sleeping, though it was clear to me that they were not.

There was a handful of other cars in the parking lot when I arrived. Three trucks, I couldn't help but notice. As I walked toward the entry, I could see the worn headstones poking out of the snow in the field. Beyond, a willow tree at the edge of a pond. I remembered this tree. It fascinated me as a child. I'd never seen a weeping willow before. Now it was larger and more gnarled, its many long fingers dipped toward the icy water. I went inside and took my place in the circle of chairs. The congregants mostly kept their coats and scarves on. Everyone looked serene and peaceful. I suddenly felt at peace, too. The silence in the room had a very soft, gauzy quality to it. Just being there gave me the feeling that I was floating along the top of warm water. Some people moved their mouths as if in silent conversation. It was hard to tell if time passed slowly or not in this room. It almost seemed to not exist at all, as if time simply marched around this little house during the hours of quiet prayer, leaving us out of its path entirely. Was I praying? I didn't know. If I was, it was for the heart enough to wait patiently, knowing that all things were passing. To be still and find comfort in time's great current, which had swept away all troubles that came before mine, and would carry mine away from me, too, and would eventually sweep me and everyone else in the surrounding chairs off the slate entirely.

Against the windowpane, a spider crawled along its web. Usually, looking at a spider gave me the creeps, but on this morning I felt at ease, peaceful. Content to watch it from the comfortable distance of my seat. Daylight caught in the silk and cast a brilliant sheen. The spider leapt from corner to corner, slinging more thread, expanding her home. If something blew the web down, she would simply spin it again. Everything she needed existed already within her own body. Beyond the glass, light reflected off the snow-covered meadow. Warmth flooded the room as the sun rose higher in the sky.

When I'd visited this meeting house as a child, my mother had asked the congregation to hold my grandfather in the light. He was a Quaker. A Friend, as they called it. His parents and their parents had been, too. My mother made this request of the group and then promptly sat back down. I'd never heard the phrase *hold in the light* before, but I felt that I understood it. Out in the parking lot, as we were getting ready to leave, she doubled over and let out a long, ugly groan, her hands on her knees. The groan lifted up at the end and became more of a shriek. It was the sound of an openly wounded person. You could hear she was not just in pain, but also perplexed by her pain, like she'd been handed a little animal that was biting her and she could not, no matter how she tried, find a way to put it down. The other people making their way through the parking lot were not alarmed. It was their steadiness, how placid they remained in the face of her moaning, that kept me from being scared.

On the way home, we made an abrupt stop at a diner where my mother ate ravenously. I realized it had been days since she'd taken a bite of food. The waitress put us in a far corner and brought me an unsolicited bowl of ice cream. This was the first time I can recall my mother seeming young to me. Normally, she watched over my sister and me with a careful gaze. Even when she was drunk, or busy with something, I never felt that we'd left her mind completely. To me, she existed within the dull, impenetrable sphere of grown people. But here I could see that I was not in her thoughts at all. Here I saw her as just a woman. A young woman. It was clear she did not possess the bound-less wisdom I'd assumed she did. There were things she did not know the answers to. Those things were lurking all around us. She would not always know what to do. She could not see what was coming next. There were things she wouldn't be able to keep us safe from.

When she finished eating, she asked me, "Do you regret not meet-ing your grandfather?" I'd been alive for such a meager scrap of time, less than a decade. I knew nothing about regret. I *knew* that I knew nothing about it. I got the sense she was really asking herself if she should regret not letting us meet. I shook my head no. "He was a dif-ficult man," she sighed, looking out the window. "We didn't talk for a long time." A display of richly decorated desserts spun slowly in a mir-rored case. I could hear the faint whir of the little motor inside. In the mirror: cakes reflecting endlessly back on themselves. My mother wiped tears from her eyes and counted some money out on the table. When we got home, Liz was at the kitchen table doing her homework. She didn't ask where we'd gone, and I never told her.

Inside the meeting house now, one woman across the circle from me was moved to speak and stood, addressing those present in a somber tone. She talked briefly about the difficulty she had finding the pres-ence of God in her middle age.

"When I was younger," she said, "I felt him everywhere." She sounded less downtrodden about it than befuddled, like she'd put her keys down somewhere and still couldn't find them after turning the whole house upside down. Everyone listened to her carefully. I was never sure how to answer the question of whether or not I believed. I often thought, with reverence, about the force that prompted the uni-verse's initial expansion. I liked to be reminded of how expendable my own body was. Just a fleck of dust. And I did sometimes feel a rippling awareness of a presence that presided above life on earth. It didn't al-ways feel benevolent, nor vengeful, but it seemed to have eyes.

The woman took her seat and silence fell again. Afterward, in the annex, some of the congregants set up a table with coffee and doughnuts. They all knew one another. I poured myself a cup and stood to the side, letting the coffee warm my hands. These people were friendly, though did not act particularly interested in me, which came as a relief. I got another coffee. I let the soft buzz of their conversations replace my own thoughts.

On the way back into Knife River, I stopped at the gas station. As I stood at the pump waiting for my tank to fill, a police cruiser pulled in. It was muddy, with a dent on the back bumper. The name of our township was emblazoned in blue and gold letters along the sides. It circled the lot before coming to a stop off to the side by the coin-operated car vacuum. A uniformed man got out of the driver's side and walked into the mini-mart. I had seen him a few times at the station. He was an officer, possibly even younger than Calloway.

As I walked into the store to buy cigarettes, the young officer came back out. Our reflections drew closer on either side of the glass door. We were looking at each other, seemingly both in recognition but hesitant to make an acknowledgment. The door swung open toward me. I stepped to the side. He held two coffees in his hands, and walked briskly past the threshold. Our eyes met. I gave a quick nod. As he passed, I heard him mutter under his breath. There was a half of a second where I couldn't understand what he said. His tone was low and gruff, muted by the tilt of his mouth. He spoke to the ground, though it was clear the words were meant for me. Then his voice, the echo of it, crystallized in my mind. *Fucking dyke* was what he'd said. He got into the cruiser and pulled roughly out of the lot. As the car turned at the exit, I caught sight of Calloway's face in the passenger window.

34

Eva was alarmed when I told her. I could tell, though she didn't say anything at first. We met for a drink at a place outside of Knife River later that week. Not in the neighboring town, but in Carthage, which was two towns away and technically in another county. Neither of us knew anyone there. The location was her idea. She'd met women at this place before, I learned. On the phone, I'd said that I needed to come over to talk in person, and she hesitated before suggesting we meet someplace else.

"Just in case," she said. "You understand." I did understand, but I was tired of having to.

There was a sign out front that read Pal's Cabin in glowing orange letters. The seats inside were orange, too, with orange glass lanterns hanging from the ceiling. It was very quiet. There were some people at the back, eating steaks. The floor was heavily worn down. No one else was at the bar. The bartender himself disappeared for long periods of time and then came back to stare at us, assessing what else we might need, before disappearing again into the kitchen. Everything looked very old. It seemed like the kind of place that might be out of business in a year or less.

Eva wore a large men's peacoat of navy wool. Her wrists looked delicate poking out from the cuffs. I realized that apart from our first run-in, this was the only time I'd seen her in public as an adult. Her presence was changed by the wideness of the open world. Out in the parking lot, I'd been struck by how small she looked. While she was locking her car, in the moments before she saw me waiting by the entrance, I imagined that she was just a stranger who would walk past me without ceremony. Thinking of this made tears come to my eyes. I pinched myself hard on the wrist, but they came to my eyes again as we sat side by side in the warmth and low light. All I could imagine were long-gone traces of herself, ghostly slivers, sitting in the same spot next to the other women she wouldn't risk being seen with in Knife River. I was one of those women now and I felt incredibly foolish.

As I waited for her to say something about my run-in with the officer, I caught a glimpse of myself in the mirrored panel on the wall and wanted to scream. What did I think I was doing there in that bleak, out-of-the-way place, sitting down with the girl I'd loved as a teenager, carefully hidden away from the eyes of her boyfriend and everyone else who might have recognized us? But another voice, one that was quieter and rang more true, asked why down deep in my marrow what I felt toward her was inextinguishable.

I had to explain what happened outside the gas station twice. Eva wouldn't look at me as I spoke. She just sat there, spinning her cup around, appearing rattled.

Finally, she said, "I think Jack was looking through my phone the other day."

I was alarmed. "You don't delete your texts?"

"Usually, I do. I don't know, he's never gone through it before."

She pushed her hair out of her face and let out a forceful breath. "I came back into the room and he kind of tossed my phone to the side like nothing was going on. Then after he left I looked at it, and the screen was still scrolled down on my text log. Obviously, your name came up a lot."

I described the man who'd walked past me coming out of the shop in more detail and she knew who I was talking about right away. "That's, like, his best friend," she said, adding moments later that she couldn't stand him. "Did it upset you?" she asked.

"What?"

"What he said to you."

"Oh." I thought for a moment. Upset wasn't the right way to explain it. It worried me. It made me feel that something I'd feared had been confirmed in one sinister, fleeting moment. I had to ask myself then what I was really so afraid of. Did I think everyone didn't already know what I was? Did I really think Calloway had no suspicions about us, and did I actually believe he didn't already wonder about Eva before I ever came back? We all lived in the same place where gossip began easily and took a long time to die. I already knew she got with him after being fired from her job over that picture. He probably felt it really was about him, like he was some special exception, like he was going to show her what he was sure she was missing.

I had a filmy, distant memory of someone, a grown man, saying to Eva, "You're too pretty for that shit." He'd come up to us out of nowhere one day in the park. I was standing right there while he said it, knowing that I was at once both invisible and the very *that* that prompted him to approach us in the first place. It was one thing to be a dyke when men didn't want to fuck you anyway. Men didn't feel entitled to me. They hardly seemed to notice me at all. My not being available didn't make them feel as though they'd been robbed of something. But Eva was always having to weave around their desires and their persistence, always having to anticipate their anger and try to keep it at bay. You could look at the way a man watched her and see he believed she owed him something. Really, I kept two versions of Eva in my memory: the way she was when we were alone in her room, and the way she was when the eyes of others were upon her.

"No," I finally answered. "I wouldn't say upset."

"Really? It's such an ugly word."

"Not to me."

That was true. It was just a vessel. An empty bowl of a word. I'd heard it so many times in so many ways. It was used to intimidate me, to identify me, to hit on me, to mock me, to compliment. It came as a question and as an insult. As a come-on. As a simple observation. Over the years, how I felt about it changed along with my circumstances. The word was a mirror. Sometimes I'd hated what it reflected onto me, other times it brought me indescribable contentedness.

"You do seem shaken up, though," Eva said.

"It wasn't what he said. It was why he said it in the first place." She nodded. Through the grimy front window, I saw that it had begun to snow outside. The flakes dissolved within a moment of meeting the ground. I finished my drink, glad the bartender wasn't around to offer another because I wouldn't have been able to stop myself from saying yes. Soon the flurry stopped and the sky stayed wet and gray. The people who were eating steaks in the back filed out the front door and left all together in one truck.

As the truck disappeared around the bend, I looked at Eva and told her, "I meant what I said about not wanting to leave Knife River without you."

"I know you did."

"Well?"

"Well, what?" She put her hands flat out on the countertop and studied them like she could see through the layers of nerves and skin. "Are you asking me to come with you?"

"Yeah, I am. If you want to."

"Have you really thought about this?"

"I've thought about it enough."

"How much is enough?"

"I mean, I know that no matter which way I turn it in my head, I don't find myself wanting it any less." I picked up a nearby saltshaker and rolled it between my palms. I asked, "What about you? Have you thought about it?"

"Of course." Her voice was soft. "You know, one of my sisters-in-law, she's a nurse, she got my father hooked up with a new doctor who's been a big help. He's on a new medication now that's cut back a lot on the tremors."

"That's good news," I said.

"It's been a relief." She looked down at her hands again. "When will you leave? Do you know yet?"

"As soon as things wind down for me here. I'm not sure exactly, maybe early spring."

"If I go with you, are we going to be together?" Her tone was cautious. I'd wondered this same thing myself many times. Simply parting ways once again seemed impossible, but so did a world where we were just friends. I didn't know what to call us. Now there was all this sex and anxiety to contend with, new water under the bridge. Did I really think we were going to run off together and live happily as a couple? I didn't want to rule it out.

I realized my face was turning red. I swiveled around the other way and pretended to cough, facing out into the restaurant. The bartender had come back and sat down at a table in the middle of the dining room floor, flopped forward with his head resting on the tablecloth and his arms dangling at the sides. His face was turned away so I couldn't tell if he was sleeping or blacked out, or just staring at the wall where there was a mural of wild horses galloping across an expanse of golden sand. His behavior was making me uneasy, so I turned back toward Eva.

"I hope we could be," I said. She looked at me for a long time. Finally, she finished her drink and told me that she would think about it. By then she had her keys in her hand and was flipping them around, running her nail over the ridges. I dropped a little money onto the countertop. The bartender didn't look up as we left.

Brenda's white town car was parked haphazardly by the curb outside the house when I turned onto my street. The screen door on the porch was open. I looked around when I got out of the car. The yard was still. The door to the mailbox hung unlatched. In the corner of my eye, I spotted Paul puttering around his garage. Our porch had been salted. His driveway and front steps had been covered, too, and I wondered if he'd done ours. It wasn't a chore Liz usually bothered with.

Inside the house, all was quiet. I stood for a moment in the entry-way, just listening, but there was no sound. The hair on my arms stood up. I crept into the kitchen then and saw Brenda and Liz sitting at the table. Brenda still had her coat and hat on. Wet footprints trailed all the way through the room. There was a palpable feeling of grief—thick and heavy and suffocating. I recognized it immediately. It had a famil-iar smell to it, somehow. Like air trapped inside a sealed box, damp paper kept in the dark, the husks of insects crumbling to dust. Liz was hunched over, her hands cupped around her face. Brenda looked upon her with a somber, contemplative expression. Neither seemed aware of my presence. I stood in the doorway, barely breathing, watching them, growing terrified.

I waited like that for a few more moments and then, when I couldn't stand it any longer, loudly asked, "What's going on here?" The ques-tion fell flat to the ground the moment it left my mouth. My sister hardly looked up. I went over to them, staring at Brenda with the hope of gaining some clue about what was happening. She motioned for me to sit. I did, and then Liz tilted her head up. There were red creases all along her face from where her sleeve was digging into the skin. Dark, puffy rings bulged out beneath both eyes.

"The medical examiner says Mom's remains are too damaged to make a conclusive ruling on a cause of death." Her voice was matter of fact, as though she were telling me the date and time. "The sheriff called an hour ago."

I looked at the two of them, suddenly consumed by a strange urge to laugh. I couldn't understand why. The impulse horrified me. My heart was racing. I felt like all the light had gone out of the world, but it took every shred of energy within me to stop a laugh from squeaking out of my lips. I'd had urges like this before, always at the most inappropriate moments. It made me want to not be around people at all. Silently, I counted to ten. It did not escape me that my sister had called on her friend before me. That was her initial, gut response. If I resented anything about that, and I'm not sure I had the right to, it was only that I had no such person in my own life. Brenda squeezed my hand under the table.

"But the paint," I said. "I thought—"

"It's not unique enough to be linked to a specific make or model from that time." She shook her head. "It's just run-of-the-mill undercarriage spray, the same kind everybody has."

"The fracture on her skull, what about that? What happened?" I was aware that the salt and pepper shakers were moving, and that something was hitting the table from below, but I did not understand that it was my own leg doing it, my own knee growing sore, until Brenda discreetly placed her hand on it. Her touch was firm and gentle. She meant to stop me from rattling the table.

"It was caused by blunt trauma," Liz said. "They all agreed on that. But they couldn't say whether it occurred while she was still alive." Her voice trailed off. There was a vacant look in her eyes. Then, "We'll never know what really happened to her."

These results weren't shocking to me. In some way, I'd half expected them, but hearing it announced like this changed everything. Suddenly, it all felt unbearably real. Even the air hurt. I tried to take only small, shallow breaths. My sister had always been the one to pursue the truth, doggedly, despite precious time and proof slipping further into oblivion with each passing year. She never gave up. She remained hopeful, in her way. It was me who was more willing to let go. Even when I couldn't, I still wanted to. I was the one to drift nearer to acceptance. I managed my dread by trying to stay close to the possibility that we might never learn the circumstances of our mother's fate. Liz was the one who fought hard against that current, wearing herself down to a ragged husk of a person and refusing to loosen her grip on the hope that one day, somehow, somebody would have to pay for what had been taken from us.

Now, my sister seemed empty. Stoic, almost. I suddenly felt very angry. "What do we do now?" I said. "There has to be something else."

"There's nothing else, Jess," Liz said. "This is it."

"No. There has to be some next step. Didn't you ask?"

"The next step is they close the case and write *undetermined* on her death certificate. It's over."

"It can't be over."

"I'm sorry," Liz said flatly.

"So we're just giving up, then."

"I didn't make this decision. I'm only telling you what they told me."

"Well, what they told you doesn't make any sense."

"I don't understand you right now," Liz said, a spike of emotion making its way into her voice. "You're the one who always tried to warn me things could turn out this way."

"And I don't understand why you aren't more upset about it. Why aren't you more angry? Why aren't you doing something?"

"You can't be serious," she said. Liz stared at me, leaning back in her chair. I knew that I was being mean and irrational. I couldn't rein myself in. I told her that I was completely serious. I demanded to know why she was willing to accept an end to this so easily. I also asked why she wasn't crying. *I* wasn't even crying. I felt insane. My voice grew higher and thinner until I could barely understand the sounds that came out of my throat.

Liz's stare turned hateful. She allowed me to go on and on, peppering her with outrageous questions until finally she snapped, shouting, "How do you think this feels for me?" I felt instantly guilty and took my voice down, saying that I knew it must feel horrible. She shook her head violently. "No," she said. "You have no idea. You haven't been here."

"That doesn't mean—"

She let out a brief chuckle, just half a second. It sounded cold and crooked. "You think because you decided to show up in October that you know anything about what it's been like for me? I don't know what all you've been up to for the past ten years, drinking yourself half to death, two-timing any woman who'll take you in. I really don't know, because you hardly ever called. But while you've been gone, doing whatever it is you've done with your life, I've been here every single day with this. I've lived with it right under my nose. Do you get that? How many times have I seen Nick Haines in the parking lot of his shop, or standing around outside the bar? And then I've had to drive past the police station every day on my way to work, knowing that they were just sitting around in there, maybe getting up to respond to some domestic dispute once a week, while her file just rotted away in the dark. I went to sleep every night telling myself that one day, the truth would come out and he would be charged. I thought sooner or later he would slip, say something to the wrong person, or maybe somebody would come forward, or he would try something with another woman and she'd escape, and go tell somebody. But now, I don't have any of that. He's off the hook for this, for good. They said they don't have reasonable suspicion. What am I supposed to do? You get to leave here and go do whatever you want. But what about me?"

She glanced between Brenda and me, her eyes nearly brimming over with tears. "I've been waiting for something to happen so I could move past this. I mean, first I wanted to go to school. That obviously didn't work out. Then I thought someday I would get married and have kids. That turned into thinking that maybe one day I would move away, or travel somewhere, or get a better job. I just kept waiting for an end to this, and the days kept piling up, and now I'm here. How stupid am I? I've never worked anywhere but the local bank. Since I was nineteen years old that's all I've done. That's my only work experience. And now with the branch restructuring I don't even know if I'll get to keep that job. I only dated that one man and I ran away from him as soon as I started to like him too much. And you know we never even slept together. Jesus Christ—" She slapped her hands on the table. She shouted, "I feel like I missed my entire life. I'm really going to die a virgin in this house wearing a fucking polyester bank teller uniform."

Brenda stared at my sister with an expression of faint horror. I leaned against the back of my chair. My eyes fell on a dried splatter of coffee on the sink cabinet doors. When I was small, I liked to crawl inside the large compartment and hide in the darkness, inhaling the sharp smell of the Ajax cleaning powder, relishing in the way it stung the delicate skin around my nostrils. I liked listening to the gurgling of the pipes, and peeling the flower-patterned contact paper on the plywood sides.

Once, I fell asleep curled up in there and woke to my sister, then about twelve and tasked with watching me for a weekend while our mother went to visit a friend, screaming my name. I later learned she'd been searching for me all afternoon. *I thought you were gone,* she kept saying, after I'd already emerged. She'd repeated this over and over, alternately hugging me and shaking me. Looking at Liz now, I could see faint impressions of her younger self lingering in the dark pools of her eyes.

I knew I was angry because I was afraid. I was afraid that an end to our mother's case would sever the only thing that held us together. What more did we share? We hardly talked about anything else. We'd gone years before this without seeing each other. And though I always felt that deep down we loved each other, and really knew each other in a way no one else could, that alone was never enough to keep us in each other's lives. Now I feared we would drift apart once more. This time there would be nothing forcing us together again.

"I'm sorry," I finally said. And I was. I was sorry that I'd left her alone. I was sorry that she never got the things she wanted. If I could have, I would've given my entire life over to her. "Everything was so unfair for you."

"I should be sorry to you, too," Liz sighed.

"No, you shouldn't," I said firmly. "You don't have any reason to be."

"I do. You were so young when Mom went missing." She shook her head slowly. "I know you probably didn't see it that way. You thought you were so grown. But I remember looking at you after I realized she was never coming home and feeling so scared. You looked like a child. You *were* a child. I knew I was going to have to take care of you some-how, but how could I give you everything you needed? I was broke, and deeply depressed. I couldn't even keep food in the fridge. I remem-ber once I tried to vacuum the floor and slipped on some water and I just stayed there, lying in that same spot on the ground for hours. It wasn't fair to you, either."

At this, I shuddered. It pained me to think of us together here, alone, in those days. Two kids in a creaky old house. We could see no light at the end of the tunnel, nothing on the other side. Help wasn't on the way. For years, I'd tried hard to convince myself that I was un-like my sister. I'd gotten out, I'd forged my own semblance of a life and came to believe that it was somehow better, that it afforded me a kind of freedom she did not have.

Now, sitting in our familial home, listening to her recount the truth of my girlhood so plainly, I felt incredibly small. I was no different now than I had been back then: helpless, frightened, propelled into each new day by denial and defiance. For fifteen years, I'd thought only of surviving into the next morning. And I had, I'd figured out a way to stay afloat in the world. But what did I really have to show for it? An idea about moving away to work outdoors, the intention always bob-bing just out of my reach, taunting me from the horizon. All my pos-sessions fit in the trunk of a car. I had nothing. No attachments, no dependents, and still I hadn't managed to take charge of my own dreams. I was afraid of the sound of my own breath, my own heart-beat, alone in a room. Afraid enough to live with women I often felt nothing for, and to keep living with them even after I'd come to almost despise them, just to have a body next to me in the dark. And now, every day I fell harder for someone who could barely handle being seen in public with me. She tried so hard to keep me hidden, and still I wanted her more and more. Pretending that I was any better off than

Liz suddenly felt like a joke I'd been telling myself for years, and had only just now come to understand that the whole joke, the setup and the punch line, was actually on me.

My sister placed her hand on my shoulder and looked me dead in the eye. "Are you okay?" she asked. I wiped my sleeves over my cheeks. Damp patches bloomed across the fabric. I nodded, though anyone could see I wasn't all right. Liz's face was gleaming, bright red. Her breath came in short bursts, halted and frantic. "I just don't know what to do," she said. "What am I supposed to do?"

Brenda slid out from behind the table and gathered up her things. She stopped at the sink to put away a stack of dried plates, and then rinsed out a few used glasses. She moved very slowly. I watched as she struggled to reach the cabinet door. I wanted to get up and help her, but Liz was now leaning the full weight of her head into my shoulder, murmuring as I patted her on the back. Brenda stood there, staring at us. Waxy pink lipstick feathered out into the lines around her mouth. Her coat hung all the way down to the ground. I could see salt stains creeping up from the hem. She was worryingly slight, even more fragile looking than the last few times I'd seen her. She nodded at me and I gave a weak smile.

"I'll give you girls some time," she said.

35

The days after the case closing did not pass easily. I checked on Liz after she went to bed every night, cracking open the door and peering in to make sure she was all right. The first night, I saw that she'd fallen asleep on top of the duvet in her work clothes. She still had her nylons on. One of her low-heeled, pleather pumps still clung to her foot while the other sat on the floor facing the bed. I wanted to go in and at least drop a blanket over her, but she looked so peaceful and unaware that I didn't want to risk stirring her. Another night, I cracked the door open and found that she was sitting upright against the pillow, still dressed, rigid as a board. Her eyes were fixed on the opposite wall. I watched for a while, growing more alarmed with each passing moment, before walking into the room and waving my hand before her face. She slowly directed her gaze toward me before smiling sleepily, as though she only just realized I was standing there. She asked me if I needed something. I asked if she was feeling well, and she assured me that everything was fine.

Despite the finality with which Liz had delivered the news to me, she continued to leap for the phone every time it rang, shoulders always slumping at the first sound of some telemarketer's recording. Maybe it was simply out of habit. All those years, she kept paying the bill for our landline, saying that it was the only number for us our mother would know if she was out there somewhere and one day tried to call. Now I wondered how long it would take her to cancel the service. I still had a little bit of hope left, too, for the unexpected. Maybe something would happen and the truth would burst open. But a week came and went, then two more. It seemed impossible that things were just done, closed, over and finished with, though it was what I'd always hoped for. Wishing for this in the past, I imagined that a hard end to it all would make me feel free. Instead, every day was like getting punched repeatedly in the gut.

I started gagging in the mornings. When I went to brush my teeth, I found myself hunched over the sink, making a sound like an old dog. Sometimes blood came out and splattered across the porcelain basin. Once I looked up from rinsing it away and spotted my sister's reflection in the medicine cabinet mirror. She was standing in the hall, watching.

"I told you that you drink too much," she declared. "You probably gave yourself an ulcer." I told her thanks and then shut the door firmly in her face. We argued often over stupid, inconsequential things. Our nerves were raw. It felt like the house was not large enough to contain our individual grief. It sputtered out of us at odd times, then cooled, and erupted again over something small like a window left open or uncollected mail. We had a very bad fight about the utility bill.

After that fight, I drove to the end of the block under the guise of going to the gas station. I wanted finally to call Maria in Acadia. I wasn't yet ready to tell Liz about it; I didn't need to give us something else to argue about. As the phone rang, I worried she wouldn't answer. It had been a long time since we'd last been in touch, close to a year. Silently, I berated myself for not taking better care of my relationships. I hadn't really spoken to anyone I used to be friendly with the whole time I'd been back home. A stray cat ambled by the front of my car. I chewed on a hangnail until it bled. But then there was her voice on the other end. If she was surprised to hear from me she didn't let it be known. We talked for a while. I told her I was getting ready to move, I wanted to go someplace new where I could pick up extra work outdoors, maybe find a rental with a small yard, did she know anything? She thought she could help me, especially with summer season coming.

"I'll talk to some people, I have a lot of friends in the area," Maria said. "Look out for my email." I hung up feeling like there was a little star glimmering out in the distance, one small and hopeful thing standing out against the dark.

During these weeks, I often got the feeling that my mother had died a second time. I found myself crying without reason. For days on end I could not sleep, then suddenly could do nothing but sleep. Food, too, became impossible. I would get ravenously, desperately hungry, but then when there was a meal in front of me I had little interest in eating it. Everything tasted like Styrofoam. I tried to keep myself focused on work but was easily distracted. I'd get up to use the bathroom and find that thirty minutes had passed while I sat on the edge of the tub, engrossed by the fine print on our shampoo bottles. I left my phone battery dead for two days and then, after finally gathering the will to look for the charger and plug it in, saw a voicemail from Eva. I didn't have the energy to listen to it. I just wanted to lie down with the lights off. But as time passed, the pressure seemed to lessen. It was gradual. Almost imperceptible. Suddenly, my sister and I were laughing together at something on the TV. My whole body didn't ache. Liz sometimes whistled as she embroidered at night.

At the end of March, we got a letter from the coroner's office alerting us to the status of her remains. *Unclaimed,* it read. There was a five-digit number at the top of the paper accompanying her date of birth. I couldn't take my eyes off it. A new identifier, like a new name, passionlessly assigned by a computer program whose sole purpose was to keep a catalog of every dead, numbered person who'd ever found their end within the county's borders. It led me to feel that she was more truly, finally dead somehow.

I called the office and learned that a funeral director had to be the one to come and collect the bones, or someone from the crematorium. It didn't rest easily with me, this idea that whatever was left of her could only be handled by licensed professionals, that only they possessed the right equipment, the right training, the right vehicle to transport her, even if she was little more than a pile of rocks. Still, imagining how I might have handled it were I allowed to retrieve her remains brought me to a dead end. Would I have set the container down in the passenger seat? What if Liz was with me, would we put her on one of our laps? Nothing felt right to me. I had the persistent, nagging sensation of having a wet wool sweater on and being unable to tug it off.

I confronted Liz with the letter when she walked in the door after work. "We have to deal with this," I said. "They've probably got her in a cardboard box on a shelf somewhere, with all the other unclaimed dead people."

"Don't say that."

"I'm serious. That's what they do. I've heard there's a closet just for remains that no one's come to collect." I followed her into the kitchen as she rolled her sleeves up and began foraging around for dinner. I reminded her again about the urgency of our response, even though I knew that it was just as much upon me as it was her to take action. The image of this closet for the dust of abandoned people wouldn't shake out of my mind's eye.

I went on until Liz turned to face me. "Stop," she said. "That's only for ashes, so calm down." I could not calm down. My heart raced as I watched her pile cold sliced chicken onto a plate. She sprinkled pepper and chili flakes over the whole thing and then picked up a slice with her fingers. "Mom wanted to be cremated anyway," she said.

"How do you know that?"

"She told me a long time ago."

"When?"

"You were way too young to remember. One day she was cleaning out the gutter and fell off her ladder and blacked out for a while. She was fine, probably just had a concussion, but she got really spooked about dying afterward and told me that if anything ever happened not to bury her because caskets were ugly and expensive, and she was creeped out by embalming." This was the first I'd ever heard about her falling off a ladder or talking to Liz about funerary arrangements. I was reminded of how many memories my sister must have had with just her, ones formed well before my life had even begun, that no other person could ever share in.

"You might've mentioned that," I replied. "At some point in this whole process."

"Well, there was no reason before now."

"I've been worrying over what we would do with her. I had no idea if we should buy a plot somewhere, or what."

"Now you don't need to think about it." We debated over whether cremation was even worthwhile. There was so little of her left. Liz agreed that we would probably be yielded a very small amount of ash and fragment. The issue of vessels came up. Nothing sat right. An urn, the polished marble kind, felt like a mismatch. A regular vase or porcelain coffer didn't make sense, either.

"We could still just bury her in the cemetery," I suggested again.

"She didn't want to go in the ground. I'm not putting her back there in the dark like that, under all the dirt with the worms."

"This would be different."

"It wouldn't, really."

"We wouldn't need to get a whole casket. Just a small pine box."

"She said cremation." Liz folded her arms defensively and gave me a look of disbelief. I countered again, bringing up the possibility of a future exhumation. At this my sister let out a gruff breath and shook her head at me in an almost pitying way. This really threw me off. I began to shout again, insisting that perhaps one day, somehow, someone would want to examine the bones again.

She looked at me steadily and said, "I think we both know that isn't going to happen."

In the end, a young man from the crematory delivered the ashes to our home. Because we did not specify otherwise, they arrived in a black plastic container with a lid. It was only about the size of a shoebox. Inside was a clear bag twisted shut with a bread tie, and inside that about two pounds of gritty, whitish dust. The day was mild enough for us to sit comfortably out on the back patio in just our light jackets. Without ceremony, Liz plucked the bag out of the box and held it up to the light. She examined it from every angle, gently prodding the bottom with her finger before passing it to me. I felt around for anything identifiable, a piece of bone or tooth, but it was mostly smooth.

It didn't really feel like she was there with us, at least not more than it usually did. It felt more like we'd finally come to the end of a very long list and were readying ourselves to move on to other things. This brought me some relief. To ease my mind in the days prior, I'd watched a video on the internet about the process of cremation. It was short, hosted by a somber, bald man in a white coat. I wanted to know every detail. I didn't want this to become another black hole in my understanding of my mother's fate, another thing to feel afraid of. After presenting the gurney and the furnace, the man tipped a mound of burned-up remnants from a big metal basin into another device that sifted everything, then ground up the larger bits into a fine dust. Everything was mixed together in something that looked like a bread machine before being packaged up and sent out.

I set the bag down in the middle of the table and asked, "What now?"

Liz pointed toward the woods on the perimeter of our property. "I thought maybe we would scatter her ashes. She liked to walk out there in the springtime."

We sat quietly for a little while, staring at the bag. I liked to think that the wind would disperse her throughout the wild expanse of forest, and that she would travel on it, unencumbered by the heaviness of earth. After a while, Liz grabbed two small trowels from the house and we walked out to the tree line, then into the woods. Snow remained in patches. We walked along little trails of muddy dirt that had been trodden down by foraging deer. In just a month or two, clusters of daffodils would spring up around the mossy rocks. Wild raspberry bushes would burst into fecundity, dropping their fruit for the bees and hummingbirds. I dipped my trowel into the bag and sent a heap of ash over the barren twigs of a forsythia bush. A breeze came and the ash went off with it, disappearing from view within moments.

We took our time with this gradual process of dispersion and parting. We hardly spoke. We were thinking our own thoughts. Images floated to the top of my mind: a sprig of forsythia blossoms in a jar on the windowsill, my mother standing above the blazing yellow flowers, inspecting their petals with a quiet awe. I had vague recollections of seeing her out here sometimes, emerging from the woods in the early morning hours. Maybe some noise would stir me awake, or I'd be up already from the sunlight or a bad dream, and I'd go to the window and spot her figure moving amid the trees. I remember she liked to collect wild berries, eating them as she walked, and snip handfuls of chives that grew in abundance at the edge of the yard. The chives would appear on our sandwiches and omelets for days after. Perhaps she was also a troubled sleeper, the way I turned out to be, or perhaps she was doing something meant to be kept from us. The more I concentrated, the foggier and more distant these memories seemed to become. How could I know if I ever really saw her out there at all?

It was still light out when Liz and I walked back into the house. The days were growing longer. *Painful* wasn't the right word for this afternoon. We had already let her go piece by piece, over so many years. This was only another part of it. We sat out in the sun room together on the chairs that overlooked the window onto the woods. As the sun set, we cried a little. It was a soft, merciful kind of sadness. It skimmed over us like a bird coming down on still water.

36

That Friday around five, Brenda called our landline.

Just as I was about to tell her that Liz was still at work she asked, "Are you free this evening?" The question took me by surprise. I'd been looking over some pictures Maria had sent of a white clapboard house in Bar Harbor with tall, unruly rose bushes growing wild around the front steps. It belonged to her friend, who was looking to rent out the renovated addition around back facing the woods. Her in-laws had lived in it before moving to Florida, and she wanted to make some of her money back on the construction. When I'd zoomed in on an image of the bedroom, I'd seen a half-circle window seat and a vaulted ceiling. There was a small kitchenette down the hall with black-and-white tiles on the floor, a small sunroom that opened out directly onto the grass. It came half furnished. The subject line read *Interested? Happy to put in a good word for you.* I was interested. Looking through the pictures made me buoyant with hope. I was about ready to move on. Since we'd scattered the ashes, our house in Knife River felt like the territory of a former life, somewhere I no longer had any business treading.

Rain fell softly against the kitchen windows. Outside in the dirt, early spring buds were beginning to emerge. I closed my laptop and told Brenda I wasn't doing anything.

"Would you mind doing me a quick favor, then?" she asked.

"All right."

"Could you bring your sister an umbrella at work?"

"You want me to go over to the bank with an umbrella?"

"And then I want you to take her out to dinner. How about Larison's? You can say hello to my brother for me."

"Why, though?"

"I think Liz could use some cheering up." Her tone was kind but firm, the voice of someone who'd taught school for many years. I didn't feel like I could say no. "I saw her this morning when I went to deposit my check," she said. "I could tell she was feeling down. I know the two of you don't have much time left here together. She misses you already, I think."

A familiar twinge of guilt came back to me. Soon I'd be leaving my sister behind in this house again. I hated to think of her alone here. I'd already found myself imagining her turning the key at the end of the day, walking into a dark and quiet room, feeling around for the light switch, no one to come and greet her.

"You'll do this for me?" Brenda asked. "It would mean a lot to Liz."

"Of course," I said. I was already digging around for an umbrella, holding the phone between my cheek and shoulder. I welcomed the excuse to go somewhere. I still felt uneasy being alone in our house at night. "I'll head over there in a few minutes."

"Go on and take the umbrella in to her so she doesn't get rained on. And then you bring her to Larison's. It's right around the corner, and Liz loves their corn on the cob." I told her I would, reaching for my jacket on the door hook. "Thank you, Jess," she said. Before I could tell her goodbye, she'd hung up.

L iz and I said good night to her manager in the bank lobby and walked out to the awning, bundled up in our jackets. She'd seemed surprised by my invitation to go to dinner, but quickly agreed.

"I'm exhausted today," she said. "I don't want to cook tonight anyway." Through the window I could see the last few tellers drawing their curtains shut, filing into the vault with their steel cash boxes. Someone ran a vacuum around the worn green carpet, knocking into a table laden with incentives for first-time accounts—toasters and blenders still in their crisp packaging. A banner offering discounts on snow tires. We continued down the street, huddled together beneath the umbrella, past all the stores closing for the evening, and turned at the last corner up the hill toward the turkey farm.

Hiram waved us over to two seats at a corner table when we arrived, facing the line of other customers mingling around the entryway. We shrugged our coats off and hung them on the backs of our chairs. People filtered in and out of the room. The waitress came and went. Food appeared before us. I thought of what Brenda said on the phone, about Liz needing help. To me, she seemed more deflated than depressed. Right after the case was closed, she'd spent so much time in bed, asleep or lying in silence, that I sometimes forgot she was upstairs at all. She barely ate. I had to cajole her into drinking just one small cup of water over the course of an afternoon. It was as if she had half disappeared.

Now, though, she got up in the mornings and moved through the day with what seemed like a resigned understanding of what was required of her to live. I noticed her zippers were often not pulled up all the way, or her sweaters were on backward, but she got dressed in new clothes every day and was more or less on time for work. She ate, but it always seemed mechanical and like the very act of moving her jaw was exhausting. I watched as she swallowed a bite of dinner roll.

"What's going on with work?" I asked. Weeks had passed since I last heard mention of the potential branch merger.

She let out a weak sigh and said, "I think they're going to close this location. They haven't confirmed yet, but I suspect it."

"What are you going to do?"

"I don't know yet. It depends what they offer me." She tilted her head to the side and bit her lower lip, thinking. "Could be some severance, could be a new job somewhere else. Or it could be nothing."

"Are you upset?" I couldn't read her tone. When the possibility of the closure first came up, she seemed unraveled by it, but now there was an air of calm resignation about her. I wondered if everything we'd gone through in the past few weeks had forced the uncertainty of her job into perspective. Or maybe there simply weren't enough feelings left for it.

After a few minutes of careful consideration she responded. "I am somewhat upset."

Gingerly, I pulled out my phone to show her the pictures of the house Maria had sent. The topic of change was already between us, and I wanted to gauge her reaction. She scrolled through, carefully examining each photo.

"This is pretty," she said. "Where is it?"

"Near Bar Harbor. I'm thinking of going there."

"What for?"

"I want to see if I can find some work outdoors. Even if it's just part time. I don't know, I'm tired of staring at pictures of broken teeth all the time."

"And you're going to move into this place?"

"Yeah," I said. "Maybe, I'm pretty sure I want to take it." I gave Liz's face a careful look. She seemed older than she had in the fall. Faint lines had appeared around her eyes. Her skin now reminded me of an oversized jacket she might slip off and put away for another season.

Finally, she said, "Good."

"You aren't upset?"

"No. Not at all."

"I thought you might want me to stay longer."

"What for?" I blinked at her. She shook her head quickly and said, "You're offended. I didn't mean it that way. You could stay home as long as you want, I just know you aren't comfortable there at the house. I get it."

"Really?"

"Yeah." She shrugged. "And now I may have to move soon. I can't imagine you'd want to live alone here. What's really left for you in town anymore?"

"Nothing, I guess." I swirled my drink around in its glass. "I mean, there's Eva," I said. "But I sort of asked her to come with me when I leave." Liz stopped eating and stared at the table. Her eyes moved from side to side, as though calculating something. "What do you think?" I asked. "Am I insane?"

"It's not my business."

"It kind of is, though."

"Well," she sighed. "I actually don't think it's such a terrible idea. You obviously love her. I can see that now." Her reaction brought me some relief, like I'd finally been granted her blessing to want this as much as I did.

"I don't know if she'll leave Knife River or not," I said.

"Hard to say," Liz said. "She's lived her whole life here, her family is here. Sort of a leap of faith to move to a place where she doesn't know anybody but you. What if she hates it there? And maybe she'll decide she doesn't want to be with you anyway."

I told Liz that I didn't feel convinced we would end up together. She asked me what the point was, then, and I tried to explain that I always regretted not asking her to come away with me the first time and that I didn't want to drive off again without her. If there was even a chance that we would be together, even if just for a short while, I wanted to take it. If I could somehow know that she was going to break my heart, make me miserable, and leave me for someone else, I still wanted her to come. Through bites of baked potato, I tried to put all this into words that Liz would understand, if not empathize with. I could see that she was listening carefully.

She remained quiet for a few moments after I finished speaking before finally saying, "I can tell you really mean all of that." Then, "But are you expecting she'll break your heart?"

"I kind of expect that of every woman, sooner or later."

"Why even bother, then?"

"It's not like my relationships have to be for life to be worth it."

"What if you knew one was going to be for life," she said. "Would you still want it?"

"Yeah," I told her. "I think I would, now."

"You know, I actually believe that Eva is a nice person." It was rare for Liz to make these kinds of declarations about others. She was seldom complimentary toward anyone, and apart from those people I knew she cared for, Brenda and Hiram, the residents at the nursing home, myself, she sometimes seemed to me to hardly be aware of other people as anything more than background noise. She moved around them as if they were potted plants, or traffic cones—just things in her way, the presence of which she had no choice but to accept.

She refolded her napkin in her lap and cleared her throat. "Last year I saw her crouching on the side of the road helping a snapping turtle get across," she said. "It could have bitten through her whole wrist but she had it by the sides of the shell and was hauling it across the median toward the stream. I wouldn't touch one of those. Everybody was honking at her but she didn't take her eyes off the turtle." Liz shrugged. "Doesn't mean you two won't ever break up, or anything. But I think she has a good heart. And I remember how she was with you back when you were teens. I never would have said it then, but I was grateful somebody was taking some kind of care of you."

This unexpected story surprised me. Liz looked a little stunned to have said it all aloud, too. I squeezed her hand under the table and she squeezed mine back. As we finished our drinks, Hiram began to clean the nearby tables. He wiped the rag in a slow, circular motion. I could see his face reflected in the wood polish. A gentle smile rested on his lips as he worked.

37

I stirred awake in the early morning hours, a feeling of quiet peace radiating down through my fingertips. I lay with it for a while. There was a sense of being alone with the world, the first one awake on the precipice of a new day. The house was silent. The leaves on the trees beyond the window lay flat and still. I stretched out beneath the quilt and yawned. My head didn't ache like it usually did when I woke up. I rested my hands on my chest and felt the steady drum of my heart. Every so often, I got hit with a feeling of real gratitude for the machine of my own body. No matter what I did, how badly I neglected myself or failed to sleep enough or drink the right amount of water, my heart and lungs kept expanding and contracting in service of my survival. Each morning, my eyes opened and perceived the world's color. This feeling usually came with an urgent impulse to take better care of myself, and then faded to an inward-pointing resentment as I failed yet again. This time, though, the prospect didn't exhaust me. I didn't meet my body as a separate entity, an instrument whose maintenance exceeded my own ability, but as something that was truly my own, which would be with me always, carrying me, pressing onward.

The floor was biting cold. I walked downstairs carefully, avoiding the planks I knew groaned or squeaked, pausing for a moment when I noticed something moving out in the trees through the back window. It seemed for a moment that there was nothing out there, just a vast tangle of brush stretching out into a wash of early, gray light. Then, another flicker. I leaned on the windowsill, gently pressing my fingertips against the cold glass. A lone deer stood at the edge of the woods. She watched me. I looked back, trailing my gaze over the taut slope of her neck, the darkness of her eyes. She appeared well fed, unlike so many of the does at the tail end of winter hobbling along the roadside with their distended rib cages, pilfering through the melting slush for grass. I thought about her life in the wild, the harshness and freedom of it. The brevity. Around every corner was something deadly, though everything she would ever need to survive was out there, too. She could not rely on any creature beyond herself, but so, too, could she never feel shame or regret. We held each other's gaze for a few moments longer before the trance was broken by the sound of a siren whirring off in the distance. I peered out the side window and saw nothing but an empty road. When I looked back, the doe was gone.

Later that day, a knock came at the front door. From my seat in the living room, I could see Calloway and the sheriff standing out on the porch. Liz got there first, and the two of them shoved their way inside where they stood with their arms crossed, frowning, looking somehow taller and more broad than they really were. Behind the sheriff was a little shelf with my sister's collection of painted porcelain birds. His jacket kept knocking into it, tipping one of the birds on its tail. I wanted to go and set it upright, but I felt frozen in place. Liz was thoroughly startled, too. She started picking at that spot on the back of her head again.

Calloway kept his eyes trained on me. He wasn't quite glaring, but he also didn't look sympathetic or even pitying. This was an impenetrable stare. He seemed not at all uncomfortable holding me in his eyes, hardly blinking or moving. I directed my gaze to the banister.

"Why do you think we're here?" he asked. Liz shook her head, perplexed.

A thought came to me that maybe something miraculous had occurred, maybe a fluke scrap of evidence had landed in front of them. Maybe someone had confessed to something.

"Did you find something?" I asked.

Calloway let out an incredulous scoff. "A 911 call came through last night around ten," he said. "Someone driving over the bridge on West River Street spotted a body lying out on the asphalt in the parking lot at Haines's Hardware. First responders went out there, turns out it was Nick Haines." We were silent. I had the sensation of teetering on the edge of something steep in the dark.

My sister spoke first. Her voice was calm, still as a mountain lake at dawn, with not so much as a ripple betraying what I knew must be crashing down inside her. "Is he dead?"

"Yes," the sheriff answered. "One gunshot wound in the upper back."

Blood coursed through my ears. My pulse galloped. His words resounded in a loop in my head, more garbled each time around, until it became static. For a moment, I felt sure it was a joke, or that I must have been dreaming. It seemed impossible. But there was the sensation of the carpet digging into my bare feet, and the air from the vent on the side of the stairs blowing at the nape of my neck. I could remember waking up that morning. This was as real as anything else.

Quickly then, my jumble of thoughts seemed to clear away, like clouds parting in a gust of wind, and there in the middle of it all was Brenda's voice last night. Her insistence, the specificity of her request, the way she thanked me before hanging up the phone. I thought of Hiram, the way he'd smiled at the end of the night, how he'd peered around the corner into the dining room at us every now and then. Checking. Heat rose up my neck. Little jolts of muted electricity rippled through my body and everything suddenly seemed to move slowly: a moth fluttering against the front window glass, the sheriff blinking and hooking his thumb through one belt loop. I had the urge to vomit, and then to laugh. I was afraid of what my face looked like, that everyone else in the room could see through it right into my thoughts and know what I knew. I tried to remain very still.

"Where were you girls last night?" Calloway asked. The way he said *girls* made my stomach turn. I had an urge to tear a rung from the banister and beat him over the head with it. He hadn't scraped his boots on the mat before coming in. Wet dirt followed his trail from the door along our carpet.

"Out to dinner," I said.

"Where?"

"Larison's," Liz answered. Her eyes were wide. She had her arms wrapped around herself and was leaning forward slightly, like there was a pain in her stomach.

"When?"

"We went right after I got off work."

The sheriff jerked his head in my direction. "You met her there?" he asked.

"I picked her up from the bank and then we walked over together."

"Did you enter the bank?"

"Yes," I replied. Everything around me seemed brighter, louder. Light caught in the badge on his chest and cast a glare in my eye. The sound of his jacket brushing up against the wall, the metal caps on his boot laces tapping together as he shifted on his feet—it was all amplified, unbearably clear and close. Even the air felt sharp.

"I brought her an umbrella and then we went to dinner," I said, relieved to hear that my voice came out steady and level.

Calloway jumped in. "How long were you in the building, exactly?"

"Sorry, but what is going on here?" Liz said, interrupting. "Are you thinking we may have had anything to do with this?"

Calloway ignored her. He looked up at the old family photographs hanging on the wall along the staircase. Our mother standing outside a church with the two of us in matching floral dresses. A portrait of some distant relative whose name I'd long since forgotten. He looked at me, then back at the photos.

Liz narrowed her eyes at him and then grabbed her purse from the back of a chair. We all turned in her direction as she fumbled around inside the pocket. It was the same handbag she'd been using for years: calf leather the color of roasted chestnuts, brushed gold hardware. The stitching along the strap was fraying now, and a spot of dye had been rubbed completely off where the bag moved against her hip as she walked. I remembered our mother's stepsister mailing the purse to Knife River from Arizona around the time Liz got her job at the bank. It arrived in a large box along with some silk blouses and tailored slacks, a simple gold necklace in an envelope—clearly things she'd culled from her own closet. We'd barely heard from this woman in the months since she'd left, and then this package had arrived out of the blue. The note inside read *good luck on your new endeavor.* My nineteen-year-old sister put these things on and suddenly looked like an adult. All the clothing still remained in her regular rotation.

"Here," Liz said, producing a folded receipt. "Look at this."

The sheriff waved the paper away. "We're just having a conversation," he said.

She walked up to him and shoved the receipt right into his chest, actually pressing her hands against his shirt and rising up on her toes to meet his eyes more directly. I could see this surprised him. He frowned and then took the receipt, looking it over before handing it to Calloway, who studied it for a long time.

"I'm going to ask you this just once," the sheriff said. "Is there anything, anything at all, you two ladies want to tell us?" The sheriff used the same tone you might use to address a couple of children who'd stolen something of minor importance.

"No," Liz said. "Of course, there isn't." The two men and my sister all turned their gaze on me. Everyone's eyes were intensely expectant. I had the sensation of many pairs of hands pressing down on my chest and back, needling their way into my mouth and ears, all trying to pull something out from within me.

"No," I said. "I have nothing to tell you."

38

Brenda took the news calmly. We arrived at her house unannounced later that day. Liz gave a quick, hard knock at the door but then immediately pulled a key from her purse and used it to let us both in. Her energy was frantic. She had wanted to go over immediately after the police left, but I'd insisted on taking a shower first. It wasn't so much that I wanted to wash as much as I wanted to sit in the tub for a while, thinking, the hot water beating down against the back of my neck. I needed some time to myself behind a locked door. Liz was waiting at the bottom of the stairs when I got out.

"I have to tell Brenda," she'd said. "I can't do it over the phone. She's going to freak out." I nodded, a tight knot hardening in the pit of my stomach. Liz left our house without a coat, just a sweater pulled over her nightdress and a pair of muck boots, no socks, that she didn't kick off her feet before entering Brenda's living room, where we found her sitting on the sofa watching *Wheel of Fortune*. No lights were on. Her tiny, pruned face was cast in a bluish glow and she put up one finger, as if to hold us in place for a moment, while the winning word was revealed. Everyone applauded. Brenda herself gave a little clap and then turned to look at us.

I took a seat opposite Brenda but Liz sat down on the floor. She dug her fingers into the carpet pile and raked her hands back and forth like a cat as she explained everything. Pink fibers loosened from the weave and accumulated beneath her nails and on her sleeves. A plate of checkerboard cookies sat on the side table next to a pair of reading glasses. She listened to my sister carefully, though she didn't look particularly alarmed, nor did she stop her to ask any questions. Liz went on for a long while. I couldn't remember the last time I heard her talk so much. She started with a fraught retelling of what exactly happened when the police spoke to us directly, including even minor details like the gloves sticking out of Calloway's back pocket—they were blue, Liz emphasized, and previously she'd only seen him with black gloves. These little things didn't seem to trouble her more than she already was, but I could tell she somehow felt they were important to the larger story.

Once she'd finished talking, she shifted into a list of observations relating to the actual visit—it was a Friday, which was the same day of the week our mother went missing. Liz had eaten some raspberries right before the police arrived and there were seeds stuck in her teeth, which were bothering her as the conversation went on. To me, it was clear that she was actually wanting to talk through her feelings and this was the easiest way to do it—a blunt naming of facts.

Soon she quieted down, thinking. Then she asked, "Who do you think did this?"

"I know he got in a bad fight not too long ago. Maybe could be the same man." Brenda's eyes remained fixed on the TV as she spoke. "Who can say? Lots of people didn't much like Nick."

"Yes, but still, for someone to actually kill him."

"Well, men do crazy things when they're drunk and angry."

"I thought you'd be shocked," Liz said, shaking her head.

Brenda picked up a cookie. "I haven't been shocked in fifty years."

Liz stood up and began to pace all around the room. She stood at the window, arms crossed, then abruptly pulled the drapes shut and walked to the bookshelf, where she ran her finger across the spines, back and forth, breathing heavily. Every so often she would say something like *I just can't believe this*. Sometimes it would be in a loud voice, other times she'd speak quietly down into her chest, though it seemed to me that no matter how she said it, she was only speaking to herself. She picked up a bowl of potpourri from a side table and held it up to her face, inhaling sharply for a long minute before coughing and placing the bowl back down and taking another circle around the couch. She seemed unable to soothe herself. I could hear her teeth clicking together from my seat across the room. Her nervousness was making me a bit panicky, but I had no idea how to calm her down.

I'd seen my sister this way before; whenever she got severely overwhelmed it seemed to spill over into the mechanisms of her body. She spiraled into repetitions, like the hair pulling, or flicking her fingers in quick bursts. Once, about a year after our mother had disappeared, I'd caught her slamming her head on the wall upstairs. I'd pulled her away and held on to her shoulders, nearly in tears, but by the time I'd gone back downstairs I could hear the same thudding noise again.

Brenda got up and straightened the potpourri bowl. By now, Liz had walked five wide circles around the sofa. Her eyes were unfocused. Brenda and I exchanged a quick look and then I heard her ask my sister to please go into the kitchen and make her a cup of decaffeinated tea. The idea of a task seemed to calm Liz, or at least take her mind off the pacing. She disappeared around the corner.

Now we were alone. The room was quiet but for the *Wheel of Fortune* song. It played on a loop as the contestant puzzled over his letters, then the show cut to a commercial break. Brenda had locked eyes with me the moment Liz left the room. I didn't want to say anything and seem crazy or risk insulting her. My nerves were wracked by the silence, but Brenda didn't seem to mind it. She barely even blinked. It felt like a long time had passed, but the same commercial for fabric softener was still going. A dry, strained cough slipped past my lips. She held a box of tissues toward me and I shook my head no. She kept her arms outstretched and smiled a little before placing the box back to her side.

"One of my nephews is a cardiologist," she said quietly. "He checked me out over Christmas while I was visiting family in Ontario."

She paused to eat a cookie. Crumbs fell from her lips and onto her lap. She didn't brush them off, they just sat there piling up on each other as she crunched away. I noticed my toes had gone half numb from curling them up so tightly inside my boots.

When she'd finished the cookie, she continued, "My heart isn't in good shape. I've chosen not to fill the prescription he gave me. What's the point at my age?" A look of mutual understanding passed between us. My toes relaxed. She offered me the plate of cookies and I took one. Liz came back with Brenda's tea after the commercial break and we watched the rest of the episode in silence.

Liz and I slept over that night on the pull-out sofa, too overwhelmed and exhausted to make the short drive back home. Really, though, I think neither of us wanted to spend the night alone in our own house. We lay there side by side, listening to each other's breathing in the dark.

"Are you okay?" I asked.

"No," Liz said.

"Are you tired?"

"No."

"What are you doing, then?"

"I'm lying here trying not to panic." She sat up in the bed, swiveling around to face me. I could just make out her features in the dim glow of the hallway nightlight. "Aren't you scared?" she asked me. I told her no. It was the truth, mostly. She whispered, "What's going to happen now?"

"Not too much, if I know this place."

"What if they think I did it?"

"No one's going to think that."

"You don't know."

"I'm pretty sure. Anyway, we both were out while it happened, at a crowded restaurant, where lots of people saw you. And there's a security camera at the bar, and you're on the footage at the bank the whole evening beforehand."

I sat up next to her and looked out the window. The moon was bright and low, hovering over the mountain ridge. A plane blinked in the distance, slowly passing into the horizon. A couple of houses down the hill had their floodlights on.

"He isn't anywhere out there," I said, pointing. "Do you know what I mean?"

"I suppose."

"You can walk into any store, anybody's home, anyplace in this entire world, and never be surprised by his face. He's gone. He's dead. You don't need to dread him anymore. You can just live your life now. Doesn't that make you feel better?"

Liz rested quietly for a few minutes, leaning back on the pillow. I could see the shadows of thoughts floating around in her eyes, gathering shape. Perhaps she was imagining walking through town, unafraid, for the first time. She could drive past the street he once lived on and not have to care; she could start taking the shortcut over the bridge by his store and not feel a rolling swell of fear and anger. I imagined the hardware shop overgrown with weeds. The roof sunken in, soft with pools of stagnant rainwater. A rock thrown through the front door. Maybe some new business would move in. Maybe someone would buy the lot and demolish it. Maybe we'd never know either way because maybe my sister would leave Knife River. The world felt suddenly open. My heart leapt at the thought of it all.

"Yes," Liz finally said. "It does make me feel better."

39

A week later, I agreed to take the rental Maria put in a word for me about and deposited some money with the owner, who'd repainted the bedroom and sent me a nice email about where to park, and what to know about the area. Even though I didn't have much to take with me, I spent a long time each day sitting on the sofa I'd been using as a bed since October, looking at my two open bags laid out before me. I folded all the clothes carefully, wrapping anything breakable inside sweaters. Each time I walked by I'd stop, look at the bags again, and feel a quick flash of panic. In some way, I felt unprepared to go, though there seemed to be little left for me to do. Liz would occasionally sneak in various things—mittens, or some cold medicine, or a few boxes of dried pasta from the cupboard. Once, a small bottle of our mother's perfume, all but dried up. She never said anything about it. I'd only find these things in there later, carefully hidden beneath my clothes.

We didn't talk about what happened to Nick Haines, either. Eight days went by, and no news came. I was jumpy, apprehensive. My heart fluttered if I heard a noise on the porch, a branch falling or the boot mat shifting in the wind, thinking it was the police back to question us. But our days were quiet. I asked the office manager from the periodontist's for extra work, wanting to make as much cash as I could before seeing what there was for me in Maine.

Then, on the ninth day, Eva called. It was late at night and I was lying awake on the couch. She began speaking as soon as I answered, barely before I could say hello. Her voice was quick and urgent.

She said, "Someone got arrested, if you didn't already know." I didn't. My sister was asleep upstairs. I thought of going to wake her right then and had even sat up, but stopped myself before standing. Blood rushed inside my ears. "It's the same guy he had a bad fight with at the Rocking Horse a little while back."

"Who is he?"

"He came here to work on one of the fracking crews, but he's been camping out ever since that all got shut down. I don't know his name."

"You heard this from Jack, I guess."

"I went to dinner with him, meaning to call things off between us, actually. But he started ranting about this right when we sat down, so I listened. I wanted to be able to tell it to you."

"So you broke up with him?"

"Tomorrow, I will," she said. "We're meeting for a drink and I'm going to tell him it's over." My heart swelled a little. I let out an awkward grunt of acknowledgment, not wanting to seem too excited. After all, I reminded myself, it was just something she meant to do. Nothing had actually changed yet.

"What happens now?" I asked. "With the guy they arrested?"

"Nothing here in town, actually, because it turned out he had all these other outstanding warrants in other states. Jack mentioned felony child endangerment and something about arms trafficking. He's getting transferred to a jail in Ohio to wait on the first trial, then to another one in Pennsylvania for the rest. It's a mess. Jack said it'll take years."

"But they charged him for Nick Haines?"

"They want to, but I heard him say they couldn't uncover anything on the scene. No tire tracks, and no footprints, because it was raining so hard all night. The one security camera Nick had was inside the shop facing the register."

"And no witnesses, I guess."

"No. All the way out by the bridge at night? No one goes there. Jack was pretty angry about it."

"Angry about what, exactly?"

"That there's nothing he can do. Apparently, the sheriff is going to retire and finally take his pension next year, so he's checked out. He doesn't care that much about this."

"I think he's been that way for a long time."

"You know, Jack actually went and checked the security footage at the restaurant and the bank to make sure you and Liz were really there at the right time. He got the coroner to rush an autopsy, just so he could know when Nick got shot that night to make sure it all added up."

"Are you serious?"

"Yeah. He was furious when it turned out you two weren't lying."

"Well." My mouth went dry. "Why shouldn't he cover all his bases?"

"Anyway," her voice was soft. "I didn't think the police would tell you anything. And I thought you'd want to know."

A stinging bloom of guilt grew in my chest. It moved into my throat, which had become tight and hot. I didn't feel like I could get enough air down it, even though I could feel the mechanism of my breathing, the contractions of my lungs inside my body. I didn't even know the name of man who'd been arrested. Asking for it felt like too much, too real. I slid from the couch onto the carpet, where I knelt at the coffee table and pressed my forehead against the surface. I tried to think only of the soothing coolness of the glass, the way my hand looked on the floor below—magnified and distorted.

Finally, I said, "I'm leaving a week from tomorrow." Silence on the other end. I listened carefully for the sound of her breathing. "Sunday," I said, as if she didn't know what day it was.

"Yeah," she said. "I thought you'd be going soon." I couldn't read her tone. I waited another moment for her to say more, but she didn't.

Finally, I said, "It's getting to be time."

"Do you feel ready?" she asked.

"Not entirely, honestly."

"Have you told your sister?"

"Yeah, we've talked about it."

There was a pause before she spoke. "Are you asking for an answer from me?"

"No," I told her. I thought about what it might feel like if she didn't come with me. A little lump started to form in my throat. I pushed it down and took a deep breath. "You don't have to tell me either way."

"What do you mean?"

"I'm going to drive by your place on my way out Sunday morning. If you're outside, then we'll put your things in my car and go. If you aren't, it's fine. I get it. We don't have to make it a whole thing."

"If I left like that, it would become a whole thing anyway."

"You don't need to tell anyone why," I said.

"I can't just disappear."

"You could say you're entering a cloistered convent."

"Oh, okay." She laughed. "That'll work."

"Or that you found a job that starts immediately or something. Seriously, though, just think about it. I'll be coming by early Sunday."

When we hung up it was nearly one in the morning. I could hear the low rumble of my sister's snores through the floorboards. She sounded like a train barreling down wet tracks. It was obvious she was deep asleep, but I found myself upstairs at her bedside anyway, nudging her on the shoulder again and again until she stirred awake. I had to repeat what Eva told me twice. Liz switched the lamp on and stared at me. Crust trailed from one side of her mouth all the way down her neck.

"You said he's in jail now?"

"Yes, for a couple other crimes. They sounded pretty serious."

"I didn't think they'd identify someone so quickly."

"Well, this guy was already on their radar."

"I guess that makes sense." She rubbed her temples. "They should've called us and let us know."

"They still may."

"I doubt it." I noticed then that her outfit for the next day was arranged on the duvet next to her, on the empty side. Her socks, pants, a shirt, all laid down in the right order. The top of the shirt rested on the pillow. It looked almost as if an invisible person were inside it, lying still, waiting for morning.

I pointed to the clothes and asked, "What's that about?"

"Easier that way." She shrugged. "I don't like to spend a lot of time thinking about what to wear in the morning."

"You don't mess them up in the night?"

"No, I'm a pretty deep sleeper. I stay on one side of the bed."

"Sorry to wake you up like this."

"It's fine. It's important." Liz yawned and leaned back on her elbows. "I'm glad you told me."

Back downstairs, I drifted off on the couch to a public-access documentary about a cave rescue. In my mind's eye, I was both on the ground outside the cave's opening and within the body of one of the lost miners. I could hear the heightened breath of the families hovering at the opening, searching the darkness for emerging bodies. Watery visions of headlamps beaming up from the bottom of a deep, black pit loomed. Mud lapped at my feet. As the credits began to roll, I jerked awake to a loud, sudden creaking. I sat upright, my hands clenched into fists. All was still. Liz's snoring rumbled on. Then another creak. It was just a loose shutter at the front of the house, shifting in the wind. My heart began to slow and I lay back down, dropping a pillow over my head to muffle the noise.

I thought about something I'd read in a magazine once, years ago, in the waiting room at the periodontist's office, when I first went in to interview for my job. The article explained that the matter of our teeth, the actual calcium, had come from massive, ancient stars that exploded long ago and sent minerals flying all across the universe. I'd had a strong urge to jump to my feet and announce what I'd learned, how reassuring and frightening it was at the same time. I looked around at all the other people, waiting, with the little miracles of their teeth just sitting in their heads. The article was placed between an advertisement for dog food and an article about solar power. It wasn't even particularly *new* news. The magazine was dated almost six months ago. Quietly, I ripped the pages out of the magazine and tucked them into my pocket to save for further review. When I got home, I read the article again. I reread it many times, actually, for a long time before I eventually lost the pages in a move. But even after that, I thought about the article sometimes as I worked on my transcriptions and when I got my own cavities filled. And it came to me again now as I lay on the couch alone in the dark, trying to steady myself.

It was soothing to think that the potential for anything was just floating around out there in the universe, waiting for the right moment to take the form of a tooth, a diamond, a sea lion, a violet, whatever, before returning to the vast, black soup and maybe bubbling up as something else again, maybe somewhere else in the universe entirely, maybe twelve billion years down the road. It made me feel a little sick, also. Like there were no guardrails, no rules. Wonderful and terrible things would keep happening all the time. Lots of things would begin as one thing and turn out to be another. And no matter how dear a person was to me, sooner or later they would be irretrievably lost. Whatever scraps of luck or vengeance I managed to come upon in this lifetime wouldn't mean much in the end. Everything I'd ever seen was on its way back to the dust pile. When I thought about it like that, I felt thirteen again—confounded and defenseless. It made me want to go back upstairs and hug my sister. Instead, I lay there, eyes shut, until I finally fell asleep.

40

In the morning, Liz went down to the basement and returned with a cardboard box. I sat next to her on the floor in the sunroom and watched as she opened the top and pulled out a half-built birdhouse. It was large, elaborate, made to look like a little Victorian home with turrets and spindles and gingerbread trimming. The base was finished, and most of the body, but it was unpainted and the roof remained in six separate pieces, unattached.

"Mom and I started to build this a long time ago," she said. "We got it at the church Christmas bazaar when you were still a toddler."

"Why didn't you finish?"

"You know," she said, shrugging. "That was around the time our father left, and then she went full time with her job, so it just never happened." We sat quietly for a while examining the birdhouse together. There were six enclosed little rooms on the inside with a dowel perch set outside each opening. In front there was a tiny door with a knob and keyhole. The porch had a shallow, lipped inlay to hold seeds. I'd never heard mention of this before. I must have passed by this box for years without knowing what was inside. Even if I had looked, I wouldn't have recognized it for what it really was: an amulet, a touchable manifestation of one of the many memories that existed only between my sister and mother. Before she was gone, it was just clutter. An unfinished project gathering dust. As the day turned to weeks after she'd disappeared, it had become a precious time capsule. Intention suspended.

"We can finish it today, if you want," I said. Liz nodded. Inside the box was a bag of different-sized screws to affix the roof and remaining walls. There was a handful of fine-tipped paintbrushes, too, and a card showing three potential color schemes and how to mix all the shades you would need from any basic assortment of craft paint. A silverfish scurried out from inside the bag when we turned it over onto the floor. We set to work wiping the dust off the house; it took some time. I was surprised my mother would've bought a thing like this at all. It was so big and unwieldy we'd have to go to the lumberyard and get at least a six-inch square post to hold it up. The post would have to get dug maybe a foot into the ground to keep steady. And then the house would need to be kept free of wasps' nests and repainted once the weather ate away at the façade. It didn't feel to me like the kind of thing she would want, but then how would I know? She bought it before I'd even formed my first memory.

"How'd you end up leaving the Christmas bazaar with this?" I asked. We'd begun sorting the little bags of fixtures; shingles and dowels and a miniature weather vane. "It's such an odd thing."

"It's for birds to nest in," Liz said, examining one piece of the roof. "What's so odd?"

"It's like a fancy Victorian dollhouse."

"The decorative elements aren't for the birds, they're for us," she said, looking at me seriously. She took the weather vane and held it up, spinning the arrow around with the flick of a finger. A delighted smile broke across her face, and I was reminded of the careful way she'd built her model planes, how meticulous she was with her embroidery, the intense concentration she applied to handicraft and the genuine love she had for it. The model planes, too, were thoughtfully embellished. I remembered one glider painted blue with dozens and dozens of tiny, perfect white stars she'd had to paint with the tip of a toothpick.

"Was it your idea to get this?" I asked, peering into one of the circular openings. There was a wispy old cobweb inside, a dead moth wobbling in the floss.

"Both of ours, really," Liz said. "There was an old man at a booth and he was selling some ready-made, and then these kits with all the pieces inside, which were much cheaper. We talked to him for a while. Mom was very impressed by the craftsmanship. It's actually made of Baltic birch, not balsa. That's a much nicer grade of wood."

"How long did it take you to get this much done?"

"We worked at it on and off for about a year." Liz leaned back on her heels. "I could've finished it myself in a week, but I didn't want to work on it without her."

"She wouldn't have wanted you to?"

"No, I don't think she would have really cared. But it was our thing, it was something we could do together, and I didn't want to miss out on that." She turned to me with one eyebrow arched. "We didn't always get along so easily, you know. So this was special."

We spread out across the sunroom floor, getting all the different pieces in order. Liz cleared her throat. "It wasn't just that she was busy with work. You were getting bigger then, and talking, so you could do stuff with her instead of just having to be looked after all the time."

"What's that have to do with this?"

"Well, you two obviously had a much more natural rapport." I picked up a little bag of shingles, just to have somewhere else to direct my gaze. "It's okay," Liz said. "I'm not bitter about it." She gave a weak smile. "You asked me why we never got around to finishing, and I'm just saying I think that's part of the reason. It was easier for her to do things with you. And it was easier for me to do things alone."

We spent awhile in silence, gluing the tiny shingles onto the sections of roof. Liz seemed unusually content. Her hands moved quickly, plucking the pieces up from the bag and attaching them in straight, even rows. No glue bulged out at the sides. No piece was crooked. My part of the roof looked slapdash in comparison, with gaps between some shingles and others overlapping too closely. I found it hard to squeeze just the right amount of glue each time, and quickly grew tired of the repetitiveness of the task. Liz's eyes were glazed in steady concentration.

Once all the shingles were affixed, we set about putting the roof together. I tried placing the segments in the right order on the floor in front of me, but found that the first two wouldn't align and one of the corner pieces was completely backward.

Liz watched quietly for a minute before saying, "Let me." I moved aside and looked on as she rearranged the pieces, giving them a quick scan before expertly interlocking the joints on each section. Within moments, a complete, single roof sat before us. She nodded, satisfied. We realized then that our only screwdriver was too small to attach the roof to the body of the birdhouse. We tried to turn the screws by hand, but of course it didn't work. I even took a dime out of my pocket, thinking maybe I'd be able to wedge it far enough into the grooves, but the coin slipped from my fingers on the first try and rolled somewhere under the bookshelf.

"Why don't we just glue it together?" I said.

"Absolutely not," Liz replied, her tone souring. "That isn't how it's done. Besides, I doubt it would even stay on, it's so heavy." I could see she was growing agitated. She picked up the screwdriver again, trying unsuccessfully to catch the notches at just the right angle. She tossed the tool down to the floor and shut her eyes, taking a labored breath before repeating the cycle again. Picking up the screwdriver, maneuvering the blade, throwing it back onto the ground and twisting the screws with her fingers, shaking her hand out after each attempt. A frenzied energy began to build around her as she repeated these steps again and again. I knew she would not stop. I knew she would sit here for the rest of the day, thinking of nothing but how to finish assembling the birdhouse. She tossed the screwdriver down harder this time. The tip left a little nick in the floorboard. In this moment, nothing mattered more to me than seeing her to the other side of the project. I wouldn't be able to live with myself, I thought, if I left town before she got to have this one thing done right. I wanted badly to restore her contentedness. The screwdriver clattered to the ground again. She let out a shrill, exasperated grunt.

Finally, I said, "You know what, I think I actually might have a Phillips head in the trunk of my car."

"Oh," Liz said, looking up at me. "That's good news."

"I'll go look." I picked one of the screws up and tucked it into my pocket. She turned her attention to the gingerbread trimming around the little porch and gables, testing its soundness by pushing around with her knuckle, adding more glue to the spots with any give. I went outside, quietly closing the door behind me.

Paul's driveway was empty, but I knocked on the front door and rang the doorbell just in case. I was relieved when he didn't answer. I didn't want to talk to him about the birdhouse, anything else really. Through the garage window, I could see his worktable laid out with spools of wire and a long rod with a spindle. He seemed to be repairing an old fishing pole. Behind the table, the finished ship in a bottle he'd shown me sat on a shelf. The sails were plump and symmetrical, billowing outward as if caught in a strong gust of wind on the open water. I looked back at our house, then down the street. No cars passed. The key was still taped in its spot on the shutter, so I peeled it off and let myself inside, pulling the roller door up just enough to duck through. Dust lingered in the air. There was a sharp, woody smell, like inside the hangar at a lumberyard in autumn. Two gloves hung off the edge of a saw table. I felt strange being in there alone, and I called out Paul's name, to be sure. My own voice echoed back to me. From somewhere within the clutter, a cricket chirped.

I began to sift through the boxes on the table. One held only loose bulbs that looked like they'd once belonged to a string of Christmas lights. There were scissors of all sizes, and protractors, razors, gasoline canisters, rope, fishing tackle, paint cans with stir sticks dried in place. I looked through the many rows of shelves, pulling out little bins and trays full of odds and ends. After a few minutes, I spotted a screwdriver and dug around in my pocket, hoping it would be a fit, but the bit was too narrow. Deflated, I moved on to the row of shelves and saw a quick flash of movement out of the corner of my eye. It was Liz, visible through the side window. She appeared for a moment in the kitchen, holding a glass up to her mouth, then again for a second in the next window as she walked back toward the sunroom. I stepped closer to the wall, keeping myself out of sight. Paul must have seen her from this same spot, doing these same things, many times over the years. I wondered if she ever saw him, too, and if their eyes ever met, if they ever exchanged a quick nod or smile.

I felt a lump form suddenly in my throat. Tears blurred my vision. Just the day before I would've said I was ready leave Knife River again. At least as ready as I could ever hope to be. Now all I could think about was this birdhouse and my sister. Leaving without finishing it together felt like leaving her without even a goodbye. I needed to know that it was assembled and painted, sitting out in the backyard, weathering the sun and snow and sheltering nests of wild creatures. I needed her to feel that its purpose was fulfilled. I looked around the rest of the garage in desperation and spotted a couple of dusty old tool cabinets up against the wall, a key on a lanyard hanging out of one of their locks. In the first, I found only some loose electrical adapters and drill attachments.

I used the key to open the second one and immediately found a screwdriver that was a perfect fit for our joint pieces. I felt a swell of triumph and made sure to note its exact placement so I could run back over to return it before Paul got back home. I knew he'd said I could come by anytime, but still I had the feeling of doing something wrong. As I went to relock the cabinet and replace the key, my hand grazed against a loose nail. I felt a sharp sting, and then the warmth of blood rising up to the surface of my skin. The cut was long and jagged. I held it to my shirt, trying to absorb any drips. The last thing I needed, I thought, was to leave my blood splattered around his workshop. I glanced around for something to wipe my hand with and spotted a roll of paper towels on a bottom shelf. In my haste, I knocked over a box labeled Lights, cringing as a loose bulb rolled onto the cement floor. The glass shell remained intact, and after wrapping my hand in a paper towel, I knelt down to pick it up. There were a few others like it in the box, along with a bag of wire caps and plastic film canisters.

And there, at the bottom of the box, lay a square of folded red fabric. The creases were precise. The cotton was dusty and unfaded. Something about it snagged in me and I paused, bulb in hand, taking a closer look. Something hard to name began coursing through my body. I felt a ripple of nostalgia. Warmth came into my cheeks. Then, fear, a shapeless, animal kind of panic. I set aside the light, picked up the fabric, and unfolded the square to reveal its printed side: little white flowers.

I dropped the fabric back into the box like it had burned me, tossing the bulb on top, and shoved the box and the paper towel roll back where I'd found them. Paul's spare key kept slipping from my fingers as I went to tuck it back under the tape at the top of the shutter after locking the garage door behind me. I ran over the gravel divide between our driveways, flying through our front door and locking it behind me. Liz was in the kitchen, setting a teakettle on the stove. I looked at her for a moment, then turned and dashed down the hall into the den where my suitcases sat open.

Behind me I heard her shout, "Any luck?" Her voice sounded garbled and distant, like it was coming to me from the bottom of a deep well. I tore through my clothes and unzipped a pocket in the lining of the suitcase, pulling out a plastic freezer bag where I'd stashed some check stubs, my Social Security card, and the packet of old photographs Eva had given me over the winter. I flipped through the pictures. I felt like I wasn't truly inside myself, but was operating the mechanisms of my body from some remote location. The pictures passed before my eyes in a blur until I got to the last one, the one of Liz working on one of her planes with my mother in the background, on the way out the door in her red kerchief.

There it was. The exact shade of red, the gauziness of the cotton weave, the little white flowers. My hands regained some of their feeling. Everything suddenly felt too real, too close, too bright. I wasn't sure what to do. I wasn't sure what to think, even. It was as though something very fragile had fallen into my lap and I had no idea what to do with it, how to keep it from breaking.

Liz called my name from the kitchen. My pulse raced as I tried to figure out how I could possibly explain this to her. What words I would use, how I would prepare for her reaction. Then, a sliver of doubt came loose in my mind, like a leaf drifting away from its branch. How could I really know what circumstances led to her scarf being there in Paul's garage? And then, how could I place that doubt upon my sister? My voice seemed to dry up inside me. I heard her call out to me again. I heard the whistle of the kettle, and then the sound of her taking it off the burner and pouring water from the spout. My breath had grown very shallow, and I noticed that I was making an effort to be as quiet as possible as I tucked the pictures back into the bottom pocket and zipped it shut. I stood up, taking a moment to steady myself, trying to wipe any hint of this from my face, before walking into the kitchen and taking the mug my sister held out to me.

We spent the rest of the day together, finishing the birdhouse. I watched as she twisted Paul's screwdriver into all the joints, connecting each bracket with a mild, contented expression on her face. We made grilled cheeses and simple salads for lunch, and ate together off trays on the floor as we used to do years ago, surrounded by the clutter of our project. Light filtered in through the windows and cast ribbons of gauzy, yellow light over everything. The sun was staying out longer, little by little, each day. She asked me about my impending move, wanting to know more about the place I'd rented and telling me that she intended to come visit once I was settled in.

Then, as she uncapped a bottle of lemon-colored craft paint left over from a different project of hers, she said, "I have to tell you something."

"What is it?" I asked.

"The bank officially offered me a relocation. I decided I'm going to take it." The branch, as she'd predicted, had extended some of its long-term employees either this option, or a severance package as part of their restructuring. "I thought at first I would take the money," she said. "But then I spoke to Brenda about it and she got me thinking. There isn't any good reason for me to stay here anymore. I'd have to find another job in town, and I can't imagine what it would even be. I wanted to leave here when I was a teenager, and then of course I couldn't. I'm lonely in this house. Why should I be here by myself?" She fussed with the cuff of her shirt for a minute before nearly shouting, "And why shouldn't I date? I'd like to try and have a relationship."

"I think you should," I replied. "I think that's great."

"I think I'll find someone," she said, shrugging. "I hope I do."

"Are you kidding?" I said. "Absolutely, you will." I looked at my sister's face and felt a surge of love and admiration. I didn't believe there was a more courageous or beautiful person in the world. "Where are they sending you?" I asked.

"Nashua, New Hampshire," she told me. "There's an aviation museum there that looks very interesting. I can get an apartment not far from the new branch. And I think it will be good for me to have a smaller place where I won't have to worry about mowing the grass or keeping the basement from flooding during thunderstorms." She explained that there was one other woman from her group who was relocating, too. "Martha. I don't mind her."

"What about the house?"

"Well, I'm going to have to put it on the market." She poured some of the paint onto a paper plate, nervously swirling it around with one of the brushes from the kit. "Brenda has a former student she's still friendly with who's a Realtor in town. We spoke to her on the phone together a couple days ago and they both kind of convinced me. She's going to list it herself. The fee is very reasonable. Of course, whenever it sells, I'll give you half the money."

"You don't need to do that. You've been here much longer than me." Just hearing her offer made me feel a little guilty. So much had already been taken from her in her life. She wasn't even out of her thirties.

"It's what's appropriate," she replied in a firm voice.

I asked my sister how she felt about all this, especially the prospect of putting our childhood home up for sale. I wondered if the magnitude of the change was overwhelming to her. I knew it would be for me.

"I don't know how I feel yet," she said.

"It's too big to see up close, maybe. When you get some distance from it then I think you'll have a better idea."

"Is that how it happens with you?"

"Usually," I said. "When exactly is this going ahead?"

"At the end of the quarter, if I don't want any paycheck delays. And of course I don't. So I need to be there in nineteen days." At first I was taken aback. That was so soon. Less than a month. It was difficult to imagine my sister in any place other than this. I thought about the house sitting empty with unlit rooms and got a little chill. Then I thought of what I'd discovered in Paul's garage and the chill spread through me, growing stronger and sharper as it went. Here was another thing too big to see up close. I didn't know what to make of it, but I knew that no matter what, Liz would soon be gone from this place. The chill didn't subside, but I could put it into a box. Just for a moment. Just until I had time alone to think.

"Take anything you may want from the house before you go," she said. "I've already put some of Mom's things aside for myself. And I'll bring some of the furniture, only what I have room for. The Salvation Army will come with a truck to pick up whatever's left for donations."

"I guess I should probably take some pots and pans."

"Anything you need." Liz poured some pale blue next to the yellow on her mixing plate. "Do you think it's silly that I wanted to finish building this even though I'm leaving so soon?" she asked, dipping a brush into the blue and painting a first coat onto every other shingle. With a different brush, she went back and filled in the remaining ones with yellow, then started the next row in the opposite direction, creating a checkerboard pattern.

"No," I told her. "I don't think that at all."

"I just thought it would be nice to be able to put it in the yard here, where it was meant to go originally." I nodded in agreement and set to work painting a shutter. While the first coat of paint dried on the shingles, Liz leaned in close to one of the spires and lightly sketched swirling candy cane stripes with a pencil before filling it all in with alternating colors. Her hand was unshaking, steady as she glided her brush over the wood, barely blinking.

"I didn't really love my life here, you know," she said. "I was just used to it. Those aren't always the same thing."

"That's true."

Liz moved on to the next spire, outlining the same stripe motif. I was only on my second shutter. "I was looking online and saw there's an aviation school attached to the museum in Nashua," she said, giving a cautious sort of grin. "I thought I could try taking flying lessons. They're giving me a bit of a pay increase, and then sooner or later I'll have money from the house."

"You should go for it," I said, my heart nearly bursting out of my chest. All my life I'd imagined her up in the sky, slicing through the clouds in the cockpit of a little plane. "I mean, why not?"

"Why not," she repeated.

We finished around dusk, and then watched half of an old movie in the living room. My sister was rapt, her eyes unmoving from the screen. Silently, she mouthed along with some of the dialogue. I learned she'd seen it already several times on this channel. It was black and white, about a woman who survives a jet crash in the far reaches of a jungle and falls in love with the badly injured pilot, who later manages to protect her from a jaguar attack despite his broken leg. Eventually they are rescued, and the woman realizes she does not want to return to her railway-tycoon husband in Los Angeles.

"I just think it's so outrageous that her hair is perfectly done in those big waves even when she's dragging around in the mud, foraging for fallen coconuts," Liz said, snorting with laughter. "I really get a kick out of old movies." At one point, I heard Paul's truck pull into his driveway. His headlights illuminated our porch, stretching long shadows out into the yard as he slowed to a halt. I heard him unload some things from the back, lift the garage door, and latch it behind him. Liz yawned and tucked a pillow under her neck, reclining back into the couch with a sleepy smile on her face.

41

For a long time that night after Liz went upstairs to bed, I sat on the couch in the dark, wondering. I had my hands by my sides, looking ahead, as though I were focusing on a presentation. In some way, I was observing two competing versions of myself, both vying for my attention, throwing their own arguments at me. There was a tremendous pressure behind my eyes, pushing out against my skull. A part of me wanted to run upstairs, burst into my sister's room, and tell her everything, if only so the pressure of knowing would not fall entirely upon me. I felt that a glaring stain had been cast on our fragile closure, and feared a future where I ended each day by rubbing at it, trying to get it out, only ruining all the surrounding tapestry in my desperation. Then the question I'd grown so sick of, the same one I'd been asking myself again and again the longer I stayed in town, joined the chorus: What did I really know?

I took a deep, long breath. I counted backward from ten. I knew that Paul and his wife had lived next to us for as long as I could remember. I knew that was my mother's handkerchief in his garage. I knew he'd acted neighborly toward me, which led me to believe he may have been neighborly toward my mother, too.

There seemed to be too many possible reasons, all innocuous and mundane, that could explain the presence of the kerchief. What if she dropped it on the driveway that day, years ago, where Paul could have spotted it, picked it up, brought it into the house to return to her when he saw her next? What if she stopped by to talk to him on her way down the road and had left it there, either by accident or for reasons unknown? Perhaps any of these things happened and then she vanished, and he put it away in that junk box, afraid that returning it to us might make him look bad? Or maybe he held on to it as some kind of melancholy keepsake. I didn't know Paul well. How could I say that wasn't the kind of thing he would do? Certainly there were good reasons to believe in Nick Haines's guilt. Other people thought so. Brenda thought so enough to remove him entirely from this world. She'd known him for decades and had felt in her gut he was a danger. He'd cleaned his truck out carefully before the police arrived at his home. He sobbed over the compact, drunk, on an isolated road at a strange hour. I thought through every damning thing about Nick, and tried to settle back down into the belief that it was him. Of course, it was him. It had to be him. I lay down and fell into a restless sleep for a while, and then jerked awake half past midnight.

I walked into the kitchen and stood at the window facing Paul's house, the same one I'd spotted Liz from when I was in his garage earlier. His front step was illuminated by a single floodlight. It cast a blue glow around the grass, drawing tall shadows from the handrail. The garage door was closed. I shut my eyes. In my mind, I ran my fingers along the kerchief again. I wished, more intensely than I ever had before, that I could conjure my mother's ghost, if only for a minute, just to ask her, simply, *who?* I sat down on the floor for a long time, half praying for some kind of miraculous confirmation to appear before me, blotting out this new glimmer of doubt. Nothing came. I tried to list my earlier explanations about the kerchief back to myself, but they didn't take as well this time. Each one seemed phony, a cheap and unconvincing prop that toppled over if I examined it too long. I moved from the floor to a chair at the kitchen table.

My gut pulsed with a cold, persistent dread. The doubts that merely needled me minutes ago now blared like alarm bells. I wanted to call Eva, but I didn't want to be soothed or reassured so much as I wanted an answer. I couldn't stand to just go back to the couch and try to sleep. I couldn't stomach the idea of waiting until morning, either, to see whether I'd view things in a more rational light after some time and rest, or maybe some logical explanation would emerge after the shock faded. The bird clock chimed one—an American long-eared owl. Something wild and unhinged began to unfold in my gut.

There was a baseball bat in the umbrella stand by the door. Liz had put it there years ago, its plain wooden handle blending in with the umbrellas. She hid these kinds of things all around the house then— a little paring knife just under her mattress, a hammer in the space between her pillow and headboard, an empty wine bottle under the bathroom sink, a sockful of coins in a potpourri jar on our mantel. One day I found a cast-iron skillet under the quilt in my bedroom; I brought it back down to the kitchen, but later found it tucked on a shelf in my closet. It wasn't that I didn't think something horrible could happen. Certainly, I knew it might. I always looked over my shoulder turning the corner onto our street, then again as I dug my keys from my pocket and walked to our door. Privately, I felt that every man who caught my eye in public, even for a fleeting moment, was just as likely to end my life as they were to go on with theirs, never giving me a second thought. But still, I couldn't bear to sleep next to these makeshift weapons, these physical representations of my worst fears. The bat's handle was thickly coated in dust. Neither of us had ever put it to use.

I brushed it off and evaluated its weight in my hands. I took a practice swing and caught sight of myself in the window's reflection, my face contorted into a snarl. For all I knew, Paul could be looking at me from inside his garage, just beyond the hedge. I knew that it would be hard to see anything clearly with the lights off, but even so I stood still for a minute, watching for any movement next door. Nothing. His windows were all dark, moonshine gleaming in the glass. I could hear nothing but Liz faintly snoring above me and dry leaves rustling on the porch. I set the bat down on the table and poured myself two fingers of scotch in a dirty coffee mug that was sitting out from the morning. There was a buzzing in my fingertips. I let the scotch sit in my mouth for a long time. The inside of my cheeks began to burn. I told myself that when I got to the bottom of the mug, I would go over to Paul's.

I'd never hit a person before, even when it might have been war-ranted, even when I'd badly wanted to. I looked at the bat and felt dizzy. It wasn't just my sister; a lot of women I knew kept one around the house somewhere. A girlfriend I'd briefly lived with taught me to put a sock over the top so that if the man tried to grab it from you, it would be easy to pull the bat down and away from him, leaving the empty sock in his hands and providing a quick moment where you could get a good crack in.

I took another big swallow and asked myself whether I was prepar-ing to hurt Paul, or prevent him from hurting me, or something else altogether. I certainly wanted to appear as though I was well capable of harm. I wanted to see how his face would change when confronted, what would flicker behind his eyes in the moment of understanding. I needed to know, even if no one else ever would. Even, I thought, if no one ever believed me, or if I kept it to myself for the rest of my days. Even if I never came out of his house alive. Or even if it turned out that there was nothing to know, and the whole idea was insane, fueled by my own festering blister of doubt, and my compulsion to pick it to the point of bursting. If I didn't go, I would never move beyond the mo-ment of uncovering her kerchief. I could see the way it would stick with me, clear as daylight; the moment my fingertips reached the fab-ric, the way the color transported me, the sinking feeling. My heart dropping like a stone in a well, and then my body, suddenly unteth-ered, floating away watching it all become small. It would come to me at night, and I would see it with my eyes closed, whether I was asleep or not. I tipped back the mug and gulped the last of the scotch.

I let myself into Paul's garage with his spare key, rolling up the door just enough to slide under before letting it back down gently, as quietly as I could manage. All the lights were off but for one dim bulb in the corner, illuminating the table with all its materials for the fishing pole repair I'd seen earlier that day, seemingly untouched. But there were new things, too: his work shirt draped over the chair back and a thermos on the table's edge. I felt it to see whether it was still warm. It wasn't. I stepped over a tackle box full of metal bolts and stopped at the door that led inside. It occurred to me that I had no way of knowing where in the house he might be. He could be right on the other side, for all I knew. Then what? I looked at my hands, both wrapped around the handle of the baseball bat. I thought about turning around and going home. No one would know I'd been here. But then I imagined placing the bat back in the umbrella holder, and trying to fall asleep knowing that I had brought myself to the threshold and then retreated. Carefully, I retrieved the kerchief from its box in the cabinet and then went to the door, twisting the knob with one hand, keeping enough slow pressure to stop the gears from squeaking. Once I felt the latch give, I waited, listening for any movement on the other side. Nothing.

I pushed the door open. Everything was dark. My eyes widened, struggling to make out the shape of anything, any movement. After a few moments I could see by the dim light of the garage the vague outline of a lamp on a table, and a coat rack, and what looked to be an old exercise bike. The floor was covered in a thick carpet. It swallowed the sound of my boots. I had no real sense of where I was going. It was only the third time I'd actually been inside of Paul's house. There was the night I'd gone to his house to sleep after my mother had vanished. The other time was when I was very small, and Liz and I were trick-or-treating. We were both dressed as dice, a bulky cardboard box around each of our middles, which our mother had painted white with black dots. I had only a fuzzy recollection of his front room, which we'd entered for just for a minute as he and his wife dug some old candy canes out of a drawer and dropped them in our outstretched pillowcases. Now, here I was feeling my way through the darkness, bat in hand, heart racing. I bumped into the back of a sofa and nearly gasped, clapping my hand over my mouth and holding it tight against my face. Standing there, breath held, I noticed a faint blue light coming from a room at the end of the hallway. It flickered between bright and dim, and I heard the low sound of voices and music. I felt my way toward it, pausing after each step.

Once I got closer, I saw a pair of work boots, and two bare feet above them, propped on an ottoman diagonal to me. I took two quiet steps toward the corridor wall, deeper into the shadows, and caught my first view of Paul. He was lying back on a recliner, his face awash in the bluish glow of the TV, his hair illuminated by a small lamp in the corner. I could see he had some kind of whittling tool in his fingers. Every few moments, he shaved little curls of wood off a small block and let them fall across his lap before looking back up at the screen. An infomercial for nonstick pans played. Eggs, hotcakes, hash browns, and sausage links slid out of the pans with ease in a fast montage set to upbeat music. Paul's eyelids drooped.

I took a deep breath and stepped into the doorframe, holding the bat in ready position with both hands. Every sensation felt almost unbearably heightened: the soft give of the carpet beneath my boots, the orange glow of the little space heater by the chair and the hot, dry air pulsing all around it. The smell of menthol cigarettes. The infomercial voiceover. The sound of Paul's drowsy, wet breaths as I drew nearer. My heart pounded so intensely my chest had grown sore. I felt like it might seize up and fail on me from sheer exhaustion. My throat, too, seemed to be on the verge of closing up.

I studied Paul's face. Silver hairs trailed from his mouth and chin down his neck and beneath his T-shirt. His nose was sharp and a little crooked. There was a pale, crescent-shaped scar behind his ear. I'd never looked at him so closely before. He was an unremarkable-looking man. Someone you'd make eye contact with in line at a store somewhere and then forget two seconds later.

He blinked, and cast a quick sidelong glance where I stood. For a flash of a moment there was stillness in his eyes, no recognition of my figure as a real, living person standing just feet away. Then he shot up in his chair and let out a quick, wordless scream.

I heard myself say, "Shut the fuck up," and then I saw myself, as if from above, walk over to the television and kick the power off with the back of my boot, still facing toward him, bat in hand. He looked utterly bewildered. I noticed through the corner of my eye that the curtain was up on the window behind his recliner, and through it I could see my sister's bedroom window beyond my own reflection in the dark mirror of the glass.

"Jess," he said quietly. "What the hell are you doing?" The sound of his voice took me aback. He did not ask in the way you would ask a stranger. There was horror in his tone, but also a degree of intimacy, familiarity. I thought I might throw up. Instead, I rested the bat on one of my shoulders and pulled the kerchief from my pocket with the other, holding it out in front of me. My hand shook. I tried to steady it but found I was unable. The first thing to pass across Paul's eyes was resignation, almost like he'd half expected this for years. Then his face seemed to collapse in on itself. He looked so fragile I couldn't stand it. I shoved the kerchief back down into my pocket and took up the bat with both hands again.

"Why do you have that?" he asked. His voice came out small. He spoke again, "When did you find that?" I took a single step toward him, bat raised, and he pressed against the chair back, his mouth hanging open like a trout.

"You tell me why you had this hidden in your garage," I demanded. Tears welled up in his eyes and began to roll down his cheeks in slow, heavy drops. Until this moment, I had thought there was a chance this whole idea might be a sick, misguided lark brought on by grief and straight scotch. But now, Paul's innocence seemed near impossible. It was the way his face crumbled when accused, the way his tears fell almost solemnly, unencumbered by disbelief. I tasted something bitter in my mouth.

"She was wearing this the day she disappeared," I said, my voice a low growl I barely recognized. He took in a jagged breath. "What did you do?" I asked. "Did you kill her?"

"No," he whispered. "I didn't kill Natalie." I blanched at his use of her first name.

"I watched her walk away for the last time with this scarf tied around her hair," I said.

"Jess," he croaked. "Why don't you put that down?" He nodded toward the bat.

I didn't lower it an inch. "Tell me what happened that day," I spat. My blood felt hot and roiling, like a river of gasoline that had just met a lit match.

"What makes you think anything did?" Paul said, suddenly sounding a bit aloof, offended even, as though my being here was entirely unwarranted, an affront to his privacy.

"Because you don't seem completely shocked that I'm here right now, asking you these questions," I said.

Seconds passed, each one excruciating. I swallowed, trying unsuccessfully to lessen the hard lump in my throat. Paul glanced at the door, then at the bat. I wondered if he was thinking about trying to wrestle it from my hands, and if he did, whether it would work. His position in the recliner put him at a disadvantage, but he was still a fairly large man. Then his eyes traveled from the bat to my face, and he seemed to deflate.

"It was an accident," he finally said. "A freak thing."

He began to speak, the words coming slowly at first, while I stood above him. He told me he'd been working in the garage that day and heard my mother say hello from the sidewalk on her way back home.

"We started talking, and then she gave me a hand with my pickup," he said. "Your mother was pretty good with mechanics." Paul paused briefly, his eyes searching mine. I felt almost as if he wanted some kind of approval from me, some indication that I agreed with him to defuse the tension, or maybe to throw me off my guard. I thought of what the medical examiner had said: *black, weatherproof paint, from the chassis of a truck.* The hair on my arms stood up. "Then we had a few drinks inside," Paul went on. "A couple hours passed."

"You invited her in?" I said, surprised.

"It was hot," he said. "We'd been working out there for a while."

"Were you seeing her?" I asked, a little dubious, but he seemed to be describing a kind of familiarity between them that I hadn't expected. "I mean, were you sleeping together?"

"Jess, I—" He looked up at the ceiling. "What has that got to do with anything?"

"How long?" I said.

Paul let out a long breath, dropping his shoulders and resting his elbows on the recliner. "I don't know, exactly," he said, not meeting my eyes. "Some time."

"How long?" I repeated.

"A year, maybe. Give or take." More tears welled in his eyes, hovering there for a moment, before spilling down his cheeks and neck. "I never meant for it to go on so long. But each time we said it was over, we'd get together again."

A swell of cold shock passed through my limbs. It wasn't that I thought my mother was celibate, or that she wouldn't have preferred to keep matters of her romantic life private. Months ago, when the police suggested she might've had boyfriends we were never privy to, it was me who had tried to get Liz to see their side, to acknowledge the possibility that her life was broader and more complicated, perhaps messier, than we would have realized as girls. But still, I'd had no inkling that anything was going on next door. I noticed a light pressure on my shoulder and realized I'd let the bat come to rest there.

"I felt bad about it," he said. "Really bad, to tell you the truth. Sick with guilt. But I'd had a tough year. Shirley—you remember my wife? Her cancer came back after a couple years of remission. She was in and out of the hospital and things weren't looking good. It was tremendously stressful."

I could picture her out on the front step with her knitted cap and her parka zipped all the way up to the top in late spring, sitting in the sunlight with her eyes closed, the bones in her hands and neck so prominent I had to force myself not to stare. There were times when she looked stronger, fuller, like she might pull through. I remembered once seeing her water the azalea bushes and there was color in her cheeks, a shiny crop of red hair sprouting from her scalp, but then a month later she was back for inpatient treatment and didn't return home for a long time.

"It wasn't that I didn't love Shirley," Paul said. "I loved her very much. But she was gone for weeks at a time, sometimes a month or more. And she was so sick. I mean, she could barely lift a glass of water to her mouth. Natalie was a real comfort to me during all this."

"So, what happened," I asked. Waves of nausea rippled from my gut. My tongue suddenly felt three sizes too large for my mouth.

"Like I said, we'd had a few drinks. Your mother always took a healthy pour. I guess you know that." His eyes flitted up to mine and then lowered back down as he went on. This comment enraged me. I felt an urge to take a swing at him with the bat, but forced myself to remain still, wanting him to continue telling me about that day.

"We decided to move the chest freezer down into the basement. My wife was coming back home from the hospital next day and she'd been asking for it to be taken out of the sunroom. It took up a lot of space, and she wanted to set up a daybed by the window in there." His eyes were bloodshot now, shining with tears. He described hoisting the freezer together, moving it in strained bursts to the top of the basement steps. I could see it all too clearly as he spoke: my mother, standing on the basement side. Paul stumbling forward over a warped floorboard. The freezer shifting abruptly toward my mother, sending her down the stairs headfirst.

"They were very steep," he told me. "The house was built almost a century ago. If she hadn't been drinking, she might have been able to—" He broke off momentarily. "The floor is poured concrete," he

346

said finally. "It would have been a bad slip for anyone, Jess, no matter what the circumstances. It was just one of those awful things."

I stared at him, blood roaring in my ears. I moved my fingers around the handle of the baseball bat, bringing it around to rest on my other shoulder.

"It happened so fast," he said, a pleading edge in his voice. "She didn't even scream. At first, I couldn't even understand what had happened. I thought maybe she'd dropped the freezer on the floor. My mind couldn't put the pieces together. But when I got to the bottom of the steps I saw that it was already over. There wasn't anything I could have done."

A sharp, crooked little laugh escaped my mouth then. Paul recoiled at the sound. I took a step closer, and he pressed his torso harder into the chair, like he'd be able to disappear into it and hide between the stuffing and coils.

"Nothing you could have done?" I said. "You can't be serious."

"You have to understand, Jess—"

"I already do understand," I said. "You didn't call anyone. You didn't tell anyone. And then what? You fucking hid her body out there in the woods? Are you out of your mind?"

"I panicked," Paul cried. He sounded like a wounded animal dragging itself off the road. "I don't know how else to say it. My first thought was to call 911. It really was. I had my finger on the dial. I pressed the first two numbers. I was about to do it. But her face was all swollen and dark. Blood was pouring out of her ear." I nearly gagged but tried to keep my face steady. "And when I tried to see it the way the cops might've, I freaked out," he said. "It looked like I'd pushed her. How could I know they wouldn't think I moved the freezer there afterward to try and stage it like an accident?" His voice grew higher, becoming more frantic by the second. "If I was alone, I swear to you Jess, I would have made the call. But I had Shirley to worry about. What was I supposed to do? Go to trial and hire a lawyer? I couldn't have even afforded a suit jacket to wear to court back then. Go to prison?

My wife was insured through my job. Even with the insurance, our medical bills were huge. I couldn't stop thinking about her lying in the hospital bed, all those chemicals they were pumping into her. And if they did put me away, and Shirley died while I was locked up? I couldn't take the chance. I couldn't risk it. She needed me."

Paul fell silent. He looked up at me, a grayish tinge in his skin, sweat gleaming on his forehead. I could see he wanted to finish the story there. That he was hoping what he'd already said would be enough, that I wouldn't be able to stomach any more and would just leave right then. He squirmed a little in his seat, seeming almost to be in pain. Nearly as much as I wanted to know what happened next, I wanted him to go through the anguish of having to tell me to my face.

"What then?" I asked.

Paul began to sob. "I knew that land was unincorporated," he choked out. "It hadn't all even been surveyed by the county. Nobody went out there back then. I couldn't think of anything else to do." He wiped his forearm under his nose and took a wet, croaky breath before adding, "I thought it would be a nice resting place." At this last comment, something inside me snapped. I lunged forward and punched him hard in the face. His skin was cool and pliant against my fist. Blood gushed from his nose. He lifted his T-shirt and pressed it there, wincing. A vivid, red bloom spread over the fabric. The bat felt like a piece of rubber in my other hand. I hadn't even thought to use it. Punching Paul hadn't made me feel any better or worse. He lowered the shirt from his face and spoke. "It ruined me, if you want to know. Absolutely fucking destroyed me."

"You're alive, aren't you?" I shot back. "Playing with all your hobbies in your garage?"

He rubbed his eyes and took a long breath. "If I'd been twenty-five, a single man, I really would have done things differently. Even now, I wish I could go back and do it differently. But I can't take it back now."

I stepped back, closer to the doorway. I was still afraid he might try to attack me. It occurred to me, too, that he might even call the police saying that I showed up like this, smelling of alcohol, brandishing a weapon and an old scarf for no reason. Who could prove where I found it? Who else but my sister or I could indisputably say that this same one had been hers, and not his ailing wife's, who had owned many head coverings, and had been the recipient of all manner of well-meaning donations, small and large, from various women in the community? I knew that Calloway would love nothing more than to arrest me for breaking and entering with violent intent. He'd scour the law for every possible charge. It wouldn't matter what I said about Paul's confession. I could almost hear myself, screaming about it from the holding cell in the back of the building, each word echoing through the empty corridor. No one there would believe me. Paul was a nice, quiet widower who'd lived in town his whole life and never caused any trouble. I was an itinerant boozer who was fucking a cop's girlfriend. The coroner had made his final judgment, their only formal suspect was already dead, and our case files had been relegated to a cabinet marked CLOSED.

I gathered myself and spoke. "Who knows about this? Who all did you tell?"

"No one." He shook his head fast, forcefully. "I told my Shirley. But only her. And she's gone now."

"Did she know you'd been fooling around with my mother?" I asked.

"For god's sake, I don't know," he said.

He told me how she knew something was horribly wrong the moment he picked her up from the hospital. They said almost nothing to each other the whole drive back. "And then nothing once we got home," he said. "She kept looking at me, nervous. Maybe she thought I'd gotten shitcanned, I don't know. Finally she cornered me and demanded I tell her what was going on, so I did. And then she didn't speak a word to me until the next morning. I found her sitting on the sofa in the living room, just staring at the wall. She was so frail. Her skin was almost green with nausea. I wondered if I should've never even told her, made up some kind of lie, but it was too late. Besides, I think she knew me too well not to know when I wasn't being honest. We'd known each other since we were thirteen years old. We met at a Valentine's Day dance, if you can believe it." His voice trailed off.

"And what? She was fine with it?"

"We were both sick over it, Jess. We weren't monsters."

"Not sick enough to tell Liz and me where to find her." He winced at this, like I'd struck him a second time. My sister's face came to me then, how pained and fearful she looked walking with her flashlight at the search party's helm, the beam landing uselessly onto muddy, litter-strewn grass. I would've lain in front of a train if it meant I could keep her from feeling the way she felt those days.

"I'm going to ask you for something," I said. Paul waited, seeming to brace himself. "Don't ever tell Liz. Ever. Not here, not if your paths cross somewhere else one day, not on your deathbed. You don't speak about any of this to her. Never."

Paul gave a firm, quick nod. "You have my word."

At that moment, a car rolled to a stop outside a nearby house and beeped the horn in two short bursts. There was the sound of a porch door opening, footsteps, then a car door opening and shutting. We heard the engine go around the corner and then disappear.

Then Paul said, "I think you ought to leave." His voice was cool, almost dispassionate. I noticed that his eyes were now nearly dry. There wasn't any pleading in his tone, and I couldn't detect any outright threat, either. He spoke to me plainly. I felt unnerved. Minutes earlier, he seemed like he was on the fringes of a total mental collapse. I could almost see the guilt devouring him. A flock of vultures in the room with us, tearing the man into oblivion, bit by bit. And within that collapse, I sensed relief, too. A kind of solace. But now, it was like he'd receded back into himself.

I turned to leave, keeping my eyes trained on him so he never totally left my view. Before stepping into the hall I paused and said, "Why was her kerchief folded up in that junk box in your garage? Why there?"

He was silent for a long minute. I thought maybe he wasn't going to answer at all. Finally, "I found it on the sidewalk that morning. Must've fallen off her head sometime before she left. I brought it in and just stuck it somewhere it wouldn't get mussed. Forgot about it while we were working on the truck, then I never had the heart to look at it again." He stared down at the carpet while he spoke. His tone was withdrawn.

I shut the door to the TV room behind me and began to run once I turned the corner at the end of the hall. I fell over a step stool, then tripped again over a boot brush. I let myself out the front door and jumped from the side down onto the slick, wet grass, where I promptly leaned over and vomited into a patch of newly sprouted daffodils. Then I ran through the brush dividing the two yards, around the back of our house, and in through the sunroom door, hoping not to wake up Liz.

For ten, maybe twenty minutes, I stood there stock-still, letting my breathing level out. Gradually, my heart slowed. My tongue tasted like spoiled vinegar. I wished I could spit it out onto the ground. Once it felt possible to move, I placed the bat back in the umbrella holder and went around the whole house closing every open curtain.

Then I sat down on the couch and thought.

Everything we'd ever wanted to know had been just across the hedge all this time. Feet away from where we ate and slept. When my sister and I stayed up all night waiting for the phone to ring, staring at maps of the trail system, getting hungrier and crazier and filthier by the day, the truth was just next door. And when on one of these nights I reached my limit and ran to Paul's porch, desperate for a dark and quiet place to sleep apart from Liz, and he led me to a spare room without comment, I must have traced my mother's last steps with my own. I wondered how he passed the hours like that, with me there in the house. Did he stay up until morning, wracked with guilt, staring at the ceiling? Did he console himself by looking at Shirley, tamping down his own doubts about the secret they kept with the idea that she was still alive, if only tenuously, and what sense did it make to jeopardize that even further by causing a big commotion over someone who was already gone from the world?

I wanted to know what moved within him when he spoke to me on the driveway just weeks earlier, or when he stood with me in his garage, and we made idle chat about his ship in a bottle. When he'd extended his offer for me to come by and borrow anything I needed, had he meant it, or was it just one of those things you say? Did some small part of him hope that I'd take him up on it and happen upon this piece of her? Maybe it thrilled him to know how close I was to it. Or maybe he hardly thought of it at all, emboldened by fifteen years of an ordinary life, indistinct from any other in town, and entirely under the radar of many searching eyes. I thought back to the earliest days, the groups of people who gathered to comb the land with us, flashlights in hand. Paul had been there.

Here was a secret, a rotten and heavy one, that sat between him and his wife for years. Then she passed, and he carried it on alone. Seasons came and went. My sister walked to her car each morning in her stiff uniform and returned home each evening. People moved away and faded into old age. New babies were born. The name Natalie Fairchild went unmentioned for longer and longer stretches of time. Maybe he started to wonder if this secret would die with him. Then a child's hand grazed bone on the forest floor, all the loose pieces began to shift into place, and now I shared in the secret, too. Some part of me was furious to have it at all, even though I'd demanded it, had gone to take it by force. I sat for a while longer. The bird clock went off: black-capped chickadee. I thought of Liz as a girl, standing up on the roof with her model plane, squinting and smiling into the sun. There were glimmers of that freer self left in her still. Seedlings. I'd seen their cautious emergence in recent weeks.

The truth was, there were always heavy things to carry. Always had been. I often felt like that was the whole purpose of a life, whether we liked it that way or not. As we grow older we are charged with the care of many fragile things, and as the years go on we are laden further all the time. We keep going even when we start to buckle under the weight, or at least we try. It took me a long while to realize that moving, whether from new place or to new person, couldn't make the load lighter. It didn't matter where my body was, or what lengths I went to trying to pretend I didn't carry all I did. The only thing that brought relief was the plain acceptance that these things were mine and my time here with them was finite. Now, I simply had one more thing to accept as mine.

Somehow, I fell asleep, and the next day I went with Liz to the lumberyard, where we purchased a stake for the birdhouse.

42

The morning I left Knife River again, the air was tense and humid with the threat of early spring thunder. All my things fit in one half of the trunk. Liz stood on the front step, watching as I brought out my last bag. She gave me a long, tight hug.

After we pulled apart she said, "I really am going to come visit you soon."

I told her that she'd better, and said that I'd be coming to Nashua, too. "Then you can take me up," I said, pointing toward the sky. "Once you get your pilot hours in."

She nodded, grinning. I did not say that I worried it would be hard to rest at night without the sound of her footsteps creaking around above me, or that I would dearly miss the hourly call of her bird clock, and her blunt manner, the gaps in her teeth and the dark hairs above her lip.

Leaning against a planter full of brilliant golden daffodils, Liz waved from the steps as I pulled out of the driveway.

I drove slowly, past the field on the other side of the woods behind our house. The grass was logged with watery mud backing all the way up to the mountain trails. I could see snow clinging to the distant peaks. Vultures circled something down in the brush. Tall weeds swayed in the breeze. I turned off the main road and onto the street that led to Eva's. The houses grew more sparse, farther back from the curb. Horses grazed behind weathered fencing. I thought of the day I'd first arrived, how many hours had passed since the moment I'd walked back into my old life. I thought of Brenda's hands, her peeling nail polish and the dark veins snaking up her wrists. I thought of her index finger poised at the trigger, hovering on the cusp of that irreversible change.

I drove down over the bridge, past the empty hardware store, the school I'd once attended, the abandoned movie theater and the dairy plant, and over onto a small road through the woods. Trees, as far as I could see, burst into leaf. Everything seemed to pulsate. Powdery, silver butterflies flitted among oak branches. A pheasant emerged from the brush and peeked around the corner. I paused, waiting for it and its gaggle of chicks to pass by. I rolled down the windows and watched as the last one disappeared on the other side. Then I kept on ahead, turning at the first white farmhouse on the right. And there, in the distance, I saw Eva, leaning against the fence, waiting for me.

ACKNOWLEDGMENTS

With deepest gratitude to:

Samantha, Katy, Whitney, Debbie, Andy, Avideh, Corina, Maria, Donna, Ralph, Rebecca, Richard, Leah, Michelle, Hope, Jonathan, Samara, Laura, Molly, Margueya, Chris, Patrick, Mary, Lynne, and Paul.

ABOUT THE AUTHOR

JUSTINE CHAMPINE's short fiction has appeared in *The Kenyon Review, Epoch,* and *The Los Angeles Review of Books*. She holds an MFA from Sarah Lawrence College and is a founding member of *No Tokens Journal*. She lives in New York City. *Knife River* is her first novel.

ABOUT THE TYPE

This book was set in Garamond, a typeface originally designed by the Parisian type cutter Claude Garamond (c. 1500–61). This version of Garamond was modeled on a 1592 specimen sheet from the Egenolff-Berner foundry, which was produced from types assumed to have been brought to Frankfurt by the punch cutter Jacques Sabon (c. 1520–80).

Claude Garamond's distinguished romans and italics first appeared in *Opera Ciceronis* in 1543–44. The Garamond types are clear, open, and elegant.